RAVELLING

Peter Moore Smith

RAVELLING

LONDON NEW YORK SYDNEY TORONTO

This edition published 2000
by BCA
By arrangement with Hutchinson
The Random House Group Limited

First Reprint 2000

CN 6625

Typeset by Deltatype Ltd, Birkenhead, Merseyside
Printed and bound in Great Britain by
Mackays of Chatham plc, Chatham, Kent

Peter Moore Smith

RAVELLING

BCA

LONDON   NEW YORK   SYDNEY   TORONTO

This edition published 2000
by BCA
By arrangement with Hutchinson
The Random House Group Limited

First Reprint 2000

CN 6625

Typeset by Deltatype Ltd, Birkenhead, Merseyside
Printed and bound in Great Britain by
Mackays of Chatham plc, Chatham, Kent

For Brigette, like crazy

Ordinarily at this hour my brother Eric would have been at his desk eating his usual Bavarian ham and brie on a wheat baguette, his cup of pumpkin soup, not too hot, a brown pear, slightly ripe, more crisp than soft. Ordinarily, as I said. But today at lunch he stood in his sterile, white-tiled, gleaming steel and bright fluorescent examining room with our mother, Hannah, who had been seeing ghosts. 'I've been seeing ghosts,' she complained. She had said it this morning, too, when Eric had come by our house to make coffee and eggs, if I wanted it, as he had almost every day for several weeks now, to check on me, to make sure I wasn't any more suicidal than usual. Eric had told our mother to visit his office at lunchtime, that he would take a look.

This was their intimacy: her acknowledging his authority, Eric's nonchalant acceptance of our mother's acknowledgment. This was the love between them.

'All right,' Eric laughed. 'Mom's nuts.'

She touched the crinkly paper that covered his green vinyl examining table, absently tearing it between her long, fragile, blue-veined fingers. She was not even aware of this, her actions having become disconnected from her thoughts long ago. 'It's like on television,' she said. 'You know how on television sometimes there's an image, like, like Bugs Bunny or something, and right next to him there's a ghost of that image, like an entirely different Bugs Bunny?'

Her face was pale, more than usual. A blue-purple vein ran beneath her temple like a trickle of red wine.

'Sure,' my brother said, somewhat bemused.

'*That's* what I've been seeing.' Almost imperceptibly, the vein in her temple pulsed. It had grown more prominent in recent years, Eric noticed, her skin whiter, finer, more transparent.

She'd become ghost-like herself.

'You're seeing double,' he said. 'With televisions that's called a double signal.' This was descriptive only, not a diagnosis.

And somewhat dismissive.

Our mother folded her arms. 'Except, my young Dr Airie, I know which image is real and which one isn't.' She was proud, it seemed, her thin lips set.

'Bugs Bunny isn't real, Mom.'

She giggled, rolled her eyes. '*Eric.*'

'Are you seeing a double image right now?'

'Not now,' she said firmly. 'Just sometimes.'

'Hmmm.' Eric, a doctor, my big brother, a fucking brain surgeon, wore a white lab coat. Beneath it, a pale blue cotton shirt monogrammed with the initials ERA, the E slightly larger, for Eric Richard Airie. He also wore a deep blue tie – silk, of course – with an elegant pattern of fleur-de-lis in gold thread. Hannah, his mother, *our* mother, wore a soft suede jacket, chocolate brown, a beige linen skirt, Italian leather boots. Outside it was sweater weather, early fall. Another Labor Day had come and gone. 'That could be her eyes,' Eric suggested, as if speaking to another doctor in the room, as if anyone else were listening. He walked to the wall, turned off the lights and removed a small black penlight from his lab-coat pocket. 'Have you been to the optometrist, to uh, Dr Carewater, isn't that his name?' He aimed it directly into our mother's pupils, one after the other, watching them dilate, and on his face was a well-mannered look of medical concern.

She blinked. 'I thought of *that*.' Hannah, a physical therapist, a hand specialist, would have known if it were her eyes. 'My eyes are fine,' she insisted. 'A little myopia never caused this kind of trouble. Besides, it comes and it goes.' She repeated herself now, saying, '*It comes and it goes, it comes and it goes, it comes and it goes,*' turning the words into a song.

'OK.' Eric sucked his teeth. 'It could just be that you're crossing your eyes for some reason.' He walked to the wall and flicked the lights back on. His sandwich was waiting at his desk. The pumpkin soup, was it getting cold? 'Can you remember when it happens? I mean, does it happen when you're coming out of a dark room and into a bright one? Does it happen when you wake up, after your eyes have been closed for a long time?' He was looking for information, clues that would lead to an explanation, data upon which to configure a theory. He was rubbing his hands together. He was growing impatient, too, hungrier by the second.

'Let me think.'

They gave the examining room over to silence for a moment and Eric looked at his clean, hairless fingers.

Hannah tore at the paper on the examining table. Then she said, 'During the day. I'll be thinking, thinking about something, I suppose, and then I, and then I just *realize* that I'm seeing a ghost.'

'You just realize it.'

'It suddenly occurs to me that I've been seeing one.'

'Thinking about what, specifically?'

Our mother paused again, eyes unfocused, and then she made her characteristic statement. 'Just lost, dear, just lost in my thoughts.' She had abandoned the crinkly paper and was now stroking the suede of her new brown jacket, combing it in the direction of the grain. When our mother wears something new, she beams, her face joyful – radiant as a young nun's. 'And there's Pilot,' she said softly, her expression dropping. 'I've been thinking about your brother.'

I am Pilot.

I am Pilot James Airie, Eric's brother, younger by five years, named after our father's passion – he flew for the airlines – a profession I have never even considered for myself.

Eric moved to the sink and pulled up his sleeves. Ever since he had gone to medical school he washed his hands compulsively, repeatedly, even at home. Ever since medical school he had been aware of the risks, the bacteria and bacilli, the microbes thriving just out of sight range. 'There's always Pilot,' he agreed.

Once, there was Fiona, too. Fiona May Airie, our sister.

Our mother hummed. It was a song no one had ever heard before, one that she made up every time she hummed it. It was, I believe, her way of trying to reassure Eric. She seemed always just on the verge of paying attention, her mind ready to wander away, her gray-green eyes unfocused and hazy. Humming underscored this quality, and it made Eric crazy. It makes everyone crazy.

I know because I do it too.

'Are you disoriented?' Eric asked, his tone saying, *look at me, listen*.

'Now?'

He sighed. 'When you're seeing these ghosts.'

'Disoriented?'

'I mean,' he laughed softly, 'more than usual?'

She sang, '*Don't be cruel.*'

'Seriously.'

'Disoriented,' our mother acknowledged. 'Yes.'

'Tired?'

'Tired,' she admitted. 'Yes, yes, that too.'

'Are you sleeping?'

'Not so good.'

'Are you, have you been talking to Dad?'

'Your father is lost—'

'—in the wild blue yonder.' Eric narrowed his eyes. He had heard our mother say this a billion times. 'I know,' he said. When she spoke to our father, which was seldom, Hannah became lovesick, unfocused, a teenage girl pining for her boyfriend.

She hummed again, a slight smile on her lips.

'What about caffeine?'

'I only drink tea, dear, you know that.'

'No coffee?'

This was a stupid question her face told him. 'Don't be ridiculous.'

'OK.' Eric dried his hands and threw the paper towel into the mesh chrome wastebasket in the corner.

Our mother's hair, which was becoming gray, which until so very recently had been light chestnut, soft as mink, fell in uneven curls around her elegant face. It was a feminine face, a doll's face, all too easy to see hurt in. It is my face, too, a patient's face, a waiting-room face, transforming everyone who looks at it into a doctor. When I am alone, my face disappears and I have no face at all. In someone's presence, especially Eric's or my father's, I am all face and no insides, I am a network of tiny muscles and porcelain skin stretched over a surface of cartilage, bone and teeth. She pushed her hair away.

'Can you *try* to worry less?'

Our mother laughed. 'About Pilot?'

'About Pilot, about Dad.' He took a step toward her. 'About everything.'

'I don't worry about you.' She placed a hand on his cheek, her fingers cool. It was always disappointing to Eric, but this is the temperature of women's hands.

'Please?'

'I can *try*.' She sang, '*I can try, I can try, I can try.*'

'Next time you're seeing the ghosts', he said, 'give me a call, describe them.' Eric took a deep breath. 'But now I have a patient coming, a real one.' He had food waiting – the sandwich, the soup – no doubt it had grown cold. 'Not that you aren't real, Mom.'

'I'm already gone.' Our mother touched her jacket, stroking the grain of the suede downward, as though petting a cat. 'Thank you, honey.' She gave my brother a swift kiss and clutched his hands, squeezing his fingers in a motherly way that means something about holding on, about not letting go, about regret.

Only mothers can do this, I've noticed. Or old girlfriends.

Eric watched her leave the room, her voluminous beige linen skirt sweeping the sterile air behind her. I imagine that he washed his hands once more because she had touched them and that he looked up to see his own movie-star, brain-surgeon face in the mirror above the sink.

* * *

I was looking in the mirror, too, staring and staring at my empty, empty face, when I decided that my brother would simply have to kill me.

Behind the house, the house we grew up in – or didn't, depending on how it's viewed – was a flagstone patio which led to an old, kidney-shaped, in-ground swimming pool. Years ago, before Fiona disappeared, we used this pool constantly, swimming in it every summer day. When he wasn't flying, our father lay in a deckchair beside it, his feet up, the *Times* spread over his chest, snoring through a smile. Our mother would bring out a tray of iced tea, a round slice of lemon over the lip of each glass – something she'd seen in *House Beautiful*, probably – and place it at the pool's edge. We could swim up, all of us kids, and take our drinks. Usually our father's had whiskey in it, too, and sometimes I would steal a sip and feel that strange stinging on my tongue, the delicious numbness that followed.

Later, after Fiona disappeared, after the yard had been allowed to go fallow, and the pool had been emptied, and the weeds had grown into it and made cracks in the concrete, my mother had it filled in with earth.

A truck arrived one day and the backyard of our house was transformed.

She mowed, tended, planted, groomed.

When the pool was filled, our mother kept a garden there, growing yellow and orange marigolds around the perimeter to keep the bugs away. She planted the vegetables of her New England girlhood. She grew carrots and potatoes, beets, radishes and parsnips, string beans and turnips. For the past several years she had even been growing rhubarb. And now, this year, early fall, tall pink and green stalks rose, their broad, purple leaves waving hello to the house.

Hello from the past.

When she came home from Eric's office that day our mother was not seeing ghosts, I believe, because she was making a rhubarb pie. Not that anyone ever ate these pies our mother made. They had a strange, rubbery flavor, I'd always thought, like a sweetened bicycle tire. But she remembered being a little girl in Massachusetts, picking rhubarb and bringing it home to our Great Aunt Jenny, who would wash the stalks and make a cone out of a page of newspaper. She'd put sugar in the cone and little Hannah would dip the stalks into it, skipping merrily back to the woods. I always imagined her bounding along, her reddish hair all crazy against a flushed face, an October wind fierce inside her pink girl's ears. When I imagine our mother's childhood it is the nineteenth century, even though she was born during the Second World War, and she wears a cape like Little Red Riding Hood.

Sometimes I imagine Fiona that way, too.

The past all blurs together.

My own past, Hannah's, my brother's. Memory's soft focus.

When I was a boy, I liked to hide in the woods behind our house in East Meadow, pretending to be the wolf boy. Alone, the English language forgotten, I'd growl, crawling through leaves. Once, a year or so before the pool was filled in, a year or so after Fiona disappeared, I sneaked into the house on a Sunday afternoon and removed a steak from the refrigerator. I snarled and tore at it with my teeth, right there on the kitchen floor. It felt slimy and tasted like blood. 'Pilot,' our mother said. She stood behind me. I was eleven, on my hands and knees, a raw piece of meat in my mouth, on the kitchen floor, suddenly made aware of my actual identity – and disappointed by it, of course. 'We were going to have that for dinner.'

'It's still good,' I said, my face hot.

Eric appeared next to her. He was sixteen. 'Jesus Christ, Pilot, what the hell are you doing?'

I am the wolf boy, I wanted to say. *I'll tear out your carotid artery with my bare hands.*

'He's pretending to be a dog.'

But today, in that same kitchen, Hannah had made a rhubarb pie, and when I came downstairs in my old blue bathrobe I could smell it, sweet and woodsy, filling the house. 'Did you see Eric?' I asked.

She only hummed.

'What did he say?'

'He said not to worry – *not to worry, not to worry, not to worry.*'

I sat down at the kitchen table while she took the pie out of the oven.

'I made a pie,' she announced.

'I can see that.' I was insane, by the way. I had moved back home at the age of twenty-nine. I had been rescued by Eric, in fact, found on the beach in California, out of money, suicidal, experiencing one senseless epiphany after another.

'It's not ready to eat yet,' my mother warned. 'Still too hot.'

The theme of her kitchen was the teapot, and on the tablecloth was a cheerful pattern of fat ones, all yellow. I traced the outline of one of these yellow teapots with my finger and examined the pie she had placed in front of me, the crust underdone, and I asked, 'Are you seeing any ghosts?'

She had a mean streak sometimes. She said, 'Just you.'

Recently I'd been feeling my hands and feet grow light and I was afraid that if I moved, I'd float away, carried up into the air the way a child's body floats to the surface of a pool when she's pretending—

'But I'm trying,' I said. 'I really am.'

Hannah put a hand over her mouth and left the room.

—pretending that she has drowned.

Sometimes in the woods, as the wolf boy, on my hands and knees stalking a rabbit or a mouse or a squirrel, *pretending*, I would stop and in a moment of embarrassed self-consciousness I could not remember who I was – Pilot or Eric. More accurately, I couldn't remember who I was supposed to be. I knew I wasn't really the wolf boy. I knew that I was only a boy, a human being, who belonged to the house with the white-painted brick walls on the other side of the trees, past the open, overgrown lawn, behind the empty, unused, cracked pool and the buckling flagstones.

8

I am the wolf boy, I wanted to say. *I'll tear out your carotid artery with my bare hands.*

That day in the kitchen, the scent of my mother's rhubarb pie strong in the air, the crust all melty and underdone, there was a dead-on collision of forgetfulness and memory. I found myself looking through the eyes of the wolf boy again. How long had it been?

That day our mother saw double, but I saw one thing.

One thing, twenty years old, clear for a fraction of an instant.

Later, I was on the phone with my brother.

'Is there anything wrong with her?' I wanted to know.

'It's too early to tell,' Eric said. 'I'm not sure.'

I suddenly realized that I was standing in the living room. I said, 'You're the brainiac. I thought you understood these things.'

His voice was dismissive, as usual. 'It could be anything,' he said. 'It's probably just stress.'

'Stress.'

'Things bother her.'

Our mother's living room had become cluttered. Mismatched pillows and throw blankets, decorator styles and patterns merged recklessly – plaids with paisleys, stripes with florals. 'I guess so.' I couldn't remember walking into this room. I remembered how it used to be so tasteful, a page from a magazine.

'And what about you?'

'What about me?' I looked at the phone. Suddenly it was black. I had never noticed that this telephone was black. It had a rotary-dial, too. I didn't remember dialing it. I looked at my finger. What fucking year was this?

'Pilot,' my brother said. 'Stop humming.'

'I really don't know, Eric. Things are weird. I'm compelled to tell you the truth', I said, 'and things aren't exactly right.'

'OK,' he said. 'OK.'

'And besides, we're talking about Hannah.'

He exhaled. 'I hate it when you call her that.'

'It's her *name*.'

'She's our *mother*.'

'Anyway,' I said, 'what about her?'

'I don't know, Pilot. It's probably nothing.'

Hannah, at that moment, was driving home from the cavernous housewares' discount store that had replaced the old K mart on Sky Highway. It was called Bed, Bath, and Beyond. Whenever she came home from Bed, Bath, and Beyond, Hannah spoke reverently of it, in a hushed voice, marveling at the selections of toaster ovens and bath towels. She was leaning down to reach for an old Joan Baez tape that lay on the floor of her cream-colored early Seventies Mercedes sports car and when she looked back up she saw two entirely distinct Sky Highways. I knew this because at that moment, at that very second, in fact, I heard a soft *beep* inside the telephone line.

'There's another call,' I told Eric. 'Hold on.' I pressed the plastic hang-up button on this old, black, rotary-dial telephone that I had never seen before in my life and I said into it, 'Hello?'

'Pilot.' It was Hannah on her cellular. I could tell something was wrong.

'What is it?'

'I've pulled over.'

'Where are you?'

'Right in front of the turnpike.'

'Is it the car?' It was a false question. I knew it wasn't the car.

'It's me,' my mother said. 'I'm seeing ghosts. I'm seeing a whole ghost Sky Highway. There's a ghost Mobil station on the ghost corner. There's a ghost dashboard right in front of me, a ghost steering wheel, everything. I don't think I should drive home.'

'I'll come get you.'

'Pilot,' our mother said. 'No.' I waited for what I knew she would say. 'Pilot, I just left a message for Eric. He can—'

'I'm on the other line with him right now, which is why he's not answering.' Which is why you resorted to calling me, I thought. 'But Mom, I can handle this.'

'Pilot, just—'

I cut her off. 'Eric?' I said. 'That's Hannah on the other line. I have to go.'

'Is she all right?'

'She'll be fine,' I told him. 'I have to go.'

I was struck by the weirdness of things. I asked myself if failure can become insanity. For some reason I thought I heard people having a conversation upstairs, even though I knew no one was home. They were saying my name. I put on some old running sneakers I found in the hallway closet. I hadn't worn this particular pair of Converse low-tops since high school, which was more than ten years ago. One of the laces came undone, slipped through the metal eyelets and into my hand. It was just an old shoelace – worn, blackened from time, frayed at one end. But millions of thoughts flickered across my mind like moths against a patio light. A shoelace. I didn't have time to tie this stupid shoe. I was off to rescue our mother, Hannah, who sat helpless, seeing ghosts, in her Mercedes by the highway.

Eric opened the door to his office and asked his secretary, 'Diane, did my mother call?'

'She's on line two,' Diane said. 'She's holding.'

He went back to his desk and clicked a button on his telephone, which was blinking red. 'Mom?'

Our mother was on the line. 'What did Pilot tell you?' She sat in her Mercedes, the light fading from the sky, seeing double.

'Nothing,' Eric answered. 'Just that he had to go, and then he hung up.'

'I'm seeing ghosts, so I pulled over.' She sighed. 'I tried to call you, Eric, but you were, you were with a patient or something, so I called Pilot instead and he said he'd come get me, but—'

'But there's no car for him to drive. He's so fucking stupid. How's he going to—'

'I guess he'll walk, that's all, and don't call him stupid.'

'Jesus Christ, Mom,' Eric said. 'He *is* stupid. Where the hell are you, anyway?'

'Right in front of the turnpike, across from the Mobil station.'

'He'll walk through the woods, I guess.'

Her voice was resigned. 'I guess so.'

They imagined me, the two of them. They saw me leaving the house through the kitchen door. They saw my black Converse All-Stars caking with mud as I stepped off the patio into the soft earth of the backyard. Did they imagine the feeling I had of the world separating from itself, its tectonic plates shifting deep beneath the forest floor, adjusting under the layers of leaves, mulch, dirt and limestone? Of the trees encroaching, preparing to swallow me the way one paramecium absorbs another?

'Will you come and get me, Eric?' our mother asked. 'Please?'

Did they know that things had become transparent again, clear as a blue sky seen through blue water? That I could actually *see* the cancer forming like a tulip bulb on the base of my mother's optical nerve? I could look through the trees all the way to the highway, through her car and through her hair and skin and cartilage and bone, into the folds of tissue around her eyes, to see the muscles dilating, the tendrils of nerves and vessels of blood, and the radical cells dividing there, and dividing again, a tumor the size of the dot over a letter i. Eric had removed his lab coat and was slipping his dark gray suit jacket on, the telephone headset wedged precariously between his neck and shoulder. 'Don't worry,' he said, and then he repeated a phrase our mother had used earlier that day. 'I'm already gone.'

The woods behind our parents' house were wide and tall and stretched all the way to the highway. Along the back of our yard the trees were deciduous – oak, maple, birch – whose leaves would drop in the fall to create a blanket of brown and gold through which, in childhood, I would crawl, breathing deeply the dry, acrid, wonderful smell. As these woods grew closer and closer to Sky Highway, however, the trees became fir and pine and their needles remained green – seemed, in fact, to grow greener – as the bleak winter wore on. There were clearings here as familiar to me as my childhood bedroom. There were trees I had climbed so often I thought of them as furniture. I remembered particular saplings that had become full grown. I could pinpoint in the woods of my memory exactly where certain bushes had gathered, where a nest of brown-feathered thrushes had lived, where a bees' nest hummed and quivered on a high branch.

I walked toward the highway.

I twisted and untwisted the shoelace, the one that had come undone in my hand, around and around my middle finger.

Winter was coming.

In the winter the woods were cold and empty, and the snow covered the ground like a white sheet of paper, and the shadows of the trees crossed the snow like black marks of ink. I'd crunch through the hard crust of ice and stand, shivering. Always there was the roaring sound of the highway in the distance, and always there was the sound of the wind in the trees. If I stayed out here long enough, I learned, I became numb, numb to the cold and more. For a time I could sit on an old broken concrete pipe in the clearing and listen to the cars on the highway and hear the high-pitched whistle of the wind in the treetops and the low falling of snow dropping from the branches and not feel a thing, become the wolf boy, my emotions too simple for language or memory.

Black-feathered ravens lit on the branches high above and called out to each other obnoxiously, like teenage boys.

The wolf boy – Pilot, Eric, whoever.

These woods in spring thawed quickly, it seemed, messily. The floor became mud and the melting of the snow created oozing black mulch, especially along the path that led to Thomas Edison, the junior high school Eric and I had attended. The tops of the trees were the first to green, naturally, and as the warm light reached the ground there soon sprouted one million fingers of fern, all beckoning seductively in the breeze.

The summer filled the woods with bugs, flies that buzzed and gnats that shot at my ears, with crawling things that scurried under rocks and burrowed through the dirt and droppings of shit. Squirrels chased each other around tree trunks, fat as my mother's teapots, gorging themselves on acorns. I would emerge from these woods in the summer covered with tiny red welts, bites of every variety, bee stings and scratches.

One of those summers I discovered a nest of tiny green snakes, as bright as tubes of neon in a beer commercial, beneath an overturned rock. They swarmed and wriggled grotesquely, each one a miniature of its full-grown future.

They would not change, I realized then, except to become larger.

I had not changed, I realized now, except to become larger.

Over the course of the next week or two I dropped earthworms and bugs into this snake nest, and I watched the tiny green vipers or whatever they were attack and swallow the insects, their whispery little tongues sliding in and out of their mouths.

I stopped for a moment, listening for the highway in the distance.

When our father was a boy he trapped mink and muskrats, then sold their pelts to Sears and Roebuck. He had kept his traps in an old box in the garage. The same summer, the summer I found the snakes, Eric discovered our father's old animal traps and set them, one by one, throughout the woods. He caught rabbits, squirrels, an adolescent raccoon and, according to him, Halley the Comet, our family cat.

That was the summer before Fiona disappeared.

And then came the summer we lost her.

And the summer after.

I was the wolf boy that summer and one afternoon I approached an empty trap and saw the scrap of meat, coagulated and raw, which Eric had placed in it. I moved my face toward it gingerly, just, as I believed, an animal – a real wolf – would do.

I backed away, though, wary.

In the fall I rejoiced at the pyrotechnics of death in these woods. The reds and golds, the explosions of leaves falling like slow-motion fireworks. In these woods death calls such beautiful attention to itself. It cascades in gorgeousness, opulent with colors. In people, death simply washes our color away, turning us blue and gray.

But Eric had lied about Halley the Comet. He had sliced our cat's leg off with a hunting knife—

Today, it was fall. I started walking again.

—a knife our father had given him. It was sleek, leather-sheathed, with a silver inlay of a rhinoceros embedded in the handle, and razor sharp.

While Hannah waited by the highway, I walked through layers of stiff, wiry branches that dragged against my windbreaker and snapped back against my face. I had known these woods so well when I was the wolf boy. I had crept through the underbrush and had buried myself in the dry, brown leaves, leaves that made a crackling sound like the paper on Eric's examining table. As a boy, I had climbed into these branches and waited for a silence to arrive like a hearse at a funeral home.

There was a path somewhere that led to Sky Highway and I remembered running along it full speed, my arms reaching to touch the leaves of low-hanging branches, my eyes closed, my head back. Where was it now? Early evening, the sun descended a single notch. Maybe it was this way. I walked into the clearing beyond which, I thought, must be the highway. Why did everything seem so unfamiliar? I could hear my own breathing, a dog panting. Toward the junior high was another path that led to Sky Highway, I remembered. I thought I heard other people, two voices in mid-discussion. Above, the sky had become chemical yellow, striped with dark gray. I stopped to consider my position. Where the hell was I? The trees had become black, too, and I realized how heavily I had been inhaling and exhaling. I had to be careful. I have a tendency to hyperventilate. Could I see my breath? No. It was still too early in the season for that. Perhaps in the morning. I had moved off the path that led away from the house and now, looking back, could not regain it. I imagined the woods had somehow subsumed the house. Sometimes, I thought, these branches will lash out and swallow cars, houses, people. Had I been swallowed, too?

Yes.

I twisted the broken shoelace around my middle finger, cutting off the flow of blood, and I felt my artery throb.

What I thought had been the path to the turnpike was merely a clearing under an enormous oak. Why didn't I recognize it? A squirrel scurried around the trunk of the tree. I walked around it to get a better look at the animal, but he anticipated me and kept always on the other side.

I was losing time.

As a boy, I had loved the way the breezes moved through the forest, and when I was the wolf boy I could close my eyes and move, feeling my way through the cracking leaves and snapping, cheek-stinging branches, hearing the sounds of the highway in the distance, smelling the burnt smell of the rotting leaves. I pushed my hands into my pockets to keep them from rising into the air like helium balloons. I dug my feet firmly into the earth as I walked. I closed and opened my eyes in a rhythm.

One of my shoes was untied, slipping on and off. But I didn't care.

I twisted the shoelace tighter around my finger – tighter and tighter.

Where was the highway? I wished I had a cigarette. I hadn't smoked in months, I realized, hadn't even thought about it. But now the darkness was drifting through the trees and I was feeling light drops of rain. Perfect cigarette weather. My face had disappeared, too, so I touched it and discovered that it was wet. Rain? Tears? When I looked at my finger I saw the familiar smear of brownish blood. I was bleeding. It must have been from the snapping of the small branches against my skin. I was inside the thickest part of the woods now. Yet I could still hear those voices and every now and then it seemed as though they were discussing my progress. I tasted the blood on my finger. It made me realize how hungry I was. I looked around with the eyes of the wolf boy, transformed. I would be coming out on the other side in a moment, I was sure of it, and I could hear the cars over the next rise, could sense the sky, smoggy and absolute, over the row of convenience stores and discount centers that I knew were there – the 7 Eleven, the Taco Bell, Marshall's, Amazing Drug Discounts, the Mobil station, Bed, Bath, and Beyond. I was Balboa nearing the Pacific. If I followed this path, it would lead me there, to Hannah, to our mother, Eric's and mine, Hannah who had been seeing ghosts, who waited for Eric to rescue her, but who had no idea that it was only me, Pilot the wolf boy, who could rescue her truly; it was only her younger son – starved for the taste of blood and bleeding – who could save her.

Hair like a trillion twisted threads of gold, a mole like a drop of blood on her collarbone, her name was Katherine Jane DeQuincey-Joy. And right now she sat on a mattress in her small apartment – the *enclosure*, as she called it – with a view of these woods and allowed the telephone to ring. She knew who it was – either Mark or Michele – and she certainly didn't want to speak to Michele. But when the answering machine answered and she heard Mark's voice, plaintive, worried, pained, she couldn't help herself. 'Hello?' she said, knowing the mistake she was making, knowing it would be the last one of its kind.

I sat down in a clearing I thought I recognized from childhood. There was a tall maple, its branches like a parachute falling perpetually toward the flattened grasses and ferns. And with the quick-falling darkness I saw behind the limbs of the trees the sky smoothing over, its colors artificial and flat. I saw the rest of the woods leveling off like a painted backdrop. I lost my sense of language. I forgot who I was. The woods, I knew, were hungry to swallow things. The woods had already taken my mother's house and I could sense the trees and moss rolling forward like a wave to wash over the entire neighborhood, subsuming cars, backyard pools, carports, entire culs-de-sac.

I had already been swallowed long ago.

I was an organ inside its body.

I twisted the shoelace, threaded it between my fingers.

The shoelace.

It wasn't long before the sky was completely dark and I could hear almost nothing in my immediate surroundings. The sound around me dropped away to an icy stillness and I heard only the cars on the highway, the faraway whir of the engines. I saw lights moving overhead and thought of my father in his little seaplane, flying somewhere. Perhaps Eric had placed surveillance devices, electronic birds and metallic field mice, all listening to the sounds of the forest, all trying to detect my whereabouts. Overhead were satellites watching the movement of the trees. Somewhere, my father piloted his little plane through the flat, backdrop sky. If I stayed perfectly quiet, I thought, and did not move, they couldn't find me.

I'd had to sacrifice my mother. I knew the woods wanted her and I wanted to help, but she was gone for now, Eric having made the move before I could find my way to her. He had simply gotten to her first.

Nothing made sense any more. But everything made perfect sense.

'What is wrong with him?' my mother was saying right now.

Eric remained silent. He turned the radio on to an all-news station.

Hannah put a hand over one of her eyes. 'And what's wrong with *me?*' The cancer cells inside her brain divided and multiplied, tendrils of aberrant DNA curling around her optical neurons. Her eyesight disintegrated one more degree.

'I think maybe we should schedule an MRI,' Eric said.

'Do you think it's neurological?'

'Well.' He was driving his sleek black Jaguar sedan. I could feel that automobile moving smoothly, animal-like, through the faraway streets. 'I don't know.' I could see out through Eric's eyes.

'Is it a symptom of something you've heard of?'

'I just want to make sure,' he said.

Hannah looked out of the window. 'Where's Pilot?'

'He's probably on his way back by now. Maybe he discovered your car, saw that it was empty—'

'Do you think we should have waited?'

'I want to get you home. Are you still seeing ghosts?'

'Yes.' Our mother began to sing, '*Yes, I am, yes, I am, yes, I am.*'

'Please,' Eric said.

'What?'

'I can't hear the radio.'

She stopped. They listened to the announcer, who described break-ins and robberies, car heists and drug seizures. There was a new war in a Latin American country. There was civil unrest in the Middle East. There was a whole new country in the Balkans. Someone had detonated a bomb at a local high school. Innocent animals were being tortured, it turned out, in the name of science. A group of scientists had found a way to extend the existence of human cells far beyond their natural life. There was reason for alarm, celebration and dismay. My brother adjusted the balance. He fine-tuned the reception. This was, after all, a Blaupunkt. He drove his Jaguar sedan evenly, deliberately, the engine droning like a politician's speech.

'Mom,' he said during a commercial break, 'do me a favor. Cover each eye and then tell me if you see any ghosts.'

Our mother covered her right eye. 'Ghosts,' she said.

'Now your other one.'

'More ghosts.'

Eric nodded.

'What does that mean?'

'It means that it's probably neurological. Aside from seeing double images, do things seem unfocused?'

It was cancer.

'Blurry?' she asked.

'Yes, blurry.'

She said, 'Maybe a little.'

They pulled into Hannah's driveway. They did not notice the woods receding into the background, slipping away from the house like a wave returning to the ocean, like one animal that has been stalking another and isn't quite ready to strike. Like the meaning of a word that escapes you. They got out of Eric's car. 'Can you walk OK?'

'I can *walk*,' our mother said. 'For Christ's sake, I can walk.'

'I'm just trying to help.'

'I'm not dead yet,' she snapped.

'Would you relax?'

'Where's Pilot? Where the hell is your brother?'

I had twisted the shoelace around and around my finger until I felt as if it would explode. I huddled down against the rough, damp trunk of a tree so no one could detect me. I knew what she meant. I knew exactly what our mother meant.

I wasn't dead yet, either.

They waited. Hannah paced back and forth across the old blue and white oriental carpet, humming nervously, her eyes unfocused, her ankles making that *crick-crick-cricking* sound. Eric sat on the old blue couch with his elbows on his knees and his fingers touching each other, tip to tip, like a spider and its reflection, his eyes on the door. It's hard for me to imagine what he was expecting at this moment. Would I walk through the door, sneakers covered in mud? Would I stay gone for ever? He went to the kitchen and straightened things up, compulsively washing the cups in the sink, the pot of coffee on the stove. Had he only been in this kitchen this morning? When he went back out to the living room our mother was holding the door open, peering into the dark front yard. 'Mom, he probably won't even come in that way.' Eric walked to the door and pulled it closed. She sighed and went back to pacing across the oriental.

Eventually my brother suggested she take an aspirin and lie down, that it might make the ghosts go away. She nodded, finding a blue Valium in her purse. But she couldn't lie down, she said.

'I have to go.' Eric held his hands out.

'Go,' she said.

And Eric left.

And so she waited alone, ghosts everywhere, doubles of everything.

And by eight o'clock I was still gone.

And by nine.

And by ten o'clock that night our mother had waited long enough. Long enough, she told herself.

At eleven she called Eric.

'He's not back yet?' My brother's voice was filled with incredulity, but not panic.

'I thought he might have taken the car to your house.' *Her* voice was panicked.

'No,' Eric said. 'He's not here. Besides, does he even *have* a set of keys for the Mercedes? And why would he come here?'

Our mother made a high-pitched whimpering noise.

'Mom,' Eric said. 'Stay calm.'

'Where is he?'

'He probably took the car somewhere.' Eric sighed. 'I'll drive by and see if it's still out there.'

But I hadn't taken the car.

I was in the woods, experiencing one amazing realization after another.

I was comprehending things.

Understanding.

Our mother sat in Dad's old blue wing-back chair by the window with her hand covering her mouth, holding in a scream. This is what happened before, she was telling herself. This is exactly how it had felt when Fiona—

Twenty minutes later Eric drove his Jag by our mother's car on Sky Highway. Naturally the Mercedes remained exactly where she had left it. He drove to our mother's house to see if I had returned in the meantime.

And of course I had not.

So Eric picked up the black, rotary-dial phone that sat heavily on the side table and, with a look of resignation, he called the police.

She waited with the telephone in her lap – black, heavy, rotary-dial. Where did it come from? She waited while she paced every inch of the house, her feet touching every inch of floor, every weave of carpet. She waited while sitting in my room on the edge of my bed, looking at the pile of books and magazines I had left there, the

National Geographics, the *Smithsonians*, the *Playboy* I had sneaked in under my shirt a few weeks ago. She waited and refused food, instead drinking endless cups of tea, all day and all night, ceaselessly, falling into a near trance to take the place of sleep. She kept all the radios and televisions on. She listened to the local news. She saw those ghosts, double images of everything, shimmery and translucent. She saw two living-room couches, two dining-room tables. Our mother saw two pool/gardens in our backyard. She saw four police detectives at the front door, but when she let them in she heard only two voices. She tried to remain calm, but her hand kept flying to her mouth and these sound – these *sounds*, just the beginning of something, something high-pitched and awful – kept coming out of her. She kept telling herself, Not again, not again, this can't be happening again. She saw two Erics sitting on the blue couch. 'Mom,' he kept arguing, 'you have to tell him.'

'When he comes back, when we find him, I'll tell him then.' She meant my father. She hadn't told my father I was missing.

'I'm going to tell him.'

'No,' our mother said, 'you will not.'

Eric sighed, rubbed his hands together. 'Are you seeing the ghosts?'

There were two couches, two blue wing-backs, two Erics, two of everything. 'I'm seeing them right now.' Her eyes were filled with tears, as well, blurring the edges.

'Stress,' he said. 'It's just stress.'

There was a doubling of cancer cells at that moment, deep inside the ganglia of nerves that let images travel electrically from her eye to her brain. They twisted like a helix around and around the wires leading to her eyes. Like the shoelace around and around my finger.

'Go out,' Hannah told him, tears on her cheeks, finger pointing to the woods. 'Go out and find your brother, goddamn it.'

Eric reached for his jacket.

Our mother put her hands to her face and said, 'This couldn't possibly be happening again, this couldn't possibly be happening to me again.'

After he left, she stood at the kitchen counter and looked at the woods, filled with double trees, double branches, double everything, and she knew that I was somewhere inside them, swallowed whole, knew I had been taken the same way Fiona had.

Imperceptibly, without her knowledge, without her *seeing*, the woods crept closer, waiting for her to turn away from the window, just for a split second, so they could roll over her, take her and the whole neighborhood with her.

She boiled another kettle of water. She poured another cup of tea.

Across the woods, across the highway, across a parking lot of dull sedans, a cheap telephone was pressed hard to a woman's delicate ear. And her eyes were closed, and her voice was hoarse, and she would be talking like this – arguing like this – for hours. And it was only this woman – Katherine Jane DeQuincey-Joy, her fingernails bitten beyond the quick, the acrid and strong taste of blood on her lips – it was only Katherine who could save me.

The telephone rang and she was on it instantly. 'Yes?'

'They found him.'

Our mother breathed in a jagged breath. '. . . oh God, oh God . . .'

'He's, he's had an episode.' It was Eric.

'An episode?' Our mother sank into the wing-back, one hand to her forehead. 'What do you mean? Is he all right?' She looked up and saw the ghost of the black, rotary-dial telephone on the ghost side table. In the background she heard voices speaking over an intercom, that faint institutional hum. She knew exactly where Eric was calling from.

'Pilot – he's, he's physically all right. I mean, there's nothing to worry about.' His voice was rushed, a vein of worry running through it, a hint of warning. 'He's not harmed or anything. He hasn't been hurt,' he said. 'He's just—'

'Just what?' Hannah looked at the picture window, silvery and reflective, and at the black sky outside. Where had I been? she wondered. Where the hell had I been?

'He's just sort of gone over the edge.'

'Over the edge? Sort of?'

Eric was regaining composure, formulating a theory. 'It's like he's experienced some kind of psychotic break.' He allowed a pause. 'Or something.' Right now he stood in the lobby of the East Meadow Community Hospital Emergency Services Center.

'Or something.' Our mother nodded, repeating him, running her thin fingers through her thinning, graying hair. Then she put her hand on the back of her neck. She saw two blue couches opposite her. She saw two gaudy chandeliers hanging over two time-worn dining-room tables. She saw two porcelain teacups on the floor near her feet, the real and the ghost of each. 'OK.' This was not unexpected. This was within the realm of what she understood about me. 'OK.' This was not even surprising.

I had gone over the edge before.

'I'm having him admitted right away,' Eric announced. 'And then I'll come and get you, all right?' He was in control again, Hannah could hear it in his voice, a tightness forming around the consonants, a liquid fluidity in the vowels.

'Did he say anything? Did he say why—'

'I don't think he even recognizes me, Mom.'

'Oh God.'

'Just hang on there. Are you seeing any ghosts right now?'

'I'm so used to it I can't tell the difference any more.' She looked around, the first smile on her lips in three days – since I had disappeared. I was all right, she told herself. Eric had called and I was all right. 'I see them everywhere.' I was alive, incoherent and insane, but alive.

'Just wait.'

'Eric, I'm waiting,' she said. 'I've *been* waiting.'

With difficulty, her breath misting in the air outside, Katherine Jane DeQuincey-Joy removed herself – as well as her pocketbook, a disorganized clutch of papers and yesterday's edition of the *New*

York Times – from her newly purchased but formerly owned, sapphire-blue VW Rabbit. It was a brightly lit fall morning. Glorious, in fact. The sun was runny as a broken egg, smearing its gooey yolk over the trees that rimmed the far side of the highway. But it stung her eyes like vinegar. Katherine had been up all last night arguing with Mark again, whom she would think of from now on as her *ex*, even though they had never really been married. And now she felt a pain forming, a thin coating of glass that shattered inside the back of her mouth when she swallowed.

She was hungry, too – she knew this because her hands were trembling – yet she had no appetite and would have to face the entire day at the clinic without a break. She let a section of the *Times* slip away. It drifted as if in slow motion, the headlines announcing new diseases, old wars, mistaken identities, all blurring their way to the ground. If she tried to retrieve it, she knew, everything would fall – her pocketbook, the papers, the rest of the *Times*, her whole life. So she just stepped over it, closing her eyes momentarily and lifting her feet.

She'd have some tea with lemon.

Katherine smiled at two nurses who walked by, then stepped in through the clinic's plate-glass doors. Her heels *clacked* down the long orange linoleum-tiled hallway. She said hello to her secretary, a large-eyed girl in a floral dress, who said, 'Maryanne MacDonald is your first appointment.'

'Thank you, Elizabeth.'

'You're welcome.'

Katherine pushed the office door open with her shoulder, throwing everything – her pocketbook, the paperwork she hadn't looked at, the sections of the *Times* that hadn't fallen – on to the hideous brown couch against the wall, let the door swing shut and sat down heavily at her desk. It was covered in papers, pastel-colored sticky notes, psychological profiles to fill out, the clinical bureaucracy getting its long fingers in right away. It had been two weeks since she'd started at the East Meadow Psychiatric In-Patient Clinic and her boxes from the old office in the city remained stacked in the corner by the empty shelves. Nothing had been hung on the wall, not even her diplomas. She'd meant to pick up something to throw over that couch – a blanket, a bedspread, *anything*. 'Katherine?' her intercom said. It was Elizabeth again, her voice sweet as music. 'I forgot to tell you, Dr Lennox wants to know if you can take on a new client.'

'Today?'

'There's an emergency client, a Pilot something-or-other, psychotic. Dr Lennox has already admitted him.'

Eyes closed, I was in a bed upstairs, my arms under the covers so they wouldn't float away. Outside the window a single branch was reaching toward the room, unfurling itself to tap against the glass, keeping me awake, warning me. I had a scratch across my face that began at my temple, crossed my cheek and ran all the way to my upper lip. I had an old shoelace wrapped tightly around my middle finger. I had a problem. I had a psychosis is what they told me later.

Downstairs, Katherine sighed. 'A pilot?' she said. 'Why the hell not?'

A voice said, 'Thanks, Kate.' Now the door was open. From behind it appeared the face of a man in his late forties, salt-and-pepper hair, slightly rumpled. It was Dr Lennox. 'He's not a pilot, though,' he said. 'That's his name. His *name* is Pilot.'

Katherine smiled. 'Get me some tea?'

'Milk?'

'Lemon.'

Dr Lennox disappeared. Katherine tried to neaten up her desk and when the psychiatrist returned, smiling, she had cleared just enough space for the styrofoam cup. 'His name is Pilot Airie,' Dr Lennox said, placing a wedge of lemon on a white napkin. 'Not even thirty years old.' He pointed to the window. 'Found in the woods near the highway, been out there three days.'

'Three *days*? Has he been medicated?' Katherine squeezed the lemon, dipping it into the water, teasing some color from the bag.

'You bet.'

I had been sedated like a zoo animal.

'Family?'

'They live in the area.'

'Full admittance?'

Lennox's eyebrows rose as if on strings. 'Absolutely.'

'Has he been in therapy?' She took a sip. 'I mean, was there any warning?'

'I don't think so,' Lennox said. He frowned briefly, then returned to his near-permanent smile.

'What's his name again?'

'Pilot Airie.'

'Unusual.'

He settled into Katherine's couch, haunches shifting. 'The mother, Hannah Airie, is a physical therapist,' he said. 'Hands, I think. She used to be with the hospital. The father's an airline pilot.'

'Explains the name.'

'More importantly,' Lennox continued, 'the brother—'

'Also psychotic?'

He shook his head. 'Other end of the spectrum. He's a consulting physician for the hospital.'

Katherine nodded. 'I've met him.' She had been introduced around – had smiled to my brother, in fact, from across the hall. Eric had lifted his hand in a small wave of hello.

Airie.

She'd thought it sounded familiar.

Dr Lennox was still smiling. 'Pilot has been in the hospital all morning.'

I lay in bed, face up. I knew the movements of every person around me. I heard the thoughts of every human being who knew me. I heard this *chattering* coming from the light fixture above my head, an electronic discussion.

Katherine shrugged. There was little to do, anyway, she told herself. Just make sure the medication was taking hold. Begin me on the snaking path toward normalcy. This is all that can be done with schizophrenics these days. 'I'll skip lunch. I'm not hungry, anyway.'

She had no idea what she was in for.

'Thanks, Kate.' Dr Lennox was standing now, hands in his

pockets, nodding and smiling. He gestured toward the door with his head.

Katherine raised her styrofoam cup.

I twisted my shoelace.

Alone again in an office with a stack of cardboard boxes, an ugly brown couch and chair, an oversized wood-laminated desk, a window overlooking the parking lot, Katherine Jane DeQuincey-Joy looked through this window, across the parking lot, at the highway, its mid-morning traffic still heavy, and across the highway to the wide patch of trees, still green but fading, yellow at the edges. I had spent three days in those woods, and Katherine tried to imagine it. Had I been quiet the whole time, she wondered, catatonic, like a predator waiting for its prey? Or the other way around? Had I grown hungry? Was I hiding from something in particular? Why would anyone name their son *Pilot*? The intercom buzzed again. 'Katherine?' Elizabeth said. 'Your next appointment is here.'

I remember Fiona in still images, like a series of old photographs.

In one of these images I just see her face, the wide cheekbones, the gray-green eyes – like mine – and the light brown freckles across the bridge of her nose. I remember the dimple on the left side of her cheek. I remember her wispy blonde hair curling at her temples. I remember Fiona, my sister, smiling shyly.

In another one of these pictures which I keep inside my head Fiona is standing by our backyard pool. There is a puddle of water beneath her. Reflective, it is shining in the light of the sun. She is smiling brightly. Fiona has a daisy-patterned towel wrapped tightly around her shoulders and she wears her red one-piece bathing suit, a matching flower made of thread positioned between her non-existent breasts. Behind the pool, on the other side of the yard, the leaves of the trees and bushes are emerald and yellow. At the base of the yard, at grass level, there is a blackness encroaching. I can see Fiona's feet splayed out, ballet style. There were lessons, I think, practices and recitals. Her toes are round and her toenails are painted a garish pink. There is movement behind her, it seems, or almost-movement, near-movement, about-to-be-movement. There is a ripple on the surface of the water. There is a rustling in the treetops. Her hair is scraggly and wet at the side of her face. The flowers of the towel are represented by a washed-out, Kodachrome yellow. In this picture of Fiona, which I have carried around inside my head because it was the only way I can remember her and because our mother has taken all the real pictures and hidden them away somewhere, there are tiny bumps of goose-flesh rising on the skin of her arms. There is a blur of red inside her mouth. There is a gurgling sound coming from somewhere inside her.

'How do you feel?' my brother was saying.

'What?'

Had my eyes been open?

'How do you feel, Pilot? Are you all right?' I was in a bed, in a bed in a hospital, the hospital where my brother worked, my arms trapped under the covers. The light above him was filled with electric voices, an argument over how I should be murdered, the methods and timing. If I could just keep them arguing, I thought, if I could just contribute to their indecision, I'd buy some time. 'Can you understand me?'

'Understand you?' I narrowed my eyes. 'In the picture', I informed him, 'there is darkness encroaching, there is a shadow falling over her, just touching her. It is the photographer.' Beneath the covers I felt the shoelace. It was still twisted around my finger, a reminder. They hadn't taken it from me. Not yet, anyway.

'Jesus,' my brother said. 'Come on, Pilot.'

'In the picture,' I said. The voices inside the light fixture continued to argue, squawking like a yardful of chickens. The light formed a halo around Eric's head.

I was in a room suddenly, a room so far and deep inside the woods that everything was white.

'We found you in the woods,' my brother was saying. 'What the hell were you doing out there?'

'Someone', I said, 'had to rescue Hannah.'

'Pilot, Jesus Christ.'

'Eric.' Inside the light fixture the voices couldn't decide. Keep arguing, I thought. Continue the debate. There was a gray nylon curtain hanging behind him. 'There is a small dot', I said, 'on the very base of her optical nerve.'

'What are you talking about?'

'Hannah.' I twisted the shoelace. I wound it around and around my finger.

'Mom?'

'You are the fucking brain surgeon,' I said. 'But you are aware of this, aren't you? You just don't want to admit it.'

'You were out there for three days,' Eric said. 'Did you know that?'

'It's cancer.' I heard a tittering inside the lights. 'I know what you're doing,' I said. 'I knew it then. I know it now.'

'What are you talking about?'

'You've followed through.' I looked at him. 'Haven't you?'

'Followed through on what, little brother?'

'All your plans.'

'Pilot, for Christ's sake.'

Eric would slip into my room at night and kneel beside my bed, as if in prayer. 'I'm going to kill you,' he would say. 'You'd better not say a word or I'll do it right now. I'm going to cut your throat from ear to ear. I'm going to take you out into the woods and hang you in the big tree. I'm going to put Drain-O in your apple sauce. I'm going to kill you like no one has ever been killed in the entire history of murder.' I would close my eyes as tightly as possible in the darkness. Sometimes I would put my hands over my ears. But Eric would pull them away. 'I'm going to take Dad's gun out of the closet', he once said, 'and I'm going to march you out into the woods, way out there so no one can hear you scream, and I'm going to put one bullet in your left leg.'

'Stop it,' I whispered.

'And then I'm going to put one bullet in your right leg,' he whispered back. 'And then another—'

'Eric, please.'

'—in your left hand, shattering all those little bones in your fingers, the carpals and metacarpals. And then I'm going to shoot you in your elbow, and that's just four bullets, there's two more to go.'

'Please, stop,' I said. His voice was velvety, like a radio announcer's.

'And then I'm going to shoot you in the stomach, and you're going to lie there and squirm and bleed all over yourself, you stupid little whiner. You'll probably throw up and taste your own stomach acids and the dinner you had, mixed with your own—'

I was crying.

'—blood, you stupid fucking little crybaby. And then, when I'm totally bored with you, when I can't think of more interesting ways to torture you, I'm going to put the gun right up to your forehead, and as slowly as I can, I'm going to pull the trigger, and I'll watch your brains ooze out of the back of your skull. Not that you've got a whole lot in there, anyway.'

I closed my eyes even tighter and held my breath, letting a blackness cover everything, and when I lifted my eyelids Eric was gone.

Until morning I'd lie in silence, waiting for him to return. Sometimes, when Eric and I were doing the dishes together, when our mother or father had left the room, he would whisper, 'I'm going to kill you,' putting his finger over his mouth to keep me silent.

I didn't doubt him. I never doubted him. And I kept silent, too.

I never told anyone.

I never told anyone.

Her hair was as insane as I was. Blonde and black at the same time, it fell in curling, twisting spirals across her shoulders, almost to the middle of her back. The rest of her was tastefully disheveled in wrinkled gray wool pants, a satiny shirt. Her eyes, like Fiona's, were green. But this woman's eyes were brighter, more focused than any I'd ever seen – wide and, at the same time, sharp. 'Pilot Airie,' she said and her voice was in performance mode, overtly professional, 'my name is Katherine DeQuincey-Joy.' Her silk shirt, pale green, open at the collar, revealed a gold chain and an antique locket with a Celtic design on it. She had a birthmark on her collarbone, a mole, as if someone had pricked her skin with a needle and a tiny globule of blood had formed there and hardened, and then it turned black.

Or were Fiona's eyes blue? I panicked to remember.

Green. Yes, gray-*green*.

I touched my face and felt the scab across my cheek. I wondered if I looked tough or pathetic. 'Hello,' I said. I decided on pathetic. I was sitting up now, although I felt impossibly bewildered.

Katherine Jane DeQuincey-Joy spoke slowly, deliberately, her eyes like twin televisions broadcasting concern. 'I am a psychologist with the clinic, Pilot, and I wanted to talk with you just for a little while just to see how you're doing. Is that OK?'

This is how I knew I was every bit as insane as her hair.

'Oh, Katherine DeQuincey-Joy,' I echoed her formality, 'I do not believe at this moment in time that I am doing so well, as a matter of fact.' The voices inside the light fixture erupted into a riot of conversation. I had just given them a fresh supply of ammunition. I had made an *admission*. Thankfully, they had not yet decided how I should be done away with.

'Really?' she said.

I nodded.

I knew that, somehow, Eric's would be the deciding vote, that he was in charge. Perhaps his communication gear was faulty. Perhaps he was out of range, trying to get through. Katherine DeQuincey-Joy had a long neck, and beneath the pale green fabric of her shirt I could see the shape of her body, her skin-colored lace bra – practical yet elegant. She said, 'Why do you say that, Pilot?'

'Can you turn out the light?' I asked. 'I can't hear you.'

She furrowed her brow. 'If I turn out the light you can hear me better?' She gave me an expectant look, eyes expanding, as if to suspend logic, as if to give me credit for an explanation that was clearly nuts. She looked at my hand, at the shoelace I had twisted around and around my aching middle finger.

'Katherine DeQuincey-Joy,' I wanted to know, 'are we far enough away from the woods?'

'You're safe,' Katherine DeQuincey-Joy said. 'You're very, very safe here. I promise. No one can hurt you. And you can just call me Katherine, if you like. Or Kate.'

'You'd be surprised, Katherine Jane DeQuincey-Joy,' I said. 'They lash out, the trees and the branches, and before you know it—'

'What does, Pilot?' She leaned toward me, hands almost touching the hospital blanket. 'What lashes out?'

'The woods.'

She paused. Could she be electronic, too? Could Eric have sent her? 'Do you hear anything, Pilot? Do you hear voices talking when they're not really there?'

'I hear arguments,' I admitted, 'but they *are* there.' I knew what she was getting at. I had trouble getting at it myself. They weren't there. But they *were*. Both things were true.

'What kind of arguments?'

'About what to do with me,' I said, 'my execution and disposal.'

'Who is arguing?'

I begged her slowly: 'I asked you, please, if you could please turn out the light, please.'

Katherine DeQuincey-Joy backed away from the bed. 'I'm sorry.' Her fingers found the light switch.

Instantly the room went dim. 'Thank you.' The murmuring of voices quieted without their electric lifeline, their wires and diodes, receptors and interceptors.

'Would you like to stay here for a while, Pilot?'

'Am I out of the woods?'

'Are you speaking metaphorically?'

I smiled. I would have to explain this. 'Katherine Jane DeQuincey-Joy, imagine,' I said. 'Katherine, please, imagine a tunnel, a man in the tunnel like an amoeba—'

'OK.'

'—and the way it moves through the solution to a problem—'
Fuck, I thought. I was losing my place.

She nodded. 'Yes.'

'—the way it swallows its pride, taking them inside, an intelligence the size of an ocean, and catching—'

'Would you like to stay here, Pilot?' she asked again, smiling. 'Stay here at the clinic for a little while, and we'll make sure you're safe, until you feel better?'

I couldn't breathe. I touched the scab on my face. My middle finger, wrapped tightly by the shoelace, throbbed painfully. 'I think that would be good.'

Katherine put her hand, her thin, cool, smooth hand – could this be electronic? no – on mine and squeezed it lightly, just lightly. Like a mother. Or an old girlfriend.

'I think that would be really, really good,' I said.

Like regret.

She smelled like lemons.

When I closed my eyes I saw Fiona's face like a prairie. My sister's eyes like twin moons on an alien horizon. Her chin was a bluff to climb over. My memory of her was a fading map of a terrain I was no longer familiar with. Everything was different now.

I missed her so much.

Katherine Jane DeQuincey-Joy was hiding her hands beneath her desk because she had chewed her nails down to nothing – *beyond* nothing – and there was a bright halo of blood around each one of her fingertips. 'I'm really glad you could come,' she was saying. 'I know how busy you must be, and—'

'I'll make time for this,' Eric broke in. 'Whenever you need me, just call, and I'll make myself available.' His hands were beautiful, Katherine noticed, the nails the perfect shape for a man, clear, with no trace of white, not dull but not shining. Dramatically, he said, 'This is my brother.' She didn't know that Eric checked his fingernails each morning in his chrome and black bathroom, holding a pair of silver clippers above a polished wastebasket.

Katherine nodded. 'So I don't have to tell you what Pilot is experiencing, what he's—'

'It's all too familiar.' Eric's face was perfectly tanned, she noticed, with wide cheekbones and blue, blue eyes. His figure was athletic, finished. His pose, however, was concerned, even distressed.

'Dr Lennox's initial diagnosis', she began, 'is, is that Pilot has some form of schizophrenia, whether it's schizoaffective disorder or—'. Eric closed his eyes, face upturned. 'But naturally we would rather believe', she rushed to say, 'that this is a response to trauma of some kind, whether real or imagined, rather than—' she cleared her throat '—well, rather than late-onset adult schizophrenia which I don't have to tell you is more—'

'—degenerative,' my brother finished. 'You don't have to tell me.'

'Dr Lennox said your mother indicated that Pilot has had other episodes?'

Eric leaned forward, his long, perfectly manicured fingers touching each other habitually. Was he aware of this habit? 'Pilot has always been psychologically – I don't know – *fragile*. He had an episode when he was very young,' he said. 'Around eleven. But we had always chalked that up to an event.'

'An event?'

'When we were children our little sister disappeared.'

Katherine was silent, her eyes wide.

'It was very traumatic, and Pilot suffered—'. Eric seemed about to describe something more specific, but then he said, 'Well, he suffered.'

'What was that particular episode like?'

He looked away. 'It wasn't like this one, really. It was more about being dissociative. He was down on all-fours, snarling and growling like a dog, pretending he couldn't understand English. He was getting lost in a game of make-believe, I guess.'

I am the wolf boy, I'd wanted to say. *I'll tear out your carotid artery with my bare hands.*

'Were there any particular symptoms of schizophrenia then?'

35

Katherine asked. 'I mean, that you can see from your medical perspective now?'

Eric ran his tongue across his teeth. 'Pilot was not always very coherent in those days and he was always drawn to the woods.' His eyes flickered toward the window. 'I guess the early signs of psychosis were present.'

Katherine couldn't help but turn and look out there, too. The sky was darkening, the blue growing deeper. 'May I ask what happened to your sister?'

'We never found her.'

'She was abducted?'

'Children are abducted every day.' My brother looked at Katherine directly for the first time, it seemed. 'And not all of them are recovered.' His head was cocked at a slight angle now.

'Of course.' She made her eyes soften, using them to reassure. 'The only reason I'm asking is that, is that I'm wondering if Pilot felt somehow responsible.' She kept her eyes on him, waiting for Eric to break the gaze. 'About your sister, that is, which might explain the dissociative—'

'We all felt responsible.' Eric kept staring back. 'But that was—' his entire tone changing '—that was twenty years ago.'

'Have there ever been any other episodes?'

'Not really. Not like this.'

'Any other traumas?'

It was a game now, their eyes playing truth or dare. He finally looked away. 'Pilot has always been shaky, you know, psychologically speaking. He's never had many friends. He's had a fair amount of trouble in school, bad grades, truancy, a lot of depression. He was living in North Carolina until recently—'

'How recently?'

'Just six or seven months ago and then he went to Los Angeles. He told our mother that he was in negotiations to sell a screenplay, but what we found out later was that he was just living on the beach in Santa Monica. Are you familiar with the area?'

'Not really.'

'There's a lot of homelessness out there. Anyway, I had to go out and retrieve him, and ever since then he's been living at home.'

'Was there any psychotic behavior on the beach?'

'He was drinking a lot, I think, and smoking grass.' Eric shook his head as though ashamed. 'Maybe other drugs. I didn't notice any deeply unusual behavior. I mean, beyond—'

'Has he had problems with substance abuse, with alcohol?'

'Some problems,' my brother said, as if he knew. 'No serious addictions, I think. But yes, some problems over the years. More with drugs than drinking.'

Katherine allowed a moment to pass, artificially shifting a few pieces of paper around on her desk. She wanted Eric to know that she doubted him, that she didn't believe he had all the answers. 'I'm trying to put a finger,' she said finally, 'on something environmental, a concern, a stresser, perhaps, anything that might have triggered this, this reaction.' She narrowed her eyes, asking, 'Is everything in your family OK?'

Too quickly, he said, 'Yes.'

'Your father, he's deceased?'

'My father? Oh no.' My brother flashed a loud smile. 'Far from it. Our parents are divorced, that's all. Dad lives in Florida.' He laughed brightly, an intense *Ha*, more like a bark. 'He's retired, but he's – well, he's not dead.'

'Could there have been—'

'Pilot and I have almost no contact with our father. Our parents divorced a couple of years after Fiona, after our sister, disappeared. They don't talk much, and when they do—'

'I see.'

He looked out the window.

'What time of year did your sister—'

'Labor Day.'

'That was two weeks ago.'

'Yes.'

'The woods behind your mother's house—'

'They picked over every inch of them looking for her, or for any

37

clue, any piece of evidence. All they found was one of her tennis shoes.'

Katherine nodded. 'When I was talking to him,' she said, 'it sounded like he was afraid the woods were going to swallow him, perhaps like Fiona?'

'Then why would he go in there?'

'I don't know. You said he was always drawn to them, didn't you? Maybe he thought he could find some other evidence. Maybe he was reliving the search. Or the abduction. Of course, I'm only guessing.'

'It was a rhetorical question.'

Katherine blinked.

Eric put his hands to his face. 'I'm sorry,' he said. 'This is my brother.'

'You've spoken to Dr Lennox?'

'I'm on my way to his office right now.'

'He's put Pilot on Clozaril, which is a—'

'I know. I'm a neurosurgeon.'

'Yes,' Katherine said. 'I forgot.'

'It's all right.'

She stood up, careful to put her hands behind her back. 'I'd like to recommend some insight therapy,' she said cautiously. 'If you don't mind. I mean, because it's not yet clear to me what might have triggered this, if anything.'

'Insight therapy,' Eric repeated.

'Nothing too in-depth.'

'Don't ask him to re-live anything, that's all. Nothing traumatic.'

'Of course not.'

My brother rose, too, and the two of them faced each other. 'Whatever you need from me,' Eric said, 'just call, anytime. I'm in the hospital Mondays and Tuesdays, and in my office the rest of the week.' He extended his hand, his nails perfectly clean, the cuticles pushed back, the skin slightly tan, hairless and smooth.

Katherine shot her hand into his, hoping he wouldn't look down and see her scabby fingertips.

'Welcome to the, uh, to East Meadow,' he said, his eyes

somewhat wounded. His grip was solid and gentle at the same time. 'It's nice to meet you, Katherine. Not my choice of circumstances, exactly, but—'

She smiled back at him steadily, saying, 'It's all right,' then pulling her hand away as fast as she could.

I was nine, leaning against my father's enormous lap, and I could smell the Bacardi he'd been drinking, like a sweet cloud that had descended over him. I begged for a sip. 'Just let me taste it, Dad, come on, *please*.' The group of men sitting and standing in a semi-circle around him all laughed. These were men from the neighborhood, fathers of boys and girls I went to school with. Each one of them clutched a drink. Each of them wore a smile.

'Looks like you've got another aviator in the family there, Jim,' one of them said. He wore large sunglasses with white plastic rims.

'Just a taste,' my father said sternly. 'Don't gulp it, all right?' He handed me the small round glass filled with ice and Coke and rum and I sipped as much as I could into my mouth before he pulled it away. It tasted like medicine and candy. 'All right,' my father said. He put the glass on the arm of his chair. 'That's enough, you little alcoholic. I don't want you to get sick.'

'I want some, Daddy.' Fiona had been watching from behind his lawn chair and now she rubbed her face against his neck like Halley the Comet.

'No, sweetheart,' our father laughed, pushing her away. 'You are *way* too little.'

'Two of them, Jim,' one of the men said. 'Two aviators.'

They all laughed hysterically, as if this was the funniest thing they'd ever heard.

'I'm not that much more littler than Pilot.'

'Just that much more littler,' our father said, holding his thumb and forefinger a millimeter apart, 'just enough more littler.'

All of these grown-ups laughed like maniacs, although to me it wasn't funny at all. Irritated, I asked, 'Can we go in the pool?' It was still light out and the air was hot, unexpectedly warm, everyone kept saying, for Labor Day. And I wanted to show off my incredible underwater breath-holding abilities.

'Just be careful.'

I grabbed Fiona by the arm and dragged her toward the house. We didn't have our swimsuits on.

'Stop it,' she said, pulling away.

'If you want to go swimming,' I told her, 'you have to do whatever I tell you.'

'I'm swimming,' she said, 'but it has nothing to do with you or anything you say, you *jerk*.'

Through the sliding glass doors that led on to our patio we could see the entire gathering of adults, many of them shifting from one leg to the other, many of them sitting with their legs crossed, each one holding an icy drink like a prize. There were two distinct gatherings, I noticed – one of men, one of women. It was going to be a successful party, I could tell. Our mother had been worried that no one would have fun, that her parties were like Mary Tyler Moore's. 'People are having a really great time,' I had already told her. 'Look how much they're drinking.' She'd sighed at this. I tried to count all the people who weren't smoking and found only three. Our pool was entirely surrounded by grown-ups. I imagined there was a person standing on every single flagstone, on every centimeter of slate. The kitchen door was wide open, too, and people were standing around inside mixing drinks, getting more chips and dip, enjoying the hot cheese fondue. I could see our mother going in and out of the kitchen door in her long, green, satiny dress, the charming hostess asking questions, making sure everyone knew where everything was.

I pushed Fiona toward the stairs. 'Go get your bathing suit,' I ordered.

She ran through the den, her little girl feet splayed out awkwardly, bowlegged as a cowboy. I followed, but not as fast. I could hear my father finishing a story, starting to laugh, giving the punchline away. I wanted to wait for the response. There was huge laughter coming up around him, like bubbles rising up from the bottom of the pool.

Then I ran up the stairs, stretching to take the steps two at a time the way Eric did.

When I went past my brother's bedroom the door was open just slightly. I peeked in. Eric and Dawn Costello the beauty queen were on his bed, their hands all over each other. 'What did you see?' Eric's face turned toward me. 'I'll fucking kill you, you little piece of shit.'

I took off toward my room and I heard Dawn say, 'He's not doing anything. He's just curious.'

In my room there was a late afternoon stillness settling. I could hear the party downstairs, the voices of men and women. I could hear the jazz music my father liked, loud but distant on the stereo. Particles of dust hung frozen in the sunlit air that came through the slats of my venetian blinds. Halley the Comet was curled up at the foot of my bed. His leg was totally healed by now, the little stump covered by scar tissue. I took a moment to scratch his big orange head, and his slitty eyes opened just a little, a curvy cat mouth smiling at me. I think it was around four-thirty, maybe five. I stepped through the piles of clothes on the floor and removed my swimming trunks from the bedpost.

As quickly as I could, I took off my clothes.

'I can see you naked.' Fiona was standing in the door behind me.

I said, 'I'll fucking kill you, you little piece of shit.'

'You're just repeating what Eric said.'

'So?'

'So,' Fiona told me, hands on her hips, 'you should try and come up with something more unique.'

We heard joyful, drunken shrieking from downstairs and then a loud splash.

'Someone fell in the pool!' Fiona ran out of my room. I slipped on my blue swimming trunks as quickly as I could.

When I got outside I saw that Trudy and Tony Malnerre from three houses down were pulling themselves out of the water, their hair smashed flat against their heads, their clothes dripping wet. 'What happened?' I asked. I wormed my way through the people to the edge of the water. 'What happened?' I looked up at the adults.

They were all laughing. Some people's faces had turned red from laughing so hard. Fiona jumped on to my father's lap. His head was fully back, his mouth wide open. I started laughing, too, but I wasn't sure exactly why. Trudy and Tony Malnerre were standing beside the pool, dripping puddles of water onto our flagstones. Tony was laughing. Trudy, his wife, was shaking her head and pointing a finger at him, sort of angrily, it seemed.

She was smiling, though.

After the laughter had calmed down and Tony and Trudy had gone inside to get dry, Fiona and I got in the water.

I cannonballed, making as big a splash as my nine-year-old body could.

Fiona tested the water with her toes, then eased herself in.

I could hold my breath underwater for a full two minutes, I reminded myself.

Two minutes at *least*.

Under the water I could see Fiona's legs dangling. She liked to hold on to the side of the pool and propel herself around, her legs pushed out toward the middle. Right now she was looking up at our mother, who was leaning down, hands on her knees, warning Fiona, no doubt, to be careful. Beneath the water, I swam toward my sister's legs, coming up underneath them, and grabbed her by the ankles.

She struggled for a moment and then I let her go.

When I surfaced, our mother was yelling, 'How many times have I told you, Pilot, not to torment your sister?' She had her hands on her hips. 'It's dangerous, especially in the pool. What if she drowned?'

'She's not going to drown,' I sneered.

Fiona was pretending to cough. I knew the difference between her pretend coughs and her real ones and these were pretend. She was always hamming it up.

'There's like a million adults around,' I said. 'No way would they let her drown.'

'Yes,' Fiona said, 'but they're all *drunk*.'

'Just try to be nice.'

'You're a shit,' Fiona told me.

'And that means both of you.' Our mother turned to face a man standing next to her. He had long blond hair and a soft mustache. Unlike most of the people at the party, I had never seen him before. And he was younger, or seemed as if he was younger, anyway, than the other guests. 'Never have kids,' our mother instructed him.

'You don't really mean that,' he said smiling. 'Not with these cutie-pies.' Now this man squatted down beside the pool and said to Fiona, 'Are you Fiona?'

Fiona nodded.

'Do you like parties?' he said.

She smiled flirtatiously.

'You don't like grown-up parties, though, do you?'

'Yes, I do.' Fiona clutched the edge of the pool. 'Yes, I do. I like grown-up parties even more than I like kids' parties.'

I said, 'I can hold my breath for a full two minutes,' and I ducked back under the surface. I could see this man talking to Fiona from down there. I could hear the voices of the party echoing strangely through the water. I could see the sky dimming above the house. I wished I could stay beneath the water for ever. Fiona's little legs kicked above me and the man – just a shadow from here – continued to speak to her, crouched low on his haunches. I saw the shadow of the woods move over the surface of the pool, which meant the sun had finally descended fully behind our house. I was just nine years old, and my body filled with a trembly kind of feeling. I loved that our parents had parties. I loved how beautiful our mother had made herself – her hair all twisted up on her head, chestnut ringlets dangling over her temples. I loved that Fiona was the kind of sister strangers wanted to flirt with, fashionable men with long blond hair and delicate mustaches. I had blond hair, too, but not *as* blond. I wished I could grow a mustache. I held my breath and this feeling for as long as I could, and when I rose from the water my lungs burst open through my mouth and I gasped for air.

'We thought you were never going to come up,' a woman in a purple pant-suit said.

'How long was I down there?' I asked. 'Did anyone time it?'

'What's your record?'

'Two minutes,' I said. 'I can hold my breath for a full two minutes. I've timed it.'

'I think you were down there about thirty minutes,' a man said. He wore a shirt with a Hawaiian pattern on it. He wore a necklace of wooden beads. His hair was too short for this look, I thought. Like the others, he held his drink in his fist. His other hand was in his pocket.

'Stop pulling my leg.'

'Maybe two and a half minutes,' he said now, more seriously.

'Really?'

'Could be.'

With the blond man's assistance, Fiona got out of the pool. He wrapped one of the daisy towels around her and padded it across her back and shoulders. 'You should go inside,' he said. 'You don't want to catch a chill.'

'Will you come with me?' Fiona asked.

Our mother smiled at the blond man. 'It looks like you've got a girlfriend,' she teased.

The blond man smiled back, palms out, shoulders in a shrug. 'I *am* single.'

They all laughed, including Fiona.

'Was it really two and a half minutes?' I noticed that everyone at this party was holding on to a cocktail glass. I saw one man staring straight into his and bringing it back and forth to his lips, repeating this over and over, the muscles of his face tensing and relaxing. I thought of all the ice in all these glasses and I wondered out loud if there was any ice left anywhere in the world. Before someone could answer me, though, I took a huge breath and pushed myself back under the water. Three minutes, that was my goal. The voices above me chattered and laughed.

When it became completely dark and my father lit the torches around the pool, I pulled myself out of the water, toweled myself dry and went back inside and changed, putting on all clean, dry clothes. Eric and Dawn had disappeared to a teenage make-out party at Brian Kessler's house. I had last seen Fiona sitting on the blond man's lap in the dining room. There had been drinks on the table, ice in the glasses. The music had grown louder in the house and it had become the new music now. This was 'Light My Fire'. This was rock. Had the blond man put it on? Fiona was still in her red bathing suit and had the daisy towel wrapped around her tiny body. But now she was wearing her red tennis shoes, untied, floppy on her feet.

She giggled and squirmed. He tickled and joked.

Later, when I went back down, they weren't there. The dining room was empty, in fact, only their glasses remained, and the party had moved completely outside.

'Don't you look nice!'

'I just put on some clothes,' I told my mother. 'Relax.' But these were my best clothes – a polyester shirt with the Declaration of Independence printed on it and a pair of white jeans.

'A young gentleman,' a tall black woman said.

'Would you like something to drink, Bob?' I heard a voice say. 'How about you?'

The population of this party had mostly moved to a single patch of flagstones beside the pool. It was the only lit area of the backyard and it forced everyone to stand together closely, uncomfortably. I had to weasel my way through these people toward the sound of my father's voice. He was finishing one of his flying stories.

My father was tall, blue-eyed with dark hair. He had a somewhat ridged brow and a strong nose. When he told stories he gesticulated wildly, his hands opening and closing for emphasis. His stories always ended the same way: with him setting his teeth together and bracing himself for some act of insane bravery, only to be saved at the last moment by an unnatural act of luck or serendipity. He was in the Australian outback, for instance, and almost crashed into a desert mountain – until an unexpected gust of wind lifted his airplane over the ledge. He was in Vietnam and crash-landed a helicopter in the middle of a strange, unknown jungle – only to discover he had landed directly on top of a secret American CIA base. I had heard every one of my father's stories by that time in my life, but hadn't tired of any of them. And I still believed them, every single word. 'Come over here,' he said to me now.

I went to his side and leaned on to his lap and looked up at his large muscly face – the face Eric would later grow into.

'That's a hell of a story, Jim,' one of the people standing around him said. 'Too bad it isn't true.'

Everyone laughed.

'It's true,' I said. 'It's totally true.' I shook my head at these people.

'I was only kidding, Pilot,' the man said. 'Of course it's true. Of course it is.'

They all smiled at me as if I was an idiot.

'Are you hungry?'

I nodded.

'Go into the kitchen,' Dad said. 'There's all kinds of stuff in there. Just help yourself.'

'Can I have another sip of your drink?'

Hilarity all around.

'Get out of here.'

I weaseled my way through the party once more toward the kitchen, just off the sliding doors on the patio. Hannah was putting her arms around some man's shoulders. He wore a white office shirt that was totally open, revealing his entire chest. They were dancing. It was only joking, I could tell. But it was dancing.

'Mom?' I said.

She kept dancing.

'Mom?'

She stopped. 'What?'

'I'm getting something to eat. Is that all right?'

'Yes, it's all right.' She shook her head in exasperation. 'Get something for your sister, too,' she said. 'Make sure Fiona gets something to eat, too. OK?'

I nodded and went into the kitchen.

There were soda and liquor bottles on every counter. There were bags of potato chips and boxes of pretzels. There was a fondue pot, yellowy cheese bubbling over. There were raw slices of crisp vegetables. There were various dips. Some guy was dancing around and pouring all kinds of different drinks. He wore a blue shirt and tie, like he had come here directly from work. But there was a big spot on his shirt where he'd spilled something.

'Are you Eric?' he asked.

'I'm Pilot.'

'A very interesting name. Can you fly?'

'Someday I'll fly. But now I'm too young.'

'What can I get for you, young Pilot? A gin and tonic? A whiskey and soda?'

'Are you kidding?'

He eyed me with mock suspicion. 'What do you mean? You don't drink?' he said. 'A drinking problem at your age?'

'You're an idiot,' I said.

He just looked at me.

I shrugged and left the room. Maybe I wasn't so hungry. 'Fiona?' I yelled. Where the heck was my sister?

Often, if I found myself alone in the house, I'd go into Eric's room, even though he had explicitly told me not to. I wanted to look at his trophies, which he kept in a tall bookcase our mother had painted sea-green. I'd run my fingers over the swimming ribbons and the gold statues of football players, their bodies caught in motion. I'd read again and again the certificates of achievement he'd received in the Thomas Edison junior high school and the Albert Einstein High athletic departments. On the top of the bookcase, all the way up, was the New York State Junior Science Prize, a large silver bowl with his name, Eric Richard Airie, etched in scrolly letters. It was way too high for me to reach, of course, so I would pull Eric's desk chair over and stand on it just so I could run my fingers along the silver rim. Someday I would have trophies like this, too, I told myself. I used to pretend that Eric would say those words: *Someday, Pilot, you'll have trophies like this, too.*

Upstairs in my room, I could hear my parents and their guests outside raising their voices. I could hear the sound of all those glasses being filled, of all those ice cubes rattling around inside them. Our mother had recently redecorated my bedroom with a racing-car motif, and everywhere were old-fashioned blue-and-white and red-and-white striped race-cars, the drivers hunched over the wheels, those funny egg-shaped helmets on their heads, the bold prime numbers – 3, 5, 7 – on their hoods. I lay down, curling up against the sound of all those voices rising into the air outside my open window, and I imagined myself in one of those race-cars. All those voices became the sound of the engines gunning around the track, and I saw myself in one car and my brother in another, and we drove side by side, not trying to out-race each other, neither one of us trying to win, but going as fast as we could, side by side.

When I woke up the house was silent except for the clinking and clanking sounds of my parents collecting glasses and emptying ashtrays. It must have been three or four in the morning, before any light had crept into the sky at all – pitch black. All the windows and doors were still open and a chill had invaded every room. It felt damp and there was a smell of wet towels. I sat up and listened for a bit, hearing my father muttering to my mother every now and then, and after a while I heard nothing, so I went downstairs.

In the living room he sat with his legs far apart, his head down, his hands holding his face.

'Dad?'

He rubbed his hands roughly over his eyes and forehead.

'Dad?'

He groaned. 'Go back to bed, Pilot.'

'What time is it?'

'It's late,' he said. 'It's really, really late.'

'I never ate anything,' I told him. 'I'm really, really hungry.'

'You're hungry.' He said this flatly.

I waited. I was still wearing my polyester Declaration of Independence shirt and the white jeans.

'You want some cereal?'

'OK.'

'So go get yourself some cereal.'

'All right already.' I made a face at him, but it was probably too dim to see, so I walked into the kitchen. Hannah was in there, humming. 'Was it a good party?' I asked.

'Was it? Oh, I don't know.' She touched the top of my head, her fingers wet from the sink.

'I'm hungry.' I grabbed a handful of potato chips from a bowl on the counter. 'Can I have a soda?'

'I'm so tired,' Hannah said. 'I'm just so tired. Have you seen your father? Did he go to bed?'

'He's in the living room.'

'Did Eric come home yet?'

'I don't know.'

'Will you turn out the lights, dear?'

I nodded again and she walked out of the kitchen with the back of her hand to her forehead.

For a while I ate the chips off the counter and drank warm Coke. Then I went out to the living room again and saw that my father had disappeared. Good, I thought. I sat down on the couch where he had been sitting and rubbed my face the same way he had. Now my face was covered in potato chip grease. I lay down and rubbed my face against the rough blue material of the couch to get the grease off. Comfortable now, I stayed that way until I fell asleep again. On the couch that night for the first time, I think, I dreamed I was the wolf boy in the woods, naked, running with a pack of dogs. In this dream the woods behind our house had grown larger and had swallowed the house. I was wild. In the dream I tore out the throat of another animal with my bare hands. I opened my eyes from this dream and saw Eric's face only inches from mine.

'You are such a fucking moron,' he was saying.

'Leave me alone.'

'I'm going to drag you out into the woods by your feet,' he said, whispering. 'I'm going to take an ice pick and push it through your hand, right through the middle, and then I'm going to push the ice pick into your ear—'

'Eric.'

'—just far enough so you can't even hear yourself screaming out of that ear but you're not dead yet, and then I'm going to pull it out and push it into your other ear.'

'Please, Eric.'

'And then I'm going to stick the ice pick into your eye.'

'Please stop.'

'And then your other eye.' At this, I squeezed my eyes shut, imagining my brother really had blinded me. I was trembling all over. 'And then I'm going to leave you in the woods for a while and I'm going to watch you stumble around, all deaf and blind, screaming like an idiot, you fucking moron—'

There was a crashing sound that came from the patio. I opened my eyes. Eric's head turned.

'What was that?' He got up and walked to the window.

'What was it?'

He slid open the patio doors and stepped through, turning on the porch light. I got up from the couch and followed him. The flagstones were covered with broken glass. 'One of the pitchers fell off the table,' Eric said. There was wind in the treetops, a faraway rustling sound. There was a ripple on the surface of the pool. 'Can you feel the winter?' he said. 'It's far away, but I can feel it.'

And I knew just what he meant.

The sky had gone gray and the sun's rays were spiking over the trees. It must have been six in the morning. There would be mixed clouds that day and the tiniest chill would invade the air, the infant beginnings of a new season.

It was coming.

'I'm going back to my room,' I told Eric. 'And by the way, you're a jerk.' I walked upstairs. In the hallway, when I passed Fiona's room, I noticed that her door was closed. It occurred to me that

Fiona never slept with her door closed. She was still too little. She was still afraid of the dark. But I didn't do anything about it. I simply went into my race-car bedroom, closed the door, closed the windows, put on my matching race-car pajamas and crawled into bed.

In one of the imaginary photographs of Fiona, she is standing in the center of my family for a group portrait. Her hands are folded together in front of her red velvet dress. A white satin ribbon is tied in a bow around her neck. Her eyes are wide open and she is smiling like only little girls who are having their pictures taken can smile – full of vanity and joy, a complete absence of self-consciousness. Her hair has been done and it curls up at the ends, sweeping down her back the way it did in the days before she disappeared. Our father's fingers rest lightly on her head. She is so little next to him that even with his arms fully extended he can only just touch the top of her head. The rest of my family sort of fades into the background in this imaginary picture. I am there wearing my Declaration of Independence shirt and white pants. Eric is splendid in a dark three-piece suit, hair feathered back. Our father, eyes blue as ice, stares ahead into the sky behind the photographer – who would that have been? – and our mother, unfocused, turns her head slightly away.

Katherine Jane DeQuincey-Joy was in no hurry to arrive at the small, lightless *enclosure* overlooking a parking lot – a highway in the distance, a strip mall beyond the hallway, quiet as the inside of a drawer – that was her new apartment. She had no furniture yet, anyway. She had no television, not even a radio. Mark had kept all those things, of course, claiming she'd come crawling back. He'd kept everything he could, even some of her clothing, old photographs of her parents and sister, and a baby blanket, for Christ's sake, that her own grandmother had knitted. What did he want with that? Katherine had brought a few boxes of books and psychology journals, the answering machine, the clothes she could pack in one suitcase. And there were the things she had collected from her office in the city, things Mark had no access to. Then, when she found her new *enclosure*, the delivery guys had left her new mattress on the living-room floor. And Katherine hadn't had the energy, strength or interest to put it up on its side and slide it into the bedroom.

So her bedroom had become a closet and the living room had become the room she lived in.

Even though it didn't feel much like living.

Now, Katherine sat in her office instead, avoiding the drive home, putting off for a few more minutes her nightly visit to solitary confinement. She sat at her desk with her hands curled like shells and her fingernails, what was left of them, to her teeth. She touched her tongue to the tip of her index finger and tasted the raw skin.

No, she told herself, flattening her hands on to the desk.

No, she told herself again.

She faced the door and forced the muscles of her mouth into a smile. She knew the very act of smiling, the deliberate contortion of the facial muscles, could activate the endorphins of contentment. She had faith in this notion, in fact. It just wasn't working right now.

There was a faint light seeping into the room, like filthy water filling up a pool. It was the sunset filtering through a smog-yellow sky over the highway. She looked at the pad of paper in front of her. She had spoken to my mother. She had seen Eric. The only one left to talk to was me.

Katherine had written each one of our names on a single line on the sheet of yellow legal paper, creating a column for each. There was our father, too – James Airie. But, of course, he wasn't available. He had probably never been available, Katherine thought.

A fucking *airline* pilot.

Typical.

Tomorrow she would try to speak with me, see if the medication had taken effect, if my thinking had become any more cogent.

Typically, the response to Clozaril was instantaneous. She wondered what would happen if she took it herself. Her brain would simply shut down, more than likely. Maybe she would try it someday. Maybe someday she'd have a psychotic episode all of her own.

The telephone rang and she picked up after a single ring, saying, 'Katherine DeQuincey-Joy'.

'Katherine,' a voice said, 'this is Dr – I mean,' he said, 'this is Eric.' He was stumbling, nervous. 'This is Eric Airie.'

'Oh, hello, Eric.' Katherine exhaled. 'I was just thinking about—'

'Listen,' Eric said quickly, 'I'm not calling about, about my brother. I mean, I know you might think this is unprofessional and if you do I'll totally forget about it and completely understand.'

Unprofessional. 'OK.' She knew what he would say next. She could feel it coming like the drop in an elevator.

'Would you like to have dinner with me?'

When had it become so dark in the sky outside the office window? The light in the room was blue. This *was* unprofessional, and not just for Eric. It was more so, in fact, for Katherine. 'Like, on a date?' She had to clarify.

'No,' Eric said quickly, 'I just – no. I mean, not like a date at all. It's just that I'm trying to deal with this, with my family thing right now, you know, and I don't especially want to go home, you know what I mean, or go out with someone I'd have to explain myself to, and you seemed like – well, you seemed like a solution. Does that make sense?'

'Half social,' Katherine said, 'half therapy.' She allowed a small laugh to come through.

'You're very understanding.'

She looked at her hands. How would she hide them? 'I'm also starving.' Should she be doing this at all? She had never met socially with a client before. But Eric wasn't exactly a client and he *was* a doctor.

'You're also very nice.'

'I'll have to put this on my time-sheet.'

'Have you—'

'I haven't spoken to your brother today. I'm waiting—'

'—for the medication to take effect, I understand,' Eric finished. 'Pilot's still pretty irrational, I know. I was going to ask, have you tried that new barbecue place on the highway?'

'No.'

'Do you like ribs?'

'I love them.' The muscles around Katherine's mouth contoured into a smile, this time a real one. She wondered if Eric could tell.

'Would you like to meet me there?' His voice wasn't nervous any more.

'All right.' Jesus Christ, how easy was she?

'Are you sure this is OK? I mean, if you think this is, if this is not right, or if you're not comfortable—'

'You're not my client,' Katherine said, even though she knew something about it wasn't right. 'Your brother is. Besides, I've been here over a month and haven't been out with anyone. And I love barbecue and I'm really hungry.'

'I'll get us a table by the fireplace,' Eric said.

'Great.' Katherine looked at the yellow legal pad in front of her, the columns she'd made for each family member. She realized she hadn't made one for the sister, Fiona, and the whole page was used up. 'And you can talk about your brother as much as you'd like,' she said. 'I don't mind.'

My mother had been sitting for most of the day in the green vinyl chair beside my bed. I was too tired to speak, but I'd look up every now and then and her eyes, somewhat unfocused, would rise to meet mine. She didn't read. She didn't look at a magazine. She didn't even knit. My mother simply sat at the side of my bed and watched my face. I knew she was seeing two of me, the image of my face separating in her vision just enough so my ephemeral double lay nearby. And if I seemed aware enough she would ask if I wanted anything. 'Water? A soda? Something to eat, dear?'

'You can go, Mom,' I said. 'I'm fine now.'

She shook her head. The room was dim, so the voices were kept behind the hallway door.

'I'm really feeling much better,' I told her. I was sluggish, though. I felt as if I'd been sprayed with still-hardening glue. All the joints of my body were turning to glass.

'I'll stay a little while longer.'

'Mom,' I said. 'Hannah.'

There was a long silence then. Hannah with her hands on her lap. Me lying face up in the tall bed in the small room. The tree branch tapping on the window, saying hello to my craziness. And then my mother asking, 'Do you want me to leave, is that it?'

'Can you see me?' I wanted to know. 'Can you see my face?' Under the covers I had the shoelace.

Hannah's eyes squinted at me.

'Is it deep?'

'What, Pilot? Is what deep?'

'The scratch?'

'It's barely there at all, dear.'

The voices in the hallway tittered and squealed, rising and falling. I tried to think of an emotion besides fear. For a moment or two, I couldn't name a single one. And then I said, 'Love,' finally remembering.

And my mother said, 'I love you, too, Pilot,' putting her hand over mine.

I could see the water on the flagstones beneath her little feet. I could see the bright afternoon light reflecting in the water, shining like gold. I could see the goose pimples forming on her arms. I could see the individual blades of grass poking up through the cracks in the mortar. I could see my sister's eyes, green as mist, the color of a pine needle. I could feel the almost-movement behind her, far back behind the pool, in the woods, a faint rustling in the branches. I could see it, see her, my baby sister.

My brother's eyes scanned the ersatz rustic barbecue restaurant, searching the room for Katherine. He wore a white shirt – monogrammed, as usual – a yellow tie, dark blue trousers. He looked formal, Katherine thought from her table across the room, he seemed dressed for dinner at a much nicer place than the Texas Barbecue Chicken and Rib Hacienda off Sky Highway. But his shirtsleeves were rolled up to his elbows and his jacket was missing – probably in the car – and he was the one who had suggested they meet here, wasn't he?

She waved.

He smiled when he saw her, walking over, his mouth like a crescent moon.

'I was beginning to think I was being stood up.'

'A patient called just as I was stepping out the door,' he apologized, touching his temple. 'She was experiencing motor impairment. I had to – well, you know. I'm really sorry.' He pulled himself up to the fake rough-hewn table. 'Jesus Christ,' he said. 'I had no idea this place was so cheesy.'

'There's nothing wrong with a little cheese.' Katherine took a sip of water. 'I like cheese.'

'Have you ordered?' He looked at her directly for the first time.

She shook her head. 'I waited.'

'I'm really sorry.'

'You're a doctor.' She shrugged. 'It's to be expected.' She left her green eyes on Eric for a moment. Usually, this was enough.

A teenage girl, hair in pigtails, with a fiery Texas-shaped restaurant logo emblazoned across her gingham dress, approached the table. 'Are you guys ready to order?' Her voice was a little too friendly for her face. And Katherine noticed a tattoo on her arm – four black, criss-crossing slashes.

Katherine laughed. 'I've been reading this menu for a half-hour.'

'I know what I want.' Eric put his enormous menu in the waitress's hands. 'The baby back rack of ribs and a Heineken,' he said.

'I'll have the chicken,' Katherine told her. 'And another glass of, of water.'

'Regular or extra spicy?'

'Spicy,' Eric said.

'I'll try that, too.'

'Try what?' The waitress was looking at a group of people coming through the door.

'The spicy.' Katherine raised her eyebrows.

They watched quietly as their waitress slouched toward the kitchen.

'It's not very healthy,' Eric said, 'but I love this kind of food.'

'Me too.'

They were silent for a moment, their eyes flickering nervously around the restaurant. Two families were here, Katherine noted, one white, one black. There were a few couples. There was a group of students from the junior college.

'How is your mother?' Katherine was squeezing her hands beneath the table. She had to remember to keep them there.

'I think she's all right. For the time being, anyway. I mean, she—'

'She must be very worried.'

'Well, I told you about California, right?'

'He was on the beach.'

'Yeah,' Eric said. 'He was more or less homeless for a couple of weeks.'

Katherine nodded. 'I was curious about that. Did Pilot accept any treatment after he came back?'

Eric furrowed his brow. 'I gave him some anti-depressants.'

'They helped?'

'We thought so. But now I don't even know if he really took them.'

Outside, the parking lot was filling up. Katherine could feel it. Families and couples were leaving their mini-vans and four-wheel drives beneath the yellow, overhanging street lamps of East Meadow. They were entering grocery stores and family theme restaurants, picking up their dry-cleaning, a bottle of wine on the way home. Outside there were faces lit by the glow of dashboards and neon. The smell of exhaust and burning oil permeated the suburban atmosphere.

'Would you rather not talk about this right now?'

Eric looked at the ceiling. It seemed to be a habit with him,

Katherine noticed, this looking up. 'What about you, Katherine?' he said. 'Where are you from, anyway?'

'I grew up in the city.' She leaned forward a bit, eyes narrowing. 'As a matter of fact, this is the first and only time I've lived outside of it.'

'And?'

Katherine exhaled. 'And I feel like I'm going to die.'

Outside the restaurant was a continuously moving stream of cars, a steady burning of gasoline and oil, a consistent grating of metal on brake pads. Katherine thought she could hear the churning of a million pistons.

'You'll get used to it.'

'Have you ever lived in New York?'

The tattooed waitress arrived at that moment with an enormous platter of food. 'Here we go,' she said cheerily. It must have been sitting in the kitchen the whole time, Katherine thought, ready to serve the instant someone made the order.

'Holy shit.'

'You said you were starving.'

My brother's face, Katherine realized, was like mine, but larger and stronger. His eyes were as blue, she thought, as the earth from space. He had the face of a winner, our father had always said, the face of the next president. 'I'm starving,' she said, 'but—'

'I went to Columbia.'

'—this is insane.'

'Brain surgery school.'

'A very good brain surgery school,' Katherine acknowledged. Now she thought she shouldn't have used the word *insane*.

'You?' Eric began cutting into his ribs. They were reddish-black, smeared with barbecue sauce.

'NYU,' she said. 'Psychology. Graduate school, too.'

He nodded. 'I'm attracted to you,' he said bluntly. 'You should know that, you know, just in case.'

Did she look shocked? 'In case of—'

'I don't know.'

Katherine laughed. 'I'm recently divorced, sort of.'

'Sort of?'

'We weren't really married.'

He smiled slightly. 'Not really?'

'Living in sin.'

'It's completely over?'

'Completely.'

'How do you feel?'

'I'm very—'.

'—fragile?'

'*Unpredictable.*'

Ordinarily, she told herself, she would never do something like this. Ordinarily. But Katherine was making an extreme exception.

In the clinic the television was on, a blur of voices and faces. I sat in front of it on a squeaking vinyl couch. Quietly, somewhere behind me, a man was weeping. My mother had finally gone home.

'I like that,' Eric said, smiling. 'Unpredictability is a good quality.'

Katherine chewed on a piece of her blackened chicken, gnawing on a sliver of the burnt, brittle skin. It tasted like wood. The sauce was way too spicy. 'You've, you've never been married?'

'Wanted to,' Eric said from behind a rib bone. 'Went to medical school in Virginia. She wouldn't come with me, though. She was like you.' He was chewing and swallowing rapidly, wolfing it down.

I'll tear out your carotid artery with my bare hands.

'Like me?'

'A New Yorker.'

'She couldn't take the idea of living in Virginia just for a few years?'

'Of living in Virginia with *me*', he said, 'for any length of time.'

Katherine laughed. 'And how did you like it?'

Through a smile and a mouthful of coleslaw, my brother said, 'She was right.'

'That's the only one?'

'The only one what?'

'The only girl you ever considered marrying?'

'I've considered it with others,' Eric said. 'She just happened to be the only one I ever asked.'

'Is this getting too personal?'

'Not at all. It's my turn, though.'

Katherine sat back. 'OK.'

'Your ex-boyfriend's name?'

She looked around, as if he were in the room somewhere. 'My ex-boyfriend's name is Mark.' It sounded right, she thought. *Ex.*

'What does he do?'

'Lawyer. Corporate finance.'

'How'd you meet?'

'High school sweethearts, if you can believe it.'

Eric leaned forward, elbows on the table. 'I can believe it.'

'We went to NYU together, too, and then he went to Law School—'

'Where?'

'Fordham.'

'And then?'

'And then we moved in together.'

'What was the problem?'

Katherine refolded her napkin. 'I didn't love him, as it turned out.'

'Oh.'

She nodded. 'It was painful . . . *is* painful.'

'Did he love you?'

'He says he did.'

'Does he still?'

'No.'

They spent a few more moments chewing. Katherine liked the relaxed way Eric leaned over his plate. She liked the way he had rolled his shirtsleeves over his elbows, the way he licked his fingers and drank his beer directly from the green bottle.

She said, 'Me, too.'

He was looking at her, a satellite dish ready to receive.

'I also find you attractive.' She immediately realized she

shouldn't have said it. But she felt as though she had waded too far in now to back out – she had to swim to the other side.

'Really?'

'It must happen to you all the time,' she said hurriedly, 'being a brain surgeon and everything.'

'Not as much as I had originally hoped.' Eric wiped his hands on his paper napkin. 'But I have met my quota of doctor groupies.'

'My father was a doctor,' Katherine said.

'That's usually the case.'

She raised an eyebrow. 'Is it?' She tried to affect a look of modest offense, but the truth is that she was embarrassed.

'Girls want to marry their dads, don't they?'

'I thought I was the only psychologist at this table.'

'Then you tell me.' Eric touched his napkin to his lips, his whole face a question. 'Don't girls want to marry their fathers and boys want to marry their mothers? Isn't that the—'

'That's what Freud maintained. Sort of.'

'Wasn't he right?'

'I don't think so, not entirely.'

'Not entirely?'

'Will you pass me that bread?'

'Are you trying to change the subject?'

'You're an extremely interesting conversationalist,' Katherine said, using her green eyes to subdue him.

Eric nodded. 'I have a lot of interests.'

'Do you want to marry your mother?'

Eric looked at the ceiling again and said, 'Good point.'

Katherine kept on smiling. Too long, she thought later, way too long.

In the spare *enclosure* overlooking the highway Katherine scolded herself. She'd been too flirtatious. It was probably the cheap wine. She'd downed three glasses of it before Eric had arrived and then, stupidly, pretended not to have been drinking anything at all, sipping ice-water the rest of the meal. Of course he knew she'd been drinking. He was a fucking brain surgeon. He could see it in her eyes – the dilation of the pupils, a slight relaxation of the facial muscles, blood congestion in the cheeks. Was she slurring her words, for Christ's sake? The truth was Katherine was afraid of my brother. The truth was she had never been asked to dinner by a man that handsome.

She'd panicked. It had suddenly occurred to her that Eric would find it even more unprofessional – his brother's therapist drinking wine at a barbecue restaurant.

At home she undressed, pulling off her gray slacks first, then unbuttoning her blouse. She hadn't shaved her legs in weeks.

In her tiny bedroom she rushed out of her clothes and threw them on the floor of her closet. Her underwear went in the laundry pile in the corner of the room. She didn't even have a hamper, not even a trash can. She'd left Mark with everything. He'd wanted it all, too. 'You'll come back,' he'd said. 'You'll come back and it will all be here, just the way you left it.' So melodramatic.

'Mark, this is not a soap opera.'

'You'll realize how much you love me, that you can't make it on your own without—'

'*Mark*,' she'd said, 'this is not an argument.'

He had brooded then, sulking around the apartment, arms folded.

Katherine *was* sorry, had been sorry. She'd be sorry for a long time, in fact. She was well aware of that. She knew she didn't love Mark. She had never loved him. And then Michele. What else could she do but leave? Katherine didn't know what the experience of love was, really. She only knew that she'd never had it. She looked at her naked image in the full-length mirror on the back of her bedroom door. She was as beautiful as she was ever going to be. Her flesh was getting softer. Her breasts hung slightly lower than they had five years ago. There were lines around her eyes. This was it. She wasn't going to get any better.

Katherine was five feet, five inches tall, exactly. She had measured herself so many times as a teenager, hoping she'd grow that extra inch or two that would make her taller than Michele, her sister younger by nearly two years. It never happened, of course. Nothing wished for that hard ever happens, it seemed. Michele had grown taller and more beautiful, her body more lithe and slender, like the stalk of a daffodil, her hair yellow-blonde like the flower itself. Michele's eyes, unlike Katherine's, were permanently soft, like she'd been half drunk, half sad all her life. Michele had never had control of her eyes the way Katherine did.

Trevor Davidson, John Taborre, Jimmy Schindler.

These were the names of the boyfriends Michele had managed to steal from Katherine when they were growing up.

And then, of course, Mark.

How could Michele have done it? What was she thinking?

Katherine's skin was pale, but had an olive cast just beneath the surface that made her overall tone like a sheet of fine writing paper. The bridge of her nose was decorated with light freckles from too many unprotected summers at the beach – like flecks of rag inside the linen.

There were too many imperfections to count.

One of Katherine's breasts was slightly larger than the other. None of the men she'd ever been with had ever mentioned it, of course. No one, in fact – not even Michele or her mother – had ever said anything about it. But when she stood in front of the full-length mirror with no clothes on it was all Katherine could see, the right breast fuller, heavier, almost a C cup, hanging lower, its nipple larger too; the left breast lighter, the skin tighter, it seemed, pulling it closer to her chest. This breast – the left one – had a single, dark, curling hair sprouting from the light brown aureole. Katherine cut it close to the skin every couple of months, but before she knew it, it was there again. Naked, she crossed into the living room where her mattress lay on the floor. She thought maybe she'd take a bath, stare at the tiles on the ceiling, sip a cup of tea. She stepped into the efficiency kitchen and put the glass kettle she'd bought at Safeway on the stovetop. When did she realize the phone was ringing? The answering machine was already speaking to someone, it seemed. 'Hello,' it said. 'You've reached Katherine DeQuincey-Joy. Please leave a message at the beep.'

'Katherine,' a voice told the room. 'It's me, Eric. Are you home?'

She hesitated, then picked up. 'Eric?' It was a cheap cordless she'd bought at the local Radio Shack. It had the strangest signal, a high-pitched squeal somewhere inside it.

'Hi.'

'Hi.' She walked across the length of the apartment, in front of the window, hoping the squeal would go away if she moved.

'I just wanted to make sure you got home all right.'

The wine. He'd known about the wine. 'Yes, of course. Are you still—'

'I'm in the car.'

'Where do you live, anyway?'

'I live down the road a bit. In the country.'

Could she hear the road he was on? 'I see.' The tires on the asphalt?

'I had a nice time.'

She didn't say anything.

'Did you?'

Katherine smiled. 'Yes,' she said. 'Thank you, I really did.'

'Anyway, that's all I wanted to say.'

Katherine looked out the window, at the parking lot and the highway beyond it. She had the same view from her office, more or less. This must be what it looks like out there, she thought. Parking lots and highways, a smattering of trees in the distance. 'It was nice of you to call.' She would have to do something about this. She would have to avoid Eric in the future.

'I'm not always such a gentleman.' He laughed a little.

'I'm sure you are.'

'You bring it out in me.'

'Ordinarily I'm sure you're a terrific bastard.' Could he hear her smiling?

'Terrible.'

'Scum of the earth.'

'You'd be surprised,' he said. 'Doctors aren't known for being such nice guys.'

She couldn't let this go any further. She changed the subject. 'I'll be speaking to your brother tomorrow.'

'I'm sure he's in good hands.'

'Well,' Katherine said, 'it's the medication that will have the greatest effect, as you know. I'll just try to make sure he gets back to normal as quickly as—'

'Pilot hasn't been normal for a while. But thank you in advance for looking out for him.'

'You're a good brother, Eric.'

'I'm not so sure Pilot would agree.'

The kettle began to scream.

'The water's boiling,' Katherine said. 'I have to go.'

'My mother drinks tea,' Eric said from the car.

'She does?'

'Maybe Freud was right.'

Katherine Jane DeQuincey-Joy stood in the kitchenette of her *enclosure*, the phone to her ear, naked, and felt the impulse to tell him, to describe herself to Eric – her uneven breasts, the hair sprouting from her nipple, the chewed nails. But she didn't, only saying, 'Goodnight, Eric.' And for some reason after she hung up the phone, she said it again, more clearly this time, to no one at all. 'Goodnight, Eric Airie.'

She would have to stop this, she told herself.

There was another message on her machine, so Katherine pushed the button.

Michele had been calling.

Michele had been calling on and off for a couple of years now, but the messages were increasing lately and growing longer, more frantic, month by month. Often, when Katherine came home from work and saw the message light blinking, she'd listen, holding her finger a millimeter above the delete button. 'Katherine,' her sister would say, 'Katherine, it's me, it's Michele. I just wanted you to know that I'm doing great, that everything's great, really great, and, and, and I'm probably going to get this new job at a, well, at this nice little bookstore. I thought you'd like that, right? I mean, how you love to read and everything. Anyway—' And if it became too much, Katherine pushed the delete button, a single depression of the middle finger, saying, *Fuck you, Michele – disappear*.

Sometimes Katherine just listened to hear her sister's voice, the desperation so far inside it, so much a part of it that it had retained a permanent quaver, a modulation like an uncertain stroke across the string of a cello. Sometimes Katherine deleted the message before she'd even heard it. She knew it was Michele, she told herself, by the way the message light on her answering machine blinked.

My brother got into his vintage black Jaguar after seeing Katherine to her sapphire-blue VW Rabbit in the parking lot of the barbecue restaurant and waited, watching, while she pulled out on to the highway. He wondered how much wine she'd had before he arrived. Perhaps she shouldn't be driving, he thought. A few moments later, he pulled out himself. He had a long drive ahead of him, but one he was accustomed to making. He put a disc into the Blaupunkt, Vivaldi's 'Four Seasons', and he whistled along with it, the even measures of music filling the car's interior.

Eric liked Katherine. He liked her tangle of crazy hair. He liked her clear, freckled skin. He liked her green, anxious eyes. He especially liked the intelligence that beamed out of them and, being Eric, my brother, he liked the idea of the challenge her eyes represented.

He thought of our mother's eyes, of the ghosts she'd been seeing, the double images and blurred outlines.

Could it be cancer?

He drove this way for a while, trying to re-live each beat of his conversation with Katherine, considering the way she used her silverware, divining her socio-economic background. He saw a strong father, middle class, an intellectual but unfulfilled mother. He saw Katherine's girlhood head behind book after book, her eventual transcendence into graduate school, her yearning for independence.

He smiled to himself.

It doesn't take a brain surgeon, he thought.

The clock on his mahogany dashboard said five after eleven. He'd wait another few minutes, and then he would call. Just to check in, make sure she was all right. Tell her what a good time he had.

Women like that.

He whistled along with the music. He stared ahead at the highway, its gray asphalt rushing toward him, the yellow lines slipping under the tires like time. He gripped the wheel and accelerated, pushing his car from seventy, to eighty, to ninety miles an hour. He was alone out here. His radar detector, clipped beneath the dash, didn't even blink. No police. He was free and clear. He turned off the music and picked up the phone, dialing information for the number.

When Katherine's machine answered he was, at first, concerned. 'Katherine,' he said. 'It's me, it's Eric. Are you home?'

But she picked up after a moment and her voice revealed everything.

I was moved from the squeaking vinyl couch in the lobby by a nurse with a wide, beautiful, brown face and soft, warm hands. 'Come with me, honey,' she said. 'Come back to bed now and rest.' Her eyes were dead, though, clouded over like the sky outside the windows. I got up and followed her, my feet shuffling in slippers I couldn't remember putting on. Later, in my room, I heard the voices in the light fixtures whispering, arguing, commenting, but I couldn't quite make out exactly what they were saying any more – they were just out of reach. I heard the long, thin branch of the tree outside tapping away at the glass. I heard the soft hum of the hospital itself. I could hear my mother all the way across the highway and the woods and the cul-de-sac. I could hear her voice. She was talking to herself, just softly, her feet *crick-crick-cricking* across the blue and white oriental rug, a cup of tea in her hands. From my hospital bed I could hear across the highway and beyond the woods and far out over the hills that lay past East Meadow to my brother in his car, the even measures of the 'Four Seasons' playing on his car stereo, his fingers gripped tightly on the wheel.

His thoughts were racing over the yellow lines quicker than his tires. I reached up to feel the scab on my face. Was it fading? I felt the shoelace twisted around the middle of my right hand like a reminder. I tried to smile – tried to move my face at all – when an aide came and turned out the overhead, quieting the voices, dimming the room. I could feel my cheekbones hardening inside my face, the skull turning to porcelain, my teeth like glass. Somewhere down the hall, a man was saying, 'Oh, please, oh please, oh please.' There were long shadows cast across my body, and my body was too thin and too long and I was as brittle as a skeleton.

The afternoon before the night of the party when Fiona disappeared for ever our mother was putting eyeshadow on, green to match her eyes, in front of the gold-framed vanity mirror she kept in her dressing room. Fiona was standing behind her, hand on her shoulder, fascinated by every application of color.

I wanted money. 'Hey, Mom,' I said, standing in the doorway, 'can I have five bucks?'

Our mother smiled through this question. 'What for?'

'I helped get the house ready for the party.'

She kept smiling. 'That wasn't out of the kindness of your heart, my dear one?'

'I helped, too,' Fiona put in.

Dismissively, she said, 'I know you did.'

'All right, then,' I bargained. 'I'll take four.'

Our mother turned to face me, one eye made up, the other bare. 'What happened to your allowance?'

'Two dollars?' I said. 'Two dollars is a joke. Lenny Haverston gets five.' Lenny Haverston lived up the street. He had everything.

'Well, aren't the Haverstons extravagant!' Our mother sprayed her hair, teased into a million specific and individual curls and the little dressing room become that much more toxic.

'Wow,' I said, 'you look great.'

Fiona said, 'You're beautiful, Mommy.'

'Where'd you two learn that?' our mother asked. 'From your father?'

'Learn what?'

'Flattery.'

I tried again. 'Three dollars?'

Our mother sighed. 'You can take two dollars out of my purse – *if* I have it.'

'Can I?' Fiona said. 'Can I, too?'

'Fiona,' she said, and then she reneged. 'All right.'

'I'm nine and I get two and she's seven and she gets two?'

'That's the way life is.' Our mother applied eyeshadow to the forgotten eye, silvery green, fading to fox brown. She closed her lid and brushed the color on, and then dusted more powder on to the brush. All she wore was a slip and a bra, shimmery yellow. I could see her feet touching each other nervously beneath the vanity.

'How many people are coming?' I asked.

'We invited absolutely everybody,' our mother said. 'Everyone on the planet, it seems.'

'Everybody?' Fiona laughed.

'Everybody.'

'Even the pope?'

'Even the pope.'

'The president?' Fiona was giggling, her face contorted.

'They did not invite the president,' I said. 'God, Fiona, you're so stupid.'

'She knows that,' our mother said. 'She's just being silly.'

'What about Donny Osmond?' Fiona asked. 'Did you invite Donny Osmond, too?'

'She invited your butt,' I said.

'Pilot.'

'She invited *your* butt,' Fiona shot back.

I laughed derisively.

'*Mom*,' Fiona pleaded.

Our mother unscrewed a tube of lipstick. 'Kiss me, you two.' She put her arms out, reaching for us. 'Because once the lipstick goes on, there's no more kissing.'

* * *

At the party were the Tischmans from next door. There were the Johnsons and the Brooks and the Daniers. There were the Joneses and the Browns and the Ellimans and the Haverstons. There were more. There were people who came to the party and left early. There were people from the neighborhood, from our father's airline, from our mother's hospital. There were four bachelors, including Paul Davidson, Karl Fuchs, Arnold Desmond and Bryce Telliman – the last one turned out to be the man with the blond hair. Equally, according to my mother's plans, there were four single women – Celia Oblena, Sherry Meyerson, Tricia Caulder and Lacy Klugman, our mother's best friend, a divorcee. There were people who came uninvited. There were people at the party whom our parents hardly knew. There were introductions. There were chance meetings, new acquaintances, old arguments. There were romantic trysts, stolen kisses, secret encounters. There was grab-ass.

That night I wandered through the party stealing sips, the different flavors weird on my tongue, from people's drinks. The women leaned down to speak to me in silly, high-pitched tones and I took the opportunity to look down their shirts. The men collared me and spoke in gruff, overly-friendly voices, slapping me on the shoulders. I smiled back at these grown-ups, wondering who the hell some of them were, recognizing others as the parents of children I knew from school.

Many of these people wanted to know who I was.

'Pilot,' I'd say.

'Are you the proprietor of this establishment?' one especially tall woman asked me.

'What are you talking about?'

'Hey, little guy,' one man said to me, 'would you happen to know where I might go to the bathroom?'

'In the pool,' I said.

'A real wiseguy,' I overheard someone say about me.

'Just like his father.'

'Pilot,' some man said. I didn't recognize him. 'Pilot.' He was rotund, with a gray and black beard. 'Why don't you run and grab me another ice-cold can of beer?' He smiled. 'Would you do that for an old friend?'

I studied this man. He wore a blue, gold-buttoned jacket, even though it was very warm out. 'No.'

'Don't you remember me?' he said. 'I met you about – well, about five years ago. How old are you now, Pilot?'

'Nine,' I said.

'That would make you about four in those days. And that would make me about forty-four back then.' He laughed drunkenly. 'So how about it, Pilot? An ice-cold one?'

I said I would, but by the time I reached the kitchen I had experienced so much additional confusion I couldn't bear the idea of making my way back out.

Plus, I didn't like the way he kept repeating my name.

And our father was standing in the kitchen door. 'How're ya holdin' up there, my boy?' he said.

I nodded, saying, 'I'm fine.' He only said *my boy* when he'd been drinking.

Our father put a hand directly on top of my head. He cupped his ear to someone at the party. 'Ice?'

'Ice!' someone shouted back. 'Yes! More ice!'

He turned to look at me. 'Shit,' he said. 'I'm not sure if we have any more ice.'

'There's ice,' I said. I saw it in the sink behind him. 'There's plenty of ice.'

He was drunk. And probably for the first time in my life I understood what that meant. I didn't know where it would lead. I only knew that he wasn't himself right now, that my real father wouldn't return until the morning.

He had placed torches all around the pool and now, the night having completely taken over the yard, they illuminated the faces of our party guests like actors in stage lights. Their smiles lit up strangely, surrealistically, and there was so much talking I could no longer distinguish one individual voice from the next, except that every now and then I thought I heard my name being mentioned somewhere in the vast conversation. I began to feel they were

71

talking about me secretly, knowing they could speak freely about me because I couldn't hear them above the din. I stood in the kitchen door like that for a long time, my father looming above me, just listening to the number of times my name was mentioned. Were they pointing, too? Were they laughing? People moved in and out of the kitchen door, moving past me like I wasn't even there. I caught glimpses of Fiona every now and then, flirting with the blond man with the mustache. Sometimes he would pick her up, and she would put her arms around him and whisper into his ear. Was it about me? She still wore her red bathing suit and red tennis shoes. What was she saying?

The view from the woods was of the yellow torches flashing gold light off the surface of the water in the pool. It was of the faces of the people at this party rising up in flashes of light, too, frozen as if in a strobe. It was of glittering drinks with shining ice cubes rattling inside the shimmering glasses. The view from the woods was of women in stylish, shining dresses, men in dark shorts and Hawaiian shirts. It was of blue jeans on the younger people and summer suits on the older ones. It was of a crowd of people surrounding a small backyard pool, a party on flagstones, a surfeit of lawn chairs. It was of two children, one nine, one seven, squirming through this crowd of adults, the adults leaning toward them from time to time, hands on their knees, pretending, with great hilarity and laughter, that these children – this little boy and girl – were the hosts.

I moved closer, imperceptible to the people in the backyard, creeping fern by fern, millimeter by millimeter, toward the house. I was the earth rolling beneath the lawn, unfurling like a blanket.

The party continued and I advanced silently, one billionth of an inch at a time, closer and closer.

Someone had put 'Light My Fire' on the stereo.

'—so anyway, Hannah,' I heard someone saying to my mother, 'I was just coming off Sky Highway, turning my steering wheel when I felt this terrible pain, this shooting pain in my hand, and I was wondering, wondering just what—'

'It could be arthritis.'

'She certainly isn't old enough for—'

'—ain't seen nothing yet, Dave. Let me tell you—'

'—been trapping animals out there, and he caught the family cat by accident, can you believe—'

'Can I help you with something, some drinks, perhaps?'

'—along came the train and when I got on all I could think about was Marcia and how I just wanted to get back to her.'

'Really?'

'Well, that was a long, long time ago.'

'Eric did, or was it Pilot?'

'—cute, aren't you, just fantastically adorable, little—'

'—about your other son, Jim, don't you have—'

'—was, flying on fumes, practically, no fucking idea in the world if I was even in the right vicinity, the Viet Cong shooting at me, snipers everywhere, and when I saw that clearing, I—'

'—get me another one—'

'—all my favorite songs—'

'—just went straight for it, I mean, you don't see that kind of thing in the jungle over there, not very often, and not where I was flying—'

'—tells this story every time he drinks, it's embarrassing—'

'—love her—'

'—are you disagreeing?'

'—no, sir—'

'I swear to God I thought you said *disappearing*.'

'What?'

'—in that part of the world it's all vegetation, all jungle, climbing vines, mangroves, weird swamps, and those people live like it's a thousand years ago, ten thousand—'

'Do they really eat bugs?'

'—had too much, I think—'

'It's the same story every time he drinks.'

'Well, I'm sorry, all right? I happen to think it's an entertaining story and I happen to be drinking sometimes when other people are around, so if you don't mind—'

'—think it's a wonderful story, really I—'

'—hell is he, anyway?'

'Excuse me, you said, but are you *disappearing* with me?'

'Oh my God, that is *so* hilarious.'

'—like you've got a girlfriend. She's not bothering you, is—'

In the woods was a stillness derived from this view of the party. In the woods out here behind our parents' house was a quiet which only a short but infinite distance enables. There was a darkness in these woods in contrast to the brightness of the faces lighting up in the torchlight. There was a rustling in the treetops. As always, there was wind in the leaves. There was unrest. There was an almost imperceptible chill arriving through the trunks and black bark of the trees that came up from somewhere deep in the ground, some great source of coldness that rose inexorably this time of year. From the woods a voice would rise off the top of the party and take on a life of its own. A flicker of light would bank off a bough. A shriek of laughter would pierce through the branches, a strain of music wafting in like perfume and in here it would sound exactly like someone was screaming, but at such a low volume that it was almost impossible to hear. I saw a man step into the woods, a man with long blond hair, a man who was thin and young, silhouetted against the dark trees. He put his hand on a trunk and let his head drop. I could see his chest heaving as if he were crying or, I thought, as if he were about to be sick.

I see her in a still image, my sister, her legs wrapped around the waist of the blond man with the blond mustache – of Bryce Telliman – her lips inside his ear. He is looking at me, a slight smile on his mouth. What is she saying? Her red one-piece swimsuit is riding high up on her seven-year-old hips and her red high-top sneakers, untied, are dangling off her feet. I can see their laces. His hair is so bleached from the sun that it is white and his skin is too tan. He seems glamorous, Bryce Telliman, as if he doesn't belong at this party, but should be at another, where all the girls are wearing swimsuits and the music is rock and roll and the people are dancing. But he is here, strangely enough, at my parents' house. And in this imaginary photograph there are other people behind them, but only in the background, and they are fading into the darkness like images in an old newspaper photograph, and Fiona's skin shines whitely, illuminated by the fiery torchlight.

He looks at me directly and Fiona regards me suspiciously from the corner of her eye while she tells him her secret. What was it? What was she saying?

Why wouldn't she tell me?

Katherine arrived at work late, as usual, as she had practically every morning since she started this job, and took the very last staff spot, walking the entire length of the hospital parking lot to the clinic, her arms full of forms she wouldn't get to, a newspaper she would never read. The section of the *Times* she had dropped yesterday still lay on the ground. She stepped over it, thinking she'd pick it up on the way home. She would have to start getting in earlier, she told herself. She would have to get her life together. Katherine held everything under one arm and pushed her fingers through her hair, realizing the familiar insane tangle was even worse than usual. In the car she had noticed a run in her pantyhose from her ankle to her knee. There was an ink stain on her sleeve she hadn't seen at home. Jesus Christ, she was falling apart. How the hell did she expect to impress anyone, much less a neurosurgeon, when she was such a mess?

She thought of the way she had flirted with my brother last night, the phone call after she'd gotten home, and her face went hot. She would pretend it had never happened.

As she entered the clinic she saw that Elizabeth had arranged a pot of tea with lemon on a tray and was filling the pot with hot water from the kettle. 'Elizabeth,' Katherine said, approaching, her voice soft.

'I thought I would save you some time,' her secretary said, whispering, 'You're late. And I thought it would be nice.'

Katherine shook her head. 'It *is* nice,' she said. 'You are the nicest person in the world. I don't deserve you.'

Elizabeth followed Katherine into her office and placed the tray on the least cluttered piece of desk she could find. 'You have David

Ogden here right away,' Elizabeth said, still whispering for some reason. 'He's been waiting fifteen minutes already. And then you have Marie Forche and after that, after *her*, I mean, you have Pilot Airie. That is your morning.'

'Thanks.' Katherine picked up the little pot and poured herself a cup. 'You can send David in right now.' She dipped the wedge of lemon into the cup. There was even a jar of honey.

I had been coated with molten glass that had since hardened around my skin. It was the medication, I guess. I couldn't smile. I couldn't frown. If I tried to move the muscles of my face, I thought, it would shatter and cut me to pieces. 'I'm sorry about the other day,' I told Katherine, entering, closing the door softly behind me.

She got up from her desk and extended her hand. 'Sorry?'

'I wasn't feeling myself.' I moved the shoelace from one hand to the other, shook hers mechanically and then sat on the office couch. I couldn't remember the last time I had felt like myself. I wondered what my*self* felt like. Perhaps it wasn't coated with glass. Perhaps it was *all* glass. I wore a pair of old gray sweat pants and a T-shirt I remembered buying at least five or six years ago, I think it was in college. I wondered why it was even here. Did my mother bring it? I couldn't remember putting this T-shirt on. I had a feeling it said something humiliating, but I was too afraid to look down and read it.

Katherine Jane DeQuincey-Joy sat in the brown office chair opposite me and smiled reassuringly. 'I imagine that's a bit of an understatement,' she laughed. 'Not feeling well, I mean.'

I tried to form a smile, too, but I could feel the glass starting to crack so I stopped. I twisted the shoelace around and around my middle finger.

Around and around and around.

'Last time we spoke', she said, 'you told me you were hearing voices, arguments in the light fixtures, that kind of thing. Have they stopped? Can you still hear them?'

I felt so ridiculous. 'No,' I said. 'I can't hear them now.' There was, however, a rustling outside her door, a gathering of feet. There were ears, I thought, pressed against the keyhole.

She nodded. 'Good.' Katherine's voice was overly gentle, as if she too were afraid the glass that had formed around me would shatter into a billion pieces. 'And you were thinking the woods were going to swallow you, or that they had swallowed you somehow?'

'It was stupid,' I said. 'I apologize.'

'It's not stupid, Pilot.' Katherine put her hand on one of her knees. I could see a run in her stocking, starting at her ankle and disappearing into her skirt, a skirt I couldn't quite get the color of. 'But you've been over all of these questions with Dr Lennox, haven't you?'

'Yes.' I had. The voices, the irrational fears, the disorientation. I felt I had responded adequately. I had answered honestly, in fact.

'Do you know what's happening to you?'

'I'm freaking out,' I answered. 'I've gone nuts.' The shoelace was cutting off my circulation. My finger was starting to swell.

'You haven't gone nuts,' Katherine said. 'You've had a relatively major psychotic episode, though.' Her green eyes widened. 'Dr Lennox thinks you may have some form of schizophrenia, which nowadays is an eminently treatable disorder. You're not crazy, Pilot, no matter what you've heard or what anybody tells you.'

Schizophrenia. The word stuck out in her sentence like a thorn.

'I'm glad you think so,' I said.

'I can see that you're responding well to the Clozaril,' Katherine said, 'which is a very good sign.'

There were interesting shadows forming on the wall behind her, as if they were hinting at the shapes of things, of animal legs, of tree limbs. 'I always respond well to medication,' I said. Of fingers curling, ferns reaching up toward the sun.

'What does that mean?'

'I did a lot of drugs in high school,' I told her. 'Grass. Acid. That's probably why my brain is so weak now.'

'Weak? Your brain is not weak, Pilot, and, as far as anyone

knows, smoking pot and dropping acid never caused schizophrenia.'

My voice felt flat and electronic, but I tried to make it sound funny, anyway. 'Maybe they just didn't do as much acid as me.'

Katherine shook her head, but I could see she was amused. 'One of the triggers of schizophrenia can often be stress. I was wondering if there was anything bothering you last week.' She looked up. 'Anything upsetting that you think may have – well, just if there was anything that upset you?'

'Last week?'

Schizophrenia. She was using the word over and over, trying to desensitize it, scrape the meaning from its skin.

'Before you went into the woods.'

'You've spoken to my mother?'

Katherine nodded.

'She's seeing ghosts,' I told her. 'She has a brain tumor.' Hadn't anything been done about this yet? All the way from here, I knew that at this moment, this very instant, it doubled, radical cells dividing.

'Seeing ghosts?'

'Apparitions, walking transparencies, double images moving across her field of vision. Why do you think I went into the woods?' My face was starting to melt the glass away.

She touched her hair and it was even crazier than yesterday. 'Apparitions of anyone in particular?'

'She has a brain tumor,' I insisted. 'A formation at the base of her optic nerve. I'm sure of it. Did you talk to Eric?'

'I spoke to Eric,' Katherine said.

'Didn't he tell you?'

She shook her head. 'Nothing about a tumor.'

'He knows it's there,' I informed Katherine, 'but he won't do anything about it.'

She looked away, constructing a hypothesis in her head, considering my diagnosis. 'Eric told me you had a sister—'

'Fiona,' I broke in.

'—and that when she disappeared—'

'Eric killed Fiona,' I said.

Katherine stopped talking.

I repeated myself. 'Eric *killed* Fiona.'

Katherine permitted a silence to enter this office. It descended like the folds of a new white sheet over the two of us. And then she began, 'You think your brother—'

'He killed her,' I said, laughing. 'And now he's going to have to kill me.'

I could see that Katherine was trying to remain calm, but that this was upsetting to her, confounding her belief in my progress, the so-called positive response I was having to the medicine.

'Pilot,' Katherine said, 'have you ever told anyone about this before?'

'No,' I said. 'It just occurred to me to mention it.'

'Just now?'

'Last week, before the episode.'

'Your mother's brain tumor,' Katherine said. 'Where do you think it came from?'

'I don't know where brain tumors come from, Katherine, I just know—'

'OK.'

'—that Eric knows and won't do anything about it.'

Katherine leaned back. I shouldn't have been saying any of this, I knew. I knew I was screwing everything up as usual. But I liked Katherine – Katherine with the shadows moving on the wall behind her, shadows of animal legs and tree limbs against a grass clearing in the day's last light, a clearing somewhere in the woods, a patch of woods somewhere in the world, a world dropping like a rock down a well, a faraway splash. There should have been pictures on the wall, I thought, something to keep the white paint from receding away for ever into nothingness and snow.

'Let's talk about this,' Katherine said.

I twisted the shoelace even tighter and my face was starting to feel normal again.

* * *

The day after the party, our mother was in the kitchen putting the kettle on for tea. 'Where is—'

'—Fiona?' Eric said.

'Yes, where is your sister?'

'I haven't seen her,' he said.

But how did he know? How did he know what she was going to ask?

'She's in bed. She's in her room,' he told her.

'Still?'

I sat on the couch in the living room and listened to the conversation between Eric and our mother coming from the kitchen. Their voices walked through the door like people entering a party.

'Maybe she's in the yard,' I heard him say. 'How should I know?'

'Pilot!' our father called. '*Pilot!*'

'Don't be flip,' our mother warned.

I got up from the couch and walked into the sun-filled kitchen. I had my pajamas on, having slipped into them when I went back to bed earlier that morning. Once through the door, I said, 'What?' even though I knew what I was being summoned for.

Our father and mother sat at the table. It was nearly two in the afternoon. 'Go out there and find your sister.'

'Maybe she's at Tracy's house,' I offered. Tracy was Fiona's best friend.

'Tracy's in Germany,' our mother said.

I shrugged. 'Oh, yeah.'

'She's out in the back somewhere,' Eric said. 'She must be.'

'Go out and get her,' our father said to me, irritated. 'I'm starting to worry.'

I went outside and stood on the flagstones. Beyond the pool was a stretch of soft grass before our yard became woods and just beyond the treeline the woods got deeper, grew thicker and darker, the way things do until a center is reached, a critical mass is formed.

'*Fiona!*' I shouted. In my pajamas I walked around the pool and across the grass and back to the treeline. '*Fiona!*' Next door, a golden retriever I had never seen before was taking a crap on the neighbor's lawn. I felt a coolness in the air, not as distinct as last night, but it was there. I yelled for Fiona once again. I heard the kitchen door, its familiar creak, opening behind me. I turned and saw my father standing on the flagstones.

He cupped his hands to his mouth. '*Fiona!*'

'She's not out here,' I said.

'Where the hell is she?'

'Maybe she's in the basement.'

Our father turned around. 'Eric,' he said, 'check the basement.'

I walked back to the house and into the kitchen. I could feel something rising inside my stomach, something slimy and alive. 'She's not out back,' I said to our mother.

Her face was a mass of little snakes moving beneath her skin, rippling and squirming.

'Does she ever go into the woods?' our father asked.

'She's too scared.'

'Could she be at another neighbor's house?' he said. 'Are there any other girls around here she plays with?'

'Just Tracy,' our mother said. Her hands were shaking.

Our father sat down at the table and put cream and sugar in his coffee. He stirred it with the sugar spoon. 'I'm so fucking hung over,' he said. 'I don't have time for—'

'Jim,' our mother said, 'the language.'

'Christ, Hannah.'

'Can I have some coffee, too?' I asked.

'No,' my parents said at the same time.

I tried to think of where Fiona might be. 'Did anyone look under the bed?'

'Why?'

'It was loud last night. Maybe she didn't like the noise. Maybe she's sleeping *under* the bed.'

Dad sighed. He thought this was a stupid idea, I could tell. But he said, 'Go look.'

I ran out of the room and up the stairs, stretching my legs and taking steps two at a time the way Eric did. I knew she wouldn't be up there. I knew she was not under the bed. But I walked into her room and looked, anyway. There were piles of clothes, strewn towels from the pool, crumpled blankets and bed sheets. I looked underneath her bed and saw only dust and a variety of headless, contorted Barbie dolls. I sat down on her bed and waited a few minutes until Hannah, our mother, stepped quietly into the room, her ankles making the softest *cricking*.

'She's not here?'

I shook my head.

'Where could she be?' She was feigning exasperation, pretending that Fiona did this all the time. But Fiona had never done this before. 'She must be somewhere.'

'She must be somewhere,' I repeated.

'A little girl can't just disappear.'

I nodded. 'She can't.'

'She'll be home any minute,' Hannah told me.

But that isn't entirely true, what I just said. Because after I looked under Fiona's bed I went around, from room to room, looking under everything. I looked under my bed, my parents' bed, under Eric's. I looked inside the closets of every room. I was looking under Eric's bed when I turned a certain way and thought I saw something, something under his desk just across the room.

And I did see something.

And then I returned to Fiona's room, and I sat down on her bed, and I could hear my mother coming, the *crick-crick-cricking* sound that her ankles made – still make – coming up the stairs.

Half-empty glasses were everywhere – on the tables, on the arms of chairs, on windowsills, on the floor. There were plastic cups and paper plates strewn all over the house. There were dark, adult-sized footprints on the hallway rug. The downstairs bathroom sink was smudged with make-up and the toilet was stopped. The light switch in the kitchen had been broken. There were new stains on all the furniture and carpets. On the grass outside there was a black scorch mark where someone had knocked a torch on to the ground. There was broken glass beside the pool. There was a stillness forming inside me. There was light coming through the trees as the afternoon progressed, but I knew that it would not last. There was my father standing in the yard, hands on his waist, his face radiating anger in bright white spikes. There was my mother in the kitchen, making cup after cup of tea.

I was ordered to go door to door to all of the neighbors' houses who had little girls and ask if Fiona was there or if they had seen her at all today.

Eric and my father explored the woods.

Hannah waited by the telephone.

I went to Marsha Grierson's house. I visited Debbie Brandice, Tracy Shaw and Bernadette Duprix. I saw some of the grown-up faces from the party last night.

'Have you seen Fiona, my sister?' I said politely. 'Have you seen her?' I tried not to appear panicked. I tried to remain calm.

'No,' they all said. 'We haven't seen her. I'm sorry.'

'That's OK.' I smiled mechanically, not wanting people to worry unnecessarily. 'But would you call my mother if you see her? Do you have our number?'

'I hope she's all right,' Tracy Shaw's mother said.

'She's probably just out playing somewhere and lost track of time,' I said easily. 'We'll find her.'

I went from house to house this way, knocking on every door in the neighborhood where I knew a girl anywhere near Fiona's age lived. But by five o'clock I had exhausted every possibility I could think of, so I went home, walking in through the kitchen.

'Did she come home?' I said. 'Mom?'

Hannah was on the telephone. She held a finger up, as if to put me on pause. 'Thank you,' she was saying. 'I'll wait.' She looked at me. The snakes under the skin on her face had hardened and now she had a permanent look of surprise. 'I'm calling the police,' she said. It's a look she would never quite lose.

I sat down at the kitchen table, exhausted, starving. I hadn't eaten anything since last night's potato chips.

'Oh, thank you,' my mother said into the kitchen phone. 'Yes, I want to talk to you about my daughter. She's, well, we can't find her, that is. We can't find her anywhere.' She twisted the white cord around her wrist. 'She's seven years old,' she said. 'Yes. No, we checked everywhere, all her friends, all the neighbors. Please, can you send someone over? Thank you. Yes. Only seven years old. Thank you very much. Goodbye.' Hannah put the phone down in the cradle. 'They're sending someone,' she informed me.

I looked at her. I tried to give my mother a look that would seem reassuring. But I only wanted to throw up. 'We'll find her,' I said. 'She's probably just out playing somewhere and lost track of time.' I waited and watched her pour another cup of tea before I said, 'I'm really hungry.'

Hannah sighed. 'Well, get yourself some cereal or something.'

'All right.'

Then Eric and my father walked in and I could smell the earth on their feet. 'Did she come home?' Dad said.

We didn't answer.

'I called the police. They're sending someone.'

'You called the *police*?'

'Yes.'

'What the hell can they do about it?'

'What if she—'

'*Hannah*.'

'I swear to God, Jim.'

Eric looked at me and I saw all the murderous hatred of his threats inside his eyes. I sifted some cornflakes out of a box. I felt as if I shouldn't be eating, but I was hungry. At the same time that I wanted to throw up, I was hungry. My hands were trembling, in fact, I was so incredibly hungry. I remember, anyway, that my hands were trembling. I remember that clearly.

Upstairs in my blue and red race-car bedroom I had the lights off. I had the radio on and I was listening to the American Top Forty with Casey Kasem. And when I heard my name called to come downstairs I understood exactly what I would be asked. For some reason, I could hardly move off the bed.

In our dining room, at the table where we only sat for holidays, there was a black man, with eyes that saw through walls, it seemed, they held so long on a single object. He wore a suit made of odd, thick material and he smelled strongly of pipe tobacco. He had a little notebook out on the table and a stubby pencil. His name was Detective Cleveland, I learned later. 'When did you first notice Fiona missing?' he was saying to my parents.

Our father pinched his eyes. 'This morning,' he said. He ran his hand through his short dark hair. 'It was—'

'It was early this afternoon,' our mother corrected. 'We had a party last night and didn't get out of bed until after one o'clock.' She shot our father a look, as if to say *pay attention*. 'It wasn't this morning.'

'OK.' Cleveland smiled. 'This afternoon. Can you tell me when you last saw her?'

'Last night,' I said.

Our parents nodded.

Eric folded his arms over his chest. 'Early last night,' he said, 'for me, anyway.'

'You didn't check on her before you went to bed?' Cleveland asked my parents.

My father said, 'No.'

My mother looked down.

'That's all right. Your kids are pretty independent, I guess. They all are these days.'

'There were a lot of people here,' our father told him. 'A big party. We were distracted.'

'You say you've checked all the houses around here where she likes to play? And you've looked out back in the woods and in all the playgrounds in the area?' Detective Cleveland's voice was quiet, with a trace of raspiness to it, like he had a sore throat.

'We checked everywhere.'

'You looked in the woods out back, all along that highway?'

'Fiona won't go in the woods,' I told him. 'And there aren't really any playgrounds.'

'What's that, son?'

I repeated it.

'Why's that?'

'She's afraid.'

'Is she a fearful girl?' Cleveland looked around the room, his eyes settling on each member of our family.

'No,' Dad said when Cleveland looked at him.

'Yes,' I said when he looked at me.

Hannah put her hand on my shoulder, which meant that Cleveland should ignore me, that I didn't know what I was talking about.

'OK.' Cleveland said. He made a note. 'When you all saw her at the party last night, do you remember what she was doing, was there anything unusual?'

'She's a seven-year-old,' our mother said.

'I know that, ma'am, it's just that I have to—'

'She was sitting on a man's lap,' I broke in.

'What man?'

'I don't know,' I said. 'He was blond. He had a mustache. He had a silk shirt.'

'Why didn't you say anything about this before?' my mother said.

'You saw him, too.'

'Who was he?'

My father's eyes started to move quickly around the room. 'Blond? With a mustache?'

Eric said, 'Did he look weird?'

I shrugged. 'I guess, weird,' I said. 'Weird, I guess.'

My mother said, 'Bryce.'

'Who?'

'Bryce Telliman. He's a physical therapist, from the hospital.'

'Mr and Mrs Airie,' Cleveland said, 'would it be possible for me to discuss this with you alone?'

Our father said, 'You two go upstairs for a few minutes.'

Eric and I left the room and went to the foot of the stairs in the hallway. We stopped there so we could listen to what was happening in the dining room. I could hear Cleveland's voice, low and raspy.

'Where is she?' I whispered to Eric.

He looked at me with lasers. 'She's dead.'

I felt my face getting hot. 'What do you mean?'

'That blond motherfucker physical therapist took her away from the party and he raped her and killed her, and we're going to find her body somewhere all horrible and hacked up into little pieces.'

I felt my eyes starting to burn.

'You're lucky,' Eric said. 'You're just lucky that it didn't happen to you. Because they like little boys better.'

Detective Cleveland had asked, 'What did she look like?' and when he said that, I knew I would never see my sister again.

I see her in still pictures.

I remember Fiona in the mornings before she went to school. I remember her hand on the banister that led to the front door. I can see her tiny seven-year-old fingers just touching it, so high up for her, the way her hair looked, the color of sand, and her shiny white boots. I can see her hand clutching the brown bag lunch that she had packed herself the night before.

I can see Fiona's red jacket with the pattern of little stars and flowers on it, her green corduroy pants.

All I really know about Fiona is here in these mental images. What can a nine-year-old boy know of his seven-year-old sister? That she liked candy? That she had a million Barbie dolls but loved only one? That she hated guns? That she loved to watch football? What is there to know about any seven-year-old? Fiona ate butterscotch pudding mix directly from the package. She found documentary news programs mesmerizing. She hated animals, was afraid of cats and dogs and mostly, she hated the woods, and would never go in there alone.

I carry this picture inside my head now.

I see Fiona's hand in another hand, a larger one. I see her standing at the edge of her bed, and she is pulling this hand backwards, her head shaking no, she doesn't want to go. Voices are being carried over the water of the pool and into the house. A flash of light is glancing off the window. I can see that her head is turned slightly toward the window and that her eyes are desperate with fear. This is the picture I carry with me in my head. This is the image I see whenever I close my eyes. She is wearing only her red bathing suit and her tennis shoes, floppy and untied on her feet. She has been told it will only be a little while, that they will be back soon, that there is nothing at all to worry about, everything is fine, Fiona, everything is all right and will always be all right and there will never be anything wrong or anyone to hurt you in your entire life.

'What did she look like?' Cleveland asked.

And I knew.

Our mother went to get a picture of Fiona that she kept on a small table in the living room. In those days, there were pictures of all of us there. This one was a year old, and already Fiona had grown larger, her face broader, more coarse. 'She's older than this now,' our mother said. It was a photograph Eric had taken in the backyard. It was just her face, a little girl's smiling, enormous, jagged-toothed face. It was framed in wood.

'Thank you,' Detective Cleveland said. 'This will do just fine for now.' He opened the back of the frame and removed the picture from the glass, peeling it away. 'I've already got two patrol cars in the area keeping an eye out and I'm going back to the station right now with this picture so we can check things more thoroughly. I'm going to have to ask one of you to stay here and call me if she turns up.' The detective got up and turned toward the door. 'I'll go ahead and let myself out.'

'Thank you,' our father said.

'Does this happen often?' Hannah broke in.

'What's that?'

'Do little, do children disappear like this very often around here?'

'Not so often, Mrs Airie, and when they do they always turn up, you know – they were off playing somewhere or fell asleep or something and they didn't know what time it was. It's possible that she wandered into another neighborhood and got lost. Don't you worry too much. I know this is nerve-racking, but we'll find her.'

Our mother nodded. Detective Cleveland backed out the door.

I ran upstairs and took one of her tennis shoes from inside the plastic Wonderbread bag and put it under my shirt. Then I ran out the kitchen door, across the yard and across the treeline. I already had that still image in my head, her hand in someone else's. I walked into the trees, following the sound of voices.

I heard them high in the treetops, first as just a whispering of my name. And as I moved slowly beyond the treeline I came to understand the voices were arguing about me. I followed them. I'd lose them at times and have to step through the soft forest earth concentrating with my ears. I followed paths I had never seen before. I knew these woods perfectly, but suddenly it was as if I had never been in them before. I could hear the voices now, moving ahead of me through the trees, ducking around branches, fighting together in the leaves. They couldn't decide on me. They had already made a determination, I thought. And when they led me into the dark thicket of underbrush into a tangle of branches, I followed. And when they led me under a fallen log and through a drainage ditch, I followed. And when they ordered me out into a clearing of tall grasses and stinging nettles, I walked out and placed Fiona's red tennis shoe upright and perfect in the middle of a patch of nothing and the voices announced something important to me by rising into a calamity of shrill screams and indecisiveness.

This was my sister's tennis shoe in the middle of the woods, where she would never come by herself, where she couldn't be dragged in kicking and screaming. I saw her, her small hand in the larger one, her head turned toward the window, that look in the eyes—

I still see it.

* * *

This is the story I have been telling myself:

It was as if it had been placed there – a tennis shoe, red canvas rimmed with white rubber, the lace still tied in a double knot. I knelt down beside it. Detective Cleveland, I understood, would regard this as an important clue. I knew the voices wanted me to hide it, bury it somewhere beneath a fallen log, throw it away, bring it back to the house and pretend I had never seen it, evidence of her arrival in these woods, proof of the existence of her seven-year-old foot stepping on the wet, black earth like an astronaut on to the moon, holding the hand, no doubt, of the person who would kill her. And when the voices ordered me to hide the shoe I became defiant. And when the voices said in a flurry of contention that they would get me, I set my teeth together in a straight line. And they told me that this would happen to me, that I would be led out here into the middle of these woods one day myself and live through my sister's experience and I knew that I had to deliver this tennis shoe to Detective Cleveland.

Light left me and I started to run. I ran through the underbrush and felt, as I would years later, the stinging of the tree branches across my face. I knew the uncertainty of each placement of my feet in the darkness, but I ran, full out, my arms wide, Fiona's tennis shoe in my hand, and I think I was screaming. And when I exited into what I thought was the yard of my parents' house I was somewhere I had never been before. There was a house so white in the suburban dark that it was hard to see. There was a pool so blue in the torchlight I thought it was filled with broken glass.

It would have to be drained.

I held the tennis shoe and as I called out I realized that I had lost the English language. I moved toward this place. This was my house, but it was entirely unfamiliar. All the lights had been turned on. The torches from the party were lit. I could not speak. There was a woman on the flagstones, her arms out to me. I saw that it was Hannah, my mother, I saw that it was her, but at the same time I understood that it was not her.

'There is no time for this, Pilot.'

As I stepped across the flagstones I held the shoe out to her.

'What is it?' she said.

I moved forward.

'What do you have?'

And when I handed her my sister's tennis shoe her voice became shrill in the dark air above the house, a strange house, an alien place. I had become a wolf boy, and among these humans I was destined to be misunderstood.

'Where did you find this, Pilot?'

I was dumb.

'Pilot, where was this? Where did you find this?'

She took the shoe from my hands.

'Pilot, if you don't tell me right now where—'

'What is it, Hannah?' My father came out of the kitchen door.

'He found Fiona's shoe, her tennis shoe.'

'Where?'

'Pilot, you have to tell me, you have to tell me where you found that shoe.' Her voice was desperate, screechy. 'You have to, have to tell me. Now.'

I knew these were my parents and I knew I was supposed to help them. I overcame my muteness and put the wolf boy away. 'In, in, in the woods,' I stammered, pointing to where I had come from. 'Back, back there.'

'Can you find it again?' my father said.

'Pilot,' my mother said, 'Pilot, do you know where Fiona is? Have you been lying to us?'

I shook my head.

'I'm getting a flashlight', my father announced, 'and we're going out there, and I want you to show me exactly where you found that fucking sneaker, do you understand?'

My mother put her arms around me and pulled me toward her. 'You have to find Fiona,' she said. 'I can't take this. I can't.'

'Call Cleveland,' my father said. 'Call that stupid cop.'

But I was lying. But I have been lying for years. I was not becoming the wolf boy; I was becoming my brother.

I have been lying for years.

* * *

When I stepped into the woods behind my parents' house and heard those voices arguing about how they would kill me, it was not to look for Fiona, it was not even that year. It was to rescue my mother, to rescue Hannah, who was seeing ghosts by the highway. And it was only me, the wolf boy, starved for the taste of blood, and bleeding, who could save her.

Only me.

And Eric was on his way.

Time folding over like a sheet. Its corners touching.

And this is the truth:

I had gone into my room and reached into the plastic Wonderbread bag containing the two red shoes and the hunting knife, and I had removed one of the shoes. I had taken it out and put it inside my shirt, holding it close to me so no one could see, and when I got out there, into the middle of the darkness, of the trees, nine years old, I placed this red sneaker in the middle of a small patch of light, light that came from the moon, I guess, and I walked away and I returned a few minutes later, as if I had discovered it there.

There were no voices.

A few minutes later, I stood in the backyard of an alien house and spoke.

'In, in, in the woods,' I stammered, pointing to where I had come from. 'Back there.'

'Can you find it again?' my father said.

'Pilot,' my mother said, 'Pilot, do you know where Fiona is? Have you been lying to us?'

For some reason, she was nervous. For some reason, her hands were shaking, just slightly. 'Dr Lennox,' Katherine asked at his door, knuckles poised to knock, 'can I speak with you, please?'

Without looking up from his desk, Dr Lennox said, as if sensing her nervousness, as if enjoying it, 'What's going on, Kate?' She could see that he was smiling, but she could also see that he didn't mean it.

'I think we should talk about Pilot Airie.' She entered the psychiatrist's office. It contained the same kind of ugly brown furniture as Katherine's. For some reason, here it looked appropriate.

'Now?' Dr Lennox said, irritated.

'He's experiencing fairly severe paranoia,' Katherine said, 'so I'm wondering about the medication you prescribed. Perhaps—'

His pen stopped moving. 'Perhaps I should increase the dosage?' the doctor asked, his smile bigger than ever.

'I think it might help.'

'I'll take another look at him this afternoon.' Dr Lennox still had not looked at her directly.

When he would see me, he would stare at my face for a long time, just looking. And my face would empty out like an upside-down pitcher pouring its contents on to the ground. Then Dr Lennox would turn back to his desk, writing something, that faint sarcastic smile of his never leaving his lips, his hair quivering like a beehive.

'Thank you.' Katherine stepped back out of his office and into the hallway. She exhaled. What was wrong with her?

From her cubicle, Elizabeth smiled warmly. 'Is everything OK, Katherine? Something I can do?'

'No,' Katherine said. 'Nothing's wrong. I'm just worried about a patient.'

'Pilot Airie?'

'How did you know?'

'I could tell,' Elizabeth said, and her face was soft. 'I could just tell.'

Katherine walked over to Elizabeth, her heels clicking, saying, 'What do you mean?' There was something wrong here, Katherine could feel it. Something wasn't right.

My own paranoia was infecting Katherine, perhaps. Like it was seeping through.

Or maybe it was guilt about Eric.

'He's different from the other patients, that's all.' Unlike Dr Lennox's, Elizabeth's eyes met Katherine's exactly, unblinking. 'Different,' she repeated, 'that's all.' And her expression was genuine.

Katherine felt frustrated. She blinked her eyes several times back at Elizabeth, deliberately holding her attention as she hadn't been able to do with Dr Lennox. 'He has schizophrenia,' she said. 'We don't have any other patients like that here. And I don't have much experience with . . . people like him.'

'I was reading about it,' Elizabeth said, as if to ask a question. She turned her wide face away, indicating a college psychology textbook lying open on her desk. 'Is he hearing voices?'

'He was,' Katherine told her. 'But now that he's on medication he seems better. He's still a bit paranoid, though – more than a bit, really – and that's why I was talking to Dr Lennox.'

The red light on Elizabeth's telephone lit up next to Katherine's name. Elizabeth picked up, her forefinger indicating that Katherine should wait. 'East Meadow Psychiatric In-Patient Clinic,' she said into the phone. 'Katherine DeQuincey-Joy's office. Can I help you?' She waited a moment, then said, 'Please hold.' She looked at Katherine. 'It's his mother.'

'Pilot's?'

Elizabeth nodded.

Katherine ran into her office. 'Mrs Airie?' she said into the phone.

'Hello, Miss DeQuincey-Joy.'

'You can call me Katherine,' Katherine said. 'Please.'

'Thank you,' my mother said. 'I was calling about Pilot.'

'Of course. I'm glad you called. I saw him just this morning.'

'Is he all right?' Her voice was hurried, concerned.

'Well,' Katherine said, 'the medication is helping tone down a lot of his symptoms. But I'm afraid he's—'

'Is he still hearing voices?'

'I don't think so, Mrs Airie, no. He's—'

'That's good.'

'—still experiencing some delusional—'

'Like what?'

'He thinks, he believes his brother, he thinks your son Eric is trying to kill him,' Katherine said as evenly as she could. 'And Mrs Airie, I'm sorry I have to ask you this, but are you well? I mean, Pilot believes you have a, a brain tumor.'

'Oh.' It was pained. I could see my mother touching her temple, her skinny finger caressing that blue-purple vein.

'Is that—'

'It's not a brain tumor,' Hannah said, almost complaining, virtually whining. 'I've been experiencing some kind of trouble with my optical nerve. There has been some difficulty diagnosing why, that's all.'

'Are you—'

'I'm seeing ghosts.'

'Ghosts?'

'Double images, like on television.'

Katherine looked out the window to the highway, at the woods beyond it. 'I understand. It seems that Pilot has taken this to mean, perhaps to mean more than it should.'

'Yes.'

'He also seems to think Eric is somehow responsible.'

'That's ridiculous.'

'Of course it's ridiculous, Mrs Airie.' Katherine walked around her desk and sat down. 'Pilot is suffering from the symptoms of schizophrenia and he's enlarging and exaggerating some of his feelings unnaturally.' Katherine wasn't sure if she believed it herself. 'I'm sorry to say it's to be expected at this point. I've only just spoken to Dr Lennox a few minutes ago, and I recommended that he increase the dosage of—'

'That's good,' my mother said, not interested in how much medication I was on. 'Have you spoken to Eric?'

'Not today,' Katherine said. She closed her eyes, thinking, *Last night I did, last night I spoke to Eric*. She felt her skin growing warm, her pulse quickening.

He pulled up outside our house and saw me watching him through

95

the window. Cleveland got out of the car – an old Chevy even then – and instead of walking across the lawn to our front door, he waved to me. I stood inside the window and pointed to my chest. The policeman smiled and waved again, telegraphing that I should come outside.

It had been two weeks.

'Pilot,' he said when I got close enough.

I looked at his face.

'I just want you to know', he said, 'that if you ever want to talk to me about something, about something maybe you're afraid to tell anybody else, well ... well, you just go ahead and give me a call.'

It seems to me I could see individual blades of grass on the lawn across the street. I could hear particular wheels against the pavement on the highway. 'OK,' I said.

'Anytime,' he said. 'Doesn't have to be now. Doesn't have to be anytime soon.' He smiled.

'OK,' I said again.

'Now', he said, 'I'll go in and talk to your parents.'

'I'm really sorry,' my brother said. 'I guess you were expecting someone else.' He stood in Katherine's concrete hallway with his hands in his pockets, his face like a begging dog. This was not his customary face.

'I just ordered a pizza.' Katherine stood in the doorway of her apartment clutching a twenty-dollar bill. 'I thought you were—'

'—the pizza guy, obviously. I'm really, really sorry. I just, well, I was going to call you, but—'

With her other hand she held together her old, blue terry-cloth robe, stained from years of wear. The air between them was like the moment before a concert, everyone taking their seats. So Katherine gave my brother a look of forgiveness, her green eyes softening. 'Why don't you come in, anyway?' she said. 'Even if you're not the pizza guy.'

'Thanks.' Eric walked into the apartment, looking everywhere, taking everything in.

'You have an unlistened-to message.' He indicated the answering machine, the red light-emitting-diode number blinking steadily.

'Michele, my sister.'

'How do you know?'

'I was here when she left it. I didn't pick up.'

He nodded. 'Younger or—'

'Younger,' Katherine said.

'Are you close?'

'Not really.' Katherine walked across the room. 'It's small,' she said, meaning the apartment. 'And not—'. She searched for the right word.

'Decorated?' Eric offered.

'Not decorated,' she said with a laugh. 'That's it.'

Eric removed his hands from his pockets. 'I went by your office and Elizabeth told me you had just left for the day. I would have called but I figured you'd be on your—'

'I was just changing.' Katherine gestured toward her bedroom. 'Do you mind if I—'

'No, please,' Eric told her. 'Go ahead and do what you were doing. I'm embarrassed now. I guess I didn't—'

'Don't be embarrassed,' Katherine said. 'You wanted to talk about Pilot, right?'

Eric was silent, meaning yes, she thought. Or meaning something else. She suddenly felt extremely ugly.

'Let me throw some jeans on.' She turned her face away. 'And I'll be right back.' Katherine went into the tiny bedroom and located a pair of faded blue jeans in a pile of dirty clothes. Did she have a blouse that wasn't wrinkled? A sweater? Anything? Jesus Christ, what the hell was he doing here? She threw her robe off as quickly as possible and – to hell with underwear – pulled the jeans on. Then she slipped her arms into the least dirty white cotton blouse. It wasn't too wrinkled, she hoped. She knew she had worn it at least once. Buttoning, she opened the bedroom door and slipped quickly into the bathroom, shouting, 'One more minute.'

'Take your time,' he called back.

The bathroom light had broken her first week here, and only one bulb above the mirror burned. Katherine had been keeping the door open whenever she used it. But now she had to squint in the dim illumination. Was her make-up all right? Fuck it, she thought. She was hideous anyway. Who cares? She left the bathroom and saw my brother at the door paying the Pizza Hut guy.

He turned around. 'Good news. Your pizza's here.'

'Let me pay you for that,' she said. 'I'm sorry.'

'Don't be ridiculous.'

'Well,' Katherine sighed, 'you can share it with me, at least.'

'I really apologize again for just dropping in out of the blue,' Eric said, closing the door and handing her the pizza box. 'Obviously—' he waved his hand around '—you haven't even properly moved in yet. It was rude of me to—'

'Stop apologizing.' Katherine rolled her eyes, sinking to the floor. 'Have a slice of pizza.' She folded her legs. 'No chairs,' she said. 'But the floor's clean.' She patted the space beside her. 'Sort of.'

Eric sank down, too, legs bending. Katherine wondered how long it had been since he had sat like this.

'I spoke to my mother,' he said seriously. He wore a dark brown suit today, the perfect color and weight for the weather. It had volumes of fabric that draped across his body like a flag. His tie was *goldenrod*. Katherine noticed the monogram on his Egyptian cotton shirt.

'Yes.'

'She told me that you felt Pilot still had some symptoms.'

Katherine held a slice of pizza in front of her mouth. 'He's no longer hearing voices, he says, which is very good, and it means he's responding well to the medication. However, he's – how shall I put this?' She placed the slice of pizza on top of the pizza box. 'Pilot's suffering from paranoia. It's not uncommon, I'm sure you know. But it means he may need more medication, or perhaps if he doesn't respond to that he'll require some other anti-psychotic.' She tried to appear as calm as possible about this, as if it meant nothing, as if everything would change. She picked up the slice again.

My brother seemed to let this sink in before asking, 'Did he say, did Pilot tell you what his paranoia was about?'

'There are a couple of things,' she answered, taking a small bite and swallowing. 'He's worried that your mother has a brain tumor which is affecting her eyesight somehow—'

'Our mother is having optical problems.'

'She told me.' She said this without pausing: 'Pilot's also convinced that you killed your sister.'

Eric put his slice of pizza back into the box. 'Oh, shit.'

She picked hers up. 'And that you're going to kill him, too.' She was about to take another bite. 'Or something like that. It's not entirely clear to me at this point.'

He shook his head. 'Well—'

'Eric.' She put the pizza down again. 'These kinds of delusions are very, very common in schizophrenia and they're what we call positive symptoms. In other words, they're in addition to what's normal behavior. In most cases, medication can eliminate positive symptoms. He's just very confused, that's all.'

Eric was nodding like he knew all this. 'It's not the first time.'

'What do you mean?'

'Pilot has accused me of, of things before.'

'Of murdering your sister?'

'Of things like that,' he said. 'Yes.'

But this wasn't true. I had never accused my brother of anything. In fact, I have spent my life protecting him.

'Whatever's going on in Pilot's brain right now', Katherine said, 'is extremely disordered and confusing, especially to him. He's more or less living in a completely different reality than we are. He also believes, for instance, that the woods tried to swallow him.' She laughed a little at this. 'None of these things are even remotely rational.'

Eric picked up his pizza slice again. 'I heard about that one,' he said grimly. 'About the woods, I mean.'

'I'm still trying to see if there was a trigger,' Katherine said. 'Is your mother's optical problem—'

'I looked at her myself,' Eric said. 'It's a mystery, if you want to know the truth. For some reason, she's seeing ghost-like images.'

'But she doesn't have a serious—'

Eric gestured with his pizza. 'She doesn't have cancer. I mean, she hasn't been in for an MRI, but it's not really indicated yet. It seems more like an optical nerve problem to me, a virus, at the very worst. What upsets me', Eric said, 'is that my own brother, that he's afraid of me.'

'I know.'

'I'm a doctor,' he said, 'but I still can't think like one when it comes to him.' His tone was almost argumentative. His face avoidant, eyes everywhere – all over the room – but on Katherine.

'It's hard.'

'Did he say anything else?'

'Not really,' she said. 'I'd like him to cycle through some more medication before I ask him too many questions. Counseling is pretty limited with patients like Pilot. Well, you know about that. There's no need for me to probe too deeply. I'm just looking for—'

'Are you using cognitive techniques?'

'Sort of.' Katherine shrugged. 'I use whatever works. I just want to make sure he understands that he's sick and that he can help himself get better.'

'Sounds like a good approach.' Eric had only eaten one slice. 'Thanks for the pizza.' He didn't even finish the crust.

'I'm sorry I couldn't offer you something better.'

'Please, I shouldn't have—'

'Stop apologizing.'

He smiled and nodded. 'Sorry.'

'Your father,' Katherine said, 'is he—'

'I can't get ahold of him right now. He's flying around somewhere. He goes flying, him and Patricia, his girlfriend, all over Florida, out to the Caribbean.'

Our father was somewhere in the clouds above us at that moment. I was in the clinic listening to the whir of a little airplane engine way, way up in the sky. In the bed next to me, a man named

Harrison was talking to himself, pleading for someone's forgiveness.

'He sounds like an interesting person,' Katherine said about our father.

'He's an asshole.'

Katherine got up from the floor with the pizza box in one hand and brought it to the little faux marble kitchen counter. 'I don't have anything to drink,' she announced, 'nothing but water.'

'There's a nice place nearby,' Eric said. 'Would you—'

'Tonight I should stay in,' Katherine said, thinking she would have to stop this here, she would have to maintain professional standards of behavior.

'But what about Friday?'

'Friday . . .'

'Dinner?'

Why was this so uncomfortable? She felt her heart beating. Why did he have to be so handsome?

She gave in, more to herself than to him. 'OK.'

Eric rose from the floor. 'I won't apologize again,' he said. 'I'll just leave.' He extended his hand, and this time Katherine took it without worrying if he saw hers. He had seen her in her bathrobe and had still asked her out. What difference were bloody fingertips going to make?

She closed the door behind my brother and stood still for a moment, hand resting on the cold door handle. She hadn't flirted this time, at least. At least she had seemed relatively professional – hadn't she? Relieved, she went back to the pizza and finished it off. She'd skipped lunch today, as usual, squeezing in more time for her clients. She'd have to give me some time, she thought, a few days at least, before we spoke again. She wondered if there was much hope for a real recovery. Despite the new medications, schizophrenia tended to be a degenerative disease. These people – we – could maintain control, she knew, but most of us never functioned quite normally after a major episode.

She went into her dark little bathroom and ran water into the tub. While it was filling, she stood in front of the sink and removed her make-up. She brushed her teeth. She put her hair in a towel. She thought of me. She thought of how much Eric was concerned.

Katherine thought of her sister Michele, her long thin body, those soft eyes.

It must feel awful, she thought, to know your own little brother is terrified of you – to believe that he hates you and so irrationally that there is no way to explain yourself.

Katherine slipped her clothes off, dropping them on to the floor, and got into the tub, now full. It was too hot at the moment, but she would get used to it. She put her head back against the tiles. She felt her skin go all prickly. Out in the other room, on the kitchen counter, the red message light on the answering machine continued to blink. Katherine had lied to my brother. She hadn't been here when the message came in. She knew it was Michele and she just couldn't bring herself to listen.

Katherine lay in the tub. I lay in my bed at the clinic. She could hear a couple talking upstairs, their voices bored but content, a radio playing. I could hear Harrison, the man next me, apologizing to no one. He was so sorry, he kept saying. So very, very sorry. The long branch of a tree tapped against the window as if to call me back out to the woods. There was a faraway rustling in the leaves. There was the faintest whispering in the light fixture. There was a cluster of diseased cells forming deep inside my mother's brain.

The next morning Dr Lennox's gray-speckled head appeared from behind Katherine's office door without warning. 'Kate,' he said brusquely. 'A minute?' His smile was painted on, it seemed.

Katherine looked up. 'Come in, Greg. Please, sit down.'

The doctor didn't enter, but stood in the doorway rocking from side to side on his heels. 'I just wanted to go over your patient list quickly and tell you that I'll be seeing Pilot Airie today, as per your request for more medication.'

'Thank you,' Katherine said.

At this moment I was studying the television. If I could see inside it, I was thinking, perhaps it could see inside me.

'You mentioned that he still has symptoms?'

She cleared her throat. 'Yes, paranoid delusions, among other things,' Katherine said. 'He thinks his mother has a brain tumor and that his brother is out to kill him.'

'That qualifies.' The doctor's smile widened. 'Did you speak to his family about this?'

Katherine nodded. 'There is some basis in fact, at least. The mother has an optical nerve problem of some sort, and the brother, well, you know Eric Airie, don't you?'

'A very well-respected physician.' Dr Lennox chuckled. 'I'm sure he's not out to kill anyone.' He looked at Katherine squarely. 'I'll speak to Pilot myself and if he tells me the same things I'll give him a higher dosage of Clozaril. All right?' His smile was more insincere than usual, she thought.

'Thanks, Greg.'

Dr Lennox started to turn away from the door, then he hung back, saying, 'Out of curiosity,' his whole face a question mark, 'is Pilot talking about his sister at all?'

Katherine was surprised. 'You know about that?'

He exhaled through his teeth. 'Well, you don't forget that kind of thing.'

Katherine touched her face. 'Pilot thinks Eric killed their sister. It's another one of his delusions.'

Dr Lennox entered the room. 'Really?'

She nodded. Then she asked, 'What really happened with that, anyway?'

'As I remember it,' he said, sitting down on the brown couch, '– and it was a long, long time ago, so I could be misremembering – they had accused someone, a man they had known, I think, of taking the little girl, but of course they never found her, never found her body, that is, and eventually they were forced to let the whole thing drop.'

'Awful.'

Dr Lennox touched his chin. 'I have two daughters.'

'I have a sister.'

He shuddered. 'I can only imagine what that must have been like.' He got up and started to leave the office, still smiling.

'Could that have contributed to Pilot's illness?'

'I don't think so.' Dr Lennox stood in the doorway again, ready to leave.

'Is it possible at all', Katherine asked, 'that Pilot *isn't* schizophrenic?'

'How do you mean?'

'Eric said he became unstable after his sister was abducted, but that he was more or less manageable for years after that. I keep thinking there must have been some kind of trigger for this particular episode. Do you know what I mean? If the first one was due to his sister disappearing, then *this* one must be—'

'*Maybe.*' Dr Lennox shrugged. 'The trauma of losing his sister could have caused a psychotic episode in childhood and it may be connected even now. Or something else entirely. It doesn't matter. I would imagine that Pilot had a predisposition to schizophrenia beforehand and that he's just extremely unfortunate. Maybe something else, if it hadn't been his sister – maybe something else would have set him off.'

'Extremely unfortunate,' Katherine repeated.

'We'll see how his symptoms change,' Dr Lennox said dismissively. 'Maybe he'll be fine. Maybe he won't.'

'I can't wait to see you.'

Katherine smiled into the car phone. 'You're being ridiculous.' Could he hear it? Could he tell she was smiling?

'Seven?' She was driving down Sky Highway toward the *enclosure*.

'Seven-thirty.'

'At your apartment?'

'At the clinic.'

Expectantly, he said, 'Bye.'

'Goodbye,' Katherine said.

And Eric waited for her to hang up.

'Goodbye,' she said again, ashamed of herself, but still smiling.

And to Katherine this meant something. That he waited, it meant something important.

When the nurse came with my medication I was like a goldfish rising up for food. Then I would sink back down to the bottom of my tank, eyes bulging, gills flexing. When I moved it was through thick water, my motions slow, inhibited. I found I could sit in front of the blue Caribbean mural in the lobby and spend more than an hour forming a single thought. At other times I felt as if I had been scooped up in a net, and now I was twitching and flopping on a countertop.

The lights in my room brightened and dimmed unnaturally, irregularly. In my room there was a finger tapping on the glass, a bright eye looking in.

She had worn her black sleeveless dress – the only nice thing she had – and fake Jackie Kennedy pearls, and now Katherine's arms and shoulders were prickled with goose-bumps. This restaurant was far too cold and Eric seemed faraway across the cream-colored expanse of linen, glimmering candles and glass. She felt the need to shout, but the hush of this restaurant, its thick carpeted floors and dim light, compelled her to speak in whispers.

'I know what you're thinking.' Eric was whispering, too. 'You're thinking this place is too fancy.'

Katherine shrugged.

'I had no idea it was this uptight,' he apologized. 'Someone recommended it to me.' A black-jacketed waiter hovered annoyingly, intrusively, nearby. A sentimental aria by Puccini played at low volume over the sound system. Silverware clinked and scraped. Few people here were under sixty. He started to laugh. 'Someone I'll never take restaurant advice from again.'

Katherine raised her eyebrows. 'Who was that?'

'Greg Lennox.'

'Did you tell him you were taking *me* here?'

'No.'

Katherine sighed in relief.

'It's hard to talk, isn't it?' Eric said.

'You do seem kind of distant.'

'That's what my last girlfriend said,' my brother deadpanned.

Katherine laughed.

'She didn't understand me.'

'What did she do?'

'She was – well, she *is* a dance instructor.'

'A dance instructor.' Katherine put her glass of wine down. 'I have to go to the bathroom.' She got up from the table and walked to the other side, leaning toward Eric. 'And when I come back,' she whispered, 'I don't want to talk any more about your dance instructor girlfriend or how distant she thought you were.'

'Got it,' my brother said.

She walked briskly away.

In the Ladies' Room she immediately looked at herself in the mirror. She looked good, she thought. Her black sleeveless dress revealed as much cleavage as she was comfortable with, dignified by the fake pearls Michele had bought for her years ago. Her messy hair was somewhat under control, for once, pulled away from her face in a silly twist. Still, she thought, her nose was too long and too pointy. Her jaw was just a bit too strong. Her bottom row of teeth wasn't perfectly straight. Her breasts uneven, shoulders too wide.

My brother, on the other hand, was so fucking handsome it was like being out with a *GQ* cover model. His blue suit must have cost a million dollars. His watch appeared to be an heirloom from the Rockefellers. Were those diamond cufflinks? He was far, far too handsome for her. The black hair, the blue eyes, the high school football star face. He was a fucking brain surgeon, Katherine thought to herself. What was he doing with her?

It was a good question. And what was she doing with him was an even better one.

She went into the nearest stall and sat down on the toilet. Someone had written something on the back of the door, but it had been rubbed off, and Katherine couldn't make out what it was. She tried to imagine a woman, all dressed up in this elegant restaurant, coming into the bathroom and writing something profane in the toilet stall. Katherine tried to imagine the rebellious state of mind this woman must have been in. Squinting, Katherine still couldn't piece together what it said.

Back at the mirror, she asked herself if she should re-apply her lipstick. No. She'd be eating in a few minutes, anyway. She looked at her eyes, burning green, and at her skin, veiled in make-up. She had cover-up on, a thin coating over her face, but beneath it she could still see the fine, tiny wrinkles forming at the corners of her mouth and the edges of her eyes. She squinted too much, probably, and smiled too much, too, like Dr Lennox, and she always forgot to apply lotion before she went to bed.

It didn't matter to her, but she knew it mattered to other people. It mattered to men, anyway. Especially men like Eric.

When she returned, their plates were on the table.

'Was I gone long?'

'Of course not,' my brother said. 'But your food's here. Don't let it get cold.'

She had ordered the duck in raspberry. It came with carrots cut into tiny slivers and small, round, peeled potatoes. 'Do you visit the city often?' she asked.

Eric cut into his steak au poivre. 'Not as often as I'd like,' he said. 'I have symphony tickets and I try to make it to at least four or five football games every year. Otherwise, I'm mostly working.'

'Giants or—'

'Jets,' Eric finished.

'Do you like it?'

'The city?'

Katherine cut a small piece of the duck and placed it gently in her mouth. It was undercooked. She had to force herself to swallow.

'I guess I do,' Eric said. 'I really like it out here, though. I mean, I'm close to my family, what's left of it, anyway, and I like having access to the country. I have a beach house.'

'And do you like your work?' Katherine asked. 'I mean, do you like being a neurosurgeon?' She tried a potato. At least that was all right.

'I love it.'

'Why?'

'Don't you love your job?'

Katherine sighed. 'I love my field,' she said. 'I love psychology. I love to read about it. I love the human mind. My job, I mean, the actual working, the enormous amount of failures, the sadness, I don't always love so much.'

'I know what you mean.' My brother set to work on his steak now, knifing away large pieces and wolfing them down. 'I was hungry,' he said. 'Is yours good?'

'It's all right.'

'What about you?' Eric said. 'You must go to the city all the time?'

'I haven't been there since I left,' Katherine said. 'I lived there all my life and now I haven't been there in more than four months.'

'Is that weird for you?'

'Very,' Katherine said. 'I feel like I'm in exile.' She looked at the large piece of underdone duck on her plate. She didn't want it now.

'Plus, our mother still believes that Fiona will return.'

'I imagine any mother would hold out hope for that,' Katherine said, 'for ever.'

'And she couldn't bear it if Pilot or I left the area. Permanently, I mean.'

'I understand.'

'It's more than the ordinary empty nest syndrome.'

'I really understand. It must have been—'

'You do, I can tell.' Eric smiled at her, and now he glanced at her plate. 'It's bad?'

'I need you to tell me something,' she said, ignoring her food.

'Anything.'

'I need you to tell me this isn't a conflict.'

Eric put his fork down. 'This is not a conflict.'

'And that we're not doing anything wrong.'

'Nothing.'

'Are you sure?'

'Katherine,' he said firmly, 'there are people who would think this is a conflict because Pilot is your patient and he's my brother, but if it's not a conflict to me – or to you – then that's all that matters.'

She held her gaze on him, looking for a sign of guilt, for any indication of insincerity. But his eyes remained steady, unblinking, and his mouth curled faintly into a smile. 'I have to be honest,' she said. 'I hate this restaurant.'

Hannah seldom dialed my father's number, but right now her long, bloodless fingers found each hole in the rotary-dial, black telephone on the living-room side table, and she dialed from memory, as if she called him all the time. She saw two of them, of course.

'Hello,' the answering machine said. It was my father's voice. 'Can't come to the phone now, so leave a message.'

'James,' my mother began, 'it's Hannah.' She touched one finger to her forehead and she told him everything.

When he opened the door to let her out of his Jaguar, Eric said, 'Do you like pasta? This place has the best anywhere, even better than Little Italy.'

Katherine smirked. 'We'll see about that.'

Inside a woman with wide hips and long black hair, about thirty-five years old, smiled broadly. 'Nice to see you as always, Dr Airie.'

Eric smiled back. 'Joannie, this is Katherine. Katherine, this is Joannie, a very, very old friend of mine.'

'Hi,' Katherine said.

'I'm not so old,' Joannie said to Eric and then she burst into too-loud laughter. 'Unless you are, too.' And then, just as quickly, she said to Katherine, 'We went to high school together, Kathy. Now he's a big-shot doctor, but he still has time to visit his old pals.' She burst out laughing again, too loud, too large. 'At least when he's hungry.'

'How's your sister?' Eric said this as if by rote, as if it was part of a routine.

'Still missing you.' Joannie looked at the ceiling in an expression of cartoonish longing. 'Still wasting away.'

My brother rolled his eyes. 'I used to date Joannie's sister.'

'They were high school sweethearts.'

'I see.' Katherine smiled weakly.

Joannie led them to a table by the wall. 'So,' she asked sarcastically, 'you two just come from the opera?'

'I took Katherine to that new French place off Sky Highway,' Eric told Joannie, shaking his head. 'A big mistake.'

'I've heard about that. Extremely fancy.' Joannie wagged her wrist.

'Too fancy. Katherine was starting to think I was a snob.'

Katherine leveled her gaze at him. 'You don't know how close you came.' She felt an urge to watch the television affixed to the corner of the room, but she forced herself to pay attention to Eric and Joannie.

'Did I save myself?'

She narrowed her green eyes to little slits. 'We'll see.'

Joannie burst into that enormous laugh. 'Well, Kathy,' she said, 'you'll like the food here, at least.' She cracked herself up completely, saying, 'At least we know you'll like the food.' When she calmed down, she said, 'So, what'll you have?'

'Spaghetti, right?' said Eric. 'Marinara sauce? A bottle of red?'

Katherine nodded. 'That would be great.'

A family was sitting nearby. The boy was twirling his noodles around inside a large spoon. His parents were arguing openly. Behind them, a television played a re-run of *Mork and Mindy*. Robin Williams pulled on his suspenders and spoke in a high-pitched baby voice. Pam Dawber sighed heavily, rolling her huge television eyes. Katherine felt odd in her black velvet, sleeveless dress watching a pair of teenagers come in to pick up a pizza at the counter, a grown man playing a video game in the corner. She tried to think of something to talk about.

'You, you knew her in high school?' she said finally.

'Joannie?' Eric said. 'Yeah. Her sister was my high school girlfriend.'

'What was her name?'

'Dawn Costello.'

'What happened to Dawn?'

'She married the guy that manages the Amazing Discount Drugs just down the road here, actually. His name is Bobby Westering. They've got four kids now, all boys. They're a really nice family, you know, church-going, active in the community.' His smile was full of irony.

'What's so funny?'

'It could've been me.'

'What saved you?'

'Medical school.'

When Joannie brought out the food, Katherine and Eric ate almost entirely without speaking, only smiling at one another from time and time between mouthfuls of pasta and gulps of the cheap red wine.

Every now and then my brother held up a forkful, saying, 'Good?'

Katherine couldn't help but laugh. 'Didn't you just eat an entire steak?'

From the bottom of my tank, I monitored the progress of their evening. I let the water flow through my gills and listened to the bubbling sound of Harrison's apologies. From my position under the water I could feel every vibration of my brother's speech, every inflection of Katherine's responses. I could feel him moving in and I could sense Katherine's welcoming gestures, her glances feeling more and more familiar as they fell across his face.

The branch tapped on the window. Harrison begged for forgiveness.

His car was insanely luxurious, Katherine noticed, with buttery gray leather seats and a mahogany dashboard. Eric put his hand on his stomach. 'I'm so full,' he said. 'Way too full.'

Katherine leaned toward him. He turned his head. She tasted his lips, the red wine, the onions and garlic. He was delicious. She put her hand behind his head, touching the smooth little hairs on his neck, and pulled him even closer. He was nothing like Mark, she thought. They were in the parking lot in front of some little Italian place off a suburban strip mall, kissing, something that never would have happened with Mark, for some reason. Katherine breathed in.

'That was nice of you,' my brother said.

She smiled. Did she really just do that?

'Time to take you home?'

'I guess so.' She wondered if she had just made a mistake.

No, she told herself. No.

Eric pulled out of the parking lot and on to the turnpike. He pushed a button and the stereo came on. It was Miles Davis – quiet and complex. My brother would have been prepared for this. He would have had everything ready.

Katherine looked out the window. It was dark and the road became a series of highway lights flashing by, the reflective tape on the guardrail flaring up in the wake of the Jaguar. 'Do you ever regret it?' she said. 'I mean, that you didn't marry Dawn?' It was a stupid question, she thought. As soon as it came out, she realized it was idiotic.

'I don't want a family. Not right away.'

'What do you want right away?' Katherine wanted to touch him, to put her hand on his leg, on his shoulder, her lips on his neck.

'This is nice,' Eric said. 'This is what I want right now. With you, anyway. The other stuff—'

'Good,' she cut him off.

'I'm sorry about that French place.'

'Too stuffy.'

'I didn't know. I really didn't.'

'I'm glad we went to, to Joannie's, though,' Katherine said. 'It was really good. Thank you. What is it called?'

'Costello's.'

Katherine repeated it. 'Costello's.'

At that moment they pulled into the parking lot of her building. She could see the window of her *enclosure* staring out into the lot like a stupid yellow eye. She had left the light on, obviously. Eric parked right next to her blue VW Rabbit. She opened the door to get out, pushing the front of her dress down with one hand.

He waited, gripping the steering wheel.

'It's not a conflict?' she asked again.

He shook his head no and she waited until he got out of the car.

In the beginning, before her eyes became so bad she couldn't drive, Hannah came to see me every morning, saying, 'How are you, sweetheart? Are you feeling better?' her hand on my forehead, as if I had a temperature, as if I would be going back to school soon.

I wasn't, though. I wasn't feeling better at all. In many ways, in fact, I was feeling worse. I'll admit, this feeling was based more on my circumstances than on my disease: the fact that I was almost thirty, in the hospital, clearly insane, heavily medicated. At times I felt I was moving toward catatonia. At times I could only sit in front of a window and watch the clouds pass by as if on a separate plane in the sky, the treetops rustling across the hospital parking lot, the woods advancing toward me millimeter by millimeter.

Hannah smiled nervously.

'I'm all right, Mom,' I said. 'Really, I'm feeling much better.' I knew she didn't want me to explain this to her and I knew she would never tell me how she was doing herself, not truly, so I just asked, 'Are things all right with you?' not expecting an answer.

But there was a knot of cancerous cells forming at the base of her spine, I knew, like a wasps' nest fixed to the branch of a tree, a tumor in the hollow beneath her medulla oblongata.

'Don't worry about me.'

She brought me rhubarb pie, of course, and tea biscuits. She brought a basket full of tiny cheeses and salamis and even a bit of black caviar. She brought a couple of news magazines. She wanted to know if I wanted anything else, a certain book, perhaps, or my Walkman and some tapes. She brought her hand to her face and touched her hair. She bit her lip. Everything looked so new to me. Did she always bite her lip like that when she was nervous? The color of our mother's hair, reddish-brown with delicate streaks of gray, when did it become like that? I was overcome by a feeling of amazement, the way I felt sometimes looking at a new car. 'How's Eric?' I asked. I had the feeling that I wasn't me any more. When I looked around, everything had that new-car look, that just-slightly-different-ness.

'He's very concerned about you,' our mother told me. 'Eric is very, very worried. He cares for you a great deal.' Every word she said was underlined. Eric was somewhere, at that moment, plotting my murder. He was developing insidious new methods of torture. He was formulating poisons, devising traps. He was rubbing his hands together like a fly. 'He's doing everything he can,' our mother went on, 'pulling all his strings, just to make sure that you're well taken care of while you're here.'

'I'd like to go home soon,' I told her. 'I don't want to be here any more.' I felt for the shoelace. This was one string, I thought to myself, Eric couldn't pull.

'That's Dr Lennox's decision.'

I put my head back. The pillowcase was overly starched and it made a crinkling noise in my ear. It seemed as if they changed the sheets every fifteen minutes. 'I know.'

'He's a very good psychiatrist,' she asserted. 'Very well respected.'

'Right.'

'Pilot,' my mother said, '*please*.'

I didn't know what she meant by the *please*. Please what? Please shut up? Please co-operate? Please stop pretending to be crazy? This room had wall-to-wall, rusty orange carpeting to match the orange linoleum tiles in the halls outside. The windows were covered in heavy robin's-egg-blue curtains. Our mother wore a tweed jacket with patches on the elbows. She wore a long khaki skirt. She wore a silk scarf, dark purple, around her neck. She wore a gold pin that I knew our father had given her, of two hands clasped together in prayer. 'Hannah,' I said, 'nothing matches.' The television, which was kept low but constantly on by my roommate, a cocaine-addicted bonds trader named Harrison Reardon Marshall, a man with three last names, erupted into a violence of red and a woman's scream. He was watching a horror movie, I think. He also seemed to be living one, the way he thrashed around in his bed, the way he breathed all night through clenched teeth, apologizing over and over.

'I don't know what you mean,' Hannah said. 'Pilot, I don't—'

'I mean,' I began, but then I realized that I didn't know, either. Despite the medication, it was still difficult for me to keep track of all the thoughts coursing through my consciousness. 'Eric cut off Halley's leg,' I told her. 'That's what I mean.'

'Pilot.'

'But that's not what happened.' I said, 'Eric cut it off with a hunting knife, the one—'

'Pilot, stop.'

'I don't want you to die,' I said now, somewhat desperate. I twisted the shoelace even tighter. Her cancer cells divided, multiplied, divided again. It happened so quickly.

'Pilot.' I could see that I was making our mother cry. 'Pilot,' she said, 'if you don't stop this nonsense they'll never let you out of here. Do you understand? Dr Lennox has to believe that you're normal, somewhat normal, at least, before he can let you go.'

I had been sitting up, I thought, but now I realized I was lying down. I sat up again. 'I'm sorry,' I said. 'I just—'. These thoughts came out of nowhere, as if someone had put them inside my brain. Did Eric have something to do with that? He was a neurosurgeon, after all, with the knowledge and necessary skill. These didn't feel like my thoughts. Perhaps I wasn't Pilot James Airie. Maybe I was looking out through his body, and my consciousness was something else, or someone else's, entirely. And these thoughts were Pilot's, this other person's, and I was only observing them.

'I have a client coming to the house,' my mother said. She worked with hands – the hands of surgeons who had smashed their fingers in car doors, of violinists who had cut their tendons with kitchen knives, of writers who had inexplicably gone numb from the wrists down.

'It's all right, Hannah, I understand.'

'Pilot, I'm your *mother*.'

'It's your *name*.'

She closed her eyes and opened them. 'I really have to go.'

'I'm really all right,' I assured her. 'I really, really am.'

'Just try and take it easy,' she said. 'Just try. No one wants to hurt you, OK? Especially Eric. And nothing's wrong with me. So stop worrying.'

'You're seeing ghosts,' I said.

'It's nothing, sweetheart. It's just my eyes. It's just what happens to an old lady's eyes.'

The cancer cells divided, multiplied, divided again. 'I'm not so sure about that,' I said. 'And you're not so old, Hannah – *Mom*. Not old enough for something like that to be happening to your eyes without a reason.'

'Pilot,' my mother said, 'you have to at least try to *sound* normal.'

'Sound normal?'

'Will you try?'

Sound normal. I wanted to, so badly. She had no idea how badly, all my life.

Hannah was growing accustomed to seeing double, though. It didn't hurt, at least. It was even beautiful sometimes. The ghosts moved across her field of vision like reflections on glass, like flower petals floating along the surface of a brook. Every morning she poured herself a pot of tea from the kettle and saw the ghost pot inches away being filled by the ghost kettle. She sat in the real chair in front of the real television and next to her were a ghost chair and a ghost TV. She lost sight, sometimes, of which object was real and which one was the ghost. She tried to pick up her ghost keys from the kitchen counter. The real ones lay nearby. She stumbled over a real wastebasket that she thought was a ghost. She reached for the real phone and was surprised to find that it *was* real. 'I'm losing track of things,' she told my real brother on the real phone. 'And these ghosts, they're not going away any more.' It was as if she was seeing the sky on the still surface of a lake. It was as if she was looking at a world full of twins.

'It's only been a few days,' Eric said, the phone on speaker, his hands touching each other, a spider on a mirror, 'and you're just reacting to stress. It's Pilot and you're worried about him. That's all. That's all it is.'

'We're all crazy in this family.' Our mother's voice was plaintive, whiny, high-pitched. 'We're all nuts.'

'No one's crazy.'

'Pilot is schizophrenic,' she said. 'Eric, for—'

'Mom, he's already much, much better. There are new drugs. There are all sorts of medical options.'

'He still thinks you're trying to kill him,' she said. 'Don't you think that's crazy?'

'It's a delusion that will go away with time. Please, Mom. I'm sure Katherine DeQuincey-Joy will help him with—'

'What do you know about her?' our mother said. 'She's new, isn't she?' Hannah sat in the living room drinking tea. Right now she tried to put her real cup into the ghost saucer. She sighed, finding the real saucer now with her real hand. She watched the ghost hand put the ghost cup into the ghost saucer.

'Katherine is very qualified,' Eric said, leaning back in his office chair. 'In fact, I've been out with her socially and she's really very intelligent.'

'You've been out with—'

'We just went out for some spaghetti, that's all. That's all it was.'

'She's your brother's analyst, Eric. Shouldn't you—'

'She's not his *analyst*, Mom. It doesn't work like that any more.' Eric sighed heavily. 'Anyway,' he said, 'she's a very intelligent, highly competent, well-educated psychologist. And her job is simply to monitor Pilot's progress on a day-to-day—'

'She wants to know why it happened.'

'True,' Eric said. 'Katherine wants to know why.'

'Eric, *she wants to know why it happened*.' Our mother paused. And Eric said nothing. 'Do you think,' our mother said after a while, 'do you think it has anything to do with—'

'With Fiona? Because it happened around that time of year?'

'I don't know.'

'Let it go,' Eric said. 'Pilot has had a lot of problems in his life. It could be anything.'

117

For every object Hannah saw, there was a ghost. She imagined that for every object there ever was, a ghost of it remained somewhere, and that she was somehow seeing into that world. Her daughter would have to be there somewhere out there. If there was a little girl, there was a ghost of her, too.

'Mom?' Eric said.

'Yes.'

'Are you spacing out?'

'I guess so.'

'You were humming.'

'Sorry.'

'I should go,' Eric said. 'But I want you to relax now, all right? I'm bringing home a prescription for you, some Xanax.'

She shook her head into the phone. 'I don't want any Xanax.'

'You'll feel so much better, Mom.' Eric leaned forward at his desk. In his drawer he had dozens of plastic containers filled with sample drugs.

'No Xanax.' She could just see him rolling his eyes, his frustration. From my position in the clinic lobby in front of the Caribbean mural, I could see it, too.

'I'll bring it anyway, Mom, and you can decide.'

'Do what you like.' Hannah had already taken three Valiums today. Besides, she didn't want Eric to know that she relied on pills. She said, 'Goodbye, Eric.'

''Bye, Mom.'

Hannah put the black, rotary-dial phone back into its cradle and nearby a ghost phone was placed into its ghost cradle. She looked at her hand, the long, thin fingers, the carefully manicured nails, and right next to it was her ghost hand, its long, thin fingers, its carefully manicured nails, the hand of a ghost woman who lived in a ghost house.

She thought of me. Pilot must be the ghost woman's son, she said to herself. He can't be mine.

I'm not sure how many other patients were staying on the ward. They all seemed new to me whenever I saw them. I had the same room-mate the entire time, though – poor old Harrison Reardon Marshall. And his problems were more drug-related than mental as far as I could see. He'd been doing crack, it seemed. And he was a bonds trader. Apparently, crack is frowned upon in the bonds trading business. There were white-uniformed nurses and medical techs everywhere. It was a psychiatric clinic, however, so most of the people here were either threats to themselves or to others. I was considered a threat to myself. The question of whether I was feeling suicidal had been put to me many times.

Whenever I was asked that question, it was always with the same gentleness, the same fearfulness, as if just asking might lead me to try.

The rooms of the clinic were carpeted in orange. It must have been on sale at the Institutional Carpeting Warehouse. The walls of the clinic were bright satin white and apple green. Many of the walls in the common areas, however, were covered in enormous, life-sized photographs of beaches or forests or canyons. There was a lobby near my room. And to escape Harrison's constant blaring of the television, I liked to sit in this waiting area and look deeply into the superman-blue Caribbean water of a photographic mural. There was a band of yellow for the beach, a band of deep ultra blue for the water, and a band of bright shining blue for the sky. It was like a Rothko painting, so easy to look at. Everything else had become so complicated, so confusing. When I looked at the television, it was just a mass of bright colors moving over the screen in no particular pattern. The sounds it made were completely unrelated to the blur of images. This was a part of my illness. In our room, Harrison lay in his bed and shivered and moaned, watching the television continually. He had tried to hang himself on his first day here, inexpertly tying his sheets around his neck and trying to find a way to attach them to the ceiling. I had watched this from a state of near catatonia, and when the nurse came in and discovered what Harrison was trying to do, I pretended to be asleep.

There was a great commotion for a while. Then, I believe, they administered a sedative.

A day later, Harrison apologized.

I don't think I responded.

'I'm sorry you had to see that.' He laughed. 'If you saw that, I mean.' He sat up in bed and looked at me. 'I've been a little on edge lately. You know what I mean? I have this little problem. And it has ruined my entire fucking life.'

I think I told him that it was all right, no need to apologize to me. I tried to, anyway, tried to make my face move even though it had been covered in liquid glass.

'Don't do drugs,' Harrison said. He was a short man, with a black beard and hair that he had forced back over a bald spot. 'It sounds stupid, but it's true.'

Then a nurse came in with our medication.

I could see this collection of bodies as if it were one. Like a number of microscopic organisms on a slide under a microscope, the people at my parents' party swirled and merged, their bodies fluid with alcohol. What was I doing out here? Every now and then I'd catch a glimpse of something – my mother's face, my father's hand gesturing wildly to punctuate a joke. There was darkness around me like an old blanket. There was a smell of ferns and earth and tree-bark. And there was my sister – her face bright in torchlight, her mouth open – laughing.

We took our medication in the morning, Harrison and I, and again throughout the day, whenever a nurse came in with a little paper cup of water and a few pills in a paper dish. I began to feel saner, more and more all the time, as each medication cycle completed its arc. Sitting in her office, I told Katherine, 'I'm feeling much, much better. I'm still, I'm still a little lethargic, you know, dazed, but I'm not hearing those voices any more.' This was more or less true, even though I suspected they were still there, whispering just out of range, so faint I couldn't hear them. 'There are no more arguments inside the light fixtures.' I forced a smile, bright as I could, on to my mouth. The truth is I just wanted to go home. I would have told her anything.

'Pilot, that's great.' Katherine's face wore the same smile as mine. I felt we were both professionals here, both of us acting our parts. 'That's really terrific.' She cleared her throat. 'And what about the woods? Are you still afraid—'

Shaking my head, I said, 'I'm not going out there again, if that's what you mean.'

She was half-sitting, half-standing, leaning on the front of her desk. She smoothed her long khaki skirt with her left hand. Today she wore a forest green sweater, too, a good color for her. 'I was going to ask if you're still afraid of them,' she said, eyes full of concern, 'if you still think they're going to snatch you.'

'That was a delusion.' I forced a self-deprecating tone into my voice. 'I know that now. I'm crazy. I'm not stupid.' I had never thought the woods would *snatch* me, anyway. I would never use the word *snatch*.

'OK.' Katherine walked around her desk to sit down. 'And what about your mother?'

'If she has something wrong with her,' I assured Katherine, 'I'm certain we'll figure out whatever it is in plenty of time. There's absolutely no reason to think she has cancer.' But she did, I knew. At that very instant, in fact, the radical cells were twisting their way through the folds of her brain. 'Especially if Eric thinks—'

'And your brother?'

'What do you mean?'

'Are you still unconvinced?'

'Unconvinced?'

'You were certain he was trying to—' Katherine sat down behind her desk, hands on its surface '—to harm you. Do you still feel—'

'Have you slept with my brother?' I felt molten glass pouring over me, hardening around my features, my face turning to porcelain and crystal, bone china and blown glass.

'What?' It was as if a veil had dropped away from her eyes. She had, I saw it. They had fucked.

'Have you slept with him?'

She gave a little shake to her head. 'Pilot, that's—'

I got up from her hideous brown couch. I knew everything now.

The way her eyes flickered away, the pupils dilating, the blood rising to her cheeks. 'You've had sex with Eric, haven't you? He fucked you.'

Katherine Jane DeQuincey-Joy, my therapist, who was fucking my brother, a murderer, was silent, looking at her fingernails. The middle one was bleeding. She'd been chewing it past the quick. It traveled, now, to her mouth.

'Eric provokes strong feelings in women,' I warned her. 'You should be very careful, Katherine.'

'Pilot.' She looked directly at me and removed her finger from her mouth. 'You still haven't answered my question.'

She didn't understand. 'Katherine Jane DeQuincey-Joy,' I said, 'ask yourself this.' I took a step forward. 'Why is he with you? What does my brother see in you?'

Katherine got up from her desk, came around it, and walked toward me. 'He's very concerned about you,' she said. 'He's very, very—'

'He's one thousand times more beautiful than you are.' I was completely brittle now, ready to shatter. 'What does he see? What does he see in *you*?' It had to be said. 'What does he want?'

She blinked her eyes. 'Pilot—'

'It's not to say you aren't beautiful, because—'

'Pilot, I think it's—'

'—you are beautiful, I really think so.'

'—time for you to—'

'But it's a way to me.'

'A *what*?'

'That's what you are to him,' I said. 'All you are. You are a way to get to me.' I shook my head defiantly. 'And it's not going to work. I won't allow it and neither should you.'

I was moving toward the door, but Katherine got up and put her hand on the knob before I could reach it. 'How did you know?' she said. 'How did you know about me and Eric? Did someone tell you? Did someone tell you something about us?' Her voice was shaking.

'I'm omniscient.'

She folded her arms. 'You're omniscient.'

'I don't mean to be,' I said. 'It's just—'

'I think the session is over for today, Pilot.' She let go of the door handle and it just seemed to open on its own.

The ghosts were multiplying in her field of vision.

The cells were multiplying at the base of her optical nerve.

Hannah found herself waking up earlier and earlier. And when she walked by the front windows in the mornings she saw two orange sunrises over the double houses across two streets. She saw more ghosts when she went downstairs, her ankles *crick-crick-cricking* against the hardwood in the hallway. She saw two right hands on the banister. One was real. One wasn't. Hannah set one pot to boil on the stove for her morning poached egg and saw two. She tried to lift the newspaper from the front door, but it was a ghost. The real one lay nearby. She tried to pick up the ghost teacup. She wondered, now, which of these items were real and which ones were transparent. It seemed, sometimes, that they had switched. Wasn't that magazine real a moment ago and wasn't the one beside it the ghost of it? Had things been re-arranged?

She no longer trusted herself.

'There's nothing wrong with your eyes,' Dr Carewater, her optometrist, had said. 'At least, there's no optical reason why you should be seeing these double images. None that I can see.'

'Perhaps I'm receiving two signals,' Hannah had suggested, quoting Eric. 'Like on television.' One from the real world, one from the world of apparitions.

'There's nothing to explain it.' He had sat down, defeated. Dr Carewater's ghost image sat down in the ghost chair nearby. 'Nothing that has to do with your eyes themselves. It must be neurological.'

Like me, Hannah couldn't watch television. She couldn't discern what was happening on the screen. She couldn't work, either. She'd been forced to refer her pianists and surgeons to a colleague. She sat in the chair by the kitchen door and listened to the AM radio news.

'Let me at least give you something,' Eric said on the phone. 'Something to make you feel better.'

Our mother cried sometimes, privately. Even when no one was there, she'd go upstairs and stand in the shower and pull the curtain, fully clothed.

Every afternoon she called me. 'Pilot,' she said.

'Hannah.'

'How are you?'

'I'm getting saner all the time.'

'You're not insane,' she said. 'There's nothing insane about you.'

'Adult onset schizophrenia, Hannah,' I said. 'That is the professional opinion of the professional psychiatrist, the official diagnosis, the actual—'

'That doesn't mean anything.'

'It means I can't trust my own thoughts. It means I can't predict my own behavior.'

She quoted Eric. 'They have drugs now, medications—'

'They only work for some people,' I said. 'Obviously not for me. Do you know what I told Katherine the other day?'

'They're working for you,' Hannah said. 'Evidently they're working for you. You sound perfectly normal. Perfectly cogent. You're just trying to rattle my old bones, that's what you're—'

'For some reason, Hannah, the only time I feel sane is when I'm talking to you.'

'I don't know if I should take that as a compliment or not.'

I changed the subject. 'How are your ghosts?'

'They're fine. Don't you worry about—'

The ghosts were fine. 'How's Eric?'

'You know how Eric is.'

'Not really,' I said. 'I really don't. He doesn't come to see me.'

'He's worried he'll upset you. He's afraid of you. He's fine, otherwise. Otherwise, he's good.'

'Did you know that he's screwing my therapist?'

'Pilot.'

'It's true. Him and Katherine Jane DeQuincey-Joy. They're sleeping together.'

'Why do you call her that?'

'What?'

'By her whole, entire name? Why don't you just call her by one name?'

'I didn't realize I was doing it,' I said.

I could feel her eyes closing as she said this. 'I knew it,' she said. 'I knew it about Eric.'

'I knew you knew.'

'Please, Pilot, you have to get better.'

'Better,' I said. 'I know. I'm really trying.' That's one thing I wasn't kidding about.

He lost his virginity with Dawn Costello when he was fourteen years old. He had sex with her sister, too – with Joannie – who was two years older. My brother had a number of girlfriends in high school, including Renee Faust, Tanya Zellwieger and Constance Johns. Of course, there were others. Girls he had been with at parties after football games. Girls he knew secretly. Girls he had brought into the woods. Girls he took into the tunnel that separates the woods from the highway island on the other side of Sky Highway. By his senior year Eric had even slept with an assistant teacher named Judith Freitag. She disappeared from Albert Einstein High under mysterious conditions. Someone had found out about them, I think. Once he got to college Eric began the systematic sexual elimination of the entire female student population. He slept with dozens, if not hundreds, of young women. I doubt he ever had to try very hard. In those days Eric's handsomeness meant more. Not that women wouldn't fall for him later on – they would. It's just that when he was in college girls walked up to him and sat on his lap. They whispered in his ear the things they planned to do with him. They led him by the hand back to their dorm rooms and walk-up apartments. I believe there were occasions where Eric had sex with more than one woman at a time. Over the years he had sex with every physical variety of female. By the end, as medical school was approaching, Eric had settled on one woman. Unexpectedly, she was not even beautiful. She even

125

might be described as plain. Her name was Stephanie, a blonde with a slim build and a white scar that ran up her forehead and disappeared under her hairline. I don't know what my brother saw in her. But it didn't matter because she refused to follow him to medical school in Virginia, even though he offered to marry her.

As far as I know, Eric never developed any unusual sexual proclivities in all that time. He never got into pain, or strange costumes, or unusual fetishes. Sex, for my brother, became like water – something that was everywhere, just reach for it. His thrills came from school, from learning about the internal composition of the human body, from understanding the function of our various parts, the structure underlying the structure. He was always that way. Even sex could not dissuade him from his life's first addiction.

He liked to dissect.

'Eric,' Katherine said into the phone, 'Pilot knows.' Eric was in his car. She was in the *enclosure*.

'Knows what?'

She was nervous, biting through a scab on her middle finger. 'He knows that we've, that we've been together. He knows about us.'

'He does not.' It was night. Eric swerved to miss a dog standing in the middle of the road, eyes silvery-red in the headlights.

'I'm telling you,' Katherine said, 'Pilot guessed it somehow. Or someone told him. Anyway, I was so flustered that I basically confessed.'

My brother sighed. 'It doesn't matter.'

'Well, I'm not sure I should be his thera—'

'Katherine, I don't see a conflict.'

'Maybe we should take a break.' She tasted the blood, raw and warm, on her finger. 'At least until he's, you know, until he's more cogent.' She was naked, pacing the small area of tiles in her kitchenette. As usual, the message light on her answering machine blinked steadily. Michele had called.

Eric's voice was querulous. 'I have a very good feeling about you, Katherine, and I don't want to let this slip away.'

'I don't either.' She looked out the window, across the highway and the parking lot. 'It's just that Pilot is my client and I, and I want to be professional, I want to help him as much as I can. It's my first responsibility.'

'He's getting better. The medication—'

'I'm not so sure about that. He really believes you're trying to get him or something, that you're trying to . . .'. Her voice trailed off.

'Jesus.' Eric was turning into his long driveway, which curved around to the front of his house. Katherine could hear the gravel crunching under the wheels of his Jaguar.

'He thinks you're using me as a way to get to him. And he really believes you, believes you had something to do with your sister's—'

He cut off the engine. 'Well, you're right,' Eric said. 'Maybe we should cool it for a while.'

'Why does he think that, Eric?'

'I don't know.' My brother sat still, one hand on the steering wheel, the other on the phone. 'He's always been jealous of me. He's always had trouble relating to people. Maybe when we were kids I could have been nicer, less of a bully.' Eric sighed. 'Christ, I don't know.'

'Is there any way to prove it to him?'

'What do you mean?'

'To prove that your sister was—'

'It was twenty years ago, Katherine.' His voice was angry now, the volume up. 'There's no way to prove anything.'

'I'm sorry.'

'I think it's best to just leave that one alone and focus on getting Pilot to function like a normal human being.'

Katherine didn't say anything for a moment. She cleared her throat.

'Katherine,' my brother said.

Her voice was small. 'I'm not used to getting yelled at.'

'Katherine, I'm sorry.'

She stared at the message light on the answering machine. Michele had called again, she was certain.

* * *

A voice said, 'Katherine, it's me. It's Michele.' Katherine paced back and forth in her little kitchen, raw fingers in her mouth, her bare feet on the cool tiles. She waited for the kettle to boil. 'I just wanted to tell you where I was, where I *am*,' Michele went on. 'I'm in Seattle, if you can believe it. Remember how you said you always wanted to live in Seattle. Well, I'm here! And I haven't seen a drop of rain. Of course, it's only been a little over a week and they're telling me it's not unusual to go this long without precipitation . . . oh my God, I can't believe I used that weatherman word, *precipitation*! Anyway, Katherine, I'm just, you know, checking in. As soon as I get a permanent place to stay I'll leave my new number, all right?' In the background, Katherine heard cars driving by. Were there seagulls? Was Michele really in Seattle? 'Anyway,' Michele said finally, ''bye.'

'Pilot,' Katherine said. I was sitting in my chair in the patient leisure area, looking deeply into the Caribbean ocean of the wall-sized mural. I saw that she was speaking to me. I saw her voice making sharp little cuts and tears in the air around me. But at the same time, I didn't hear her. At the same time, I didn't hear anything. 'Pilot,' she said again. 'I want to talk to you. Would that be all right?'

I turned my head away from the Caribbean mural toward Katherine Jane DeQuincey-Joy and said mechanically, 'It would be all right.' My voice was made by a faraway sound-making machine.

'I just want to clear something up, OK?' Her voice was urgent, red-tinged at the edges.

'OK.'

'Your brother Eric and I are just friends, and that's all.' Katherine pulled a chair up so she could face me. 'And until you leave the clinic we're not going to see each other.' She made so many patterns in the air I couldn't see the mural for a moment. 'Not socially, anyway.'

'It doesn't matter,' I said.

'It matters to me.'

'Whatever.' In the distance, where the tropical blue water

shimmered, it seemed almost like this picture was moving, as if the water were real. Or perhaps it was the air around Katherine's head, the atmosphere made all shimmery by her hair.

'If you'd like,' she said, 'I can arrange for you to have another therapist, someone else. That way—'

'No,' I said. 'No. I want you, and you don't have to stop seeing Eric.' I attempted a reassuring look.

I'm not quite sure what she got, because she asked, 'Why do you think Eric is trying to hurt you, Pilot?'

'Because he took Fiona', I answered, 'and because I know all about it.'

'I see.'

'And because he told me he would kill me if I ever said anything.'

He came up behind me in the hallway. I could hear the shower running in our mother's bedroom. It was less than a month. There were still neighborhood searches. There was still a vigil at the East Meadow Presbyterian. There was still a moment every night on the news where they showed her little face. He put his hand over my mouth.

'You want a hunting knife?' he said. 'Is that all?'

I shook my head, no.

'If I get you a hunting knife you'll give me the other one?'

Again – no.

'Do you want to go where Fiona went?'

It was getting more and more difficult to move my face. My mouth had hardened. My eyes had been locked.

'He told you that?'

'Yes.'

'When?' Katherine said. 'When did he say that?'

'After he did it, when we were kids. A million years ago, a million-billion—'

'He *told* you that he killed Fiona?' The word *told* was like a sheet of glass shattering all over my face.

'He put his hands around my throat.' This was an exaggeration.

'When you were boys?'

'Yes, then.'

'Pilot,' Katherine said, 'are you hearing any voices right now?'

'No.'

'Do you think anyone is putting these thoughts into your head?'

'No.' But there was rushing sound coming from somewhere behind her. There was rippling in the Caribbean water.

'Do things seem *real* to you lately?'

'Real?' I asked. I wasn't even sure what she meant.

'I mean, are you having any trouble understanding what's going on around you, Pilot? You seem distant.'

'The medication,' I said. 'I'm taking more of it. Dr Lennox—', and my voice stopped without my consent.

'OK,' Katherine said. 'OK.' The little blades of her voice cut into the blue air all around me, swirling into the water of the mural. I looked down to see my own hand on the armrest of this chair, the blackened shoelace twisted around my middle finger. I saw Katherine's hands on her lap, each of her little fingertips scabbed over, nails bitten to oblivion.

From her office, she dialed Dr Lennox's extension. 'Greg,' she said, 'it's me.'

'Kate.' Dr Lennox's voice was good-natured today. 'What can I do for you?'

'I'm sorry to bother you about this again,' she said. 'It's just that I'm having, I'm having difficulties with Pilot Airie.'

He cleared his throat. 'What kind of difficulties?'

'Let me start by asking you something,' Katherine said. 'Is it possible to be left with only one symptom of schizophrenia? I mean, after the medication has taken effect?'

'One symptom?' he said. 'I don't understand.'

'He's paranoid.'

'Pilot Airie—'

'—is paranoid,' Katherine repeated. 'He thinks his brother is out to kill him and he believes Eric was responsible in some way for his sister's abduction.' She touched the simulated woodgrain on her desk. With her index finger, she traced the fake whorl of a knot.

'Well,' Dr Lennox said, 'that sounds odd. All of his other symptoms are gone? Are you sure about that?'

She said, 'I'm not positive, of course, but he seems fairly rational right now, otherwise. He's not hearing voices. He's not hallucinating. At least he says he's not. The increased dosage is making him sluggish, I think. But overall—'

'Paranoia is not just a symptom of schizophrenia,' Dr Lennox reminded her. 'Schizophrenia may be only one of Pilot's problems.'

'True,' Katherine acknowledged.

The doctor cleared his throat again. 'Perhaps he's ready for some cognitive therapy,' he said. 'Help him to re-organize his thinking.'

Katherine allowed a few seconds to pass. She could hear the doctor's insincere smile through the intercom. She'd been hoping for more information, something concrete.

'Is there anything else, Kate?'

'No, Greg – but thanks.'

'I'll talk to him.'

''Bye.' Katherine put down the phone gently. She had wanted to tell him about the relationship she was having with Eric, to clear things, but for some reason she hadn't.

For some reason, she had allowed it to become a secret.

An omission.

But since I knew, she told herself, and since she had offered to stop seeing Eric, to get me another therapist – wasn't that enough?

So why did she continue to feel like a criminal?

On the yellow pad of paper near the phone she kept a list of numbers. It included the contact names for her clients. My mother's was at the bottom. Katherine dialed that number now. It rang several times, and just as she was about to hang up, someone answered.

'Airie Residence, Hannah speaking.'

'Mrs Airie,' Katherine said, 'this is Katherine DeQuincey-Joy.'

'Katherine DeQuincey-Joy,' Hannah said absently, as if she had never heard the name before.

'I wanted to tell you that I spoke with your son this afternoon, with Pilot, and that he seems to be doing fine. His symptoms are actually diminishing quite a bit.'

'I'm very glad to hear that,' Hannah said. Did her voice brighten at all? Was she pleased?

'I thought you would be. Pilot is responding well to the medication. He said he's no longer hearing voices or believes the woods are going to swallow him. He has relaxed a bit about your optical condition, although I think some of his concern is appropriate. I mean, you *are* his mother and he obviously cares for you.'

'Thank you,' Hannah said. 'Do you think Dr Lennox will release him soon?'

'I don't see why not,' Katherine said. 'And I want you to know that I won't be an impediment to that in any way. But—'

'But what?'

'But I did have one question.'

At the other end of the line, Hannah twirled the telephone cord around her wrist. 'Go on,' she said.

Down the corridor, I sat in front of the Caribbean mural and twirled the shoelace around my own finger, tightening and tightening.

'Pilot seems to be exhibiting one last symptom,' Katherine said, 'and it is Dr Lennox's opinion that it is more likely to be a symptom of something else.'

'Of something else?'

'A thought he's having.' She paused. 'He's paranoid, Mrs Airie. He still believes your other son, he believes that Eric, is out to, well, that he wants to kill him.'

'I know,' my mother said resignedly.

'More importantly, he believes Eric had something to do with your daughter's—'

'Fiona?'

'Yes, with her disappearance.'

'Like what?'

'He thinks Eric . . . killed her.'

'Oh.' It was a small sound.

Katherine imagined my mother in an elegant house, with beige carpets and tan velvet furniture, with white flowers in glass vases on rattan tables. 'Mrs Airie,' Katherine said, 'the reason I ask is not to bring up unpleasant memories. In fact, I really hate to do that. It's just that I think whatever is causing these thoughts or feelings in Pilot may be what triggered this episode.'

'Sounds plausible,' my mother said.

'It's clear, however, that Pilot is no longer a threat and that the medication has helped greatly. I mean, it *is* making him a bit sluggish, but that should go away over time. And, even though I can't speak for Dr Lennox, I don't see why Pilot won't be released in the next day or two. But we'd like to recommend continuing therapy, insight therapy. I believe it would greatly improve his—'

'I'm a physical therapist,' Hannah said. 'You don't have to convince me of the benefits of therapy, Miss DeQuincey-Joy.'

'I'm sorry. I just—'

'It's all right,' my mother said brusquely. 'You would handle this counseling yourself?'

'I would like to. If you'd rather, I'm sure Dr Lennox can recommend another qualified—'

'No, no,' Hannah said. 'I'd *like* you to do it.'

'Oh,' Katherine said.

'Would you come out to my home for the sessions?'

'I could,' Katherine said. 'But if we don't do it at the clinic it would have to be a separate financial arrangement. I'd be happy to oblige, however, and I'd charge as little as—'

'I'm sure Pilot would rather do it here,' my mother said. 'Have you discussed this with Eric?'

'No,' Katherine said. 'I haven't spoken to him about it.'

'I understand you and he are friendly.'

'I find Eric very, very nice, Mrs Airie. I'm new here and he's been, well, he's been nice to me.'

'Yes.'

'You have two fine sons, Mrs Airie.' Katherine waited for a response. She pictured our mother looking around her perfect house for anything that was out of place. She imagined Hannah picking up a fine glass figurine, examining it for particles of dust.

The truth was, Hannah was standing in her dirty nightgown, her fingers tracing a line along the edge of a pile of ancient *National Geographics*. 'I'd like to speak to Eric about the therapy,' was all she said. 'And to Pilot, too, of course.'

Katherine looked at her cluttered office, the papers strewn everywhere, the ugly furniture. 'Of course,' she said. 'Absolutely.'

With the smallest turn of his head, Dr Lennox indicated the hideous brown three-person couch, the same kind Katherine had in her office, opposite his equally ugly brown chair. I sat down, hands gripping the edge. 'How's it going, Pilot?' he said almost absently. 'Are you feeling better?' His eyes seemed fixed on a point somewhere behind me. I turned and looked, but there was only a wall back there, a display of diplomas and certificates, faded pictures of his children, an overweight woman I assumed was his wife.

I said this as clearly and as brightly as I could: 'I'm feeling much better, Dr Lennox. Thank you.'

Behind him was his desk, its surface clean and open, the window overlooking the parking lot, the highway in the distance, a mass of trees forming at the edge of it. The leaves were changing now, I noticed, turning from green to yellow to gold. The pyrotechnics of death.

'I spoke to Kate and she said you aren't experiencing anything unusual any more. Is that true?'

'No more unusual than usual,' I said good-naturedly.

'Good.' Dr Lennox laughed. 'No more voices?'

'No.'

'No irrational fears?' He was smiling.

'No.'

'No feelings you can't explain?'

I shook my head.

'No visual hallucinations?'

'Not unless I'm hallucinating you.'

This was insane asylum comedy. This was institutional burlesque.

'And I'm glad to see your sense of humor is intact.' Dr Lennox chuckled. 'Always a good sign.'

'I'm feeling much better,' I said. 'Really.'

He leaned forward now, hands on his thighs, saying, 'Kate has one concern that she wanted me to address.'

I knew what was coming. I anticipated it like a blow to my face.

'She's says you're afraid,' the doctor went on, 'afraid that your brother, that Dr Airie—'

I literally winced.

'—is trying to hurt you.'

Dr Airie. I'm Pilot, I thought, Pilot the schizo boy, and Eric is *Dr* Airie. 'Are you telling me I'm paranoid?'

'What makes you think he would try to harm you?'

I couldn't help it. I felt compelled to inform him. 'When we were children,' I said, 'our sister was – they said she was abducted from our house during a party our parents had on a Labor Day weekend.'

'I know.'

'She wasn't.'

'No?'

'Eric killed her.'

Dr Lennox leaned back in his chair, an aura of incredulity settling over him. 'OK.' He smiled. 'And you confronted him with this?'

'In a manner of speaking.'

'How did he respond?'

'I ended up in the hospital with the symptoms of schizophrenia.'

Dr Lennox closed his eyes and nodded very slowly. 'Yes, you did.'

'Do you see what I mean, Dr Lennox – *Greg*?'

'I have to admit, Pilot, that I'm not sure I do. It sounds very complicated and ... circular, in a way.' He rubbed his hands together. 'Let me ask you something.'

I waited.

'How do you know?'

'I remember.'

'Recently? You remembered this recently?'

'All my life.'

'A lot of things we remember from our early childhood, especially things that seem traumatic, are not necessarily real memories. Do you follow me?'

'This was real,' I said. 'Absolutely—'

'Pilot,' he interrupted, 'it may seem like a real memory, I know it does, and that doesn't invalidate your experience of it, but it also doesn't necessarily mean that it actually happened the way you remember it.'

I twisted the shoelace around and around my middle finger. I said, 'OK.'

'I just want you to consider the possibility that what you're remembering might be closer to, say, a dream, or a nightmare even, than it is to a memory of something that actually happened.'

I waited for a moment, considering whether I should argue. I wanted to get out of here, though. Desperately. 'I'll try,' I said.

Smiling, Dr Lennox said, 'What would you think about being released from the clinic?'

'I'd like that,' I said quietly. 'That would be excellent.'

'You would go back to stay with your mother?'

'I've got nowhere else to go.'

'What about your brother?'

'I have to deal with him, too, I guess.'

The doctor looked at me and then he said, 'OK. But I'm going to ask that you stay on the medication. Would that be all right with you?'

'No problem.'

'And I would like you to have some counseling with Kate.'

I hesitated, then said, 'All right.'

He seemed concerned. 'Would you rather someone else did it?'

I thought for a moment, wondering if I should tell Dr Lennox that Katherine and Eric were fucking. But I decided against it. 'No,' I said. 'Katherine's good. She's fine with me.'

'Great.' He clapped his hands against his legs. 'Why don't we check you out tomorrow morning, then? Is that enough time to get ready?'

I tried to regain my positive attitude. 'Ready when you are, Doc.'

Dr Lennox looked at me, his eyes fixing somewhere in the middle of my body, taking me in, I supposed, objectively.

I could feel the muscles of my face moving beneath my skin. I rose from the couch.

He said, 'I'll see you later, Pilot.'

'I have one question.'

'OK.'

'What am I?'

'What do you mean?'

'What is my diagnosis?'

He looked at that place on the wall now. 'A diagnosis is just a word, Pilot,' he said. 'Just a way for us to describe and categorize illnesses and conditions. It's not an identity.'

The definition of *psychotic* in the *Diagnostic and Statistical Manual of Mental Disorders*, Fourth Edition – or the *DSM*-IV, as it's known in the trade – is this: 'delusions or prominent hallucinations, with the hallucinations occurring in the absence of insight into their pathological nature'.

Does that sound like me?

Did I fail to see my own 'pathological nature'?

Definitions of various forms of schizophrenia, according to the *DSM*-IV, are as follows:

Schizophrenia is a disturbance that lasts for at least 6 months and includes at least 1 month of active-phase symptoms (i.e., two [or more] of the following: delusions, hallucinations, disorganized speech, grossly disorganized or catatonic behavior, negative symptoms). Definitions for the Schizophrenia subtypes (including Paranoid, Disorganized, Catatonic, Undifferentiated, and Residual) are also included in this section.

Schizophreniform Disorder is characterized by a symptomatic

presentation that is equivalent to Schizophrenia except for its duration (i.e., the disturbance lasts from 1 to 6 months) and the absence of a requirement that there be a decline in functioning.

Schizoaffective Disorder is a disturbance in which a mood episode and the active-phase symptoms of Schizophrenia occur together and were preceded or are followed by at least 2 weeks of delusions or hallucinations without prominent mood symptoms.

Delusional Disorder is characterized by at least 1 month of non-bizarre delusions without other active phase symptoms of Schizophrenia.

Brief Psychotic Disorder is a psychotic disturbance that lasts more than 1 day and remits by 1 month.

Shared Psychotic Disorder is a disturbance that develops in an individual who is influenced by someone else who has an established delusion with similar content.

In Psychotic Disorder Due to a General Medical Condition, the psychotic symptoms are judged to be a direct physiological consequence of a general medical condition.

In Substance-Induced Psychotic Disorder, the psychotic symptoms are judged to be a direct physiological consequence of a drug of abuse, a medication, or toxin exposure.

Psychotic Disorder Not Otherwise Specified is included for classifying psychotic presentations that do not meet with criteria for any of the specific Psychotic Disorders defined in this section or psychotic symptomology about which there is inadequate or contradictory information.

'He really thinks you killed her,' Katherine said.

My brother sat up against the wall, pushing the sheet off his chest with one hand, rubbing his face with the other. 'He really does?' His voice was pained. 'How could he—', but he stopped himself.

Katherine pulled her portion of the sheet up to her chin. It was getting cold out, an early winter this year, and the heat hadn't come on in her building yet. They were in the *enclosure*, on the mattress on the floor of her tiny living room, all the lights off. 'He does,' she was forced to say. 'It's irrational, I know, but he really thinks—'

'Did he tell you how? Did he say *how* he thought I killed her, for Christ's sake?'

Katherine sighed. 'He didn't say anything to me about that. Perhaps he said something to Dr Lennox. I know Greg talked to him about it this afternoon. Pilot's – well, he's very vague.'

Eric closed his eyes in frustration. 'He's so crazy.'

She reached up, palm open, to put her hand on his shoulder. Eric was muscular, she noticed, without being overly defined. He had the body of a handsome man, she thought – not a vain one. 'You're a good brother,' she told him. 'Pilot will get through this.'

'How can I be a good brother if he thinks I killed Fiona?' Eric shrugged off her touch. 'What kind of a brother is that?'

'At least he's being released.'

'It's not too soon?'

'The medication will keep his mind from slipping back into the psychosis. I mean, you know about that. And other than the paranoia, Pilot's fine. I'm not even sure schizophrenia, or even schizoaffective disorder is the right—'

Eric wasn't listening. 'Our mother is practically blind from this, from this optical aphasia,' he said, his voice revealing the slightest tremble, 'my brother is a paranoid schizophrenic and my father is flying around somewhere off the coast of Florida with his whore.' His voice was becoming pinched. 'What the fuck has happened to my family?'

Katherine put her head against the skin of his arm. Eric was too warm for this, really, and it made her own skin feel prickly. 'Maybe you should have a little counseling yourself.'

Eric sighed, shaking his head.

'Why not?'

'It's just that someone has to be strong through this, you know. Someone has to be able to handle things without—'

'Going to therapy is a sign of weakness?'

'I didn't say that.'

'Well,' Katherine said, rising up against the wall next to him, 'you do whatever you think is best.'

The two of them sat together this way for a moment and listened to the sound of the cars on the highway beyond the parking lot. She heard an ambulance go by, then an eighteen-wheeler. Finally, she broke the silence. 'What do you remember about that night? I mean, do you mind talking about it?'

'About—'

'About the night your sister was—'

'I remember very little about it, actually.' He faced the window, away from her, and a rim of light flared off his cheekbone. 'It was a party my parents were having. It was hot. An Indian summer, I guess. They used to have a lot of get-togethers in those days, you know – barbecues, cocktail parties. I was upstairs with my girlfriend, with Dawn Costello, Joannie's sister, the one you met, and then we went to a party a few blocks away. I got really, really wasted and eventually I came back to my parents' house, and went to sleep. The next morning Fiona was gone.'

'What happened after that?'

'There was a search, you know, which started out small and became enormous. I mean, her picture was on television, my parents were on the news. It was horrible.' He shook his head. 'And we, and no one ever found anything. Except Pilot.'

'He found something?'

'He found the tennis shoe she was, she had been wearing. It was out in the woods somewhere and he found it.'

'In the woods.'

'And that's really all there is to remember,' Eric said. 'That, and how everything just sort of went to shit afterwards. You know, my parents got divorced. They kept blaming each other, our father was worse about that, really, blaming our mother, I guess, and Pilot was crawling around like a dog, even barking.'

'Tell me about that.'

'About Pilot?'

'It sounds like he had an episode of psychosis.'

'I guess that's what it was.' Eric shrugged. 'Pilot wigged out. He decided that he was an animal and he started, I don't know, he would crawl around through the woods on his hands and knees, and he stopped talking for a couple of weeks, just growling and barking. It was comical, in a way. I think he'd seen something on television about the wolf boy, the one they discovered in France. Later on Pilot said he felt as if he had lost the power of speech. I'm afraid I, I think I wasn't so nice to him in those days.'

'You were a kid.'

'I was five years older. I should have been more—'

'Still.'

'Well,' Eric said, 'there's not a lot more to talk about, really. Fiona was gone. Pilot was crazy. My parents were divorced. I just studied, you know. I just lost myself in textbooks and sports.'

'And now you're a big-shot.'

Eric sighed. 'Whatever.'

'Praised be the fall.'

'What?'

'Praised be the fall,' Katherine repeated. 'It's an old medieval idea about the fall from heaven, the fall from grace. They said praised be the fall because without it, without the fall from Eden, we would never have known the blessings of Christ.'

Eric let a small burst of air out through his lips. 'OK.'

'Without the tragedy your family suffered you might never have become a doctor,' Katherine said.

Eric nodded. 'A lot of things would have been different.'

'You're rather amazing', Katherine said, 'for coming out of that experience the way you did. You should be proud.'

'I just wish Pilot had come out of it – and who says I'm all right?'

'He will,' Katherine said. 'It's not too late for him.'

His face turned toward her now. 'They accused someone.'

'Who?'

'There was a man at the party the police suspected, but since they never found Fiona – I mean, since there was no body, and no evidence besides the sneaker, they had to let him go.'

'Do you think he did it?'

'People saw him playing with her. The last time anyone saw her, she was with Bryce Telliman.'

Katherine was quiet.

'That doesn't mean he did anything,' Eric said. 'Does it?'

'No,' Katherine said. 'A lot of people like children. It doesn't mean anything.'

'I used to wish he had done it,' Eric said. 'That way I could have killed him.'

'You think he didn't?'

'I don't know. I just, when I was younger, I just wanted to kill whoever had done it, you know. I just wanted to hurt someone, make someone pay.'

'Did you ever tell anyone about that?'

'What do you mean?'

'Pilot thinks you want to kill him. Maybe your brother feels guilty about Fiona, feels responsible, so he thinks you want to make *him* pay.'

'Pilot,' my brother said, just saying my name, I think. Just to hear himself say it.

She saw Fiona.

Hannah was in the laundry room unloading the washer. Nearby, another set of ghost hands unloaded a ghost washer. On the floor were piles of laundry, dirty dishtowels, floral patterned sheets, striped pillowcases, each with their ghost companion. She thought she heard something at first, something like footsteps behind her. Fiona used to help Hannah with the laundry when she was a little girl. She liked to get inside the basket of warm clothes after they came out of the dryer. She liked to fold the big sheets with Hannah, her mother. She wanted to turn the fabric over and over in her tiny hands until it was a tiny square.

Hannah saw her.

Everything Hannah looked at had a ghost. Perhaps she was just getting used to the idea of ghosts. Out of the corner of her eye, she saw a little girl run by, flashing by the door. She saw the flash of red that was Fiona's bathing suit. She saw the one red sneaker. It was her. Hannah definitely saw Fiona.

Didn't she?

She dropped the towel she was holding and next to her her ghost hands dropped the ghost towel. She went into the kitchen. There were doubles of everything, glassy transparencies, shimmering overlays of color, a film of opacity blurring whatever fell in her eyeline. What was wrong with her? Had Fiona been in here? Why shouldn't there be ghosts? she asked herself. Why wouldn't her daughter be trying to reach her?

'Hello?' Hannah said into the room. 'Hello?'

There was no answer, of course, only the dry sound of the highway in the distance, the wind in the treetops. The usual neighborhood hum.

Hannah felt foolish. She turned to go back into the laundry room, but as she turned, she saw – she *thought* she saw – that flash of a red bathing suit, the one sneaker, the little-girl flesh, pink and perfect, moving by the kitchen window. Was Fiona outside? Was she trying to get in? Hannah went to the window again. Was someone playing a trick on her?

Outside was restlessness itself. Outside were leaves dying on the tree limbs, were quavering branches, high up, ready to fall. Outside was too-long grass that hadn't been cut in weeks, since I had gone into the hospital, was wind-blown debris from the woods, her garden unkempt, and everything she saw outside had a ghost. But where was Fiona? Hannah opened the kitchen door and looked out into the yard. She rubbed her eyes, hoping to clear away the double images, and squinted into the daylight. It was eleven in the morning, or around then. It was early in the day, anyway, wasn't it?

Perhaps it was one of the girls from next door. A young family had moved in, with two daughters, little girls around Fiona's age. No, Hannah corrected herself, around the age Fiona was when she disappeared.

'Is someone out there?' she said. 'Hello?'

Sometimes, when she stepped outside through the kitchen door, she expected to see the pool, expected to see the glimmering water, the flashes of sunlight on its surface. She expected to see her children, to see Eric, me, Fiona, splashing in the pool, my father beside it in the lounge chair, newspaper unfolded on his chest, sleeping. Instead she saw her garden, the leaves of rhubarb, the vines of pumpkin and squash twisting around and around each other. It was such a mess. Hannah sometimes worried – irrationally, she knew – that Fiona would one day come back through the woods, still seven years old, and not recognize her own home.

Where is the pool? she would think.

She pictured Fiona coming back through the woods.

Fiona would be a grown-up woman now, was the truth. It was possible, it was still possible, that Fiona was somewhere, *was* grown-up, living a life, not remembering. It was possible. There was a boy in Arizona Hannah had read about who had been abducted as a child and was raised to the age of eighteen or twenty before he remembered, before he realized he'd had a life elsewhere, before the memories of his real childhood came flooding back – that he'd had real parents, a real house, real brothers and sisters. They can repress memories, children can make their minds do anything, Hannah thought, disassociating from the truth completely.

But today, wearing an old floral house dress with a bottle of Xanax in her pocket, doing the laundry, seeing double, waiting for me to become sane and return home from the hospital, Hannah thought she saw her daughter.

It was the cancer. It was the knot of cells in her optical cortex blurring her vision, her wishes bleeding into her sightline.

She thought she saw Fiona in the kitchen from the laundry room. She thought she saw her running by the kitchen window. Was it just wishful thinking? Were her eyes playing tricks? Of course they were. She closed the kitchen door on the outside and turned around again. She walked back into the laundry room. She touched her face and realized it was wet. Had she been crying? Was she going insane, too? Like me. Crazy with grief. People said that, didn't they? She continued to lift the laundry into the basket, folding as she went. It had been so many years. She pretended that

Fiona was outside in the yard, seven years old, playing a game. When Hannah pretended like that, she felt some relief. And sometimes she forgot, even for a second, that Fiona wasn't there and it felt a little better that way.

'Risk factors for suicide', according to the *DSM*-IV, 'include being male, age under thirty years, depressive symptoms, unemployment and recent hospital discharge.'

Me, me, me, me and me.

Eric was standing behind me, jacket thrown over his shoulder, when I gathered the few things Hannah had brought me, the bits and pieces of clothing, books, and toiletries I'd needed for my stay. 'Mom can't drive you,' Eric said apologetically. 'Her eyes, you know. And there's no one else.'

'It's all right,' I told him. 'There's no need to apologize.'

'I know you don't want to see me.'

'Eric,' I said, 'what are you talking about?'

My brother shrugged. 'I guess we'll talk about it later,' he said. 'Anyway, how are you feeling? Better, I guess. I mean, they're letting you out, anyway.' He was acting nervously. Why was he so nervous? Or, better yet, why was he acting?

'I feel much, much better,' I told him. 'Really.' It's what I'd been saying to everyone. And it was true, mostly.

'We were all pretty concerned about you,' he said. 'We still are.'

I looked at his face, a face that had turned out to be our father's face. There was something slightly plastic about its handsomeness, as if it had been pre-formed. 'Thank you,' I said.

'You think you'll be all right at Mom's?' he asked. 'I mean, I know you might not be entirely comfortable moving back in with her, I know I wouldn't be, and I thought—'

'Where else am I going to go?'

'You could stay with me.'

I said this flatly: 'Mom's will be fine.'

'Pilot,' Eric said, 'I just—'

'It's all right.' I finished stuffing all my things into my bag. 'It's fine, really. It's really fine. I'm all medicated up now. I can't go crazy', I laughed, 'even if I want to.'

Eric tossed his car keys from one hand to the other. They made a jangling sound. He wore his usual blue tie, white shirt, navy suit. He wore a concerned smile. He wore his hair differently, I thought, parted in a new way. I thought it must have had something to do with Katherine DeQuincey-Joy. 'I got a new haircut,' he said. He saw me notice it, I guess. 'It looks stupid, I know.'

'It looks good,' I said. 'Very stylish.'

Sarcastically, he said, 'You've always been so big on style.'

I changed the subject. 'They want me to keep up with the counseling.' I twirled my finger around my temple. The shoelace was threaded around my fingers.

He nodded. 'I think it's a good idea.'

'They think they've got the schizophrenia thing under control', I said, 'with medication.'

'Clozaril,' Eric said. 'Very effective.'

'But I have other . . . issues, they tell me.'

'Pilot,' Eric said, 'you don't have to tell me any of this. I'm your brother, and I'll do whatever it is, whatever I can do, to help you. I promise. But you're not obligated to—'

'It's all right,' I said. 'It's just that I know about you and Katherine.'

He looked at his hands.

I took a final look around the room to see if there was anything I had missed. On the windowsill were get-well cards from my mother's friends. I decided to leave them.

I had already said goodbye to Harrison and some of the other patients and nurses I had met.

'Let's go,' I said.

Eric repeated me, saying, 'Let's go.' Minutes later, in the car, he said, 'I'm not trying to kill you.'

I laughed. 'You're not?'

'Pilot, why the fuck would I want to kill you?'

'I know,' I told him. 'I know what happened. I know exactly what happened to Fiona.'

'What happened to Fiona?'

'I know what you did to Halley, too.'

'You have to let it go, brother.' He closed his eyes, turned the key in the ignition. 'It's in the past.' The Jaguar's engine started.

'You were practicing,' I said.

'Pilot.'

'To become a doctor.'

'I can't believe this.'

'Which is why they never found her.'

'Jesus Christ, Pilot.'

'Because she's in a million little pieces, isn't she, Mr Junior Scalpel?'

From the woods I could see bodies moving around the pool. Shadows from here, the party-goers' faces flared up every now and then in the torchlights, drunken smiles frozen on their lips. I could see flames through the trees in yellow-gold flickering stripes. Voices of men and women co-mingled in the boughs above me – laughing shrieks, arguments, passionate conversations, chatter. I saw him stepping in, a blond man with long hair. I saw the way he moved, his body swaying, a man who had been drinking too much. It was as though my senses had been heightened, sharpened on a stone. I could pinpoint individual conversations swirling into the woods from the party. I could sense the rising and falling of a woman's chest. I could smell the perfume and aftershave and alcohol on the bodies of these people. I could hear my father, his voice bellowing arrogantly, and my mother, hers soft and accommodating. The man who walked into the woods put his hand against a tree, his body leaning into his arm. He looked down, his chest heaving. He was going to be sick. But when he looked up, I caught that eye-flash of recognition, the light in his face that said he saw me, too. I could have spoken to him then. I could have said something – anything – and it would have been impossible later. If I had said something, if he had said something, then everything – everything that ever happened in my life after that – would have been changed. But he didn't. And I didn't. He stepped out beyond the treeline, then, on to my parents' lawn.

'I've been out flying,' he said. 'Patricia and me were—'

'Patricia and I.'

'Yes,' my father said. Hannah was always correcting his grammar. It had always annoyed him and she knew this. 'Anyway,' he said, 'I got your message.'

'It's Pilot.'

My father's teeth came together. 'What now?'

'James, I think he needs you. I think this time he—'

When Eric and I drove up to the house that morning Hannah came out to the driveway in her floral housecoat, saying, 'Oh, Pilot, I'm so, so sorry I couldn't come and get you myself.' I got out of the car and she placed one cool hand on my cheek and the other around my neck. Her old cream-colored Mercedes sports car sat parked in front of the house, covered in dust, dead leaves, brown whirlies. 'How do you feel, sweetheart?' she said. 'You know I can't drive any more. It's this darn thing with my eyes. It's nothing, but, but, how are you?'

'I'm fine, Mom,' I said, as I'd been saying to everyone, as I'd been saying over and over and over to everyone. 'Much better.' Eric was behind me, lifting my small, overstuffed duffel bag from the back seat of his Jaguar and shutting the door.

He nodded. 'He seems fine,' he said to our mother. 'He seems normal, anyway.'

There was an implication in my brother's voice.

'I am,' I told them both. 'I'm fine. I'm so full of anti-psychotics and anti-depressants. Who wouldn't feel great?'

'Of course he is.' She pulled me toward the front door of the house, leading me by the arm. 'Of course.' I had a feeling she didn't want the neighbors seeing us out here, even though everyone who knew us from the old days had moved away. There were children in the neighborhood, in fact, new generations of young families moving into these old houses. 'Well,' Hannah asked, 'are you hungry? Both of you? Either of you?'

The medication I was taking left a hollow in my stomach that felt better when empty. I shook my head. I was supposed to take my pills with food, naturally, but I felt much better not eating. Plus it was around eleven in the morning, the wrong time of the day to eat.

'I'll have something,' Eric said. 'I had to skip breakfast.' He shot me a quick look. 'I'm starved.'

I thought I could see clouds forming in my mother's eyes. I thought I could see the years multiplying on her face. The blue vein that ran like a trickle down her temple had become almost purple. Her hair was a notch more silver, her skin whiter. 'How are your eyes?' I asked.

'My eyes?' As if she didn't know what I meant.

We stopped on the steps leading to the front door. 'You just told me you couldn't drive because of them. Are things getting cloudier, or—'

'They're – they're all right,' she said unsteadily. 'They're good.'

'You're not seeing double any more?'

She laughed a nervous laugh. 'I'm getting used to it, I guess.'

'You can't drive,' I said flatly.

Now Eric was the one who laughed. 'It wouldn't be a very good idea.'

I looked at our mother. 'Is it because you can't see the road,' I asked, 'or because you can't see the dashboard?'

'Pilot.' Hannah walked in the door.

Eric brushed past me, carrying my bag. 'Pilot, do you ever remember a time when she paid attention to the road?'

'You have a point.'

Inside the house, Eric sat down on the old blue living-room couch, tossing my bag beside him. 'Now that you're home,' he said, 'you can look after Mom while we figure out what's going on. It's nothing serious, so don't worry. It's probably just an infection in her optical nerve or something, something benign. In any—'

'It's because I'm old,' Hannah interrupted. She was picking up outdated magazines from all the little tables and putting them in stacks. There were *Peoples, Times, National Geographics.* 'It's because I'm an old lady.'

'You're not an old lady,' I told her. 'Why do you say that?'

She walked into the kitchen. 'Because it's true.'

Eric got up from the couch and followed her, shrugging.

I went in after him. The yellow teapot-motif kitchen was brilliant with late morning light, more gold at the moment than yellow. Outside, just past the yard, the woods rustled and shook in the fall breeze. My mother and brother looked at the woods and then back at me uneasily.

'Don't worry,' I said. 'I'm not going out there.'

'Do you feel all right about being so close?' Eric asked. It sounded almost genuine, like concern.

'What do you mean?'

'Katherine,' he said, 'Katherine told me you were having fears that they would, you know—'. He left it hanging.

'Eric,' Hannah said, 'he probably doesn't want to talk about it.'

'I'm not afraid of the woods any more,' I said. 'If that's what you mean.'

And I saw the anger flashing across my brother's face. 'Just me,' Eric said.

'Eric.'

This is the manner of a tattletale: 'Pilot thinks I'm going to kill him.'

'He does not.' She started placing things on the counter, reaching into yellow cabinets and pulling out cans of tuna, boxes of crackers, all kinds of colorful packages. There was Jello. There were Oreos. There were Lays potato chips.

'He thinks I killed Fiona.' Eric sat down heavily on a kitchen chair. He loosened his tie and unbuttoned the top of his shirt. He rubbed his hands together. 'He thinks I did it, Mom, that it was me.'

Our mother grabbed a bag of Wonderbread from the bread box and started putting sandwiches together, taking pressed ham out of the refrigerator and slapping it between the spongy, white slices.

She slathered plain French's mustard on as if it was the principal ingredient. She put two of these sandwiches each on two small plates which were decorated with little yellow teapots and set them down on the kitchen table, one for Eric, one for me, even though I had told her I wasn't hungry, even though I was standing on the other side of the room.

She said, 'What do you want to drink?'

'Is there juice?' Eric asked.

She went to the refrigerator again and removed a carton of orange juice. She poured two small glasses. 'I can't find the big glasses,' she said. 'These will have to do.'

'These are fine,' I said.

Humming, she set them down. I wasn't even sitting at the table. I was standing in the archway that led to the dining room, twisting that shoelace around and around my middle finger. What color had this kitchen been when Fiona was alive? When did the teapot-motif start?

After a few bites of his sandwich, Eric sighed. Then he said, 'I'm sorry about that, Mom. It's just—'

'Apologize to your brother.'

Eric looked at me.

I nodded. What difference did it make?

'I talked to your father last night,' Hannah told me. 'He says he wants to see you.'

Eric rolled his eyes. 'Where has he been?'

'He's been out flying.' She started to wipe the counter. I could hear the girl in her when she spoke about our father. Our mother had never seen another man after he left, had been permanently heartbroken by this second loss, had never even tried to see anyone else, as far as I knew. 'Out flying that damn airplane,' she said. 'Your father is lost,' she went on, and Eric and I knew exactly how she would finish this, but she surprised us, not finishing. We looked at each other across the kitchen – it was the kitchen our mother had put in, I remembered, the summer she and our father had decided to sleep in separate rooms.

* * *

Our father was a tall man, an inch or two taller than Eric. He had a square jaw and gleaming blue eyes. He had a two-seater seaplane that he flew off the coast of Florida. He lived only a mile or two from the water. Years before, before the beginning of time, our father flew test jets for the Air Force and he lived in California briefly, before he met our mother, and then he became an airline pilot for TWA, and then he met Hannah, and then he had us, and all the rest.

After Fiona disappeared, our father hardly came home at all. He took the most difficult, time-consuming flight routes the airline offered. He flew all over the world, one flight after another, with just enough time in between to check our report cards and ask if there had been any news about his daughter. When I was in college we learned that Dad had been flying to and from Atlanta all these years and that he had a girlfriend there, a woman named Patricia. He announced to our mother one night that she could have everything – the house, the money, the retirement – as long as he could take just enough to buy a small plane.

Hannah had grown so used to not seeing him anyway that it would make little difference, she supposed. He had blamed her for Fiona's disappearance, too. They had not slept in the same room, in fact, since Eric went to school.

The summer of the yellow teapot kitchen.

Our father wore a salt and pepper beard. He had broad, muscular shoulders, blue, blue, blue eyes – eyes like Eric's. I dialed his number, sitting in the living room on the old blue couch. Upstairs, Hannah ran the water for a bath. I could hear it filling the tub.

'Hello?' came a voice.

'Patricia?' I said. 'It's Pilot.'

'Pilot?' she said. 'How are you?' Patricia's voice was always overly enthusiastic, bordering on desperate.

'I'm much better, thanks,' I said, feeling a bit like I'd been programmed to say these words. 'I'm really much, much better.'

'I'm so glad to hear that.' She was distracted, I could tell. I felt like I had interrupted something. 'Let me get your dad. He's in the other room. *Jim!* I heard her yell. '*Jim, it's Pilot! Pilot!* Hold on,' Patricia said into the phone, 'he's coming.'

The phone was transferred from one hand to another.

'Pilot?'

I could hear the television in the background. It sounded like one of those Second World War documentaries.

I became soft. 'Hey, Dad.' I felt as if I was in trouble.

'Pilot, Jesus Christ, are you better?'

I said my line.

'We weren't here, you know. Otherwise we would have called right away. I didn't talk to your mother until—'

'It's all right. Where were you?'

'Island hopping, you know.'

'Sounds great.'

'Can you tell me what happened?' His voice was filled with something like amazement, something beyond concern, like I had accidentally gone to the moon. Was he almost proud?

'There's not a lot to tell. I had a psychotic episode,' I said. 'I had a schizophrenic reaction. I was afraid the woods—'

'What do you mean?' he said. 'Were you hearing voices and—'

'Exactly,' I said. 'It was just exactly like it is on television – voices, uncontrollable thoughts, irrational fears, the whole nine yards.' It was an expression I thought he would like, the language of football, the whole nine yards.

'And what did they do for you?'

'They medicated the hell out of me. I'm taking a new drug. It really makes a big, big difference,' I said. 'I don't have any more symptoms at all. I'm fine now, totally back to normal.'

'Well,' he said uneasily, 'that's great, Pilot.'

'So.' I examined the black telephone I held on my lap. The last time I had used it, I remembered, I was going crazy. It had always been a black, heavy, rotary-dial phone. It had always been that way, I told myself. I recalled the amazement I had felt looking at it. I really had been nuts. 'So how have you been?' I still had the shoelace around my finger, the reminder.

'We're having a lot of fun, Pilot. Just living day to day.'

'How's Patricia?'

'She's great.'

'Great,' I said.

Our father cleared his throat. 'What would you think of, uh, what would you think about coming down here for a while? You could stay on the couch. There's not a lot of room, but there's plenty of space to roam around outside, and we could take the plane out. There's this little island I found, I call it Nowhere—'

'Well, Dad, thanks,' I said, 'it's just that they kind of want me to do some, to do some therapy, you know, and I kind of have to—'

'Therapy.'

'Right.'

'I guess that makes sense.' I heard gunfire coming from the television. I heard the narrator's voice describing something about the Pacific Theater, the Japanese Navy.

'Has Mom mentioned anything about her eyes?'

His voice hardened. 'What's wrong with your mother's eyes?'

'She's seeing ghosts, she says. She's seeing weird transparent things, double images. I don't know. Eric says it's nothing, but, but, but she can't drive. I guess I kind of need to look after her until she gets that straightened out, too. I mean, that's another reason—'

'Christ almighty, we're having all kinds of problems here, aren't we?'

I tried to make this sound funny: 'I guess we're falling apart, Dad.' It came out pathetic.

There was a pause. In this pause I believe I could have lived and died a million times. In this pause, I believe, entire generations of people could have lived and died. Civilizations could have risen from ignorance and destroyed themselves with knowledge.

'The offer stands,' my father said firmly. 'Anytime,' he said. 'Anytime you want to come down, Pilot, we'll take the plane, just you and me if you want, go anywhere, or at least as far as those little wings can carry us.' He got cute when he talked about his airplane.

'Thanks, Dad.'

'You take care of yourself.' He was desperate to get off the phone.

'I will.'

'I'm serious.'

I knew he was serious. He was never anything but serious. He was, after all, my dad.

In the last spot in the clinic parking lot, the following Tuesday, Katherine Jane DeQuincey-Joy started her sapphire-blue VW Rabbit and, instead of driving to the *enclosure* across from the strip mall, she took Sky Highway to Exit 10, which led down a narrow road into Foxwood Court, the cul-de-sac of houses where Eric and I had grown up. Katherine had never been out this way before – had, in fact, only imagined what my childhood home looked like. She had thought it would be modern, sterile and beige, with sleekly designed blond wood furniture adorned by glass vases filled with water and stark branches. She pictured oriental prints on the walls, pale watercolors, black and white photographs. She imagined spare, tightly woven Berber carpets. She thought there would be shelves of hardbound textbooks and a telescope placed handsomely in front of a window.

She was wrong.

Our house, like so many others around here, was early Fifties colonial, made of white-painted brick and covered on one side by ivy. It stood in the shade of overly large trees, two maples and an oak. It had a two-car garage filled with the detritus of our childhoods, with a ping-pong table, every imaginable sort of game, a full wet suit hanging in front of the garage window like the body of a dead man.

Katherine pulled her car into the street behind our mother's cream-colored Mercedes and sat there for a moment, making sure she had a pad of paper in her purse, making sure she had her thoughts gathered together properly, making sure of things, in general – that this was even the right place.

Katherine had imagined everything wrong, but she was still right – all the pieces still fit together properly.

Sometimes a person can imagine everything wrong and still be right. Sometimes. And I think it helps to be crazy.

Even though she was seeing double, seeing two old oaks in the front lawn, two each of our neighbors' houses with cars too multiple to count, our mother had been watching from the dining-room window, hands folded under her chin, waiting for my therapist to arrive. 'Katherine DeQuincey-Joy is here,' she said when she saw the two VW Rabbits pull up behind her two Mercedes. As it always had, my mother's voice carried easily – cutting like piano wire – through the walls and ceiling to where I sat in my bedroom looking at my feet. I had been positioned this way for an hour, for some reason, not moving except to breathe. It was the medication, which made me sluggish to the point of catatonia. I think it was the medication, anyway. I had started to put a sock on and had just stopped, mid-motion. Catatonia, of course, is one of the many symptoms of schizophrenia. I had become totally catatonic in the woods, as a matter of fact, to the point where I was absolutely frozen, could not move at all. My memory of the three days I spent out there was returning a little bit at a time. If Eric had wanted to kill me, I thought, he could have done it then, so easily. Anyone could have. It was as if I had been caught in one of his traps.

'I'll be right down,' I said now, the spell broken.

I put the other sock on, not even checking to make sure it matched, rose from the single bed and descended stiffly downstairs, my hand touching the macramé weavings of animals my mother had hung there years ago – an owl, a sparrow, a hawk.

Katherine stood in the middle of our living room, smiling nervously at Hannah. Poor Katherine. She wore a black suit today, with a gray silk shirt, a triple string of pearls. Her mass of hair, at day's end, had frizzed into a collection of blonde-brown curlicues so twisty and confused it was hard to believe it wasn't alive. She looked up at me and I could see the relief in her face. Hannah can be a bit intimidating to strangers. Her absentmindedness comes off as cold, and that day, with her eyes unfocused, she was particularly strange.

'Hello, Katherine,' I said.

'Pilot.'

My mother asked, 'Can I get you something, Miss DeQuincey-Joy? Some tea, perhaps?' It was as if she was repeating a line from a movie.

'No,' Katherine said. 'No, I think I'm fine, thank you.'

I looked at my mother. 'Where should we do this?'

'Oh,' Hannah said, touching a finger to her lips, 'I hadn't thought about that.'

'Wherever you're most comfortable, Pilot.'

I tried to make a joke, saying, 'Then I'm afraid we'll have to leave the country.'

Hannah smirked. 'Why don't you use the living room?' She pointed to the stairs. 'I'll go to my room and listen to the radio.'

I said, 'That's fine.'

Katherine looked smilingly at the furnishings.

Hannah stood by the stairs for a moment, her frail hand on the banister. 'Well,' she said, 'all right, then. Have fun.' It was an odd thing to say. She turned and walked up the steps to the second floor. 'Help yourself to whatever's in the kitchen if you need anything.'

'Thank you, Mrs Airie.'

I could see that Katherine was taking in the living room, the mismatched pillows and drapes, the blue and white oriental on the floor, and the relic from the Seventies – the ancient blue couch.

'We're finally alone,' I said, as if we were lovers.

'Your mother has a beautiful house.' Katherine was trying to be sincere and I could see that it was difficult.

'It's insane,' I said. 'Even crazier than me. It was more orderly once. Once, it had a design to it, a visual approach, a point of view. Now it contains everything. Everything and nothing.'

Laughing, Katherine sat down in the high-backed leather chair my father used to sit in to read his spy thrillers. 'Is this all right for you, Pilot? I mean, would you be more comfortable somewhere else?'

'It doesn't make any difference to me.'

'Let's begin, then.'

'All right.' I sat down, feeling the grain of the coarse fabric.

'How are you feeling?'

'A little slow,' I admitted. 'Sluggish.'

'You've been taking your medication?'

'As directed.'

'Good.' Katherine opened her bag and pulled out her pad of yellow legal paper. I could see a fresh wound on one of her fingers, where she had recently chewed past the skin. 'So I trust you've had no voices or, or strange thoughts?'

'Just from my mother,' I said. 'And I'm pretty sure she's real, unfortunately.'

Katherine wrote something on her legal pad. Then she leaned forward. 'Pilot, I know we haven't really talked about this until now because our main concern was making sure you stayed—'

'Sane?'

'I was going to say rational.'

'Same thing.'

I twisted the shoelace, just to check if it was still there.

'Anyway,' Katherine said, 'I think we should talk about some of the feelings you expressed to me at the clinic last week.'

'About you sleeping with my brother?'

'I thought we had worked that out.'

'Sorry. I'm just being a wiseguy.'

'I think we should talk about what happened to your sister.'

'Eric happened to her.'

'That's what you mentioned before,' she said. 'You should know he finds that deeply troubling.'

'Of course he does,' I said. 'No one wants to get caught.'

Katherine sighed. 'Can you let me try to explain something to you?' she asked. 'I don't want you to think I don't believe you or that I'm calling you a liar, because I'm not. I absolutely believe that you're telling the truth. But I want you to listen to a theory I have. I just want you to listen. Just listen. Would you do that for me?'

I shrugged. 'All right.'

'Here goes.' Katherine's hand was pressed flat against the pad of paper, bloody fingertips pointed toward me. Her other hand held a small silvery pen. 'Because you're a human being, Pilot, you have a very complex and active brain.' Her fingers started to stroke the smooth paper, the way Halley the Comet would gently paw at a sweater. 'Unfortunately, your brain is not, is not as chemically balanced as it should be, and that's why you suffered that, that scary episode. Now, one thing we know about schizophrenia is that it doesn't alter the logic part, or thinking part, of your brain. Are you following me so far?' Her tone was that of someone talking to an animal or a retarded person.

I nodded. I knew all this. I had read about it a million times, in fact.

'Anyway,' she continued, 'what is affected is the sensing part of your brain. You're hearing voices, you're getting disordered imagery through your eyes. So the logic part of your brain – which is completely intact – tries to make sense of all that wrong sensory data and tries to do the logical thing, but nothing really makes sense, right?'

'Nothing made sense,' I said, nodding. 'That's what I remember.'

'And the result is crazy behavior, because you're trying to interpret what the right thing to do is based on the information you're getting.'

'OK.' I unraveled the shoelace from my ring finger, then twisted it around my middle finger again, raveling it back.

She seemed to be looking at it. For the first time, I thought, Katherine noticed my shoelace. 'Pilot,' she said, 'when you were suffering from all those chemicals rushing around in your head I think some things got, well, got re-ordered, you know, re-shuffled, and re-organized, and they didn't get put back in the right places after you started taking the medication, and that's why you have these feelings about your brother.'

'I see.'

'And what I would like to try to do is, is try to help you clear all that stuff up.'

'So, Katherine,' I said, 'you don't think I'm lying. You think I'm nuts.'

'No,' Katherine said.

'You think I'm stupid.'

'Pilot, I don't think you're crazy or stupid or anything. I think your brain is lying to you. I think you're getting some bad information. And it's hurting people. This is your family we're talking about, your brother, and he loves you.'

I considered the idea. I sat back, saying, 'It's possible,' twisting and untwisting the shoelace – raveling, unraveling.

'Of course it is.'

'Anything for my brother's girlfriend.'

Now Katherine reached up and touched her forehead. 'OK,' she began, 'like I said, I'm not Eric's girlfriend. I went out with him a couple of times for dinner and I think he's a very nice man, but as long as you want me to continue being your therapist I don't have to see him. We talked about it and both of us feel that is the right thing.'

I repeated her. 'You and Eric talked about it.'

'Does that make you feel any better?'

I leaned forward on the couch. I said, 'It didn't suddenly occur to me, Katherine Jane DeQuincey-Joy.'

'What?'

'That Eric killed Fiona.'

'What do you mean?'

'It's a fact I've been hiding all my life.'

The essential feature of the Paranoid Type of Schizophrenia is the presence of prominent delusions or auditory hallucinations in the context of a relative preservation of cognitive functioning and affect ... Delusions are typically persecutory or grandiose, or both, but delusions with other themes (e.g., jealousy, religiosity, or somatization) may also occur. The delusions may be multiple, but are usually organized around a coherent theme. Hallucinations are also typically related to the content of the delusional theme. Associated features include anxiety, anger, aloofness and argumentativeness. The individual may have a superior and patronizing manner and either a stilted, formal quality or extreme intensity in interpersonal interactions. The persecutory themes may predispose the individual to suicidal behavior, and the combination of persecutory and grandiose delusions with anger may predispose the individual to violence. Onset tends to be later in life than the other types of Schizophrenia, and the distinguishing characteristics may be more stable over time. These individuals usually show little or no impairment on neuropsychological or other cognitive testing. Some evidence suggests that the prognosis for the Paranoid Type may be considerably better than for the other types of Schizophrenia, particularly with regard to occupational functioning and capacity for independent living.

'He wanted to kill me,' I told her, 'when we were kids. Eric wanted to torture me.'

'Did he ever do it?' she asked. 'Torture you, I mean?'

Once, just after Fiona disappeared, when I was ten, I think, Eric located me in the woods, had come looking for me out there, in fact. I was hiding in a particular bramble of bushes, playing with a nest of tiny, newborn, almost hairless mice. I heard my brother's dry voice behind me. 'Do you know what that man did to her?'

I turned around. 'Shhh.' I put my finger to my lips. 'There's mice here. Check it out.'

'Fuck the mice,' Eric said. 'Don't you want to know?'

I shook my head.

'He raped her. Little tiny Fiona. He raped the shit out of her. He tied her tiny little stick arms together behind her back, and he spread her little legs open, and he raped her. He stuck his huge, mean penis directly inside her tiny little-girl vagina.'

'Stop it,' I said.

'Why?' Eric said. 'Don't you want to know what happened to our little sister? Don't you care?'

I put my hands over my ears, but Eric slapped them away from my head.

'Then he fucked her in the ass.' He was whispering now. I was starting to cry, I think. On the outside I felt as if I was melting, my face getting all hot, but inside I was dividing, losing language. 'He pushed his enormous, man-sized penis into her tiny little asshole.'

I said, 'Please, Eric.'

'It could have been you,' Eric said.

'No.'

'It would have been you if you were just a little bit younger. They like boys better, everybody knows that. They're called *pedophiles*.' He over-pronounced it.

'No, they don't.'

It was getting more and more difficult to squeeze out my words. And now, some of what Eric was saying seemed hard to understand, as if he was speaking a new language, something I hadn't heard before.

'He's out of jail now, you know. They released him. And he'll be coming after you. He probably wanted you to begin with. He wanted to fuck a little boy instead of a little girl and now he's angry that he didn't get to. Oh yes,' Eric said. And when I opened my eyes I saw his face, but it wasn't his face. It had too many muscles in it. 'He's definitely coming back. He'll probably fuck you in the mouth first—'. I had never thought about this before, had never heard of anyone doing something like that. '—fuck you until you gag, until you practically choke to death, and then he'll tear apart your ass. You'll be lucky if he kills you before he cuts your penis off. They like to eat children. That's why they can't find Fiona's body. That's why she's gone, because he ate her.' It seemed as if I could hear Eric now, could hear Eric's voice, but at the same time I could not understand what he was saying, the words themselves. I was the wolf boy. I let my eyes roll back into my head. I was clutching at the dirt next to me.

* * *

'Dissociating,' Katherine said. 'It's something children do to deal with situations they don't like.' She touched the tip of her silvery pen to the yellow pad of paper. 'Let me ask you something, Pilot.' She leaned into the question. 'When you were out in the woods recently, before you came to the clinic, did you feel like the wolf boy?'

I thought about it. I had lost the power of speech out there, I remembered that. I had forgotten myself. 'Maybe,' I said. 'I just remember everything becoming extremely concrete, more solid than it should be, everything flat and artificial.'

'You couldn't speak, though.'

'No,' I said. 'I couldn't. I just, all I could do was see things and hear things, you know, just the trees, the highway, and there were all these thoughts, thoughts that didn't seem to be mine, exactly.'

'Do you remember having that experience as the wolf boy, that same concrete reality feeling?'

I thought back. I remembered bringing my face closer and closer to Eric's trap, then pulling away. 'Yes,' I said, 'I guess I do.'

'You had a traumatic experience when your sister disappeared, and then your brother teased you cruelly. He shouldn't have.' Katherine's face softened. Her eyes, emerald shards glowing, brought their focus into mine.

'Why did he do that?' I said.

'Perhaps you can talk to him about it now.'

'What good would that do?'

'He could apologize.'

'That's ridiculous.'

I knew that Hannah was listening upstairs. I could see her face responding to everything we said.

'Pilot,' Katherine said, 'it's not ridiculous at all.'

Eric left me there, deep inside those bushes, where I had found the nest of baby mice. I remember that my face became hot for a while and then I remember feeling the liquid glass pouring over me. I took a small pointy stick and pushed it, one by one, into the heads of the little hairless mice inside the nest. Their tiny skulls made a popping sound when the stick poked through. And the remaining ones started squeaking and wriggling around frenetically, a panic settling over them. I imagined the little mouse parents coming back and finding the little mouse babies all dead like this, their tiny skulls crushed. So I picked up each of their little dead baby mouse bodies and flung them outside of the bushes, knowing that it would be worse for the mouse parents this way, to come home and find them missing.

Find them missing. Find them missing.

I pawed at the dirt beside me. My throat felt rough, like I had been growling.

Find them missing.

They were in bed again, the *enclosure* dimly shadowed, lights out, their clothes on the bare floor beside them, both huddled under a thin sheet and Katherine's only blanket, a white summer throw she had managed to keep after the break-up with Mark. A wind was building steadily outside, beating itself like a giant moth against the apartment complex windows.

'I was a mean kid,' Eric said, his voice resigned. 'I had a tough time growing up and I picked on my little brother. I'm sorry about that now.'

'Did you tell him those things?' Katherine asked quietly.

'Those things,' he repeated, as if not quite listening. There was something faintly amused about his expression, she thought. It was the same expression she had seen on Hannah's face. 'It couldn't have been those particular—'

'About what happened to Fiona? About her being tied up, raped—'

He rubbed one of his eyes. He said, 'I don't remember saying anything like that.' Then he paused, and after a moment he said, 'I couldn't have. Because that was all before.'

'When did you do this, then? Do you remember when?'

'What day?'

Katherine felt this was important to know. 'When did you, when did you torment Pilot like this? How old were you?'

'I was a kid,' my brother said. 'It was all before Fiona disappeared. All before.'

'So Pilot would have been nine years old or younger?'

'I guess so.'

'He remembers it differently.'

Eric sighed. 'Obviously,' he said. 'But I only wanted to threaten him. I just wanted to scare him. I felt, I felt like I had to be good all the time, you know. Good in school, good on the football team, good in science. I could be bad around Pilot, *to* Pilot.'

She cleared her throat. 'I think', Katherine said softly, 'that at some point he'll need to, to talk to you about that stuff.'

'Yeah.'

'He found it pretty traumatizing.'

'Do you think it contributed to his illness?'

She thought for a moment, biting her lip. 'Not really,' Katherine said. 'Brothers and sisters are rough on each other, that's all. It's part of the family mechanism. As the oldest sibling your position in the family was threatened by him, so you found—'

'—found a way to put him down.'

'And you know more about brain chemistry than I do. His condition may have been triggered by trauma, but not created by it.'

Eric turned and put his feet on the floor. 'What a shitty brother I was.'

'You can make up for it now.'

He reached back to put a hand on Katherine's leg. 'How?'

'You can be very, very nice to him.' She curled into him, wrapping her body around his.

'That's your expert psychological advice?'

'Yes,' Katherine said, 'it is.' She slid down in bed, so she was completely tucked around the curve of Eric's body, facing the window. Then, conspiratorially, she said, 'I told him we wouldn't be seeing each other until after his therapy was over.' Across the parking lot outside was a broken street lamp. It flickered on and off, glowing yellow light like the tail of a firefly on a summer evening.

'That could be years.'

'Years,' Katherine said. 'I don't think so.'

'He'll know.'

'You know what's weird?' she said. 'Pilot told me a while ago that he was omniscient.'

At that moment I was standing in my mother's kitchen, my bare feet on the cold tiled floor. My hand was on the refrigerator door handle, but I hadn't moved in over ten minutes. Upstairs a radio was playing.

Behind the woods, across the highway, down the turnpike, in Katherine Jane DeQuincey-Joy's *enclosure*, my brother turned, pushing Katherine's tangle of hair to the side and nestling his chin into the hollow of her shoulder. 'Strange.'

'How *did* he know?' she asked.

'About us?'

'About us.'

'Good question,' Eric said. 'He just knew, I guess. He sensed it somehow. Pilot's intelligent, if nothing else.'

'You didn't tell him?'

'I haven't seen him lately. I've been afraid to. I've been afraid to talk to him about anything.'

Katherine shook her head, somewhat bewildered. 'What about your mother, could she have—'

'I didn't tell her, either.' Eric paused for a moment. 'Or maybe I did,' he said. 'Maybe he found out about it from her somehow.'

The wind beat against the glass of the complex again and the entire wall rattled. Katherine thought this flimsy building would blow over if it became much stronger. She saw my mother now, imagined her sitting in her old lady's bedroom, drinking a cup of tea, listening to the same wind blowing through the same treetops outside, seeing two of everything, eyes permanently unfocused.

'How is she, anyway?' Katherine said.

'I don't know.'

'Do you think it's something serious?'

'I think it's some kind of infection in her optic nerve, viral, bacterial, I don't know.'

'Is that common?'

'It's a bit unusual.'

'What do you do for it?'

'There are medications. The passage of time often helps with things like this.'

'She's still seeing ghosts, then, I take it.'

'Says she is.'

'Double of everything?'

'Double.'

Katherine shook her head back and forth in amazement, her face like an egg inside a basket of hair. 'How did I get mixed up with you people?'

'Weird, aren't we?'

'What an understatement.'

'I'm sorry.'

'One year ago,' she said incredulously, 'less than a year ago, in fact, I was living with a lawyer and lived in the city. I had a whole different job, a different man in my bed, different clients coming to my office, a different boss.'

'Some things are better,' Eric said, 'aren't they?'

His hand had found its way around her belly. His finger and palm felt large and warm to Katherine there, pressing lightly into her skin.

'Yes.' She giggled. 'Some things are much better.' She closed her eyes against the flickering yellow street lamp. If Eric was going to stay here, she thought, she would have to get blinds.

Later, she looked at me for a long moment, her eyes revealing the formulation, I could tell, of a question she believed would be difficult for me to answer. 'I think we should talk about—' she began, then stopped. She touched her eye, pushing something out of its corner. Then she started again, saying, 'I wanted to ask you, Pilot, to ask if you can sort out your feelings and thoughts about your brother for a moment.' She put one hand flat on the yellow legal pad. The other was poised above it, holding her silvery pen. 'Do you think you can do that for me?'

I still had my shoelace and now tiny pieces of it, little time-blackened shreds, were starting to come off in my hands. I picked and picked, tearing bits of the end off and dropping them on to my leg. After a minute of this, I'd brush the little tearings on to the floor. 'I'm not sure I know what you mean.'

'I'll ask you some questions, that's all, and you just answer me as honestly as you can.'

Upstairs, Hannah listened, eyes clouded over. Cancer threaded its way through her optical cortex.

I sat up in the old blue couch and registered its rough fabric from time to time with my hands. 'I can try.'

I can try. I felt as if I had been saying this a lot lately.

I had been saying it for years.

'Can you tell me what, what happened when Fiona disappeared?' Katherine was looking directly at me. 'I mean, if Eric did it, if Eric took her, can you tell me how he did it, precisely, and what happened, step by step, as you remember it?' She wore the gray suit and the green satin shirt. The suit was lined with silk. I knew because I heard it rustling beneath the gray outer fabric. Her hair was messier than usual, lights and darks all mixed together. Today it was colder outside. A wintry wind had arrived. Brown leaves swirled in the yard.

'You know,' I said, 'I feel much better. I feel much more animated.'

'That's good.' Katherine smiled. 'That's great, in fact.'

'And you know,' I said, 'there was a good side of Eric.'

She leaned forward. 'What do you mean?'

In the living room, I sat up on my mother's couch. I tore a little piece of the shoelace off and dropped it on my leg. Katherine watched me. I saw her register the shoelace. Still, she didn't say anything about it. 'I mean,' I went on, 'I'm not saying that I don't, that I don't love my brother.' I took a deep breath. 'He could be nice sometimes, and not just – well, you know, not just a bastard.'

'How was he nice?'

'This is going to sound weird,' I said, 'but it really was a positive experience.'

'Don't worry about how weird it sounds right now. We'll worry about that later. Besides, maybe it's not so weird.'

'He got me into grass, when I was eleven or twelve, I think. He turned me on to marijuana for the first time.'

'Really?' She was smiling.

'I was trying out for the football team,' I told Katherine, 'the Thomas Edison junior high school Chargers. I was terrible. And Eric would come to watch. Our father was flying somewhere, usually, and when Dad was home, you know, he was sleeping most of the time. So Eric came.' I laughed a little bit, my eyes closed. 'I thought he just wanted to humiliate me, you know, see how pathetic I was. But he was, I don't know, he was there with his girlfriend, with Dawn Costello.'

'Dawn Costello.'

I thought I saw something flicker across Katherine's face.

'Yeah,' I said, 'she was beautiful and he watched me get slaughtered. I mean, I don't know what I was thinking. I was thinking, I guess, that because Eric had been the star running back for the Junior Chargers, then I'd be at least good enough to make the team, you know. He used to come for every practice. He'd come and watch from the bleachers. This was junior high and Eric was already in high school.'

Katherine nodded.

'Anyway, when they called out the names for the team, I wasn't on there. I was missing from the list. My name was—'

'You didn't make it.'

'No.'

'Was that disappointing?'

'I guess it was. I was crying, I remember, and I wouldn't take my helmet off because I was afraid the other kids could see the tears on my face.'

I stopped talking. I was looking at the little bits and pieces of the shoelace I had piled on my leg. I'd have to stop, I thought, or I'd tear the whole thing apart and there would be nothing left.

'Pilot?'

'What?'

'So what happened?'

'Oh.' I looked up. 'So I went and sat on the bleachers and waited for Eric. He almost always walked home with me. Thomas Edison junior high, it's just on the other side of the woods from here.' I pointed to the window. 'And he said goodbye to Dawn, and then they—'

'What happened to her?'

'To Dawn?'

'Yes,' Katherine said. 'What happened to her?'

'I don't know. She's still here somewhere. She has a family.'

Katherine nodded. 'OK, go on.'

'So he said goodbye to Dawn and started walking home. And I followed him, wearing my stupid helmet the whole time because I was still crying, because I could never stop once I started. I was all hot under there, too, but I just followed him, and instead of taking the usual path, Eric walked into the woods, the deeper part.'

'Weren't you afraid of the woods when you were—'

'No,' I laughed, 'that came later. That's only recent, that fear.' I paused for a moment. 'Fiona was afraid of the woods,' I said. 'Not me.'

'Why not?'

'I don't know.' I felt my face. I remembered the scratch that had been there. It was finally gone. How long had it been gone? 'You'd think I would be afraid, right, the kind of kid I was?'

She shrugged.

'So we went into the woods', I continued, 'and Eric went to this clearing. It was one of those places, you know, where kids smoke pot and drink beer. Cigarette butts everywhere, bottle caps.'

'Is it still there?'

'The clearing? Yeah,' I said. 'Of course it is. Kids still use it, I'm sure. Anyway, we sat down on this old piece of concrete tubing someone had left out there—'

'Were you still wearing the helmet?'

'I didn't take it off for a while, because I was still crying, you know, always a crybaby, my father said.'

'Go on.'

'And Eric, he told me this story.'

'What did he tell you?'

'He was fourteen.' I pushed the balls of my hands into the sockets of my eyes. 'And there was a kid in his class named Henry Addler. Henry wasn't a big kid or anything, but he was unpredictable, the kind of kid that could fly into a rage, you know, the kind of kid teachers are afraid of because he's so crazy. Naturally, perhaps stupidly, Eric wasn't afraid of Henry Addler at all. Eric was the smartest kid in class – and not a nerd, either. He was by far the best science student and he was also the best athlete. Altogether that made him pretty much the most popular kid at Thomas Edison. Henry Addler was the most unreasonable kid. They were both superlatives, I guess, and that made them friends, or at least they had some weird kind of mutual respect.'

'So what happened?' Katherine was interested, leaning forward.

'Eric was doing homework for Henry and in return Henry was stealing white cross tablets from his mother's medicine cabinet and giving them to Eric.'

'Isn't that an amphetamine?'

'Yeah. Eric was really into speed. It helped him with sports.'

'Go on,' Katherine said.

'Anyway, all this time that Eric was telling me this story, I was sitting there with my helmet on and my face all hot because I was crying. And Eric was rolling this joint.'

'Had you ever seen one before?'

'I'd seen them, I think, but I had never smoked one. And I didn't know Eric would show me how to smoke it that day. He was just telling me this story about Henry Addler and the white cross.'

'Finish the story,' Katherine said.

I sighed. 'What happened was, Eric gave Henry the wrong homework somehow. Not on purpose, he said, but something went wrong and Henry turned in his biology homework and got a big, fat F. So Henry Addler didn't say anything about it at first. At first he didn't even tell Eric. What he did was to give him a new kind of pill. He said his mother wasn't taking white cross any more. Now she was taking something else. And he gave Eric four little yellow pills instead of the one white one he was used to.'

'Yellow?' she said. 'Were they—'

'Valium,' I finished. 'And he said Eric should take four of them to equal one white cross.'

'Did Eric take them?'

'That's what he told me. He took them right there, he said. He used to take speed in fifth period so he was super athletic for after-school practice.'

'He must have just passed out, right?'

'Henry Addler pulled out his homework, the one that had the big fat F on it and showed it to Eric. He said, "You screwed me and now you've just taken poison and you're going to die."'

'He said that?'

'I don't know what he really said. All I know is that Eric told me all this when I was sitting on the concrete pipe in the woods with him and that's when he handed me the joint.'

'Did you take your helmet off?'

'I finally took it off', I said, 'and Eric showed me, he showed me how to inhale. He told me how I wouldn't really feel anything the first time but that I'd get used to it. I know it sounds weird but it was really ... nice.'

'But Eric must have panicked about the pills. I mean, didn't he think he was going to die?'

'He said he didn't care if he died. He said he didn't give a shit if he died. And then he said, then he said all he could think about was me.'

Katherine was quiet. She was looking at her pen, which until now had been poised in mid-air above her yellow legal pad.

'He said he didn't give a shit about anybody else,' I continued, 'about any of his friends or our stupid parents, that he just gave a shit about me and he didn't care if I didn't make the football team. The football team, he told me, was all bullshit, and he said that Coach Parks was queer, anyway. And guys were always snapping towels at your ass in the locker room and the whole school just resented you, anyway.'

Katherine smiled. 'He made you feel better about being rejected from the team.'

I nodded. 'Sometimes Eric could be nice.'

'I guess all brothers can be nice to each other sometimes.'

'Yeah,' I agreed. 'Even Eric.'

'Do you think about that?'

'About what?'

'About that moment, when he said that to you?'

'It's all I think about,' I confessed. 'After Fiona,' I said, 'he's all I ever thought about.'

He would take me to the movies sometimes and in the theater he'd put a huge bag of popcorn between us.

For years he bought me comic books.

When he learned to drive, Eric took me everywhere, like a chauffeur.

When I was thirteen and wanted an electric guitar, our parents wouldn't buy me one. But Eric did. It was a Hohner telecaster copy with a leopard-print pick guard and silver pick-ups. He even got me some lessons. This guitar still sits in a corner of my room. I haven't touched it in years. I remember the first time I touched it, though, my fingers awkward on the strings. 'You'll be a rock star,' he told me. 'Just remember me when you're famous.'

'So what happened to Henry Addler?' Katherine asked.

Eric's face went slack. 'Henry—'

'The boy who gave you the yellow Valiums and said they were poison.' She knew she was breaking her confidentiality agreement with me, but she couldn't help it. She wanted to know the rest of the story. There was a curiosity inside her.

'Pilot told you about that?' Eric was almost laughing, shaking his head, hands on the table in front of him.

'It's quite a story.'

He had come by her office at noon that day to take her to an unplanned lunch, and now the two of them were sitting inside the brightly lit Subway Sandwich at the Crestview Shopping Plaza on Sky Highway. Katherine had forty-five minutes and she wanted to know.

Eric sighed. 'I took the yellow pills, the Valiums, and Henry told me—' he started to laugh '—told me that he'd poisoned me.'

'That's what Pilot said.' Katherine smiled. 'You must have been terrified.' She brought her sandwich to her mouth, turkey and lettuce, but decided not to take a bite. She held it there while Eric spoke, then put it down and sipped her 7Up instead. The booths here were full of businessmen from the nearby office park. They all wore the same gray suits, the same wine-red ties. They all brought their sandwiches to their mouths at the same time, chewing in unison.

'I thought if I could make myself throw up,' Eric said, 'I would be all right.' Today he wore a deep blue shirt beneath a dark brown suit. Armani, Katherine guessed. His tie was brown, too, just a shade lighter.

'Did you?' She finally took a bite and immediately wished she could spit it out.

'I couldn't,' Eric said. 'I couldn't make myself throw up for some reason.' He looked at his own sandwich now, a ham and Swiss. 'I've never really been able to do that. I guess I had no future as a bulimic.'

'Obviously.' Katherine swallowed.

'And by that time', said Eric, 'the Valiums were starting to have their effect on me.' He swirled his fingers in front of his face.

'You were getting bleary?'

'Everywhere I looked all the colors were running together. It was like I was seeing through a fish-eye lens. You know how it feels.' He bit into his sandwich again, chewing slowly.

'Sounds like one of those government anti-drug films they showed us in high school.'

He nodded, swallowing. 'That's exactly what it was like.'

'So what did you do?'

'I went to my coach and told him that Henry Addler gave me some weird pills.'

'You could tell your coach something like that?'

'Coach Parks. He was terrific.'

'Really?'

'Sure, and he knew right off the bat what they were. In those days all the suburban housewives were taking those yellow and blue Valiums. He knew just what I had taken and he also knew they weren't going to kill me.'

'So he didn't take you to a doctor?'

'Nah,' Eric said, 'I only would have gotten in trouble and then I wouldn't have been able to play for a couple of games.' My brother laughed. 'He needed me, so he let me sleep it off in his office.'

Katherine didn't really want this sandwich, she decided. It happened to her often when she ordered lunch, especially lately. She was hungry, but she couldn't eat. 'You put a different spin on it when you told Pilot the same story.'

Eric swallowed, then sipped some of his large Coke through a straw. He wrinkled his brow. 'What do you mean?'

'I mean', Katherine said, 'that you told him you were afraid you were going to die and that your only thought was of losing him.'

Eric took a long sip. Afterwards, he rubbed his eyes with his fingers. 'That was a long time ago,' he said finally. 'I don't remember what I told Pilot. I said I was a bad brother. What do you—'

'Pilot remembers it as something *nice*.'

'What do you mean?'

'Something nice.' Katherine shook her head. 'You told him that story and gave him his first joint after he didn't make it on to the Junior Chargers.'

'His first joint.' Eric looked down, examining his hands. 'Out in the woods, right? After his practice.'

'You thought only of losing him, you said.' Katherine brought her eyes up from her 7Up to meet his.

My brother looked at his hands.

'You weren't such a bad brother,' she said. 'Even Pilot doesn't remember you as being a bad brother all of the time.' His eyes were such a bright color, Katherine thought, an amazing blue. And his clothes were so incredibly clean. She wondered if he dry-cleaned his suits each time he wore them.

'So things are going all right with him?'

'I don't know,' Katherine said. 'We just started. It's hard to tell. It could take a little while.'

'Has he said anything about our mother?'

'What do you mean, about—'

'About her eyes?'

'No,' Katherine said. 'Why?'

'They're getting worse.' He pushed his ham and Swiss away and leaned back in the booth, hands behind his head.

'What's wrong with them?'

'I spoke to an ophthalmologist. If it's what he thinks it is, her vision could deteriorate dramatically. It's bad enough already. But she could go blind from this. Completely.'

'I'm sorry to hear that.'

He bit his lip. 'I don't know what to do.'

'Could it be psychosomatic?'

'Of course it could. But I've just never heard of anything like that. Psychosomatic blindness is usually total, not gradual.'

'It's not, not bad that I'm telling you about Pilot, is it?' Katherine asked. 'I mean, I guess it's pretty unprofessional.'

'Katherine,' Eric said, leaning forward, 'I'm a neurosurgeon. Pilot has schizophrenia. By talking about it with me you certainly aren't hurting him. In fact, you're helping him. I can illuminate whatever he's telling you in therapy. And', he finished, 'if he tells you something that you don't think I should know, don't tell me.'

Katherine smiled, hiding her hands beneath the table. 'All right.'

'All right.'

'I still don't think he has schizophrenia,' she said.

'Why not? I thought Dr Lennox—'

'All of his symptoms went away so fast,' she said. 'Practically the instant he took the Clozaril.'

'It's a new medication, it's very effective.'

Katherine shook her head just slightly. 'Still.'

Eric looked at his watch. He looked back at Katherine. He said, 'Time to go.'

Hannah sat in her bedroom with the window partly open and the cold air coming into the room like thousands of bees and the cancer multiplying into a hive inside her brain. She could hear our voices, Katherine's and mine, coming upstairs through the floor, could tell when I was launching into a story, could hear the question marks at the end of Katherine's sentences. She could make it out, if she wanted to, could listen to everything, if she chose. It was early evening, already dark, but Hannah watched Fiona playing with a ball in the backyard. She saw her little girl running back and forth to the trees, jumping rope, squatting beside the pool and filling her plastic pail with water. Fiona wore the red swimsuit she had worn the day she disappeared.

But now she had re-appeared. She re-appeared every day, in fact, forming out of the mass of colors and shimmering light the world had become to Hannah.

Our mother's vision had blurred to where she wasn't just seeing double any more. Everything seemed ghostly. Only at very close range could she make anything out. She couldn't read or watch television at all.

The only thing she could see clearly – and it was something she wouldn't tell anyone about – was Fiona. She could see my little sister helping set the table downstairs. She could see Fiona pouring herself a glass of juice in the kitchen. She could see Fiona curled up in front of the television.

Fiona.

She could see Fiona.

She couldn't tell anyone, could she? She couldn't say that she'd been seeing the ghost of her missing daughter around the house. She couldn't. It was bad enough that I was crazy.

Voices rose through the vent.

'This is going to sound weird,' I was saying. And Hannah

strained to listen. Our voices were faint, though, almost as indistinguishable as the colors in the room.

Not the noise of them, Hannah thought, but the people in them. The people in the voices were faint.

'You didn't make the team?' she heard Katherine say. Hannah smiled. She remembered that day, too. She remembered Eric and me coming home through the woods. She remembered the way we smelled of marijuana smoke when we came into the kitchen.

'Pilot didn't make it,' Eric had said.

I'd put my helmet on the kitchen table.

'Good,' Hannah had said, smiling, 'I don't want two boys playing football, anyway.'

'Coach Parks is queer,' I had said.

'Pilot,' our mother had said.

'He is.'

'That's a very serious accusation.'

'Whatever,' I had said.

'You boys smell funny,' Hannah had ventured.

'We came through the woods,' Eric had said firmly. 'That's what we smell like.'

'No,' Hannah had said. 'It's something else.' She had known what it was, of course. She had not been so stupid in those days that she wasn't aware of the smell of marijuana.

I remember waiting, terror in my throat.

'Never mind,' Hannah had said. 'Dinner's almost ready. Why don't you boys wash up and then help set the table.'

I'd gone upstairs. And our mother had opened the oven to check on the chicken pot pies she had been heating up. Our father had been flying somewhere, in the wild blue yonder. The radio had been tuned to an easy listening station. Hannah remembered that they were playing an instrumental version of 'Bridge Over Troubled Water'. It was the day, she thought, that she realized that music no longer moved her. It was the day she had understood that her confidence had left her completely, only to return momentarily and only with the assistance of red wine. She'd go to work every morning for the next ten or fifteen years, literally holding people by the hands – surgeons, violinists, sculptors – helping them bring the movement back, the delicate muscles which had cramped, the swollen knuckles that had stiffened from arthritis, the bones that had been cracked, showing these people how to clutch a ball, how to stretch a tendon to reach a note, how to grip a fine, sharp instrument.

Now she leaned back and listened to us, to Katherine and me, talking downstairs.

'Did you take your helmet off?' she heard Katherine say.

'Yeah,' I said, 'I finally took it off, and Eric showed me – he showed me how to inhale it.'

Hannah smiled. She had been right about the marijuana. Of course she had been right.

'I feel like we're having an affair,' Katherine said.

There was a pause, then, 'Is that good or bad?'

She shrugged. 'It's exciting, anyway.'

They had a free weekend, Eric and Katherine, and wanted to spend more than a single evening together. So they were unpacking. Eric was, at least, carefully removing his clothes from his brand-new black leather overnight bag and placing each item – sweaters, socks, shorts and jeans – inside the drawers of a white particle-board dresser in the all-white bedroom of his all-white beachhouse. Outside, waves sloshed on to the shore and a high-pitched wind whistled through the eaves.

Katherine had thrown her things next to the bed, sat down and kicked her shoes on to the floor. Now, with her hair splayed out on the mattress behind her, she lay back, watching my brother like an obedient pet. He had bought this beachhouse, he had told her on the drive down, completely unfurnished and then he had filled it with cheap, modern catalog furniture, everything white and light wood. Everything here seemed relentlessly practical, she thought, and, at the same time, flimsy.

'You are so incredibly tidy.' Katherine rolled her face to see him walk to the closet.

'A little obsessive-compulsive disorder never hurt anybody.'

From the bed, she laughed.

'Are you hungry?'

She could hear the autumn waves smashing themselves up against the shore outside, the shrieking wind. Katherine rose from the bed and then moved toward Eric steadily, her face to his face, and put her lips against his, not kissing, just pressing lightly against him, just touching. My brother stiffened at first and then relaxed into it. 'Come on,' she said. 'Let's go outside,' pulling his arm. 'Let's go out and look at the ocean.'

Her hair, long and blonde and black all at once, curling and spiraling like the seaweed washed up on shore, and getting tangled hopelessly in itself, whipped around her eyes and mouth in the salt wind. She kept brushing it away and smiling apologetically, as if it could hurt Eric somehow. The cold wasn't stinging yet, but it gave her that numb feeling. She should have brought a hat. Or at least a bandeau. She said, 'My family used to spend Thanksgivings at the beach.' Katherine noticed the choppiness of the water – far, far out, how gray it was. Her skin tightened around her body. She wore an old jean jacket, but it wasn't enough. 'My sister and I would play out in the sand all day. We didn't care how cold.'

'That sounds nice,' Eric said. 'Two girls.' He wore a brand-new blue sweater – cashmere, of course. His face was perfectly unshaved, complete with movie-star stubble. 'You never talk about your sister.'

Katherine nodded. 'Michele.'

'Why not?'

'Because there's nothing much to talk about.'

'Do you speak to her often?'

'I haven't spoken to her in two years.'

Eric put his hands in his pockets.

She was shouting a little over the wind and the waves. 'You look like a model in an aftershave commercial.'

He turned to smile back, completing the effect.

'Thank you for taking me here,' she said. The sun felt warm, at least. She'd have to be careful about sunburn, though. Katherine had taken her shoes off and was pushing her feet into the cold, damp sand. She had tucked the shoes, a pair of old loafers, under a large piece of driftwood near the top of the beach. Now she walked up and wrapped her arms around my brother's waist and curled her toes.

'Thank you for coming here,' he said.

Katherine's insane hair swept around in the wind and punished them. 'Sorry,' she said.

'About what?'

'My hair.'

'I love your hair.' Eric took her hand and they resumed walking. It was nearing sunset, the light glowing more yellow, more gold, sucking up all the light from the day. This was one of those posters, Katherine thought, a couple on the beach, hand in hand, a sharp silhouette against the setting sun.

'Do you come here alone sometimes?'

'No.'

'Really?'

'I thought I would.' He was yelling a little, too. 'I planned to, anyway. When I first bought the place I thought I would come here alone all the time, but, but it's not the same, you know, when you're by yourself. You just end up staying indoors and reading. I might as well stay near the hospital if I'm going to do that.'

'I would come here every weekend,' Katherine said. 'Every free minute I had.'

'Alone?'

'Sure, alone. I think it's wonderful.'

He smiled. 'You're pretty wonderful.' It was a quarterback smile, all perfect teeth and handsomeness. She had never been with anyone so handsome. It was almost unreal, she thought, his beauty. She remembered what I had told her, that he was more beautiful than she was.

Katherine forced a laugh. 'Are you trying to make me blush?' She wondered if it – if all of this – was actually happening.

'Can I tell you something ridiculous?'

'Absolutely.'

'You're not like anything, you're not like anyone I've ever met,' Eric said. 'You're totally, completely different from everyone else. I hope you, I hope you're willing to hang around for—'. He looked away. Way up the beach were a man and a black Labrador retriever. '—for a little while, anyway.' The Lab was bouncing and jumping at something in the man's hand.

'I'm not going anywhere,' Katherine said.

'I mean, I'm not always that easy to get along with.'

'Eric.'

'It's part of being a doctor, I think, or just of being me. I'm kind of, kind of highly strung, you know. But, but, Jesus Christ, Katherine, you're learning everything about my childhood, what a crappy kid I was, what a terrible brother I was to Pilot—'

'Eric, you weren't—'

'—and you still seem to like me.'

'—a bad brother, you were—'

'Which either means you're crazy yourself, and that's—'

'—a very, very nice, normal—'

'—fine, that's all right, or—'

'—brother, perfectly normal.'

'—you're exceptionally wonderful, which is what I believe must be the case.'

'Eric, come on.'

'I'm really crazy about you, Katherine.' He looked at her again, the same smile, only more sensitive this time, something bashful in the eyes.

Did he know he was doing this? Was it under control?

Katherine smiled. 'I grow old . . . I grow old . . . I shall wear the bottoms of my trousers rolled,' she said. 'Shall I part my hair behind? Do I dare to eat a peach? I shall wear white flannel trousers, and walk upon the beach. I have heard the mermaids singing, each to each.' She wanted to break the spell, say something weird. 'I have heard the mermaids singing, each to each.'

'What?'

'It's a poem.'

'A poem?'

'By T.S. Eliot,' she said. '"The Love Song of J. Alfred Prufrock."'

Eric pulled her body into his. 'I'm cold,' he said. 'And you're talking about poetry from freshman English.'

Katherine put her arms around his neck, then, saying this: 'Let me warm you.'

She was fumbly – nervous. They'd had sex before, of course, but only at night, and for some reason, it wasn't the same. Here, at the beach, waves crashing romantically outside, a high-pitched wind howling, the room filled with light, she breathed unevenly, the air coming into her lungs jaggedly, a kind of romance sucked out of the situation, but replaced by another. Eric seemed larger here, the muscles of his body writhing more effortlessly beneath the surface of his skin. She went down on him, hands on his thighs, digging in with her fingers a little, and he did the same for her, lifting her entire body to his mouth. She wasn't particularly small, but when he did this she felt tiny and light. And when he was inside her, on top of her, moving in and out of her in a building rhythm, his chin locked around her shoulder, his whiskers rough on her skin, he whispered to her, saying he loved her, couldn't stand not being near her, thought of her, only of her.

He actually said these things.

Mark had never said anything when they had sex. Mark had been as silent as stone.

But today Katherine was silent. My brother had a hand placed on the small of her back, and his mouth was next to her ear, and he was whispering, '*Katherine.*'

She came then, biting her lower lip, only a small sound escaping, and it rose from somewhere deep in her throat, from somewhere else, some*one* else, it seemed.

When Eric came, he clutched her thighs, pulling her legs up and leaning hard into her, and his chin lifted, back arched.

A few hundred miles away, I stood in front of the kitchen sink with my hand over my eyes. Hannah was upstairs waiting for me to bring her some tea.

Katherine and Eric hadn't changed positions once.

He was on top. She was on the bottom.

Missionary.

They were on a mission, I thought at the kitchen sink.

I could see everything.

This is the difference, Katherine was thinking, between men and women. Women come first and men never see them in their delirium. Men never get to see this behavior clearly. But the women lie there, accommodating, holding them by the back of the neck, with their minds clear and their bodies satisfied, when men come.

'That was so nice,' Katherine said softly now. 'You are so nice.'

'You are so beautiful,' Eric told her.

They lay like this for a while, locked together, their bodies too warm to be touching, but touching. And she thought of Michele. And she thought of Mark, whose eyelids would flutter when he came, who was so feminine and soft, like she had been today.

'What do you look for in a chicken?' Katherine asked. In the little grocery store in the tiny beach town they were selecting poultry. She had hardly done this before.

'Interesting question,' Eric said. 'Tenderness, I suppose.'

'Featherlessness,' Katherine said.

'Also a good quality.'

Katherine lifted a small one from the refrigerator case and placed it in their basket. 'Does this one look good to you?' It was covered in clear plastic wrap, its skin the color of a pale human's – like mine.

'I don't see any feathers,' Eric said. He started to walk toward the produce aisle. 'Carrots? Celery? What else?'

'Thank you,' Katherine said suddenly.

'For the chicken?'

'Thank you, Eric, for taking me here, taking me—'

'You,' he said, pushing the cart over to her. He walked around it and placed his face against her cheek, kissing her jawline. 'You are the one to thank.'

'No.'

'And Pilot,' he said.

'Pilot?'

'Pilot for going crazy.'

'*Praised be the fall*,' she said.

Eric smiled, but didn't seem to hear this. 'You know,' my brother said, 'when I'm with you, when you're here with me, I have no doubt that he'll get better, that he'll be all right.'

They were in the vegetable aisle now, surrounded by green beans, broccoli, carrots. There was a stack of large oranges by the cash register. 'Oranges?' Eric asked. 'Grapes?'

'Oranges,' Katherine answered. She was smiling stupidly now, uncontrollably. 'Grapes.'

I had been sitting on the back steps that led out of the kitchen, watching the woods rustle and groan under the fall wind. Behind me, I could hear my mother washing the dishes. Porcelain and silver clink-clanked in the sloshing water. I believed I could even hear the song she was humming, the melody changing every bar, mutating and shifting with consistent irregularity. 'Pilot,' she said eventually and I heard the tap cut off.

'Yes?'

'Is there anything out there?'

'What do you mean?'

'In the yard, I can't see properly, you know, is there anything—'

'There's the same things there always are.'

'Are there ...'

'What?'

'... children?'

'Mom, come on.'

'The little girls from next door, I thought. Perhaps—'

'No, they aren't out there right now.' I got from the steps and went into the kitchen, closing the door softly behind me. 'It's just trees, bushes, the pool – the same old stuff.'

She hated it when I called it the pool. It was the garden now. 'Is it terribly overgrown?'

'It's not too bad.' She stood at the counter, her hand holding the edge like Fiona's hand on the edge of the pool. 'Do you want me to weed it out?'

'Eric already said he would.'

'OK.'

She brought her hand up to touch her face.

'Are you all right, Mom?'

'I thought I saw something, that's all.'

'Saw what?'

'Just something.'

In his black Jaguar, she asked, 'Whatever happened to the tennis shoe?' Eric drove. Katherine sat in the passenger's seat with the groceries on her lap. 'Eric?' She knew she shouldn't bring it up. She couldn't stop herself.

He didn't look at her. 'It was turned over as evidence.' His voice was hardening. She could see his jaw muscles tighten.

'Your family never got it back?'

'I don't remember.'

'Only one of them was found?'

'Only the one.'

'Where did Pilot find it?'

'Pilot found it on the first day that we, that we looked for her.' Eric rounded a corner without slowing, powering through. Katherine thought she felt the wheels slip, just slightly. 'And he couldn't really remember where, exactly, that he was when he picked it up.' He reached for the radio dial. He touched it, but didn't turn it on. 'We never did find exactly where. At least, Pilot was never sure.'

'Evidence?' Katherine said. 'Evidence of a struggle, maybe, or that she was trying to leave a trail?'

'Possibly. Fiona was very little. I doubt she was thinking about leaving a trail.'

'He didn't remember where he found it?'

'It was a very confusing day, Katherine. Probably the most traumatic of his life.'

'I can imagine.' She looked at him, saying, 'That would have been important to know, wouldn't it? I mean, if they had known exactly where, exactly—'

'It didn't matter. They went over every inch of those woods.'

'I guess they must have.' She thought for a moment, biting her fingernail, tasting the blood. 'Was he always so forgetful?'

'Pilot?' Eric stopped at a light and looked at Katherine. 'Pilot was always very forgetful,' he said, shaking his head. 'Just like our mother.'

My father kept walking to the window to look at the sky. Patricia, his girlfriend, watched him through the kitchen door. On television Florida State was beating Nebraska. He'd sit on the couch for a few minutes, muttering at the game, then he'd get up again, hand in his pocket jiggling keys, leaning over one of the wicker chairs in the sun room, his face to the glass. The sky was clear – clouds scattered like a few leaves on the lawn in early fall. Patricia leaned back from the sink and watched him at the window. 'Jim,' she said finally, 'what are you doing?' She turned off the tap.

He said, 'What?' even though he heard her.

'Why do you keep going to the window?'

'You know, on the weather channel they said something about the possibility of a storm. I just thought—'

'It's Pilot.'

'—I'd look and see for myself.'

'You're worried about him.' She moved across the beige living-room carpet toward my father. There had been a new message from Hannah.

He look down, ashamed. 'Yeah.'

And my mother never called.

Patricia spoke with her whole body and the way she came closer to him, so openly, made him use his voice.

'I keep thinking something's really wrong with him,' he said.

'Maybe.'

'Something I should do.'

'Call him.'

'Something I should say to him.'

She put a hand on his shoulder. She said, 'Call him.'

He looked at her. 'It's that easy.' It was a question.

'It's that easy.'

They stood together on the beach again and this time it was night, and the clouds billowing up in the sky made the horizon turn black, and the last filtered light of the descending sun misted over the countryside behind them. 'I was a terrible brother,' Eric was saying. 'I wish I could have—'

'Eric.' Katherine put a hand on his chest. The water was gentle right now, for some reason, the tide low.

'I want to make it up to him.' My brother turned his face away dramatically. 'I want to, to find a way to feel better,' he said, 'some redemption. The things I used to say to him.' He closed his eyes.

With his eyes closed, she thought, he looked like a statue. 'Eric,' Katherine said. 'Magical thinking. You're smarter than this. You're a brain surgeon, for Christ's—'

'I was really bad,' he said. 'Abusive, there's no other word for it.'

'Do you have any idea how cruel my sister and I were to each other?'

'Really?'

'Terrible. Evil.'

'Is that why you don't speak with her any more?'

She looked at her fingers. 'I guess it is, probably.'

'But I was—'

'No, Eric. You're unfortunate, that's all. Your brother has an illness. But you didn't give it to him. No amount of sibling rivalry could have given him what he has. It's chemical, completely biological.'

'He thinks I killed our sister,' he said. There was something in his voice. There was something almost like crying in my brother's voice.

'Pilot is irrational, Eric.' Katherine touched him again. 'He has all kinds of disordered, distorted thoughts.'

'Katherine, I understand these things. It's just, it's just that I guess I'm irrational about it, too. I mean, it's different when it's your own family.'

'You really are being irrational.'

'I can feel bad, can't I?'

'You can.'

'I wish I could help him.'

'You're helping him so much already.' Katherine held his hand. 'You don't even know.'

'What wouldn't you do for your sister?'

'A lot,' Katherine said. She looked at the ocean. 'There's a great deal I haven't done, as a matter of fact.'

Katherine wore a black skirt, a black jacket. She wore a silver chain around her neck that held a mysteriously twisty Celtic symbol. She wore a look of concern. 'I was asking you, Pilot,' she said, 'last week I was asking if you could tell me what makes you feel, what makes you feel so strongly that Eric is responsible for Fiona's, for Fiona disappearing. Do you remember?'

I rubbed my eyes. I was sitting on the blue couch again and the living room seemed to have gathered more magazines, knick-knacks, and dust since last week. 'The sneaker,' I said. 'The tennis shoe. It was in his room.' I sipped my tea. Hannah, almost completely blind, had placed a pot and two delicate cups on the coffee table. Katherine and I had started the session by pouring ourselves jasmine tea.

'But you found the sneaker in the woods.' Katherine was certain she'd caught me in a mistake of some kind. 'I thought you found the—'

'It was in Eric's bedroom.' I shook my head. 'I *said* I found it in the woods, that's all. I lied.'

'Pilot,' she began, 'you—'

'I *lied*, yes. All the time. For years. Constantly. About everything.'

'Why did you lie? To protect Eric?'

I nodded. 'Something like that.'

Katherine made a mark on her yellow legal pad. Her silvery pen made the slightest scratching sound when she wrote. Looking up, she asked, 'Where in his bedroom did you find it?' Her face carried the slightest pain, something around the eyes, I thought. Something like disbelief.

'Under his desk,' I said, 'in Eric's incredibly tidy, perfectly organized, everything-in-its-place bedroom under his desk, exactly where he must have put it.'

Katherine sighed. She touched her hair. It was insane again today, crazier than me. 'OK,' she said, 'so the sneaker was in Eric's room, that's what you remember. Does that mean he's responsible? Does that necessarily mean that he killed her?'

I looked at the ceiling. I knew our voices were carrying through the ventilation system up to my mother's bedroom. I knew she was listening, facing the window, eyes closed. I used to sit by that grate myself and listen to the grown-up conversations coming from down here, the arguments about money, about our father's next flight, about how he was never around, and later about who should have been watching her, watching Fiona that night, and why the hell did it have to happen to them. So now I whispered, 'I found something else. I found something that I never told anyone about.'

Katherine leaned forward, whispering, too. 'What was it?'

'I found a knife.'

She leaned back, speaking aloud. 'You found a knife.'

'Inside one of the shoes.'

Gently Katherine cleared her throat. 'Do you, do you still have it?'

I smiled. I twisted the shoelace around my finger, twisting and twisting.

Katherine looked at me quizzically, her brow furrowed. 'Pilot, if you really have a piece of evidence, a twenty-year-old piece of hard evidence in the disappearance of your own sister—'

'And tell my mother that her boy, her favorite boy, the successful one, the *good* one, killed her only daughter when he was a teenager?'

'*Pilot.*'

I smiled, 'Isn't there a statute of limitations on that, anyway?'

'Really, Pilot, do you have it? Do you have the knife?'

'Not only do I have the knife,' I said, whispering again, 'I have the other shoe.'

'Why are you whispering?'

I pointed to the ceiling. 'Hannah is listening.'

'Pilot,' Katherine said, 'why haven't you done anything with these things all these years? Why haven't you—'

'I couldn't talk about it.'

'Why not?'

'Because I was sane.'

'Sane?'

'You can only talk about these things if you're crazy.'

'Pilot.' She shook her head.

'Have you heard of repression, Katherine?' I said. 'Or did you miss that day of psychology class?'

She rolled her eyes. 'OK. When did you remember these things?'

'I remembered them all my life. It occurred to me to remember them out loud, though, right before I went crazy, Katherine.'

'Are you implying something?'

'Implying that a neurosurgeon may have access to psychotropic drugs that could, for instance, stimulate a psychotic episode in an already unstable and susceptible mind?'

She suppressed a laugh, I could see it. 'Pilot, that's very, very implausible, what you are saying—'

'Katherine, I'm serious.'

'What are you going to do?'

I looked up. 'I don't know.'

'You don't want to bring this evidence to the police?'

'Are people required to testify against their own brothers?'

'That's a legal question,' she said. 'I don't know the answer.'

'I'm not sure if I could.' I unraveled the shoelace, which had grown blacker and blacker, unfurling it from my finger. How long had I had this thing now? 'How is Eric, by the way?' I said. 'How was your weekend together? Was it romantic?'

Katherine leaned forward and took a sip of her tea. It was probably cold. 'Eric is fine,' she said. 'Just fine. Have you spoken to him?'

'Not directly.'

Katherine cleared her throat once again. 'Not directly,' she said, eyebrows raised.

'Remember, Katherine Jane DeQuincey-Joy,' I told her, 'I'm omniscient.'

'Pilot,' she said, 'do you really have these things?'

'Really.'

'Where?'

'In a very, very safe place.' I rose from the couch. This session, as far as I was concerned, was over.

'Pilot,' she said, 'you have to tell me where—'

'You should stop chewing your nails like that.' I went to the stairs. 'You're going to bleed to death if you're not careful.'

It was amazing to me how cold California could be on the beach at night. As cold as winter in the east, it seemed. I stayed out on the beach for a solid week, from one Wednesday to the next. I tried not to fall asleep, the fear keeping me up, the fatigue overwhelming me, my eyelids slipping from time to time, flickering open and shut. Sometimes I lay down on the sand. Sometimes I found a piece of grass by the Santa Monica Boulevard and propped my head against a palm tree and listened to the sound of the rushing waves on the one side and the sound of the car engines revving on the other. After a few days of this, I called him. I called Eric. And two days later, immediately, in fact, he came out and found me. He took me to an expensive hotel, bought me some new clothes, flew me back business class to New York, delivered me to our mother. And then came a few weeks of padding around the house in my bathrobe, and then Hannah's double vision, and the moment of clarity, or insanity, or whatever it was, and the clinic, and Katherine . . . .

Before, I had been in North Carolina, staying on after college. I had been sleeping with a married woman whose name was Jorie. I had been writing screenplays that nobody liked or wanted or even understood, stories about cold families, sibling rivalries, stories like mine, but with magic endings, miraculous recoveries, completions.

Before, I had been a ghost, just like my mother said.

But out on the beach none of that mattered. I had come out there, ostensibly, to sell my screenplays, and I had been calling Jorie, telling her I was staying at the most expensive hotel in Beverly Hills, that I had even gotten an agent. I had made up these wonderful scenarios for her, these elaborately beautiful lies. She swallowed them all. But the real truth was I was walking up and down the Santa Monica beach every day, my skin pink from the sun and my eyes red from lack of sleep, spending what remaining money I had on hot dogs, greasy French fries, sodas, and grass. I met a girl out there named Selena and when she wasn't too drunk she'd sit by me on the sand at night. I wasn't hearing voices yet, only hers, which was real. I wasn't imagining electronic surveillance devices in every seagull that flew by. All of that came later, after I got back to New York.

I only wanted to sit out there and watch the waves with Selena.

'Where are you from?' Selena said.

I told her I was from North Carolina.

'You don't have an accent.'

'Where are *you* from?' I said, trying to change the subject.

'Texas . . . Corpus Christi, Texas.' She had a long drawl and, on top of that, a raspy, alcoholic voice. 'I drink way too much for my own good,' she told me. 'I know that.' It was the world's greatest understatement. 'But I'm a nice person, and no one has ever been able to explain to me what good will come of it if I quit the drinking.' *The* drinking. She looked at me then, as though I could explain it to her, or that I should try.

I shrugged. 'Maybe none,' I said. 'Maybe no good at all.'

'Out here you're either into drugs or drinking, or both, or you're crazy,' she said. 'I ain't seen you drinking or shooting up.'

I laughed, reading her implication.

She had blonde hair and small breasts and a stocky build. She had fine little stubby hands, brown with dirt, blackened under the nails. She had an infected gash on the inside of her left calf which she tended to by tearing little bits of her own skin away from it, keeping it raw and bloody, making sure it would never heal. In the daytime I'd try to find a nice piece of shade somewhere beneath one of the trees that lined the parking lots. And when the sun went down enough I'd pace up and down in front of the water, getting my pants wet up the knees, daring myself to walk in. Each night was different. Each night was the same. Each night after it became dark and cold, so surprisingly cold for California, I would find a new place, away from the other homeless people, and try to get some rest without sleeping. It wasn't easy. After a few days of this I think I did begin to hallucinate, not from the craziness – because I wasn't crazy yet – but from the fatigue and lack of food. And each night Selena found me. She was the only person who never heard me tell a lie, I guess because she didn't matter.

I was standing in the water up to my waist, the salt waves splashing over my chest. The sun was dissolving into the water faraway to the west like an enormous tablet of vitamin C. To the left, the Ferris wheel of the Santa Monica pier spun itself in delirious, stupid circles. Kids were laughing somewhere behind me. What if I walked out there? I thought. What if I stepped, one foot at a time, into the ocean, my eyes closed? I could hear a group of children behind me, a family flying kites, a bunch of friends packing up their beach towels for the day, ordinary fucking human beings. I knew that beyond this ocean the world dropped away to nothingness. Columbus was wrong, I knew this. The world was flat and after a time at sea you'd come to the edge, where the water spilled like a waterfall into pure space. I considered, for the first time seriously, killing myself. I thought of Fiona just then and I remembered where I had placed the tennis shoe and the knife.

I remembered. I remembered with the clarity of an all-blue, football-stadium sky. I remembered looking under Eric's desk that day. I remembered seeing the plastic bag and pulling it out, seeing inside it the tennis shoes, the knife all bloody wrapped up in there. I remembered the smell of the blood. I remembered removing the bag to my own room and stashing it temporarily under the covers of my bed. I remembered the fake search after that, going from house to house throughout the neighborhood, pretending to find the one red tennis shoe in the woods. I remembered all of it. I remembered our father cursing and our mother's lower lip trembling and how steady Eric's nerves were and the look he gave me when I presented the tennis shoe to our parents. I may not be the most credible of human beings. I may even be crazy on many levels. But this is what I remembered that day on the beach in Santa Monica, up to my legs in the water, up to my neck in my life.

So I stepped back out. So I stepped out of the water and on to the beach. I found Selena behind one of the refreshment stands, by the trash cans. She was sober for a change. 'Where have you been?' she said.

'I was in the water.'

'I can see that.'

'I remembered something.'

'What's that?'

'I remembered that it was my brother who killed my sister.'

She was nonplussed. 'He did?'

'Yes.'

'What did you think happened to her?'

'Everyone thought . . . we all thought she was abducted.'

'By aliens?'

'By a man named Bryce Telliman.'

'A girlfriend of mine was abducted by aliens,' Selena said. 'She remembered it, too. She had been abused by them.'

'Are you saying I'm crazy?'

'I'm saying you have to believe what's in your own head', Selena said, 'and more than that you cannot do.'

'I'm going to call my brother,' I said. 'Selena, I'm going to call my brother.'

'Will he come and get you?'

'Yes.'

'You don't belong out here, anyway,' Selena told me. 'You're a little bit delicate, if you know what I mean.'

I nodded. I knew what she meant. I loved her suddenly. I wanted to marry her.

'Come sit by me for a while,' she said. 'And then we'll go and make your phone call.'

When I sat down, Selena put her head against my wet shoulder. And together we watched the last light coming through the trash cans behind this refreshment stand. I would get up with her later and she would lead me to a telephone, where I would call Eric collect. Two days later, I would be on a plane, flying business class, being treated like royalty as far as I was concerned, way up there above the American plains, sitting next to him.

But right now I said, 'You should do something about that.' I indicated the gash on her left leg, right along her calf.

'Do what?'

'Go to a hospital?'

Selena made air come through her nose in a way that meant something like forget it, what's the point. And when I left her to meet Eric she would squeeze me in the way that meant something about regret, about not wanting to be let go. 'Hospital,' she said. 'Right.'

This is what Eric said the day he found me: 'Pilot.'

Just that word in that voice, and immediately I knew it was time to go. Immediately I knew everything.

'Eric,' I said back. I tried to smile. I was looking up through the bright yellow sunlight at him. It was early in the afternoon and Selena and I had been sitting on the curb by the bike path that ran along the edge of the beach. Selena had been tending to her wound. I had been scratching myself, my skin so dry from the sand and salt water that it felt like canvas, peeling away.

'What are you doing?'

Selena rose up and stretched like a cat. 'Time for me to head out.'

'Eric, this is Selena.'

Eric looked at me in bewilderment.

''Bye,' Selena said, clutching me for that quick moment, and then disappearing, falling in behind a group of rollerbladers.

I'd never see her again.

'Pilot,' Eric said, 'it's time to go, all right?'

I got up, too. 'Where?'

'Home.' My brother put his hand on my arm, escorting me like a prisoner. 'I've got a car around here somewhere,' he said. 'And I've got a hotel room at the airport Hilton.'

'I'll help you find it.'

'It's red,' he told me. 'It's a red Mustang convertible. I rented it at the airport. It costs seven dollars to park here, you know.'

'Isn't it ridiculous?'

'I couldn't believe it.'

I waited a moment and then I said, 'Thank you for coming.' I meant it, too. I hadn't known how I would've gotten back without him.

My brother stopped for a moment and rubbed his eyes against the California sun, saying, 'I didn't tell Mom.' He had grown older, I thought, and more handsome. He had grown completely into his doctorhood, his air of authority having traveled with him all the way out here.

'Whatever.'

'But I want you to tell her when we get back.'

'Tell her what?' I really didn't know what he meant. I was so hungry, so bleary, I really didn't know what there was to tell.

'Pilot.' He shook his head. 'You've got to get it together. Jesus Christ, you are all fucked up. If you need help, I'll get it for you, OK? Whatever it is, whatever you need. But, please,' he said, 'please, just let me know what's going on, will you?'

'OK,' I said. 'All right.'

'There it is.' He indicated a red Mustang convertible at the far end of the Santa Monica beach parking lot. And on our walk across he was silent, so I started pointing to various things of interest.

'That's where they shoot *Baywatch*,' I told him. 'And at that refreshment stand you can get weed, if you know the right thing to say.'

On the plane the following day, high above America, Eric said, 'Pilot,' and he shook his head in stern disappointment.

I almost laughed. 'Come on.'

'Pilot,' he said. 'Why?'

I slid the shade down over the window. I looked at my brother. I offered my face to him. 'I wanted to, wanted to get out of where I was, Eric, to get away from things. I thought I could sell a screenplay or something. I don't know.' I could never talk to Eric. I could never explain myself to him. 'I thought I could get somewhere.'

'Did you try?'

'Try what?'

'Try to sell a screenplay?'

I slid the shade up now. Outside, the clouds rolled beneath us. It is a sensation, no matter how much I've flown, that has always amazed me. We were actually in the air, actually *flying*. 'I left them in a bag,' I said. 'When I first got out there, to the beach, I left them in a bag and they were stolen.'

'Were they your only copies?'

'I had them on disk,' I said. I slid the shade down again.

'Do you have the disk at home somewhere?'

'The disk was in the bag, too.'

'Jesus Christ.' He shook his head again. 'What the hell are we going to tell Mom?'

I could hear the jet engines in the airplane turning, the huge turbines screaming. 'I thought of something,' I told him then. 'While I was out on the beach. It was just a couple of days ago, really. It was the day I called you.'

'What?'

'Where I put the other shoe.'

He didn't hesitate. I believed he had been preparing all his life for this moment. 'What other shoe?'

'Fiona's.'

'Pilot,' my brother said through his teeth, 'what the fuck are you talking about?'

We were sitting in the business-class section, cold drinks on the little pull-down trays in front of us. A movie was playing on the screen, but we had declined the complimentary headphones. No one was listening, I thought, so I spoke aloud.

'The other shoe,' I said. I pulled the shade down again. I couldn't decide whether I wanted it up or down. 'I found it, you know, under your desk, all those years ago.'

'Pilot.' He was rolling his eyes, practicing every gesture of denial.

'And I told everyone that I had found the one shoe in the woods somewhere, but I hid the bag, the Wonderbread bag with the other shoe and the knife in it.'

'Pilot,' Eric said, 'you are really losing it this time.'

'For some reason, I've never let myself think about it until now.' I sipped my orange juice. 'But what did you do with her? Where is she? Where's Fiona?' My voice was calm, I thought, reasonable, despite the screaming content of what I was saying, despite the insane loudness of this accusation.

'Pilot,' Eric said, 'that's all, OK? No more of this.' He looked at the gray leather of the chair in front of him. Oddly, he reached out and touched it. Then he sipped his ginger ale and rubbed his hands together.

'I hid the other shoe and the knife, the whole bag, where no one could possibly find it, where no one in the world could ever think of looking.'

He waited a moment. 'When we get back I think you should, you should try some counseling, all right?' He was trying hard to be nice, I could tell. 'I know someone who I think can help you.'

'Fine,' I said.

'And maybe you could try to find a job or something.'

I shrugged. 'I'll do it.'

'Pilot,' he said, and he faced me, 'I'm your brother. I'm trying to help you. I really am. But I can't if you're accusing me of . . . of . . . of weird shit. There's no other shoe, Pilot. The police looked everywhere. Whoever took Fiona took her with the one shoe on. Do you understand me? And there was no knife.'

'But I know where it is. And whatever happened to that hunting knife, Eric? The one you cut Halley's leg off with?'

'You're having some kind of hallucination, Pilot. You're having a paranoid delusion, is what you're having. Do you know what I mean?'

'No.'

'You were out on the beach for how long? Were you eating? Were you sleeping? You had some strange dream and you're thinking now that it was a memory. For Christ's sake, you were staring into the sun too fucking long.'

'It's very clear.'

'Memories aren't clear, little brother. Dreams are clear. Hallucinations are clear. Memories are like—'

'I'm not sure about that.'

'Can I give you a sleeping pill? Something to relax you?'

'No,' I said.

'Go on,' my brother told me, 'please take one.'

What difference did it make? 'All right.'

He reached down to get his briefcase and from it he pulled out a bottle of pills. He handed me the whole thing. I didn't know what the hell they were – the bottle was unlabelled – but I have never questioned an offer of free drugs. I put one into my mouth, crunching the sour, dusty tablet against my molars.

'Take two,' Eric said.

I chewed another.

'I can't believe you,' he was shaking his head, even laughing. 'I really can't believe you.'

And then I asked, 'What are these, anyway?'

Some of the medications reported to evoke psychotic symptoms include anesthetics and analgesics, anticholinergic agents, anti-convulsants, antihistamines, antihypertensive and cardiovascular medications, antimicrobial medications, antiparkinsonian medications, chemotherapeutic agents (e.g., cyclosporine and procarbozine), corticosteroids, gastrointestinal medications, muscle relaxants, nonsteroidal anti-inflammatory medications, other over-the-counter medications (e.g., phenylephrine, pseudoephindrine), antidepressant medication, and disulfiram. Toxins reported to induce psychotic symptoms include anticholinesterase, organo-phosphate insecticides, nerve gases, carbon monoxide, carbon dioxide, and volatile substances such as fuel or paint.

Katherine leaned forward in our father's old wing-back. 'And you believe your brother gave you, that he gave you drugs to make you experience hallucinations, psychotic hallucinations?'

I looked at her directly. My face was made of metal. My eyes were glass. 'There's no other way to explain it, is there?'

Katherine cleared her throat. 'When did Eric give you the drugs? When could he have—'

'The pills on the plane, maybe.' I shrugged. 'I don't know. He's very clever.'

'And he did it because—'

'Because he wanted everyone to believe I was crazy, because I was finally telling the truth about what happened to Fiona, because he has everything to lose if—'

'Is it possible,' Katherine said, 'even remotely possible that all this business about the shoe and knife was hallucinations? Memories are tricky, Pilot. Sometimes they seem real, but they're not.'

I untwisted the shoelace from my middle finger. 'If I hallucinated the shoe, why would I have this?' I held it out, dangling it in front of her like a hypnotist's watch.

Katherine took it in her open palm and without looking up, said, very matter of factly, 'You have the shoe.' It was a question.

'And the knife.'

She looked at the shoelace. It was completely black, frayed at the ends. 'You've had this since—'

'Since they found me in the woods,' I said. 'Haven't you noticed it?'

'It's out there?' Katherine looked at me with a sudden realization. 'The other shoe, the knife—these things are out there in the woods somewhere, where you hid them? Is that what you're thinking?'

They gained material, then. Somewhere out in the woods, these items came into being, particles forming around the nucleus of an idea like the cancer cells forming around my mother's optical nerve.

'Yes.' I exhaled heavily.

'Pilot,' Katherine said, 'I think we should end our session early today.' She still had the shoelace in her open palm, as if it were a small animal, something wounded. 'Can I keep this?' she asked me. 'Do you mind?'

At the clinic, Dr Lennox leaned back in his chair and rubbed his eyelids until they were pink. 'I guess,' he said sadly, 'I guess the question is this.' He put his hands on the desk in front of him. He seemed tired. His smile, though permanent, was wearing thin. 'If Pilot Airie is handing you evidence, Kate, actual evidence from a crime, or at least what he believes is actual, should you investigate?' He paused now, looking out the window behind her. 'And I don't know the answer. I mean, we're not the police here, are we?'

She was standing in the door, leaning against the jamb, arms folded. 'Pilot's still making delusional, paranoiac accusations about his brother,' she said. 'Not much of it makes any sense, but it's deeply entrenched. I mean, he will *not* let go. But the thing is, it's not bizarre.'

'Not bizarre.'

'It's not—' she searched for a word '—crazy.'

'You're saying it's possible.'

'I'm not saying Pilot isn't delusional, but he's not talking about having his brain removed by invisible little men or a secret cave inside his body where pink elephants live. He's talking about something that is . . . well, at least it's based in reality.' She stepped forward. 'Which is not psychotic. It may be wrong, but it doesn't indicate schizo—'

'True.' The doctor nodded, his fingers to his lips.

'So I think we should, I mean, I should—'

'Is there anything else?'

'What do you mean?'

'Is he exhibiting any other symptoms of schizoid affective disorder or schizophrenia, anything at all?'

'Not really. He seems a bit sluggish still, that's all.'

'That's not much for the diagnosis, is it? Exactly what are his accusations?'

'Primarily, that Eric had something to do with their little sister's abduction twenty years ago.'

'What else?'

'Pilot's suggesting that Eric gave him drugs to, to make him psychotic, to make him seem crazy, so no one would believe his accusations.'

'Dr Airie is a neurosurgeon.' This was as if to say brain doctors are incapable of wrongdoing.

This was my brother's advantage. He'd used it for years. He was Eric Airie, floating like air through the advancing defense to score the touchdown, untouched.

Katherine nodded. 'Yes, he is.'

'I'm wondering', Dr Lennox said, 'if we're dealing with a simple case of a brother's jealousy.'

'Cain and Abel?'

'Something like that.'

'And they're fighting over—'

'Their mother.'

'It's so Freudian.' Katherine laughed. 'I guess it's possible.'

'Sometimes Freud's OK.' Dr Lennox smiled. 'Sometimes.' He looked at his desk, which was a mosaic of pink and yellow sticky notes. 'Anyway, Pilot's not a patient of the clinic any more, Kate. He's your client, and it's your decision about what to do with him. You don't think he's a danger to anyone, do you?'

'He's perfectly sane,' Katherine said. 'I mean, otherwise, he's totally rational, taking care of his mother and the house. It's weird.' She was shaking her head.

The doctor shrugged. 'Try the library,' he said. 'Look up all the old articles about the case, see what really happened to Pilot's sister, or at least what the police think happened.'

'I might do that.'

'Something could turn up that can help you.' Dr Lennox leaned back again, hands behind his head. 'I have to ask, though, Kate, what is your aim here? How are you helping Pilot with this?'

'Sudden psychotic episodes like his are usually brought about by extreme trauma or stress, right? And Pilot experienced nothing like that, not according to him or his family, anyway. Nor do they report noticing any gradual symptoms, except maybe that trip he took to California.' Katherine walked forward into Dr Lennox's office, approaching his desk. 'I want to know what caused his psychosis. I think if I knew,' she said, 'I could help him, I could help his whole family.'

'And you want to know', Dr Lennox said matter of factly, 'what happened to Fiona.'

Katherine could not help but admit it. 'Yes.'

'That's not necessarily going to help the family, though, is it?'

'Do you think the truth can hurt?'

Dr Lennox gave her a look and lifted his hands just slightly. It meant she was on her own.

Our mother lived in a swirl of soft colors and blurs. The only clear image that moved in front of her eyes at present was her daughter, Fiona, our sister, who glided about the house and backyard with the clarity of a photorealistic hologram, sharp at the edges, colors vivid and bright. Fiona even whispered in Hannah's ear sometimes, coming up behind her, telling her the little things daughters tell their mothers, asking if she could go into the pool, could she have ice cream after dinner, could she stay up past nine. Other voices, real ones, mine and Katherine DeQuincey-Joy's, rose from downstairs through the ventilation. Hannah heard my voice on the telephone, my voice and Eric's arguing – bits and pieces of conversation rising up like mist.

Hannah listened to the radio sometimes, too, but mostly she listened to her daughter's laughter in the backyard.

If that's what it was.

She saw memories more clearly now than her present reality.

It was all in her head, according to Eric.

'Pilot,' she said sometimes, and her voice was so clear and sharp it cut through every wall of the house.

I'd come into her room. 'Mom?' I'd have been out in the backyard raking the leaves. Next door, a new family had moved in and two little girls, nine and ten years old – sisters – one blonde, one brunette, had arrived with them. They giggled and squealed, their voices shrill and joyful.

'Pilot,' Hannah would say, 'I think we should have pork chops for dinner.'

'Pork chops?'

'Could you go out and get them?'

I nodded, then remembered she couldn't see me nodding. 'I can get them.'

'Do you know how to prepare them?'

'Will you come down to the kitchen and tell me?'

'Those children, the new ones next door – girls?'

'Little girls,' I said. 'One blonde, one brunette.'

Hannah cleared her throat. 'I'll come down now.'

Twice a week I drove my mother to the hospital, where a therapist, a woman not unlike my mother – but an expert on eyes, not hands – led her through a series of exercises to help her regain the ability to squeeze her eyeballs into focus. I'd sit in the lobby and try to read a magazine, but end up just looking at the pictures of celebrities and television personalities, the actors and rock stars.

'It's painful,' she'd say on the way home.

'What's that, Mom?'

'The squeezing, the tension around my eyes.'

'What does she have you doing?'

'Squinting, mostly.'

'Does it help?'

'Am I getting more wrinkles around my eyes?'

Sometimes when I came into her room, she didn't even know I was there. Sometimes I'd come in and she'd whisper, 'Fiona? Little baby, is that you?' and I'd have to back out as quietly as I could, not making a noise, and then, five minutes later, re-enter, but boisterously, so she'd know it was me.

Eric wanted to know how she was.

'She's going blind,' I told him. 'Crazy, too.'

'What do you mean, crazy?'

'She's seeing ghosts,' I said.

'No,' Eric said, 'they're double images.'

'No,' I said, 'they started as double images, and now they're ghosts. She thinks Fiona is in the house.'

'I'm coming over,' he said to me.

'You're seeing ghosts,' he said to our mother.

'I'm seeing blurs,' Hannah told him good-naturedly. 'All blurs and swirls.' She was different around him. When Eric was there she behaved as if she were in public.

Eric gave me a stern look. '*Pilot*,' he said.

'What?'

He opened his hands, as if to say, *See*?

'Are you hungry?' Hannah said. 'Do you want something?'

'Eric doesn't have time to eat,' I said. 'He's too busy screwing my therapist.'

Eric sighed.

'Well, you *are*,' I said.

Now it was our mother's turn to say it. '*Pilot*.'

I rubbed my finger where I had been twisting my shoelace. I didn't have it any more. I had given it to Katherine.

It was called Cassavettes Sports. And beneath the layer of fake trophies, game jerseys and signed pennants was evidence of multiple renovations. Katherine imagined a suburban archeology, the decades peeling away layer by layer until the weak wooden structure was revealed beneath, the sub-layer of gypsum and particleboard. 'He gave me a shoelace,' Katherine said, her eyes avoiding my brother's.

'A shoelace.'

They sat as far in the back of Cassavettes as possible, trying to avoid the large television monitors that blared the sports channels at top volume. There were two men at the bar. There was one other couple near the front eating chicken wings.

Katherine felt exposed, as if someone would discover her.

'He's been carrying it around,' she said, 'nervously wrapping it around and around his fingers. I had noticed it.' She shrugged. 'But I hadn't thought about what it meant.' She took a sip of her sour white wine.

'I noticed it, too.' Eric opened his hands to her. 'But I didn't think it meant—'

'He says it's from—' she said this as though she were ashamed, looking down '— he says it's from your sister's shoe.'

Eric sighed. 'That shoe', he said, 'was taken in evidence by the police a million years ago.' He shook his head. 'Pilot doesn't have that shoe. It's impossible.'

'He says it's from the other one.'

My brother rolled his eyes. 'There's no other one.'

'Well,' Katherine said, 'there *has* to be another one somewhere, right? And Pilot says he has it.'

Eric put his head in his hands. 'My family is so fucked up.' He pulled his dark, cropped hair, his face mock crazy, all frustration. 'What the hell is going on?'

'Eric.' Katherine reached across the table and touched my brother's arm. 'What if Pilot really did hide it somewhere all those years ago? What if inside all this confusion there's some kind of truth? Maybe he really found the evidence in the woods that day and he's confusing it with a time when he found an old football under your bed or something. What if this other piece of evidence could lead to the real, to the real abductor?' She waited a second, then said, 'Jesus Christ, Eric, he says there's a knife, too.'

'A knife.'

'He says it has blood on it.'

'Oh God.' As far as Katherine could see, Eric did not believe it. He sighed heavily. 'What are you going to do with the shoelace?'

'Who was the police detective assigned to the case?' she asked. 'Do you remember?'

'How could I forget? His name was Jerry Cleveland.' Eric chuckled. 'He was the most incompetent detective they possibly could have—'

'Was he young?'

'He wasn't that young.'

'Do you think he's still around?'

Eric pushed his beer away. 'I don't know, Katherine.' He looked around, then, trying to locate the waiter.

'I'll try to find him,' she said. 'Of all people, he'll know what to do with the shoelace, right? Come on, Eric, what if it still has some of that man's DNA on it? That's admissible now. What was his name?'

'The man they accused?'

Katherine nodded.

'Bryce Telliman.'

'What if the shoe or the knife or something has his fingerprints – or anything. Isn't it worth checking into?'

'Katherine,' Eric said, 'my brother is crazy. He's schizophrenic, all right? He's heavily medicated, yes, but that doesn't mean all of this isn't some paranoid reac—'

'I think it's worth looking into for Pilot's sake,' Katherine said. 'And I don't think he's schizophrenic. I don't know what he is, but it's not that. He doesn't have enough symptoms. And who knows, you might even find the person who, who took your sister. Hiding the evidence may have been the act of a very troubled boy and after all these years Pilot's become confused about where he found it. I don't understand why you're resisting. He might really have this stuff.'

My brother sighed. 'Do you have any idea what this will do to my mother?'

Katherine was silent.

'Do you?'

'No,' she said.

'She already has some bizarre psychosomatic blindness and this is the kind of thing that could—'

Katherine touched his arm again, stopping him. 'Let me contact this detective, Eric. How many other little girls has this man taken and, and hurt all because he wasn't caught after he took your sister?'

The muscles of Eric's face seemed to tighten now, gathering beneath his skin like that twisting bundle of snakes.

Katherine released Eric's arm and sat back. They sat together without talking for a moment and Katherine sipped her wine. Eric examined his glass of beer. 'Can I see it?' he said finally.

'See what?'

'Can I see the shoelace?'

It was in her purse, the brown leather one that sat at her feet under the table. I had seen her put it in there, in fact, just last night. 'Oh,' she said, 'it's, it's at the office, in a drawer, it's—'

My brother nodded. And she could see that he didn't believe her.

And that is when it began, the doubt inside Katherine, growing like Hannah's cancer.

And the awareness of her doubt growing in my brother's mind.

She drank more wine. She was terrible at lying. 'I'll show it to you later,' she said. 'Tomorrow, if you—'

'Don't worry about it.' He looked down. 'Just take it to the police. Find Cleveland, or whoever is in charge of that kind of thing, and, and let's get this over with.' He touched the rim of his beer glass. 'I have to get something else.' He grimaced slightly. 'I don't want this any more.'

* * *

When the phone rang and it was my father, Hannah caught her breath like a teenage girl about to be asked to the prom.

'Are you all right?' he said.

'I'm fine, James. I was just—'

'Listen,' he began right away, 'about Pilot.'

'He's much better,' she said. 'He's really—'

I was in the kitchen. I had been hanging around in there lately, watching old movies on the little black and white on the counter. I could hear that it was him just from the tone of her voice. I could feel his presence through her. She was in the living room on the black rotary-dial, of course, the only telephone either one of us used.

'I want him to come down, at least for a little while. I can make arrangements to have someone look after you, Hannah. I just think it would be good for him to get away from that house, OK?'

She nodded. 'I can take care of myself.'

'I've already spoken to Eric. He's going to have a nurse come and watch out for you. You know, just in case of, of, of whatever might happen.'

'I'll be fine. That's totally unnecessary.'

They were silent for a moment, each in their living rooms, phones to their ears, and then he asked how she was.

I was to fly down to our father's cottage in Florida and stay with him for a month. Fishing, hiking, fresh air, a trip in his seaplane. It was supposed to be good for me. A nurse was coming to take care of Hannah. 'It will be great to see you,' our father told me on the phone. 'Think of it as a break – like a break from life.' I could hear his smile through the miles of fiber optic cable. When he smiled, it was genuine. 'Anything you want,' he said. 'Sleep late, watch TV all night, read, go for a walk, a swim, fishing. You name it, you got it. Sound good to you?'

It sounded bizarre to me. It sounded so alien I could hardly imagine it. 'Sounds great.'

I was on a plane three days later. I had my medication in my backpack, enough to last a month. I had Katherine DeQuincey-

Joy's home phone number in case I needed to talk to her at any hour of the night. I had a warning from Eric not to drag our father into any of my craziness. I had a feeling I was moving beyond the present moment and that I could see what would happen to all these people sitting around me on this airplane.

The blur.

The woman next to me would get a divorce within the year. The man across the aisle would die in a car accident. The little blonde-haired girl who ran up and down the aisle throughout the entire flight, much to the disapproval of the flight attendants, would be running just like this through a mall in Greensboro, North Carolina, away from her mother, and a man would grab her by the wrist and lead her outside to the parking lot, to a virtual city of gray vans and blue sedans. The police would find this little girl by the highway, scratched, but largely unhurt, dazed, with little memory of what had happened. The story would be considered so common by the local reporters that it would not even make the papers. I looked down through the airplane window and saw all those infinitesimal lives unfolding into the next year and the next decade and the next century. I heard all of their conversations and thoughts.

I knew them. I knew everything about them.

At the airport, my father was there to greet me. Patricia, his girlfriend, stood nearby, smiling nervously.

Their faces lit up with recognition – truly happy, it seemed, to see me. My father had become more gruff since he retired from the airline. He had become a character from a Hemingway novel, I thought. When he was younger, he was smooth, a city man. But he had become more and more grizzled, countrified, macho, since he moved down to Florida. He had been developing this persona for years, the one he had always wanted.

Patricia hugged me a little too hard, as though she really had missed me. 'Sweetheart,' she said, 'it's so good to see you.' But she had never even known me.

'Hi, Patricia.'

'Pilot,' Dad said. He had his hand extended. It was brown and wrinkled. It had become, somehow, an old fisherman's hand.

I gripped it as firmly as I could, trying not to seem limp-wristed, sissyish, trying not to seem like a fragile mental patient. Like myself.

He clapped his other hand around mine and pumped. 'Glad you're the hell out of that woman's icy clutches.' He meant Hannah.

I rolled my eyes. 'It's not like that.'

Dismissively, he said, 'There's nothing wrong with you, is there?'

'Jim,' Patricia cautioned.

I tried to be funny. 'Nothing that a lot of strong anti-psychotic medication can't take care of.'

'Psychotic,' my father repeated, shaking his head. 'The car's this way, Mr Psychotic. Got any more luggage?'

'No.' I had a duffel bag and the backpack.

We walked out to the parking lot. The sky here was white, I noticed, with white clouds descending like a sheer white curtain, against a thin, faded green horizon. This was winter in Florida. I had been here once before, years ago, but hadn't looked at these things. There was a wet smell in the air, a dampness.

'I'm sorry I didn't come up,' Dad said.

'It's all right.'

'It's not all right. I was having all kinds of problems down here and I couldn't get away.'

'What problems?'

Patricia laughed. 'He was trapped off the coast on the little island, when you—'. She stopped herself, then went on, saying, 'And he couldn't leave, you know, because of the hurricane warnings.'

'How long were you out there?'

'Two weeks.'

'What did you eat?'

'Fish.' My father grinned hugely. 'And I bagged a possum.'

'That's disgusting.' I grimaced. 'You didn't eat it, did you?'

'He ate it.'

'I was hungry.' My father laughed and opened the car door of his sleek, blue, four-by-four-off-road vehicle. 'I was tired of fish, too.'

I got in the back.

'You comfortable?' my father asked. 'It's a long drive home.'

'I'm fine.'

Patricia turned to look at me. She was concerned, I could tell. She was worried about my mental health. I gave her my sanest, most rational look. I was glad my father had found her. She was kind, I had always known that. 'I made sandwiches,' she said smiling. 'They're in the cooler.' There was an old red cooler beside me. 'But if you don't like them we can stop somewhere and get something else, anything you want.'

'Sandwiches are great,' I said. 'I love sandwiches.'

Patricia held her smiling gaze on me a beat too long. It made me feel pathetic. I went to twist the shoelace around my finger, but of course it wasn't there.

My brother sat at his desk and neatly folded the waxy paper his sandwich had been wrapped in. Today it had been cream cheese and olives on pumpernickel, a winter peach and warm squash soup – although he hadn't finished the soup. He thought of me arriving in Florida. He imagined me getting off the plane, the long walk through the airport with my bag in my hand, finding our father at baggage claim. Could he see that my hair was becoming long? Could he sense that if it weren't for the bag I was carrying my hands would float away? He dropped the remains of his lunch in the wastebasket. He got up from his black lacquer desk and washed up, scrubbing his fingers. My brother closed his eyes and saw the Florida landscape slipping beneath the wheels of our father's four-wheel drive.

I rode back in memory to the fishing trips he took us on when we were kids. It was a Ford Grand Torino then. Fiona was a toddler and our mother would lay out the dusky plaid picnic blanket in the shade somewhere near the edge of the trees. Fiona would come down to the edge of the lake and clap her hands together, giggling and burbling. If anyone caught a fish, she'd dance, her bright four-year-old face like a cartoon image of happiness. Only once did anyone actually hook a fish large enough to keep. It was on our father's line, of course, a shimmering large-mouth bass sixteen inches long, dangling like an enormous shining locket on a pendant. It was probably the biggest fish that little suburban lake could maintain. We always stopped at a deli on the way, and while we fished, Mom assembled sandwiches from cold baloney, soft rolls, hot mustard. There was cool macaroni salad and thin slices of Swiss cheese. I used to pretend not to know how to put a worm on the hook just so our father would show me again, just to have his body curling over my body, just to see his fingers move like that and have his face so close to mine. I used to pretend that our family lived in a cabin just behind the line of trees on the other side of the lake, on the other side of where Fiona and our mother were.

Fishing, our father always said, is tranquillity interrupted by violence.

In the car, just now, he was saying, 'I picked something up for you, Pilot. It's behind you, in the way-back. Can you see it?'

I turned around in his car. There was a brand-new fishing rod, red lacquered, in separate pieces, held together by a single piece of orange tape. 'A fishing rod,' I said.

'I figured you wouldn't bring your old one.'

'I hadn't even thought about it.' I took the rod on to my lap and turned it in my hands. 'I was just thinking about when we'd go to the lake, you know, when we were kids.' I thought he would be glad to hear that.

'That was nothing,' Dad said. 'You just wait till you get your line in the water in a Florida lake.'

'It's good fishing?' I felt like Hemingway saying that.

'You can't lose.'

'Tranquillity interrupted by violence?'

My father laughed, remembering what he used to say. 'All violence,' he said. 'Nothing but violence.'

I said, 'Great,' and then I realized my voice may not have sounded as enthusiastic as I wanted it to.

'You don't have to fish if you don't want to.' Patricia had removed her seat belt so she could sit sideways in the car, her back against the door, facing us. I pictured the door opening, her body falling back on to the highway.

'Absolutely,' our father said. 'You don't have to do anything. I just thought that you might—'

'I'd love to fish,' I broke in. 'I really would. It's just what I needed.' I could see him smiling even though I was looking at the back of his head. I could see his eyes beaming at me in the rear-view mirror. I could see the relief on Patricia's face, who could see his face directly, who was living directly under the influence of his face, and I could see the reflection of his smile in hers.

'Excellent,' my father said. He drove for a while, and then he said, 'Superb.' We drove in the glow of his approval for several miles on this Florida highway and then he turned on to an exit. He also turned the radio on. 'They play country music down here,' he said.

'Your father likes country music.'

'It's all right,' I said. 'He's entitled.' I never much liked that kind of music. It always seemed too simple to me, like a soundtrack to a movie in which you can see the ending coming a mile away.

If my life was a movie, the soundtrack, I thought, would be like *Jaws*, a single heartbeat beating louder and faster, fear and its quick release, stupid and insistent.

When anyone caught anything, or even if they just thought they did, Fiona would rush down to the edge of the lake and our mother would follow behind her by a few paces, bending over, her hands out just in case she had to catch her, just to make sure nothing happened, to make sure she didn't fall in. I was fairly little myself, only six years old, I think, too little to cast the line out on my own. But I remember Eric swinging his rod back and casting his.

I remember how beautiful he was, how graceful his body.

And when our parents weren't looking, he would threaten me with the hook, come after me, saying he'd gut me like a bluegill.

My father's radio played Loretta Lynn, and the Florida suburbs that led eventually to the airport swished by my window in a flurry of fence white and brick red and lawn green. When we got to their cottage, I knew, our father would ask what it was like in the clinic, did they treat me all right, did they restrain me at all, tie me to the bed? I would tell him that it was fine, that it was like a vacation in many ways. And I would consider telling him exactly what had put me in there, but I would hold back. Today, I would hold back. I had to plan the moment, had to break it to him just right. 'And when you were in the woods,' he would ask me, 'what was going through your head? What were you doing out there for three days?'

'I was thinking a million different things,' I would tell him. 'And I didn't know which ones were right and which were crazy. And I can't really remember a lot of it.'

'Were you afraid?' he would ask.

And I would tell him that I had never experienced such fear, which was not a lie. And I would tell him that I was thinking fondly of him, which was one.

I remember Fiona as a still photograph. I remember the green grass behind her, the shadows of saplings crossing her body. I remember the garish yellow dandelions in her hair. I remember the baby smile turning up the corners of her pink mouth, that slight but permanent upward curving. I remember the deep dimple in her right cheek (I have one, too). I remember the little red shoes she wore – always red – the pink and blue floral dress. In the background are trees, a blue-black rippling lake, a cobalt-bright sky covered unevenly with lacy clouds. I remember Fiona's hands held together in front of her, caught mid-clap, captured in that split second of baby-joy. I can see our red and black plaid picnic blanket behind our little sister spread out on the grass. I can see our mother sitting on that blanket, unfocused in the lens, her auburn hair in an early 1970s' twist, long curls dangling beside her ears, a short yellow dress. The details are there. In these photographs of Fiona that I carry in my head there is always her face in center focus. There is always her smile. My sister's smile.

'Did you talk to him?' I asked.

'Did I—'

'Did you speak to Eric?'

We were in a borrowed rowboat far out on a Florida lake, me and my father, our lines in the water, our poles propped against our knees. 'I spoke to him,' our father said, nodding. His face told me that he knew what was coming, that he had been prepared for this conversation.

'Do you know about Mom's eyesight?'

'She's having some trouble with her vision, is that it? Eric told me a little.' He teased the line.

'She was seeing ghosts,' I said. 'At least that was how she put it. It was like she was seeing double, I think. But now she's having trouble seeing anything. There's a nurse coming to the house to take care of her.'

'She'll be all right.'

'Did he tell you about Katherine Jane DeQuincey-Joy?'

He gave me a questioning look.

'My therapist.'

Shrugging. 'I knew you were in therapy.'

'He's sleeping with her.'

'Who?'

'Eric, your son, my brother, he's—'

'With the therapist?' My father smiled. He laughed a little bit, too.

'It's funny?'

'Pilot, what difference does it make?'

'A lot.'

'Why don't you get another one?'

'Because if I can convince her,' I said, 'I can convince anyone.' Even as I said this, I realized how stupid it sounded.

My father cleared his throat. He began to reel his line in, very

217

slowly, steadily, teasing it in the water the whole way. 'Do you like it here?' he asked.

'At the lake?'

'Florida.'

I looked around, as if I could see the whole state from this rowboat. 'I like it.'

'You can stay as long as you want.' He looked at me directly. 'You don't have to go back in a month. If you want to, if you want to, you can stay here for ever.' He reached over to me, his hand coming toward my shoulder. The little rowboat swayed a bit at the shifting of weight.

'I don't know,' I said.

'Think about it.' His hand was resting on my shoulder, lightly at first, then pressing down.

I turned my body just enough, just so he'd release me, then I began to pull my line in, as well. The little boat rocked in the calm water. I thought I felt something tugging at my line, but it turned out to be nothing. It was cold out here, but not so cold that we could see our own breathing in the air.

'Ghosts?' my father said abruptly.

'That's what she calls them.'

'Of anyone in particular?'

I knew Hannah had been seeing Fiona, had seen her running around the backyard, had felt her little-girl breath on her neck behind her in the kitchen. I had heard my mother call out to her. I had listened to her whispering to my sister through the ventilation.

I looked back at my father steadily. I said, 'Fiona.'

He cast his line into the water. 'We don't know that she's dead.' He wouldn't look at me. 'How can your mother be seeing the ghost of someone who might not even be dead?'

'She's dead.'

'Pilot.'

'Eric didn't tell you?'

'Eric told me you were having trouble with it still and I can see that now.'

I knew what Eric had told him. I knew everything. 'I know what happened.' Around the lake I could sense the rustling of the trees, their roots quietly reaching into the water, curling up through the black silt and rotting leaves at the bottom.

'About what?'

'Everything. Everything that happened that night.'

'Shit, Pilot. Your mother has—'

'I know what happened.'

His manner changed quickly. His teeth clenched together. He even closed his eyes. 'What happened, son?'

'Eric killed her.'

Our father's shoulders slumped down. 'No,' he said. It meant he was disappointed in me. He wasn't surprised, just let down.

'I found the evidence, Dad.'

'The shoe?' He was incredulous.

'Both of them,' I said. 'Both shoes – and a knife.'

'This is all some kind of psychological bullshit,' my father said derisively. 'This is not even—'

'I'm not crazy.'

'Have you talked to the therapist about this?'

'Yes.'

'What does she say?'

'She says I'm confused.'

'Listen to her.'

'I'm trying,' I said. 'I really am. I want it to be confusion.' I wasn't sure if I believed this, as I said it. But I thought it would be good for him to hear.

Of course, we didn't catch anything worth keeping. But my father had steaks in the cooler and we set up a barbecue pit at a roadside rest-stop. From where we were I could see a public restroom down the road. Men lurked in the trees just beyond it. My father, I believe, had no idea what was happening or even that anyone was there. We sat at the picnic table eating our grilled steaks with raw tomatoes and onions.

'Next week', he said, 'the plane will be ready.'

'What's wrong with it now?'

'Just getting a tune-up.'

I nodded.

'So,' Dad said, 'do you want to go out to the islands?'

'The islands?'

'Off the coast there are hundreds of little islands – beautiful, perfect little places.'

'OK,' I said.

'We can bring a tent, stay a few days.'

'Sounds great,' I said.

'There's one in particular I'd like you to see.'

'An island?'

'It's uncharted. I call it Nowhere Island.'

'Sounds really—'

'Of course, there's no phone or anything. You think that would be all right for you?'

He was challenging me. He was challenging my resolve to remain sane. He thought it was a decision I had made, that I had chosen to be crazy like this. 'I can make it,' I said.

Dad took a huge bite of his steak. 'How's your meat?' he asked while chewing.

'Perfect,' I told him. 'Excellent.'

'You always did like steak,' he said.

'We all did.'

'Your mother's eyesight is bad?'

'It's pretty bad,' I said. I watched the cars zooming by on the highway. Men moved in the shadows of the trees on the other side. If my father knew about them, he didn't let on. I laughed a little bit. 'She likes to suffer. She likes to suffer silently.'

My father laughed at that.

At this moment my mother was speaking to my sister. She was asking Fiona to come inside, saying it was too cold out and that it was getting dark. Fiona's ghost stopped at the edge of the lawn and turned her head. Her eyes seemed to ask for one more minute, just one.

Please, Hannah begged her daughter silently, *please, dear, come inside.*

Dad cleared his throat. 'You know,' he said, 'I want you to clear all this up, all this about Eric – killing Fiona – I want you to clear it all up with your therapist first, all right? I mean—'

'You don't believe me,' I said. 'But it's all right. I don't always believe me, either.'

'It's not that I don't *believe* you,' Dad said. 'I mean, I'm sure you *think* that's what happened. But you know, Pilot, you can't always trust your own brain, you know what I mean?'

'Dad,' I said, 'I've lied to you my whole life and for the first time I can trust my—'

'There are a lot of things that happen when you're a kid that get all twisted and distorted in your mind when you get older. You can't—'. He stopped talking.

'Can't what?' I asked.

'You can't just accuse your own brother like that.'

'I have proof.'

'Just do me a favor.'

'What?'

'Just talk it all through with your therapist.'

'That's what I'm doing.'

He was dropping the dirty dishes into the cooler now. Later he would simply leave it all for Patricia to clean. 'Good,' he said. I would help her, standing in the kitchen, the two of us.

'I won't talk to you about it any more,' I said.

'I think that's a good idea, too.'

'I don't mean to upset anyone.'

'Pilot,' he said, 'I know you're having a hard time. I know you are. Don't feel bad about that. I've read about these things. It's not you, I know, it's just some chemical thing that went wrong in your head or something, something that got out of whack, that's all.'

Out of whack. 'I hope you're right.'

In the trees on the other side of the highway, there were men moving further into the dark. I imagined them reaching out for each other, their rough beards scratching against each other's faces. I saw them slipping further in. I looked at our father's innocent face. I wished so much that I had inherited that face and not Eric.

* * *

On the highway were cars carrying sailboats on trailers. Seafood restaurants, boat dealerships and bait shops lined the sandy roadside. The Atlantic ocean roared nearby, just a mile or so away. I couldn't see it, but I could feel the pulsing of its waves against the shore in the near distance. I could smell the salt in the air, stronger here, and the wind on my face was much softer than it had been. We pulled off eventually, stopping in the parking lot of an enormous airfield.

We had stopped to say hello to the plane.

No one seemed to notice the two of us walking across the expanse of weed-broken asphalt, and we entered the hangar with only a nod from a passing mechanic in a bright orange jumpsuit.

'Jim,' he said.

Dad just wanted to touch it, I think, and wanted me to touch it, too. He believed it was a therapeutic act.

For me. For him. For the plane.

'Touch it, Pilot,' he encouraged. 'Go ahead.'

It was the kind that lands in the water, a Cessna or Piper Cub or something, with little boat-like runners instead of wheels for the landing gear. At the moment, however, it was inside this dimly lit cavern of sheet metal, its front panel opened up to reveal the mechanical engine. Dad peered in, an educated look of concern on his face, masking, I thought, his true face of confusion.

Inside this hangar were at least a dozen other single-engine planes of similar sizes, and outside on the small airfield I had noticed another twenty or so, all of them in various stages of disrepair, all of them red and white or blue and white or yellow and white. Our father's plane, one of the smaller ones, had three red stripes running down the length of the body and across the underside of the wings. It had a serial number painted in red on the fuselage. It had two seats in the front and a tiny area in the back for supplies and storage. I supposed another person or two could fit back there as well, but it would be a tight squeeze. The inside was beige, like a car. This was the first time I had seen his plane outside a picture. Every year Patricia and our father sent us a Christmas photograph of the two of them standing next to it. It was always decorated with an evergreen wreath and it was always taken from a new angle. Usually, Patricia penned in some joke like, *Merry X-mas from your father and his girlfriend! (And from Patricia, too).*

Touching it, I said, 'It's pretty great, Dad.' Its fiberglass coat was not as smooth as I thought it would be. My hands were blackening with soot. It needed to be cleaned, I realized.

He ran his hand along the fuselage.

'Flying's one of the easiest things in the world,' my father said. 'I could teach you.'

I wondered if a person diagnosed with schizophrenia was allowed to pilot an airplane. I imagined answering the questionnaire.

Have you ever been diagnosed with a mental illness?

Long ago, Eric had taken flying lessons. But he stopped when Hannah begged him to. And then Dad left us, anyway, and it didn't seem to matter any more. I had always thought I would learn to fly because of my name at the very least.

We walked back out of the hangar, which was dimly lit and oddly quiet, into the harsh Florida daylight. It was around four in the afternoon by then and the sun shone with a brilliant glinting intensity off the windshields of the little airplanes out there. We got back inside Dad's four-wheel drive, each of the doors closing with a solid click.

'It's a great-looking plane, Dad,' I said after a moment of just sitting there, after I realized I was supposed to say something. 'Really cool. Beautiful.'

He wore a look of disappointment that I could only think had something to do with my reaction. It hadn't been inspired enough, I guessed. 'Wait'll we get it up in the air,' my father said. 'Then you'll see what I mean.' He started the engine. It was cold, but I rolled the window down anyway.

A beige tablecloth, beige plates, beige candles flickering – Patricia had set the table beautifully, even romantically – a dinner for three. She poured us each a glass of sweet white wine. She had arranged little wedges of various cheeses on round crackers on a beige ceramic platter in the living room. She had an easy listening station playing at low volume.

'Your mother never knew how to live,' our father told me when we saw all of this. 'It took Patricia to teach me how to enjoy life.'

She came out of the kitchen, clearly happy to see us.

'You didn't have to go to all of the trouble,' I told her. 'I feel like you've been working all—'

'What else am I going to do?' she said. 'There's mushroom soup all ready and just in case you didn't catch anything—' she winked at me '— I made stuffed sole.'

'Sole's good,' our father said. He settled into the couch.

'Stuffed sole,' I said, marveling.

I felt as if I should shower first. I went to the bathroom so I could at least wash my hands. In there I looked at my face in the mirror and tried to see my father in it, who I had been looking at all day. He wasn't there. I only saw Hannah. I saw my pupils dilating, as if I were looking out at the horizon.

When I came out I smiled.

The furniture here was nothing like the furniture we grew up with. Everything was wicker, for one thing, and very new. There were warm beige carpets on the floor. There were batik prints on the wall from exotic places. My father's aerial photographs – pictures of sky, mostly, and of the ocean's horizon – were framed and hung in squares of four above key pieces of furniture. There was a covered sun room in the back the size of a living room. At the end of the sun room was an outdoor hot tub. There was a fireplace. There were soft beige throw blankets draped everywhere.

I remembered, suddenly, that I hadn't taken my medication. I went to look for my backpack, but then I wondered how the chemicals would react with the wine. Fuck it, I thought. I decided simply to enjoy the wine. I looked around to see if any inanimate object had come alive. I listened to the dim lamps for any sign of voices. But there was nothing unusual. I'd take a double dose of the medication tomorrow, I told myself. I wouldn't go insane again in a day.

I tried to imagine our mother in this house. I tried to see her walking barefoot like Patricia across the earth-toned flooring to seat herself in one of these comfortably upholstered armchairs. It was impossible. Hannah could not exist in a place like this.

'This is such a nice cottage,' I said to our father. 'I'm sorry I never came here before.' I sat down on the cream-colored couch next to him.

'It's her place,' our father said. 'I just live here.'

Patricia had entered the living room from the kitchen again. She had long thin arms and shapely legs. She had dark, curly hair that hung around her face the way a much younger woman's does. It was a new hairstyle for her, I realized. When she was younger, when our father first met her all those years ago, she must have been incredibly beautiful – sexy. She seemed always to be cringing a little bit, though, as if waiting for someone to scream at her. 'Don't listen to him,' Patricia said. 'He has quite a lot of influence over this place. He just thinks decorating is for sissies, but he knows what he likes and he's quite vocal about the things he doesn't.'

'You've been doing some decorating, Dad?' I teased. 'Looking at fabric swatches, picking out window dressings?'

My father snorted. 'Anything on tonight?' He never liked being made fun of.

'There's a Hitchcock I haven't seen before,' Patricia said.

'Nah.' Then he turned to me, saying, 'You don't like Hitchcock, do you?'

'Whatever you want to watch is fine.' I would probably go to sleep early anyway, I thought. I ate a cracker. I sipped the wine.

'Anything else?'

Patricia handed him the newspaper. 'Why don't *you* look?'

I saw his eyes scanning the listings. 'It's Monday and there's football.' He winked at me.

Patricia rolled her eyes. 'I'd hoped you wouldn't notice.'

He laughed.

'We don't have to watch football,' I said.

'He can't stay up that late, anyway,' Patricia said. She slid down on the couch next to my father, putting her arms around him.

'I'm getting old,' he said. 'I can't stay up late any more and then I'm up all night pissing, anyway, because my prostate is shot.'

I tried to smile, but couldn't.

'When you get old,' he told me, 'your prostate is the first thing to go.'

'You're getting better,' our father's girlfriend said.

'Old,' he said again. He looked at her. 'Old is worse, not better.'

'Then I'm old, too,' she said.

I could hear a dog barking somewhere.

I imagined our mother, truly old, talking in the dark of her bedroom to the ghost of her daughter.

Katherine Jane DeQuincey-Joy pulled her VW Rabbit into a parking space in front of the East Meadow County Library and sat for a moment, the engine idling, asking herself if she really wanted to do this. What was the expression? Opening a whole new can of worms. She imagined twisting the can opener and the wiggling, squiggling mass of earthworms oozing out on to a clean kitchen counter. A person's brain, she thought, did not look unlike a mass of worms. And it was her job, at least in a manner of speaking, to open her clients' brains, unraveling the wiggling, squiggly, twisted mass of thoughts and emotions that made their lives – our lives – so complicated and unhappy. She turned the engine off and examined the building while she finished the already cold styrofoam cup of lemon tea she had bought at the 7 Eleven on the way. The library was white, modern, with large two-story-high slits of glass to let light in. The little institution was encircled by trees and the parking lot and patch of grass surrounding it hadn't been swept or raked all season.

Katherine opened the car door. It was a Sunday and she wore old blue jeans and a soft, gray sweater she'd had since college. She closed the car door solidly and walked across the leaf-strewn parking lot in the wet November air. It had been a mild winter so far. Some rain, but nothing very cold yet.

This was a new library, built within the last five years. She wondered if they even had records of newspapers from twenty years ago. Opening the glass doors, she saw across an expanse of gray institutional carpeting to the stacks of books – just metal shelves with wire dividers. It was early – the place had just opened at ten – but already the children's nook was filled with toddlers and their young mothers, women Katherine's age, women whose lives had gone as planned, women whose lives had had plans to begin with. She scanned the room for the periodicals. She hadn't been in a public library for so long it was almost embarrassing, since graduate school, really. Behind the librarian's desk was a double entrance marked, *Reference*. She'd start there. She walked up to the long-haired man at the counter and asked, 'Do you keep microfilm of old newspapers here?'

'We have a complete record of the *East Meadow Gazette*,' he said, with a hint of apology in his voice. He was in his early twenties, with a blond beard and a soft voice. 'And we have the *New York Times* on computer via the internet.'

'Can I take a look?'

'Sure thing,' he said. 'Follow me.' The young man led Katherine through the double doors and into a white utilitarian room with rows of metal computer desks. 'One of these days,' he said, 'we'll have everything on computer.' He laughed. 'And then I won't have a job any more.' He indicated which desk she should take by pulling out a chair for her and gesturing. He must have been a waiter, Katherine thought. 'I assume you're starting with the *Times*?' he said. 'May I ask what kind of thing you're researching?'

'I'm looking into a crime, one that was committed in East Meadow about twenty years ago.'

He put his hands on his hips. 'Was it a bad one? I mean, a famous one?'

'It was an abduction, just a little girl.'

'You'll want the *Gazette*.' He pointed to the microfilm machine in the corner, which looked as if it had never been used. 'I'm Edward, by the way. Do you know how it works?'

Katherine shook her head.

'Let me show you.' He pushed the plastic chair back under the computer desk and walked across the tile floor to the microfilm machine.

She sat down.

He showed her how to scan through the pages of the *East Meadow Gazette*, going all the way back to the year Fiona was taken, to the day of the last party at my parents' house. There was no index, no search button, only her eyes. She moved steadily to Labor Day of that year and scanned more carefully forward from that point in time. It would be a couple of days, she thought, before reporters would have learned of the abduction. She slipped the film forward a few pages, and there it was.

Girl Abducted from Foxwood Court, Reward Offered.

The article said exactly what Katherine expected it to say, indicating only enough information to provide a description of Fiona ('a sandy-haired seven-year-old, freckled, with green eyes') and little more.

The police, it said, were investigating.

Three days had passed since Fiona disappeared when this article was printed.

Three days since the party.

Katherine tried to imagine what each member of my family's mental state must have been after three days of not knowing, of waiting while the police conducted their search. She considered my father, who worked frantically with the detective, trying so hard to remember another detail, anything that might lead them to his daughter. She imagined Hannah, who crumbled into a mass of tears and grief, not to awaken from it for several years. She imagined Eric taking over the household, the oldest child stepping in. She saw him at the kitchen counter preparing food, making my lunches, learning to thrive on the stress.

She imagined me.

Three days after my sister had disappeared and Katherine imagined I would have been retreating. I would have been pretending to be the wolf boy by then, on my hands and knees, learning to crawl and growl. It was a common form of dissociation, actually, she thought, a typical childhood response to trauma, disappearing into fantasy, escaping into the realm of make-believe.

It was true.

And what if I was right – this thought had flickered across her mind more than once by now. What if my brother had killed Fiona? Disappearing into a fantasy may have been the result of a more practical concern.

I may have been hiding, Katherine realized.

I may have been afraid for my life.

Before moving on, she scanned the article again, looking for any detail, any image or word that, twenty years later, would seem out of place. Fiona was 'taken', the article said. The girl was 'last seen by the family around mid-evening'. She had 'no history of running away'.

There was a cloudy black and white picture of my sister in the corner of the article, more difficult to make out because of the heavy contrast in the microfilm. 'The missing child, Fiona Hannah Airie,' the caption said, 'seven years old.' She counted the years for a moment, imagining all that time going by – a life. She spooled the microfilm forward, day by day, scanning the headlines as she went. An ad appeared, paid for by the newspaper, no doubt. It had a picture of Fiona, different from the one used in the article, more evident in the microfilm. It was a class picture of a second-grader, all big teeth and freckles. Our family had offered a reward of twenty thousand dollars, a great deal of money in those days. On the following day, a larger article appeared. It was the Sunday edition, the human interest version. There were pictures of our whole family, with Fiona s face circled and highlighted. It described the party, the night she disappeared. 'At an ordinary Labor Day barbecue in Foxwood Court', the copy began, 'a little girl disappeared. She was a seven-year-old much loved by family and friends.' This article identified a 'suspect', a man seen talking with Fiona at the party by 'one of the Airie boys', a man who seemed to have disappeared around the same time she did. The article did not give the man's name.

What was the name Eric had told her? Katherine couldn't remember. Had she written it down?

The suspect had been brought in for questioning, it said. But nothing had been determined. A single piece of evidence had been located in the woods behind the Airie house. The article didn't say what it was, but Katherine knew it was the red sneaker. It didn't say that I had found it, either. It hardly mentioned Eric and me at all, except to list our names in the caption of the family photo. James Airie, our father, was a handsome man, Katherine thought – like Eric. He looked exactly like him, in fact. Our mother didn't look that much different to Katherine then than she did now. Not as thick around the middle, perhaps. But she had the same cloudy eyes, the same faraway gaze.

It was a look Katherine recognized in me.

Finally, in another piece two days later, the paper identified the detective. It was the name Eric had given her. Detective Gerald Cleveland. He even sounded like a cop. 'In comments to the press,' this little news item said, 'Detective Cleveland indicated there have been advancements in the case but nothing definitive. "We have not yet resolved whether Fiona Airie was abducted and is presently alive somewhere or if she was killed."'

Katherine wondered if Fiona had been kept alive up to this point. Was she tortured before she was killed? There were cases of abduction, she knew, when the trauma actually led to a complete loss of memory. Fiona could be alive somewhere, not even aware of the first seven years of her life. It had happened before. But where would the little girl have been taken? And by whom?

Behind her, Edward, the young librarian, stuck his head in the door. Katherine could see his reflection in the glass of the microfilm machine.

'Everything going all right in there?'

She realized now she'd been in here for more than an hour.

'Perfectly,' Katherine said. 'Thank you.'

She moved forward in time again, going day by day through the weeks that followed. Only small items about the case appeared now. Katherine had to replace the scrolls of microfilm several times. Eventually, though, nearly a year from the day my sister was taken, an article announced that a memorial service was to be held in her honor. It wasn't long after that, Katherine knew, that I had my first episode of psychosis. It was more likely a case of severe dissociation, she thought, probably misdiagnosed.

I had forgotten how to speak. I had been discovered eating raw steak on the kitchen floor.

Katherine pictured Hannah and my father, me and Eric, all of us standing at the front of the town Presbyterian church, our neighbors and the community behind us, the lawyers and dentists and insurance salesmen of East Meadow, their wives and children, and possibly even the person who abducted my sister.

Eric stood on the flagstones by the filled-in pool and considered the things our mother had planted that summer – the rhubarb, red beets, parsnips and russet potatoes. These were fall vegetables, food that should have been reaped and stored away for winter by now. The garden was overgrown, though, untended since Hannah's blindness, and the vegetables were rotting in the hardening earth. He sighed. He'd have to come out here himself one of these days and tear everything up before a frost came and made it impossible. He remembered the pool here before it had been filled in, the water in the summers, the light flashing across its surface, blue and gold. Across the lawn, next door, were the new neighbors. Their two girls – what were their names? – just six or seven years old, squealed and screeched as they ran around together playing some convoluted imaginary game. They'd sit quietly for a few moments and touch each other's hair, and then they'd leap up, shrieking, their voices like whistles. It always startled Eric to hear children playing. Especially girls. It sounded to him like they were being hurt.

Like someone was after them.

Like what happened to Fiona. Only she didn't scream, did she? Or someone would have heard.

'What are they doing?' It was our mother's voice behind him. Eric turned around and saw Hannah standing on the patio by the kitchen door. She wore her yellow robe and soft moccasins. Her gray-laced chestnut hair was in disarray.

'What?'

'Those girls, why are they screaming?'

The two little girls actually stopped what they were doing for a moment and looked at Hannah. She was the crazy old lady next door, my brother thought – a fearful, timid thing, seldom seen.

'They're just playing, Mom.' Eric smiled in the girls' direction. 'Just playing.'

'What are *you* doing out there?' It was an accusation.

'I'm not doing anything.' He began to walk toward the house, his shoes making stiff sounds on the slate. 'I'll have to come out here and take care of this garden for you one of these days, that's all.'

'I haven't been able to—'

'I know, Mom,' he said, 'it's all right.'

'—do anything around the house. I haven't been—'

He walked up the steps to the kitchen door where she stood, and he lowered his voice. 'How is your vision? How is it today?'

'Non-existent,' our mother told him. 'All blurs and swirls.'

'I made an appointment for you,' Eric said.

'Another neurologist? Another ophthalmologist?' This was derisive, sneering. She had been through two cycles of antibiotics.

'A psychiatrist.' She moved from the door, and Eric slipped by her. 'Close the door, Mom,' he said. 'It's getting cold.'

She saw Fiona rising from the side of the pool in a flash of sunlight. Hannah shut the door quietly, knowing this was not possible, knowing this was winter, the pool was a garden now. She began to shake. 'I'm not going to take anything.'

'What do you mean?'

'I won't take any medication. Not from you.'

'Mom,' Eric said. 'What are you talking about?'

They were in her yellow-teapot kitchen. She shuffled across the tile floor, hands exploring the air in front of her, until she reached the counter. She placed her hand flat and turned to face her oldest son. Her blindness was so great today that she couldn't find the eyes in his face. It was just a smear of pink. 'What did you give to him?' she said.

'What did I—'

'You know what I mean,' she said, her voice a bit louder, shaking. 'What did you give to him? To Pilot?'

'Mom.' Eric's voice was going up in pitch, his throat closing. 'Pilot's on anti-psychotics. I wouldn't give him anything—'

'What did you give him?'

'Mom,' Eric said, 'what are you talking about?'

She reached for the stove and grabbed the kettle off the burner. She moved to the sink and filled it with water. 'I'm having tea,' she said unsteadily. 'Do you want some?'

Eric sat down at the kitchen table, put his elbows on his knees and his hands together. 'Mom,' he said, 'come on.'

Hannah was crying, just a couple of tears running down her face. She heard the two girls squealing next door. Our mother thought she heard her own daughter out there with them. Could they see her, too? Could those little girls be playing with Fiona? 'You gave him something,' she said. 'I know you did.'

'How could I do that', he said, 'and what on earth would I give him?'

Hannah put the kettle back on the stove and lit the burner. 'I don't know what you gave him exactly,' she said. 'How would I know?'

Eric sighed. 'My whole family has gone nuts,' he said to himself. Then, to Hannah, 'Take it easy, Mom, all right?'

'I know,' she said. 'I know I'm nuts.'

The two of them waited for the water to boil, waited while the little girls next door played in shrill, high-pitched delight. When the kettle whistled, too, it was almost indistinguishable from the siren whistle of those little girls.

Hannah said, 'Honey, do you want some tea?'

'Oh, Mom,' Eric said to her, but not really to her.

At the base of her optic nerve the little cancer cells divided and multiplied, the mathematics of death mounting against her.

* * *

Where did it begin? Was it something inside her? Or was it something inside Eric? Did he look away when he told her how he felt? Did his eyes dial left, even a single notch, when he said that he loved her? Or did his pulse flutter the wrong way? Did it fail to flutter? Doubt begins like a single cell, then splits and multiplies and enlarges exponentially until it is a question. And a question, no matter how absurd – *Consider these: is there a God? Did Eric kill Fiona?* – implies belief.

In doubt there is faith.

Katherine was starting to believe me.

For some reason, this question had been pressing. For some reason, the telephone felt cold against her ear. 'I was wondering if I could speak to a detective,' Katherine said. 'I don't even know if he works there any more. His name is Cleveland.'

'Please hold.'

Katherine sat at her desk at the clinic and waited with the cold phone to her ear while the police receptionist put her through. There was also the thin, barely audible drone of a radio announcer on the line. The announcer's voice was smooth and steady, but coming from so faraway she could barely make it out. 'This is Detective Vettorello,' a young man's voice said finally. 'How can I help you?'

'Actually, I was holding for Detective Cleveland.'

There was a slight pause during which the radio announcer announced the next record, something by the Staple Singers. 'Detective Cleveland. Um, Detective Cleveland has retired,' the man said. 'Quite a while ago. Perhaps there's something I can help you with?'

Katherine cleared her throat. 'Well,' she said, 'it's about a case that Detective Cleveland worked on many years ago, and I'm not sure if—'

'Are you a reporter, ma'am?'

'No,' Katherine said. 'No, I'm not.'

'What case?'

'It was an abduction case, many years ago, as I said, here in East Meadow, a little girl named Fiona Airie was—'

There was a sound of paper shuffling on the detective's end. There was faraway laughter. There was something going by on squeaky wheels, a mail cart, Katherine imagined. 'How many years ago did you say that was, ma'am?'

Katherine said, 'About twenty.'

'That's *way* before my time,' Detective Vettorello said, laughing. She could hear those wheels squeaking again. Perhaps it was his chair moving around the tiled floor. 'I have to ask, though, ma'am, why you are interested in this case.'

'I think I may have some new evidence.' She hardly believed it herself.

'You have evidence for a case that's twenty years old.' Obviously, he didn't believe her at all.

'Maybe,' Katherine said. 'Well, a piece of it, anyway.'

'What's your name again?'

'Katherine DeQuincey-Joy.'

'Very nice.'

'Thank you.' Now there was a noise. At her door, she could see that Elizabeth was motioning. Someone was waiting outside. Katherine tried to wave her away. Whatever it was, it could wait.

'I'll have to check into that,' the police detective said. 'What was the kid's name again, the one that was—'

'Fiona Airie,' Katherine repeated. Elizabeth was making a face at her. 'Elizabeth,' Katherine said, 'whatever it is can—'

The door was pushed open from behind her and Eric walked in.

'Hello, Katherine,' he said.

'Eric.' Katherine held up a finger, indicating that he should hold on a moment. Had he heard her use Fiona's name? 'I'll have to call you back.'

'Miss DeQuincey-Joy,' the detective said, 'if I can just get your num—'

'Really,' Katherine said. 'I'll call back. I have to go.' She put the phone down softly. Had Eric heard her?

He was standing over her desk. 'Who was that?'

Katherine tried to smile. 'Nothing important.'

235

Eric slumped down on the hideous brown couch. He put his face in his hands.

'What's wrong?'

'Everything.'

'What do you mean?'

'My brother and now my mother.'

'Your brother's out of your hair,' Katherine said. 'At least for the moment.'

'How did all of this happen?' Eric looked at the ceiling.

Was that it? The look up, the eyes casting about for answers?

Katherine got up from her desk and sat down beside him on the couch. She put her arm over his shoulders. 'I really think Pilot is much better now.' She wasn't sure if she was lying or not. She wasn't sure about anything.

Eric sighed. 'Now my mother is crazy, too, and she won't take anything for it.'

'They can't figure out what's wrong?'

'Nothing's wrong with her. It's entirely psychosomatic.'

'Will she see a psychiatrist?'

He shook his head.

She allowed a moment to pass. 'I have a patient coming.'

'I want to see you.' He put his hand on her leg. 'I want to see you tonight.'

Katherine hesitated. 'It's just that—'

'What?' Eric said. 'It's just that what?'

'I'm awfully tired, that's all.'

Eric stared at her. Katherine could see that he was on the edge of something, that he was barely – just slightly – disheveled. 'It's my family, right? You think we're all crazy.' His tie wasn't pulled perfectly into his collar. His jacket was ever so slightly wrinkled.

'Come on, Eric.' From where she was sitting, Katherine could see the shoelace on top of her desk. She got up from the couch, went over to it and slipped it into her hand, closing her fingers around it tightly. 'I really have to get to work,' she said. 'Paperwork, you know, and I have a lot of—'

'It's OK, I'm going.' Eric smiled. 'Have you spoken to the, to the police yet?'

Katherine lied again. 'No.'

'Are you going to call them?'

'I've been thinking about it,' she said. 'And I'm starting to think that you're, that you were right about that. I think Pilot's just delusional and it would only upset him to find out that his evidence was, was—'

'Not real?' Eric smiled. He rose from the couch, moving toward her. 'Just out of curiosity, can I see the shoelace?'

'Oh,' Katherine said, 'turns out it was in my purse and I left that one at home.'

Eric nodded. His eyes flickered to the window. 'Just throw it away, I guess.'

'I will,' she said. 'But—'

'But what?'

'What should I tell Pilot I did with it?'

'How is he?' my mother asked.

'He's the same and getting more and more like the old man and the sea.' We were talking about my father. I paced the tiles in Patricia's kitchen. Whenever I got on the phone, she and my father fell silent in the living room.

Hannah spoke into the black rotary-dial. 'Tell him I said hello. Patricia, too.'

'How are you, Mom?'

'I'm fine.'

'Your eyes?'

'Better, I think.'

'Really?'

She was quiet for a moment, and then she said, 'I spoke to your brother.'

'And?'

Again, silence.

'What did he say, Mom?'

'How are you, Pilot?'

'I'm better,' I said. 'Completely.'

'He's acting strange.'

'What do you mean?'

'I don't know. There's something, though. I don't know what it is.'

Patricia walked into the kitchen, an apologetic look on her face. 'Mom,' I said. 'I have to go.'

'Call me soon.'

'You know I will.'

In third grade Katherine had told her friends that her mother was a movie star. In junior high she had contrived a mysterious skin condition to escape the indignities of gym class. Sometimes – no, *often* – she'd had to fake her orgasms with Mark, moaning convincingly into his ear. But every time she lied, even when someone was just asking what she thought of an ugly sweater, Katherine became all too aware of her own face, of her own hands, of her own movements, awkward and telling. Did she feel the same awkwardness with Eric, the same tightness in the mouth, the dampness of the palms? Did she know where to put her hands? Did Katherine know where to look?

But this time, this lying – was innocent. Lying to a liar, it seemed, was a form of telling the truth. Or at least a way of getting at it.

Now, Katherine told herself, someone else was lying, too. It was either the crazy one – me – or the sane one – my brother. It has to be one of us.

And it was.

And it was becoming more and more difficult to tell which of us was the crazy one.

She stood at the window in her office and waited for Mrs Kelleher, her next patient, to arrive. Is Pilot delusional? she asked herself. Is Eric a murderer? She went to the phone and buzzed Dr Lennox on the intercom. 'Do you have a minute?' she said. 'It's Kather – it's Kate.' She put the phone on speaker, so she could keep her hands free.

'Half a minute,' Dr Lennox's voice said. She heard some movement, then he said, 'What is it?'

'Is there a drug that can *make* someone psychotic?'

'All kinds of drugs.' She could hear the insincere, condescending smile on his face.

'But is there one that reproduces the symptoms of schizophrenia exactly?'

'That's sort of what LSD was meant to do, but it didn't work out.'

'One that lasts longer than a day.'

A hiss of static. Then, 'I'm not sure what you're getting at, Kate.'

'Let me put it this way.' Katherine put her hands flat on the surface of her desk and leaned toward the telephone. Her fingertips were getting bloodier and bloodier, having reached a state of permanent irritation. She was trying not to chew them. But it was automatic. 'If I wanted to make someone seem crazy,' she said, 'if I wanted them to *go* crazy, without them knowing, how would I do it – if I had to use drugs?'

'I'd find a way to increase the levels of dopamine in their brain,' Dr Lennox said.

'How could you do that?'

'A big shot of dopamine would do very nicely.' That smile was coming through the phone.

'No shots.'

'Major doses of amphetamine might do it, too. In pill form.'

'Amphetamines. But you'd be able to tell someone was on something. I mean, wouldn't there be other indications?'

'There would,' the psychiatrist said. There was a pause, a crackling sound coming through the phone, telling her she was on the speaker in Dr Lennox's office, too. 'Anyway, Kate, I'm in a meeting right now. Can this wait until later?'

'Oh,' Katherine said, 'of course it can. I didn't realize—'

'As a matter of fact, Dr Airie and I were just going over some medication schedules. Perhaps he can help you.'

Katherine sat back in her chair.

'Hello, Katherine.'

'Eric,' she said weakly. 'Well, sorry to interrupt you guys. Talk to you later.' She pressed the hang-up button on the intercom. She felt the skin of her face tightening across her skull. She felt her neck getting hot, her palms sweating.

There was a knock. 'Katherine,' Elizabeth said through the door, 'Mrs Kelleher is here.' It was her next appointment – Mrs Kelleher and her control issues. Mrs Kelleher and her obsessive need to clean. Mrs Kelleher, Katherine thought just now, who could not be helped.

'All right,' Katherine said. 'OK.'

'I'm really sorry about hanging up on you like that,' she said into the phone. 'It was—' and she paused. 'Anyway, it was very important.'

'That's all right,' the detective said. 'Where were we?'

'I was about to give you my number.' Katherine watched the door. For some reason, she expected Eric to burst through at any moment, accusing her of deceit, his finger pointing. 'My name is Katherine DeQuincey-Joy, as I said, and I'm a psychologist with the In-Patient Clinic here in East Meadow.' The door didn't move, of course. She turned to the window and looked at the trees across the highway. They weren't going to move, either, were they? Katherine was beginning to feel things the way I was feeling them. I was getting inside her.

'The information you're using,' he asked, 'does it come from a confidential meeting?'

'I have permission from my client to go to the police.'

'Your client . . . he's—'

'The official diagnosis is schizophrenia,' Katherine said.

'That's a type of psychosis, correct?'

'Yes.'

'A word of advice, ma'am.' Vettorello cleared his throat. 'You might want to get that permission in writing.'

Katherine sighed.

'And what's the number?'

She gave him her number at the office.

'Fine,' he said. 'And the little girl's name again, the one who was taken—'

'Fiona Airie,' Katherine said.

'Just making sure I got it right the first time.' Something on Detective Vettorello's end of the line made that squeaking noise again, like little wheels that needed oil. 'Fiona Airie,' he said slowly. 'Interesting name.'

'It's Scottish, I think.' Katherine was losing patience. 'How long before you'll be able to look into this?'

'Well,' he said, 'those are pretty old files, which means they're upstate in the house of records. Could take a couple of weeks.'

'But I have new evidence.'

'Is it physical evidence or testimony or—'

'It's a shoelace.'

'A shoelace.' The detective allowed a moment to pass. Was he laughing? 'You'll have to come down here and show me what you've got, anyway,' he said. 'If it's evidence that could change things I can re-open the case based on it. I mean, once I look at the case files and see how it all fits together. Otherwise—'

'There's no way I can speak to Detective Cleveland?'

'Detective Cleveland is retired.'

'Because he would know,' Katherine said, 'without having to look, he would—'

'I'm not even sure if he lives around here any more, Mrs DeQuincey.'

'DeQuincey-Joy, with a hyphen.'

'Sorry.'

Katherine said, 'When can I come to see you, then?'

'You want to come by first thing in the morning?' the detective said. 'I'll buy you a coffee.'

Once again she was sure it was the pizza guy. Walking in, Eric said, 'You think I did it, don't you?' He stepped into her little living room, a vein bulging on his temple. 'You think I killed my sister and that I drugged my brother to make him go insane.' His voice was shaking. My brother's eyes were everywhere but on Katherine.

He had the posture of a man who couldn't believe what was happening. He had the look of an innocent man.

'Come on.' Katherine shook her head. 'I don't think anything of the sort.'

'Then tell me why you're asking Dr Lennox those questions about, about—'

'Eric,' Katherine said, 'I have to find these things out for Pilot. He's my client. He asked me these questions and I have to provide him with the answers, all right? As a doctor you should understand that. Of course you didn't drug your brother. That's ridiculous. I have to prove it to Pilot, though, OK? He's a smart guy. He'll know if I'm telling the truth or if I'm just feeding him a line of bullshit.'

Eric shook his head. 'Pilot is paranoid,' he said flatly, dismissively. 'Schizophrenic.'

'I know he is, Eric. I mean, well – he's paranoid, anyway.' And almost more as an aside, she said, 'Schizophrenic I'm not so sure about. Besides.' Katherine walked up to him, placing a calming hand on his chest, unbuttoning the top button of his overcoat. 'Don't you think I trust you? Haven't I demonstrated that by now?' She kissed his chin. She gave him her most imploring expression. She could feel something inside her recoiling from the lie, like an animal backing away from a trap.

'Did you go to the police yet?'

'I've decided to take your advice,' she said, 'and when Pilot gets back I'll ask him to produce the whole shoe or the knife or whatever he says he has, and if he can – which I doubt – then I'll go to the police, and only then.' She rubbed his shoulder. 'OK? Is that all right?'

Eric let out a breath. 'All right.'

'Plus,' she said smiling, 'I don't really feel like tracking down some old crotchety detective.'

Still wearing his gray overcoat, he walked away from Katherine, sat down on her mattress and put his hand to his forehead. 'It's not that I don't want you to help Pilot,' Eric said, 'because I do. I really do. It's just that you don't have any idea what it would do to my mother to open up all those things again. They'd have to question her all over again, you know, about what happened. I don't think she could take it.'

'I know.'

'She'd lose it completely.'

'How is she?'

He looked at the ceiling, hands back on the bed. 'The weird thing is, she doesn't seem to mind going blind.' He was shaking his head in disbelief. He closed his eyes against the overhead light.

'Is she actually losing her eyesight? I mean, is she—'

'She says things are very blurry. She can't really get around outside of the house any more. She goes out into the yard, you know, and that's about as far as she can make it. She can't drive. She can't even take a walk in the neighborhood.'

'Any luck in convincing her to see a psychiatrist?'

He shook his head.

'Does she know Dr Lennox?'

'I think she does, actually.'

'Maybe she'd talk to him.'

There was someone at the door, and this time it *was* the pizza guy.

'You like black olives?' she asked Eric.

'Do you have any wine to go with it?'

'Sorry, only water.' Katherine paid for the pizza, put it on the floor and sat down, legs folded.

He looked around at the small empty room. 'When are you going to get furniture?'

Katherine laughed. 'What was he like?'

'Who?'

'Detective Cleveland. What was he like, do you remember?'

'He was a detective, you know. Not that smart.'

'Rumpled overcoat, skinny black tie, used the word *situation* a lot?'

'Something like that.'

'Was he nice?'

Eric said, 'I don't remember him being especially nice. He was black.'

'Do you remember if Pilot liked him?'

'What are you getting at?'

'I'm thinking that Pilot may have manufactured this new evidence because he wants to, because he wants to reconnect with the past, you know what I mean? I have a feeling what he's doing is trying to bring, to bring Fiona back somehow. He wants the search to keep going.'

'That actually makes sense.' Eric was sitting across from her now, still in his overcoat, eating a slice of greasy pizza. He seemed placated for the moment. Maybe she wasn't such a bad liar after all. Or maybe the Airie family was rubbing off on her. She felt that thing inside her, deep in the chest, slipping deeper in. The way to get good at lying, she realized, was by surrounding herself with liars.

And when they went to bed together that night Katherine closed her eyes and saw those imaginary photographs of Fiona that I carry around in my head. She could almost hear the shutter click. She saw a little girl standing against the background of a bright blue, shimmering pool, wearing a red bathing suit and red lace-up tennis shoes. Katherine saw Fiona's eyes glinting red and silver in the glare of the camera flash. She saw the woods in the background, and did she see them moving almost imperceptibly closer to Fiona, the shadows encroaching? Eric slid his large hand behind Katherine's back, reaching, it seemed, inside her, touching that thing inside her, something alive, and the pushing, insistent motion he made, the hips thrusting up, hers pushing down, made Katherine imagine a knife being thrust with the same motion into Fiona's little-girl body, somewhere deep in those woods, the party torches flickering yellow in the distance of the yard. Katherine saw the earth turning up as if under a plow. Katherine saw Fiona being buried somewhere, placed inside the earth. She felt Eric's sinewy, brain-surgeon hands pulling her closer to him as he thrust himself again and again into her, and she saw those hands, as I have seen them so many times, cupping the dirt into the grave of my sister.

And Katherine came. She came thinking of this little girl's body being covered by a last handful of blackness, and the sound Katherine made when she came was a very soft one, a very small one, the same sound she might have made if a long knife had been going into her and there was no use screaming.

Sometimes I'll be driving or watching a baseball game or doing anything and I remember her. I remember her from some vantage point I never knew I had. I'll see her from above, for instance, our whole family together – at the lake, maybe, the picnic blanket spread out, our mother making sandwiches. Sometimes I just see her face, wide open, a slight smile telling me her emotions. Sometimes I see her from the woods, a little girl worming her way through all those adults crowded on to the flagstones. Or I see her in her bed, face turned to the side, cheek squashed against the pillow, eyes shut tight, and I just want to lean over and wake her up.

In the large, empty parking lot of the East Meadow County Police Headquarters, Katherine used a pair of old nail clippers she kept in her purse to cut the shoelace in half. She didn't want to give Detective Vettorello the whole thing because she knew she wouldn't be getting it back. So she put one half of the shoelace in her purse, then she placed the other half in the glove compartment. She took a deep breath. She was nervous, evidently, although even she couldn't understand why. The police had always made her nervous. Katherine opened the door and lifted herself out, then walked steadily toward the double glass doors of the suburban institutional building.

Before entering, she smoothed the fabric of her skirt and made sure she didn't have too much hair in her face.

Inside, she was greeted by a long empty corridor lined with unmarked doors. To her left, a single receptionist, a heavy girl no older than twenty-one, sat at a tidy counter. 'Can I help you, miss?' she said.

It was eight in the morning. Katherine hoped she wasn't here too early. 'I'm here to meet with Detective Vettorello,' she said. She smiled at the receptionist, who had a ring through her eyebrow.

'One minute,' the receptionist said, her finger poised in the air. With her other hand, the receptionist dialed an extension and waited. Then she said into the phone, 'There's someone here to see you, Dave – someone very attractive.' Smiling, she held her finger up at Katherine, a gesture that meant *Wait, don't go until I say*.

'Katherine DeQuincey-Joy,' Katherine said.

'Katherine DeQuincey-Joy?' The receptionist put the phone down. 'It's six doors down on the right,' she said. 'There's a big room and he sits right in the middle of it. He's the goofy-looking guy – you can't miss him.'

'Goofy,' Katherine said. She turned away and walked down the corridor, her heels clacking on the green tiles. When she was halfway down the hall, a door opened and a big man with short, dark hair and bad skin came forward to greet her.

'Miss DeQuincey-Joy?'

'Hi,' Katherine said. 'You must be—'

'Detective Vettorello.' He offered his hand. 'Dave Vettorello. Come on in.' He led her into a large room filled with cubicles. Only a few people were there and they mostly seemed to be eating breakfast. Over his shoulder, Detective Vettorello asked, 'Did you, did you bring the evidence?'

'I did.' Still walking, she reached into her purse and pulled it out. 'It's only half a shoelace, really.'

'Half a shoelace?' Detective Vettorello stopped. He was a large man, built like a football lineman, with broad shoulders and a gut that protruded over his belt. He wore a blue short-sleeved shirt. His wool tie, in black and white stripes, hung outward over his stomach, the skinny end longer than the short end. He took the shoelace and held it up in front of his pink, acned face. 'This thing is over twenty years old?'

'Something like that.'

'It was cut recently.' He brushed his finger over the newly cut end.

She nodded. 'That's the way it was given to me.'

The detective continued to lead Katherine into his drab, brown cubicle. It was orderly and unkempt at the same time, with tattered bits of paper stuck everywhere and little notes written to himself on yellow and pink stickies. The big man sat down hard on a small, squeaky task chair. He pulled another one forward for Katherine. 'Sit down,' he said, 'please.' When she sat, she heard the squeaking of the wheels just like she had heard over the telephone. 'I'm still waiting for those files to come from Albany, you know, but they're on order, and I talked to a few of the older guys about this case, guys who knew Cleveland, and they told me they had a suspect back then, a known sex offender—'

'Bryce Telliman,' Katherine said. She had asked me for his name.

'You know his name?'

'He was the man accused of abducting the little girl, Fiona—'

'—Airie, right,' Vettorello said. 'They just couldn't find enough evidence to make anything stick.'

'He was a sex offender?'

'He had been arrested once before, apparently, for soliciting an undercover officer in a public restroom.'

Katherine sighed. 'You guys have got to stop arresting people for that.'

'Yeah,' Vettorello said, laughing. 'I know.' He held the time-blackened shoelace up to his face again. 'The truth is', he said, 'I'm not sure what the heck to do with this thing.'

'Can't you match it to the original evidence?'

'The evidence is probably long gone,' he said. 'There will be pictures of it, sure, but we won't be able to match it except by sight.'

'What about testing it for blood or DNA?'

'Oh, I don't know,' Vettorello said. 'It's so old.' He looked at it. 'And I can't see anything on it. I mean, it looks like it could be twenty years old all right, but a shoelace like this could come from anywhere.' He contorted his face. 'And the fact that your patient is psychotic—'

'Pilot had a psychotic episode. He's not psychotic. In fact, he's very much improved.'

'Well,' Vettorello said, 'it still doesn't make it any easier getting people to take him seriously, you know what I mean?' Vettorello dropped the shoelace into a little plastic bag. 'But it's not up to me.' He sealed the little bag with his huge, stubby fingers.

'Whose decision is it?'

'It has to go up the chain of command.' The detective smiled, pointing to the ceiling. 'But', he said, 'I'll send it over to the lab and ask them what they can figure out about it.'

'There's more coming,' Katherine said. She realized that this was just teasing him, but she wanted to be taken seriously.

'What's that?'

'Pilot says there's more.'

'More?'

'More evidence. He claims to have the shoe that goes with the shoelace and also, he says, a bloody knife.'

'A bloody knife?' Vettorello laughed. 'Now we're talking.'

'But Pilot is, he's away right now, visiting his father, and I have no way of finding these things without him.'

'So,' Vettorello said, 'right now we'll just see what we can find out about this shoelace.'

Katherine worried that Vettorello's good-natured smile was designed to humor her – the way Dr Lennox smiled at everyone, vague and deceitful – but she smiled back. 'I have to get to work.'

'I'm sure you do,' Vettorello said, his chair squeaking loudly. 'A lot of crazies out there.'

I sat in my father's living room and watched old movies with Patricia, dutifully taking my medication as indicated. She'd bring me a glass of orange juice, in fact, whenever it was time, a nervous smile on her face. I tried to imagine her with children, but I couldn't. She was someone's girlfriend. Even at forty-five or however old she was, Patricia had the look of a girl you take to a restaurant, the one who will go home with you, not the one you go home to. 'Thank you,' I said, taking the glass of juice and reaching across the coffee table for the plastic amber bottle with the child-resistant cap. Her face asked me how I was feeling. But I turned to the television, not answering.

Outside, there were palm trees, long fronds drooping over the warm Florida winter.

Later, Katherine dialed the listing she had found in the white pages for Gerald and Carla Cleveland. It rang for a few moments, and just as she was about to hang up an older woman's voice came on the line and said brightly, 'Carla speaking.'

'Hello,' Katherine said, almost startled. 'May I speak to Gerald Cleveland, please?'

'May I ask who's calling?'

'My name is Katherine DeQuincey-Joy.'

'One minute, please, Miss Joy,' the woman said pleasantly. Katherine heard her put the telephone down and then the words, 'It's your mistress.'

Now a man's voice came on the line. 'Hello.'

'Detective Cleveland?'

'Used to be Detective,' he laughed. 'Now I'm just Jerry.'

'My name is Katherine DeQuincey-Joy,' Katherine said. 'I'm, uh, I'm—'

'We really can't buy anything, Miss Joy, I'm sorry—'

'Oh, I'm not trying to sell anything.' Katherine laughed. 'I'm a psychologist.'

'A psychologist? It's a psychologist.'

'Yes,' Katherine said, 'and I wanted to ask you about a case, one you had a long time ago.'

'A case? Oh, I'm completely retired from police work—'

'I know,' Katherine said. 'That's what they told me at the station, but I have a patient who, it turns out, has been withholding evidence for over twenty years, evidence you should have had, and I thought you might like to know about it.'

Katherine heard a long, sad sigh. 'What case was it?'

'There was a little girl named Fiona Airie. She was abducted. Do you—'

Jerry Cleveland cleared his throat. 'Oh, yes,' he said. 'I remember her very well.'

'Do you remember the details of the case, sir?'

'Yes,' he said, 'yes I do.'

'My patient is Pilot Airie,' Katherine said. 'Fiona's brother. Do you remember that he found one of her tennis shoes in the woods?'

'The sneaker, I remember. The boy found the sneaker in the woods.'

'And no one could recover the other one.'

'Never found it, no.'

Katherine turned to the window. There they were, the treetops rustling in the fall breeze. 'Pilot claims to have the other sneaker.'

'Says he's got the other one?'

'And a knife,' Katherine said. 'A bloody knife.'

'That kind of evidence would have made all the difference back then,' Cleveland said, laughing. 'All the difference.'

'I was wondering if I could meet with you,' Katherine said, 'talk about the case. My patient is, is a very troubled person. He had a psychotic episode recently and a lot of his thoughts are very, well, they're disorderly.'

'I can imagine.'

Just at that moment, Dr Lennox popped his head in Katherine's door. 'Kate,' he said smiling, 'I have some possible answers to your question from yesterday,' he said. 'You got a minute?'

Katherine held her finger up to Greg Lennox the same way the receptionist at the police station had done to her this morning. 'Can I speak to you later, Jerry?' Katherine said into the phone. 'I have a visitor right now.'

'Why don't you meet me at my office?' Cleveland said. 'Come by Sky Highway, the Oak Road Exit, 514. I'll be there all afternoon.'

'Terrific. I'll probably see you around four,' Katherine said, writing down his address. 'Is that OK?'

'Fine,' Cleveland said. 'Bye now.'

'Goodbye.' Katherine hung up.

Dr Lennox walked in. 'I hope I didn't interrupt anything important.'

Katherine smiled. 'No.'

'Anyway,' the psychiatrist said, 'there's a new drug. It's sort of a synthetic neurotoxin, not unlike some poisonous snake venoms. If you took enough of it at once, your neurological system would overload and you'd die. But if you took it in very small quantities over a period of time, it might cause your brain to sort of get excited, tense up, as it were. The result could be a psychotic reaction.'

'How do you get it?' Katherine asked.

'That's just it. It's used after certain kinds of brain surgery,' Dr Lennox told her. 'It kind of excites the brain back into action. And a clever brain surgeon – they're famous for their cleverness – could probably get his hands on some.' Dr Lennox put his hands behind his head. 'Dr Eric Airie, for instance.'

'How would it be administered?'

'Easy,' Dr Lennox said through a large smile. 'You could put it in someone's food.'

'Really?' Katherine said. 'In food?'

He nodded. 'There are probably other ways to do it.' Dr Lennox folded his legs, leaning back. 'But the thing about it is that the body produces something so similar naturally that it would never show up in a blood test. In fact, I don't think you could detect it at all unless you were specifically looking for it, and even then . . .'

'It would be difficult to detect.'

Lennox nodded. 'Extremely.'

I was outside an enormous discount book store in a strip mall, the kind where there would be nothing anyone would want to read. It was the only public telephone I could find anywhere. 'Katherine,' I said. 'It's me.' I had left my father's four-wheel drive idling at the curb with the door open.

'Pilot,' Katherine said, a bit surprised. 'Are you back?'

'No, I'm still in Florida,' I said. 'I just wanted to, just wanted to check in, you know, that's all, see how things—'. I stopped talking. A little boy with a blond crew cut waited for his mother outside the discount book store. He cupped his hands against the window and looked in, trying to locate her, I supposed. Wasn't she keeping an eye on him? Wasn't she watching him?

'I'm glad you called,' Katherine said. It was in the late afternoon, the time of day Katherine told me I could call because she didn't have any patients. 'How are you feeling?'

'Sane,' I told her. 'Completely, totally—'

'Have you been taking—'

'Yeah,' I answered, 'all the time.'

'That's good.'

'The shoelace?'

'I took it to the police.' I thought I could see Katherine turning in her chair, looking at the trees across the highway, the yellow winter light filtering through a smoggy sky. 'They're going to examine it.' She brought her finger to her mouth and bit on a tattered piece of skin.

'Really?' I was surprised.

'And they're having the files for the investigation sent down from Albany.'

'That's excellent.' I imagined the stack of police files being removed from a cardboard carton in a huge warehouse somewhere, someone placing them in a handcart and pushing a trolley into the mailroom.

'Are you enjoying yourself?' Katherine asked. 'Are you having a good time with your father?'

'Given the circumstances,' I said. 'Given that I'm watching football constantly and constantly fishing, and so forth.' This phone was an old one. There were profanities written all over it – threats, slanders, propositions.

Katherine laughed, then asked, 'Have you spoken to your mother lately?'

'I can call her from the house,' I said. 'She's the same. Still seeing ghosts.'

'And your brother?'

I let a moment pass by reading about the offers for sex written on the payphone. Then I said, 'No, I haven't talked to him in a while. Have you? I mean, besides sleeping with him.'

'Pilot,' Katherine said, letting it go, 'do you remember the policeman, the detective, his name was Detective Cleveland, who investigated your sister's—'

'I remember him.' I remembered a gray man in a gray suit with big gray features. I remembered the way he leaned down when he spoke to me, hands on his knees, the way he called me *son*. 'What about him?'

'I've contacted him,' she said. 'I want to ask him about the case, if there's anything that he remembers, if anything has been bothering him about it all these years.'

'Not a bad idea,' I told her. 'What does Eric think?'

'I just wanted to make sure it was OK with you.'

'It's just fine with me.'

The little blond boy's mother came out of the discount book store at this moment and said, 'Talbot, *comeer!*' The little boy went to her and she dragged him by the hand, never taking her eyes off me – a strange man at a public telephone in a strip mall.

I saw Talbot's eyes turn toward me, too, a look of dim realization passing over his small, toothy face.

'So,' Katherine said heavily – and, I thought, a bit distractedly – 'you've been feeling all right, then? No strange sensations? No voices? Nothing unusual?'

Hadn't I told her this? 'I'm perfectly sane, Katherine. There's nothing wrong. There's absolutely—'

'I have to ask you,' Katherine said. 'When you came back from California, was Eric around a lot?'

'Yeah,' I said, 'he was with me all the time, at my mother's.'

'Did he come over to your mother's for dinner?'

'Sometimes,' I said. 'But mostly he was there in the mornings.'

I noticed that this little boy, Talbot, was on the other side of the bookstore window now, cupping his hands and looking out at me through the glass. Evidently, I fascinated him.

I stuck my tongue out.

'Describe it,' Katherine said.

'What do you mean?'

'What would happen, generally, in the mornings when Eric came over?'

Talbot's mouth dropped open. His eyes grew wide.

'I'd wake up and Eric would be in the kitchen with our mother, making breakfast.'

'Did you eat anything?'

'Just coffee, mostly. Sometimes I'd let him make me some eggs.'

'Your mother—'

'—drinks tea,' I finished. 'Why?'

Katherine didn't answer, just as she didn't respond to my questions about Eric. 'Pilot,' Katherine said, 'how many pills are you taking right now? I mean, how many a day?'

'Three,' I said. 'But sometimes I miss one.'

'Do something for me,' she said. 'Reduce it by half. You can cut those pills in half, right?'

'Sure,' I said. 'They have a little notch in the middle.'

'From now on, take half a pill three times a day instead of three whole ones, all right?'

I realized how cold it was out here, even though it was Florida, and that I had forgotten to wear a jacket, and that there were few cars in the parking lot, and that the sky was more green than blue. 'OK,' I said. Talbot was making a funny face at me, stretching his mouth open with his fingers. Behind him, I could see his mother, a large-boned woman with mouse-brown hair, looking at whale calendars and *Star Trek* calendars. What month was it? I couldn't remember. I couldn't remember what month it was.

Jesus Christ, it was cold. Could I actually be in Florida? It was probably Blue Whale month. Or Klingon Battle Cruiser month.

'But if you start feeling strange,' said Katherine, 'if you start feeling at all unusual, hearing voices, seeing things, fearing things, then please go back to your regular dosage right away.'

'Fine,' I said. 'The medication just makes me groggy and stupid, anyway.'

'And call me.'

'Call you.'

'Pilot,' Katherine said, and I knew she was looking at her watch, 'I have to go now. But will you call me in a few days?'

'Of course I will,' I said. 'Don't worry about me.'

'It's my job to worry about you, Pilot.'

Talbot stuck his pink little tongue out at me from the other side of the glass. ''Bye, Katherine,' I said. I could see his tongue flattening against the window, touching the glass. I remembered the taste of glass from my childhood, the sooty, filmy sensation of my tongue on a window.

'Goodbye, Pilot.'

I hung up the phone, taking a step toward Talbot, and he panicked and ran to his mother. November, I think. It had to be November. But he had no reason to be afraid of me.

Katherine followed Jerry Cleveland's directions on to Sky Highway, scanning the numbers over the doorways. When she saw it, though, she thought she must have made a mistake. She pulled her sapphire-blue VW into the lot and looked around. Huge red, white and blue streamers hung from wires that had been strung across high poles. Everywhere were banners advertising amazing deals on pristine condition, previously owned, reconditioned automobiles. An older black man wearing a plaid jacket and white pants walked up to her car window right away. She rolled it down. 'We have some incredible things to show you, Miss, absolutely incredible things. Why don't you pull right over there—' he pointed to an empty space '—and we'll walk around and take a look at a few models that will absolutely blow your—'

She recognized his voice. 'Detective Cleveland?' Katherine said. 'I mean—'

'Miss Joy!' The old man laughed.

'You're a used-car salesman?'

'I was an average detective,' he said smiling. 'I'm a *great* used-car salesman.' He waved his whole arm. 'Go ahead and pull in over there, then we'll talk.'

Katherine pulled her car into the space he indicated and Cleveland was right behind her, opening the door. 'Thank you,' she said, stepping out. 'It's DeQuincey-Joy, by the way, with a hyphen.'

'Come right in and I'll pour you a nice cup of coffee, Miss DeQuincey-Joy with a hyphen.'

Katherine followed him into the small dealership offices, where three other salesmen sat around a portable radio drinking coffee and smoking cigarettes. Cleveland led her into the back office, the one that had a MANAGER plaque over the door.

'You're the manager?'

'Nah.' He shrugged. 'But that guy's never around, so we use his office when we want some privacy,' he said. 'Take a seat.'

Katherine took the old gray metal folding chair opposite the old gray metal desk in the center of the room. There was one other chair and on the wall was a colorful poster of a burgundy-mist Mercury Cougar.

'Coffee?' Cleveland said.

Katherine shook her head.

Cleveland sat down, too. 'Now,' he said, 'I want you to explain to me once again what it is you're after, young lady. I'm afraid I didn't get everything that was going on with you on the phone there.' He spoke methodically and carefully. 'Just that you've got some new information about that missing child. Is that true?'

'Well,' Katherine began, 'her brother, Pilot Airie, is my client.'

'You're a psychiatrist?'

'Psychologist,' Katherine said. 'A counseling psychologist. I don't have a medical degree.'

'OK.'

'Pilot Airie, my patient – he claims to have some new evidence.' Katherine looked out the window. It was a bright day and the chrome of hundreds of cars sparkled in the sun. 'Well, not new, exactly, but evidence that he's held on to since, since it happened.'

Cleveland was scratching the back of his head. 'That was more than fifteen years ago, Miss DeQuincey-Joy.'

'Twenty.'

He sighed. 'What kind of new evidence does he have, anyway? Do you have it?'

'I have part of it.' Katherine removed the half shoelace from her purse and placed it on the empty desk.

'A shoelace?' Cleveland picked it up. 'This is from a shoelace?'

'Don't you remember?' Katherine asked. 'Pilot Airie found a single tennis shoe in the woods and no one could find the other shoe.'

Cleveland nodded. 'I remember the shoe. Is this the lace from that shoe?'

'No. This is the lace from the *other* shoe.' Katherine tried to pull the whole mass of her hair toward the back of her head. When she released it, though, it all just fell back into her eyes. 'Pilot says he found both of them all those years ago and that he found a knife, as well. A bloody knife. He says he found them in his brother's room and that he hid them.'

'The other brother,' Cleveland said. 'What was his name?'

'Eric,' Katherine said. 'He's a doctor now.'

'Does he know about this?'

'Most of it.'

'Boy, that must make him feel good.' Cleveland dangled the half shoelace in front of his gray face. Then he said, 'This has been cut in half – recently.'

Katherine smiled. Vettorello had noticed the same thing. 'I did that,' she said. 'The police have the other half.'

'It's not going to tell them much.'

'That's what I'm worried about.'

'They can probably verify if it's the right age, but they can't do much more.' He smiled and shook his head. 'You're going to need the rest of the evidence to confirm anything. The knife, for example. Do you have that?'

'That's a problem,' Katherine said. 'Pilot's telling me he's not sure where he put it.'

'I thought you said he's had it for twenty—'

Katherine looked at her hands, which were small and white in her lap, the fingertips chewed beyond recognition. 'Pilot had a psychotic episode and he said he moved the evidence during that time.'

'I see.'

'And in the process he remembered having the evidence in his possession, but then he doesn't quite know what he did with it.'

'This was recently?'

'Two and a half months ago.' Katherine cleared her throat. 'He was discovered in the woods behind his mother's house after a three-day search.' Katherine looked across the desk directly into the old man's eyes. 'What was your opinion at the time?'

'What do you mean?'

'I mean, that man – his name was Bryce—'

'Bryce Telliman.'

'Yes,' Katherine said. 'He was the lead suspect?'

'According to the papers,' Cleveland said, 'and that seemed to be what the family and most other folks wanted to believe.'

'Did you agree?'

'I thought he might have done it. There wasn't any real evidence pointing to him, though. That man was a homosexual. Why would he be interested in a little girl?'

'Were there any other suspects?'

Cleveland shifted in his chair. 'Everyone at that party was a suspect as far as I was concerned.'

'Anyone in particular?'

The older man rubbed his hands together and Katherine could actually hear his rough skin. 'I have to say I never really considered the boys,' Cleveland said. 'Either one of them.' He paused for a moment and scratched the back of his head again. 'I always thought it was the father.'

Katherine leaned forward. 'What made you think that?'

'Bryce Telliman,' Cleveland said, his voice pitched high. 'It was *his* theory.'

'Bryce Telliman had his own theory?'

'Sure he did. He said he saw the way the father looked at the little girl and he thought it was creepy. That was the word he used – *creepy*.'

'Creepy,' Katherine repeated. 'Did you investigate the father at all?'

'We asked him some questions but, Miss DeQuincey-Joy, you've got to know, we didn't have a lick of evidence. We never even found the girl's body.' He smiled thinly. 'No body, no murder charge, you know what I mean?'

Katherine nodded. 'Pilot hasn't spoken much about his father.' She said this more to herself than to the old detective.

Cleveland touched his chin. His eyes flickered back and forth.

My father kept going over checklists. 'Propane stove?' he said. 'Habachi? Briquettes? Starter fluid? Matches?' We were packing.

Patricia only smiled, repeating, 'Yes, yes, yes, yes.' She had thought of everything, of course, especially of the food we would eat. It seemed she always thought of everything, taking care of my father like a nanny. Patricia had even packed Christmas decorations.

It was my father's job only to worry about the plane.

Only that.

I made certain, of course, to bring my medication, a backpack full of books and the single blue canvas duffel bag I had brought with me from East Meadow.

The take-off went easily, as take-offs go. The truth is, I had never been flying with my father before and was a little more than nervous when we rose from the choppy water like a seagull, rushing forward on the surface until the wind caught our wings and lifted us into the air. That morning it had seemed to me it was getting cold, but my father said it would be warmer on the island. 'It catches those Caribbean winds,' he said. 'It's different out there.'

'It's beautiful,' Patricia reassured me, shouting over the engine. 'You'll really love it, Pilot. You really will.'

'Trust us.'

In the air I could see the coast of the United States falling away. There were no sailboats at all, only waves, slate blue and flat in the gray winter daylight. I sat in the front with my father and Patricia sat in the back, where there was barely enough space for even her, we had brought so many supplies. Dad turned to me, though, not her, asking, 'Are you all right, son? Are you comfortable?'

An overcast day, with a solid cloud stretching all the way to the horizon. 'This is great,' I told him. 'This is awesome.' I said this through clenched teeth. I could feel all those snakes beneath my skin coiling and slithering. I never could express enthusiasm – even when it was genuine.

The engine was loud and cold air leaked into the cabin of the little red seaplane in squealing fissures through the fuselage. Dad turned to me with a conspiratorial smile. 'Your mother would never have gone flying like this.' He said it as if she were dead.

'You're right,' I agreed. But I also knew that he never would have invited her.

'I'm glad you could come.' He had to shout this over the noise of the engine and the wind coming into the plane.

'Have you ever taken Eric up here?'

'He's always too busy to visit,' my father said. 'The big brain surgeon has more important things to do than visit his old dad.'

'How much more flying', I asked, 'until we get there?'

My father mocked me. 'Are we there yet? Are we there yet?'

'Well,' I laughed, 'are we?'

He turned his wrist so he could see his watch. He wore it military-style, face on the inside. 'About an hour,' he said. 'Can you handle the wait?'

Patricia leaned toward us, saying, 'If you guys are hungry, I mean, if you're hungry right now, I packed some sandwiches and sodas for the ride. I have everything handy. Plus, there's coffee.' She was leaning over me, directing this mostly to my father, and as she did so she pressed her right breast against my left shoulder. It felt surprisingly large and soft. Was she even wearing a bra? I had never thought of Patricia's breasts before. She turned to me, as if acknowledging my thoughts. 'Pilot,' she said, 'would you like something?'

'Coffee,' I said. 'I'll have some of that.' For once, I had skipped it this morning. I had been trying to stay away from any stimulants for a while. It had been Katherine's suggestion, actually. But now I thought I needed some. I watched Patricia, my neck craned around, with the new thought about her body under her clothes, as she poured from the Thermos into the cap.

'It's black,' she said. 'Is that all right with you?'

'Perfect.' She looked so uncomfortable back there, surrounded by all the things we had packed. 'Do you want to switch seats?' I said. 'Are you sure you're all right back there? You're not all scrunched up?'

She closed her eyes and shook her head. 'I'm just fine. I ride in this crazy airplane of his all the time.' She smiled warmly. 'You sit up there and enjoy the view.'

I took the Thermos cap of coffee and sipped. It tasted like bitterness itself. We flew in silence, then, the propeller roaring in our ears, the fissures of air screaming through the little cabin. The waves of the ocean flattened out below us as we climbed higher and higher into the atmosphere, and the coastline receded further and further into the distance. I couldn't help it, I tried not to, in fact, but I thought of Patricia and my father in bed, her on top of him, her breasts hanging down, her hands on my father's shoulders. It was not an erotic thought. Rather, it was scientific. They're just two people, I said to myself. They must do it. They must have sex, at least every now and then. The air inside the cabin seemed to get warmer somehow. Maybe it was the coffee. 'There it is,' my father said. When he pointed it out to me, it was an infinitesimal speck on the distant horizon. 'Our very own private paradise.'

I laughed. That tiny little place. 'How can you even see it so far out there?' I said to him. 'Your eyes must be amazing.'

'I've got good eyesight,' he said, 'but I've learned to anticipate it. I know exactly when it will appear.' He made a popping sound with his mouth. We came closer and I could begin to see the contours of the little speck of land, the tiny cove in which he intended to land.

'It's beautiful,' Patricia said over my shoulder. 'Isn't it beautiful, Pilot?'

'It is.' I turned to face her and saw at the same moment that the coast had disappeared completely from sight, as if it had been swallowed by the ocean. I thought of the medication I carried in my backpack, the amber plastic bottle of pills with the child-proof cap. I turned back and the little island had come even closer now, was actually a distinct green and brown shape in the middle of all that blue.

The blue of the ocean had grown considerably lighter, the sky less cloudy, the sun more yellow.

'We'll be landing soon,' my father said in his airline pilot voice. 'Make sure everything's put away.'

I teased him, saying with a nasal voice, 'Please make sure your seatbelt is securely fastened and that your tray table is in its upright position.'

He laughed.

'Also, make sure your carry-on luggage is stowed safely beneath the seat in front of you. Thank you for flying Airie Airlines'

As we came toward the island, Dad gradually lowered the trajectory of his plane so it would set down in the still water adjacent to the small patch of sandy beach at the island's periphery. When we hit the surface everything changed – suddenly we seemed to be going much faster than we had been – with a hard swish into the waves and a few bumps as we bounced off, and then the final approach to the little beach.

Patricia clapped.

'It's not always this smooth,' my father confessed, turning off the engine and opening the door.

Dad and I waded out into the cold sea water and pulled the little plane closer to shore. We anchored it firmly to a large palm tree with a long nylon rope and then he went back to carry Patricia, piggy-back, on to the dry ground. It was noticeably warmer here. 'I can't believe it,' I said, my face to the sun. 'How is this possible?' I hadn't even noticed the sky clearing. It was cobalt blue overhead, crystalline clear.

'How is what possible?'

'The weather. How is the—'

'Warm winds,' Dad said. 'We're just inside the gulf stream. We've traveled to a different part of the world, into a whole different weather system.'

Nowhere Island.

It was somewhere, however, somewhere not far off the coast. It was an empty island, though, bereft, completely unclaimed, according to him, and probably owned by the government. I guessed it was too small and not far enough out in the ocean to be used as a resort island and a bit too far out for people with boats to get to. We walked the entire perimeter as if on a military inspection, Dad pointing to this and that. The foliage in the center was deciduous, it seemed, not tropical. There were regular trees here, the same kind I'd seen in North Florida, their leaves still mostly green. On the shore were a few old palms leaning in their languid, lazy way toward the water. The earth itself was hard, dry island dirt, trampled and dusty.

'Do real people come here?' I asked my father. 'I mean, you know what I mean.'

'You don't think I'm real?'

'I didn't mean—'

'There are other people who know about it,' Dad said, laughing a bit. 'But there aren't many folks with their own seaplanes.'

At the little island's center was a clearing. Some stones had already been placed in a ring. I thought of the clearing in the woods behind our house, sitting with Eric and smoking my first joint. Vaguely, I remembered sitting there more recently, frozen between wanting to rescue Hannah on the highway and wanting to hide from everything, completely catatonic. I walked out of the clearing, going to the highway—

'This is where we'll camp,' my father said.

I nodded. 'OK.'

We walked back to the plane and to Patricia, who had been sunning herself on the little beach, and we began unloading, getting ourselves completely wet in the chilly surf as we carried everything on our shoulders to the shore. There was a tent, two coolers of food, my father's fishing gear, a little radio, cooking supplies. There seemed to be enough here for a year on the island, significantly more than enough for the two weeks we intended to stay.

'Jesus Christ,' my father said finally. He looked at Patricia. 'Fuck me.'

'What?' I said.

'It's my fault,' Patricia said. 'What is it?'

'*Fuck! Fuck! Fuck!*'

'Dad,' I said. 'What?'

'Where are the fucking sleeping bags?'

I looked around, as if I would find them lying on the ground nearby. 'It's all right,' I said. 'We'll go back and get them.'

'No.' This was firm.

'Then what are we going to do?' I said.

Patricia said, 'It gets cold here at night. I'm so sorry. I don't know what I—'

'I'll go,' Dad said, his expression resigned.

'By yourself?' I looked at him like he was the crazy one. 'Why don't we all go?'

'It's better if I go by myself.'

'You shouldn't fly alone,' Patricia said. 'Jim, you really—'

'Help me push the plane back out,' Dad said to me, 'and when I get back you'll have the camp all set up and everything will be fine, all right?'

'You're going to be too tired,' Patricia said, 'way too tired to make that whole trip and back. We should all—'

'It's not that far.'

My father made a gesture with his hands, putting them in front of his face, palms inward. He closed his eyes. This body language meant *shut up or I will kill you*. I remembered this gesture from childhood. So we untied the plane from its mooring and pushed it back out into the water, where my father jumped in. I was totally wet.

Before he got on the plane, he said, 'I guess you're wondering how I'm going to fly with wet pants, right?'

'Well,' I said, 'it does seem as if it would be kind of uncomfortable.'

'I'll tell you a secret.' He came closer to me and lowered his voice. 'I fly with no pants on.' He got on the plane, then, saying, 'and once I get near the shore, I put them back on. So if you want a good laugh, think of me out there, flying with no pants.'

I waded back to the shore and said to Patricia, 'He asked me to tell you not to worry.'

'I can't help it,' she said. 'Why does he even say that?'

I realized, then, that I had left my backpack, with my bottle of pills inside it, on the plane—which, at that moment, was rising into the sky.

A former Air Force pilot, an airline pilot for many years, my father cursed himself in his small, single engine seaplane somewhere not far off the coast of Florida. He cursed Patricia, too. And me. He had two three-hour flights ahead of him, one home, one back to the island, and he wouldn't have any time to rest if he wanted to get back before dark. Thankfully, it was still early. The sky was clear out, too, a fine day for flying, he thought. And more often than not, it was true, he preferred flying solo. Dad thought of me now, his second son, the crazy one, the failure and disappointment, and considered my handicaps, my mental frailties, social awkwardness, physical inabilities. He'd always supposed that our mother was neurotic and he felt that, through no fault of my own, I'd inherited these traits from her. He may have been right.

Alone in the sky, my father thought the plane seemed quieter than usual. Too quiet? With someone else up here, it was all engine and propellers, the popping of air pressure in his ears, shouting over the roar and the fissures of squealing air. He kept a box of cigars in a secret place under his seat and he reached for it now. At least he could have some time by himself. Hell, it wasn't so bad. He wondered if I was getting any better, if the medication was taking hold, smoothing over the rough edges. Finding the cigars, he righted himself, groping inside the box for the cutter and matches. He couldn't seem to get his hands on the cutter, so he placed the round end of the cigar inside his mouth and bit down, tearing a small hole. The tobacco was acrid on his lips. He spat some of it on to the floor. He found the matches and, taking his eyes away from the window momentarily, lit up, sending clouds of puffy gray-blue smoke into the cabin's interior. It tasted wonderful. He'd only stopped smoking in the first place because Patricia had threatened to leave him.

He hoped she and I had started to work on setting up the tent by now, and was sure that by the time he got back with the sleeping bags we'd have everything ready, including dinner.

It was perfect, actually. All he had to do was fly.

Eventually, the coast of Florida came into view. My father could see it as a point of land first, just a bit of green rising off the blue in the far distance, and then it grew larger incrementally, the beach sweeping upwards and above him like an enormous wave of earth to that solid layer of clouds which had been there earlier. He had only to follow the land north for another hour and he would arrive at the little landing area in the small cove, where we had taken off earlier this morning.

He considered Eric now and my accusation. Would Eric really do something like that? Would he have killed his own sister? My father thought of Eric as a little boy. He remembered the football games, the science fairs, the academic achievements. Eric had become a neurosurgeon, a man with a highly developed mind, capable of tremendous complexities. Morality was a function of intelligence, my father thought to himself. It must be. Then he remembered some of my brother's experiments, the way Eric dissected animals in the garage and left their carcasses rotting on the table, the smell of disintegrating flesh out there. Once, the boy had opened the skull of a field mouse while it was still alive, asking himself how long can a mouse survive without a brain? So Eric had tortured animals. OK. A lot of boys do that. He had done that himself when he was young, hadn't he, trapping muskrats and minks in the woods and selling their coats to Sears and Roebuck. He had done it for money. Eric had done it for science. It was still torture.

Dad thought of me in comparison. I had too much imagination. I was too much inside my head. As a kid, I drew pictures – sensitive, symbolic images. Later, I wrote romantic songs on my guitar. I cried easily, weeping whenever other kids made fun of me. I was never good enough at sports to learn anything from them, to know about teamwork, about controlling my emotions, about sportsmanship and honor between men.

My father's memories of Fiona, I believe, were even cloudier than mine. He remembered, mostly, her smell, the way her skin felt when she was a baby, incredibly soft and velvety. He remembered how soft her hair was, too, how fair. He remembered the week before her last Christmas when she was six, and the Barbie doll and Barbie house she'd wanted. Like me, my father remembered her as a still image, the background barely shifting behind her. He saw a close-up of Fiona's freckled, dimpled face. He recalled the thin straps of her little red bathing suit on her sun-pink shoulders. He saw the light in her eyes from the flames of the torches by the pool. My father remembered Fiona on that last night through a haze of drunkenness. He hadn't been watching his own children. He remembered, mostly, flirting with some stupid woman, what was her name? Doris Schott. He remembered that he had made plans to meet her later on, at a hotel, and that the meeting had never taken place because Fiona was gone and after that nothing mattered at all. He remembered calling Doris from a payphone on the side of Sky Highway, saying he wouldn't be coming, but he knew she understood. His daughter had disappeared for Christ's sake.

Quite steadily, my father turned the plane, banking it just slightly against the coastal wind.

With some difficulty, Patricia and I managed to set up the tent. Mostly it was her telling me what to do and me doing it awkwardly. I had never been very good with my hands. Patricia had dark hair and skin that had been tanned so often in the outdoors that it retained the permanent color of parchment. She had large, brown freckles across her collarbone. She had a reddish nose and ears and cheeks. Her smile was warm. Her eyes were deep brown. 'Your father usually starts the fire right away,' she said. 'It's not a camp until there's food.' She wore an old pair of blue jeans and a soft flannel shirt. She was nothing like Hannah.

267

It occurred to me that Patricia and I had never been alone together before. 'Do you want me to start a fire?' I asked her. 'Is that what you mean?'

'If you can,' she said.

'I can try,' I said. 'I just hope I don't set the entire island in flames.'

'Like *Lord of the Flies*?' she said, laughing. 'Don't worry. We'll put plenty of rocks and sand around you.'

'Just don't call me Piggy.'

It was still before noon, early enough, and I felt normal. Things appeared normal, anyway. I knew my medication was in the plane and that the plane would not be back until later, probably early evening. I had been taking less and less of the medication, cutting the tiny pills in half, as Katherine had indicated. But I had yet to go an entire day. I kept checking the treeline around the little clearing. If I noticed it moving, if I thought it was ready to reach out for me, then I'd know I was going crazy again.

Then I'd know.

Patricia and I gathered as much wood for the fire as we could hold in our arms. We found a patch of relatively dry driftwood on the other side of the island and we carried it in two trips back to the little clearing. 'I'll bet he did this on purpose,' Patricia said finally.

'Left the sleeping bags at home?'

She was nodding, arms folded, her feet resting on the woodpile. 'Just so he could go flying by himself.'

'Sounds plausible.' I started to stack an arrangement of wood. We were encircled by the sea, by the island itself, by this little clearing, I thought, and now I was making a fire in this circle of stones.

'He likes to be alone,' Patricia said, smiling apologetically. 'Are you like that, too? You probably are.'

'I guess so,' I said. 'I find myself alone pretty often.'

Her face softened. 'He's really worried about you. He probably doesn't say it, but he cares about you a lot. He really—'

'Is there a newspaper or something? How do we get this started?'

'We have starter fluid.'

We had stacked the wood the way I imagined my father would have done. Patricia went to get the starter fluid and some matches. When she returned, she handed them to me ceremoniously. 'The man should do this.'

'Well, he isn't here.' I doused the wood with the fluid, then dropped a lit match on top of it. The whole thing exploded into flames. 'Is that how he does it?'

'That's the way it's done.'

She was being condescending, I knew, treating me like a child. But for some reason I didn't mind. I was probably acting like one. I glanced at the treeline. From here we could see the ocean and I wondered if my psychosis might cause me to fear the water as well as the woods. The waves licked the shore. They receded. They came back. They went away again. I wasn't afraid of the waves in Santa Monica, I remembered, where I had sat for hours – days, actually – on the beach, mesmerized by their repetition. As a matter of fact, I had walked into them, hadn't I, totally unafraid. But I wasn't psychotic then, either, I told myself. Just depressed. I felt jittery. I had brought some books – an old literature anthology, a science fiction novel. But I had left them in the seaplane, too.

Even though it was uncomfortably warm, Patricia and I sat by the fire until the wood began to burn evenly.

'Aren't you hungry?' she said. 'I can start cooking something, anything you—'

'No,' I told her. 'I'm not hungry.' I hadn't had anything but the coffee she had given me on the plane, but for some reason, probably nervousness, I wasn't hungry.

'Would you like to play cards?'

'Patricia, I'm having a bit of trouble concentrating right now,' I confessed.

'Are you—'

'I left my medication on the plane,' I said. 'I mean, don't worry about me or anything. I'll be all right. It's just that—'

'You're a little nervous. I understand.'

I nodded, then I pushed a little stick deeper into the fire. Was the fire going to come alive somehow, I wondered. Would it reach out for me the way I thought the woods had at home? There were so many possibilities for craziness here. The sea, the fire, the wind, the earth.

All the elements.

'Let me know if you need anything or, or just want to lie down.'

'I'm all right. I think I am, anyway.' I played with the fire some more.

'He'll be back soon.'

Patricia and I waited, sitting on the sandy ground, toying with bits of wood. I got up from time to time to walk through the little forest to the other side. I circumnavigated the beach. The sun moved in its natural arc from the sky's highest point to the west. A wind rose from the east, blowing across the little island, causing the leaves of the trees to shiver and rustle. I wondered, had to wonder, if I was imagining it.

In the woods behind my mother's house, Katherine moved slowly, a step at a time, trying to think like a psychotic. Where would I have put the evidence? she asked herself. She had never been out here before. In fact, she had hardly been inside any forest. She certainly had never been in one like this: a suburban strip of deciduous maples and oaks, on one side the highway, on the other a cul-de-sac of houses. The season was nearly over now, the leaves all descended and crackling, frozen underfoot. It was winter, to be truthful, and the cold moved through the tree trunks like a million slippery eels gliding around waterweeds at the speed of wind. Katherine tried to remember the way I had described these woods to her. She knew that when I was at the hospital I had imagined the trees creeping forward, moving toward me almost imperceptibly. I thought they would swallow me, lash out across the expanse of asphalt highway and draw me inside the way an amoeba swallows its food. She knew how I had pretended to be the wolf boy when I was little, free of language, untouched by humans. Is that what I was afraid of? she thought. That I'd be swallowed by the woods and become the wolf boy again?

Katherine asked herself this: where would a wolf boy hide a plastic bag of evidence?

It was an absurd question.

Near my mother's house she found the path and stepped along it gingerly, trying not to disturb anything or make a noise. She had the strange feeling that she could be discovered out here and get into trouble. Then, just beyond a thicket of bushes, she saw a clearing. In the distance, she could hear the highway, the hiss of tires, the whir of engines. She imagined our boyhoods taking place in these woods, Eric's and mine. Eric's first kisses with girls. My first joint with Eric. There in front of her was the broken concrete pipe. Was this the same one? It had to be. Around it, cigarette butts and crushed beer cans littered the earth. Katherine looked inside the hollow, but there was nothing in it besides some old, disintegrating *Penthouse* magazines. She sat down on the pipe for a moment and put her hands on her knees. There seemed to be a stillness enfolding her, quiet like the inside of a trunk. Beyond the highway sounds was something quieter. It was the sound of the branches moving in the wind. It was the sound of winter birds fluttering high up and of leaves settling. It was a single, simple pulse in her ears. It was a stillness Katherine could understand going crazy in.

And now it was broken – Katherine was almost thankful – by a pair of girls' voices. Up ahead, two junior high girls laughed their way into the clearing and, seeing Katherine there, stopped talking. They moved past her, heads down, one of them muttering a faint, 'Hello.' One was blonde and thin, the other a brunette and heavier, wearing far too much make-up. Katherine only smiled, remembering her own dreadful junior high experience. Then she had a thought. She got up and called after them.

'Excuse me!' Her voice felt loud and awkward. 'Excuse me!'

The girls stopped. They turned around and looked at her, astonished.

'Excuse me,' Katherine said again. 'Do you mind if I ask you a question?'

One of them, the dark-haired one, looked frightened. 'Sure,' she said. 'OK.'

'Do you come through these woods often?'

'Sometimes,' the blonde one said, more boldly.

The other only shrugged.

'Do you live around here?'

'We live on Willow Road,' the brunette said. She spoke as if confessing.

'Do you walk through here every day?'

'Almost,' the frightened one said.

The other said, 'Not *every* day.'

'Did you ever see a man hanging around in here? Sandy-brown hair, about twenty-five, thirty years old, around two or three months ago?'

'The Airie guy?'

'You know him?' Katherine said.

The one who had been silent was now bold. 'He's the one who went crazy, right? My mother told me.'

Neighborhood gossip, Katherine thought. She said, 'I'm his psychologist.'

'Sorry.'

'Oh my God, did he do something wrong?'

'No,' Katherine said. 'No, nothing like that. I was just wondering if you ever saw him in the woods and, if you did, what part of the woods you saw him in, where he might have hung out.'

'He used to just walk around, really. I figured he was harmless.'

'Didn't they find him out by the highway?'

'Do kids hang out by the highway?' Katherine asked.

'Certain kids do,' the brunette said.

'What do you mean?'

'You know what I mean.'

Katherine wasn't sure, but she nodded, anyway.

'There's a tunnel under the highway,' the blonde one said. 'I would never go in there. But some girls go in there all the time.'

'I see.'

'Edwina Carlson goes in there.'

'Who's she?' Katherine said.

'Just a girl.'

'Can you tell me which way the tunnel is?'

'Just walk straight to the highway,' the blonde one said, 'and then walk in the direction of the shopping plaza.'

'Are you really going to go there?' the brunette said.

'Why not?'

'Be careful.'

'And look out for the Tunnel Man.'

She walked away from the two girls cautiously, a little frightened now. But then she chided herself, how stupid it was to let a couple of teenagers scare her like that. What could possibly be so scary in the tunnel under the highway? That's where the bad kids go, Katherine said to herself, the pot smokers and the girls who allow boys to touch them under their clothes. She remembered secret places in Central Park when she was in high school, the nervous laughing inside a thicket of bushes, tremulous hands groping around beneath her shirt, how a boy could lose his breath by just touching the rough material of her bra. The wind was stronger now, bracing, the afternoon wearing away. Following the path the girls had been walking, Katherine found the highway and began to travel north, the sounds of late afternoon traffic whipping by over the embankment to her right. It was nearing rush hour.

She looked around. This was where they found me, she realized, alone and raving, incoherent, psychotic, on this path near the highway. This must have been where I had hidden the evidence, too. Katherine closed her eyes and tried to imagine what I had been feeling that day. I believed, at that point, that Eric was out to kill me. I was clutching a plastic Wonderbread bag with a tennis shoe and a knife inside it. I felt that the woods had swallowed me. I was aware that my mother had cancer forming around her optical nerve. All my life I had believed my sister had been taken out here somewhere and killed by my own brother.

Where would someone in that state of mind hide something? Katherine asked herself.

Then, far up ahead, she saw it, the tunnel. It must be in there, she thought. I must have hidden the evidence somewhere inside the tunnel. There was a trickle of water coming out. In the spring, she told herself, it must fill halfway up with the thaw. Katherine had to step on some carefully placed rocks to cross the deep puddle forming at its base. She poked her head around the corner and saw that it was just large enough for a normal person to stand inside. Anyone over six feet would have to duck.

She stepped in. There seemed to be something blocking the other end, because the light was dim, darker than it should have been at this time of day.

'Hey,' a voice shouted.

Katherine squinted. Was someone down there?

'Hey,' the voice said again.

'Hello?' Katherine said.

'Get ... the ... flying ... fuck ...'

'I'm just looking around,' said Katherine. 'Nothing to worry about.'

'... out ... of ... my ...'

'I don't mean any harm.'

'... tunnel.' There was a man, she could see now, standing in the middle of the long tube. He had emerged, like the troll in billy goats gruff, from an enclosure of cardboard and plastic.

'My name is Katherine DeQuincey-Joy,' she said to the silhouette. 'I'm a psychologist.'

'Katherine DeQuincey-Joy,' the man said, 'you are a major pain in my ass.' It was the voice of a forty-year-old man.

'Can I ask who you are?'

He came forward, sloshing through the liquid grime.

Katherine took a step back. How fast could she move through the woods, she asked herself, and get to the highway?

'I am no one,' he said. 'No-fucking-body.'

She could see him clearly now. He was homeless, evidently, or, more accurately, this was his home, and he wore the usual overgrown thicket of black and gray facial hair, the heavy coat, the orange wool hat. 'Of course you're somebody,' Katherine said, thinking he must know everything that's around here. Perhaps he saw something. Perhaps he had seen me that day, she thought. 'I was just wondering if you could help me.'

'Help you?' His tone was derisive.

'Yes,' she said. 'Help me.'

It was a good ten degrees colder in here. She shivered.

'Why would I?'

'To be nice?'

He laughed. 'I am the man who lives in the tunnel and frightens children. I am not nice.' There was a halo of light forming behind him. The homeless always made Katherine think of biblical figures. It was their hair, she thought. 'I am the direct opposite of nice.'

'I just have a couple of questions.'

He rolled his eyes, and she could see his whites in the gray light of the tunnel. 'Hit me,' he said. 'Lay it on me.'

'There was a, a man found out here, right around here, anyway, I think,' Katherine said. 'His name is Pilot. He was, he was sick, you know, seeing things and—'

'I know Pilot,' the Tunnel Man said. 'I know him.'

'You do?'

'What do you want?' he laughed now. 'His stuff?'

Katherine couldn't believe it. 'Do you have it?'

'No . . . I do not have it. But perhaps . . . perhaps I know where it can be found,' he said teasingly.

'Where?' She stepped forward, his face coming into clearer focus in the dark. She could see that he was actually handsome, with delicate features beneath all that hair.

He threw a hand in the air, startling her. 'I cannot tell you my name and I will not tell you my name,' the Tunnel Man began, 'but I will tell you that I know the Pilot of whom you speak, I know the secrets and the daylight particles that fall through the cracks in hospital floors, and that I knew, know, will for ever be advised, of where he left things, where things are hidden and placed accordingly, each along their lines, by their kind, color-coded.' He smiled at Katherine, yellow-toothed. This was an act, she knew. He had been far more lucid just a moment ago. He was pretending to be insane. This was *schtick*.

'Pilot told you where he hid his things?'

'He hid himself, didn't he?' the Tunnel Man said. 'Pilot of the golden light, dream of the weary dark, trembler under blankets, didn't he? He hid himself well.'

Katherine heard the reason beneath the Tunnel Man's strange locution. From here she could smell him, as well, the alcohol stench. 'I'm Pilot's friend, too,' she said. 'A good friend.'

'Friends are found in the places of transport', he said, 'at an hour when only the criminals are expected to depart.'

'Pilot was your friend?'

'. . . of a friend of a friend of a friend . . .'

Katherine smiled at him. 'I'm wondering if you might help me find where Pilot hid his things. It's very important, and he asked me to help him. Can you help me help our friend Pilot?'

The Tunnel Man walked back and forth quickly within the confines of the small tunnel, his feet splashing in the water. Katherine wondered why he hadn't died of exposure before now. 'Thinking, thinking, thinking,' he was saying. 'How do I know about you? What are your credentials?'

'Well,' Katherine started to say, 'I'm—'

But he cut her off. 'How do I know that Pilot is living and that a simulacrum has not been placed in his place and that you are not party to the council of time, when all lost—'

Katherine held out her hand. She reached into her purse and extracted a twenty-dollar bill, extending it toward him. 'He wanted me to give you this,' she said. 'He said you could use it.'

The Tunnel Man looked at the money, his eyes narrowing comically, a smile forming beneath his beard.

'He wanted to offer his help to you,' she said.

The Tunnel Man moved forward, toward Katherine, shuffling, sloshing. 'He thought,' he said. 'Pilot – he's a thinker.'

'Pilot is very thoughtful,' Katherine said, 'yes.'

Close enough to reach, he snatched the bill, brought it to his nose, and sniffed. More *schtick*, Katherine realized.

'Will you help Pilot now?' she said. 'Will you?'

The twenty disappeared somewhere inside the Tunnel Man's

layers of clothing and now his arms made little circles in the air. 'Helpfulness is next to cleanliness,' he was saying, 'cleanliness is connected to the funny bone, the funny bone's connected to the brain stem and the brain stem leads down, down, down in the ground, the underneath of things thinking, always thinking.'

'Where did Pilot hide his things?' Katherine asked hopefully.

The Tunnel Man looked incredulous. 'I just told you,' he said. 'Didn't I?'

'I didn't understand.' Was it lost somewhere in his word salad? Katherine wondered.

'Understanding the moon landing.'

'Where?' Katherine asked.

The Tunnel Man shook his head.

'Will you show me?' she pled.

'I knew Pilot,' the Tunnel Man said, his face held up. 'He came and talked to me until the winds and trees made him afraid and my tunnel turned to him, curling, a wave over him, unsmiling, and so I went out and said hello to the highway and they came for him.'

'You went for help?'

'Pilot is all right?'

'He's fine,' Katherine said. 'He's with his father.'

The Tunnel Man smiled. 'Fathers are feathers.'

'Show me,' Katherine said. 'Show me where he hid his things. Please.'

He looked left and he looked right. He touched his fingers methodically, one by one, each dirty fingertip touching the next. 'Can you return?' he said. 'On the day after the day after the—'

'Can I—'

'I'll have to find you the things,' he said lucidly, 'all the evidence, the naughty evidence, and if you come back in three days—' he held three blackened fingers up '—I'll have everything ready for you.'

'You can't show me now?'

'Three days,' the Tunnel Man said. 'A blink.'

Katherine wondered if it would even be worth coming back here in three days. Was this homeless man even remotely competent?

Was he lying? Did he really know me? Was he only hoping for more money? Katherine smiled as warmly as she could. This man, the Tunnel Man, either didn't know or he was simply unwilling to tell her now. 'Three days,' Katherine said. 'And then I'll be back.'

On Nowhere Island the night came and the light dropped from the sky and there was no sign of my father. Walking down to the beach every fifteen minutes, my hand over my brow in a salute to the descending sun, I squinted my eyes for any speck of darkness in the corner of the sky that could be his little seaplane. There was nothing, though, only the cold creeping in through the medium of a strengthening wind. Patricia had packed sweaters, at least. I kept my one eye on the treeline around the small clearing where the tent was, waiting for it to move an inch, to creep forward a single millimeter. Would it strike out? Would it grab me or Patricia? I couldn't remember then if I had ever actually seen the woods strike out in my craziness or if I had only been waiting for them to do it.

'There must be a storm coming,' Patricia said. She smiled reassuringly. 'And he has to wait for it to pass, that's all.'

'He'd fly in a storm.'

'No,' Patricia insisted. 'No, because I ask him not to.'

I didn't see the sense in disagreeing. He would fly in a storm, though. My father always drove above the speed limit without his seat belt. He ran the lawnmower without the safety guard. He kept his handgun, the safety off, by his bed. He would fly in a storm if it suited him. And, as it was, the sky was only wind and cloud. There wasn't any rain yet. At least not out here. 'Maybe something's wrong with the plane,' I said. 'And that's why he can't come back.'

'That's possible,' said Patricia. She kept eyeing me, looking for signs of schizophrenia, I suppose, waiting for the craziness to start. I kept looking at the way she looked at me, trying to see if she was seeing a crazy person. The treeline remained where it was, however, and the ocean became only choppier in the wind.

The sky stayed empty.

I paced the circumference of the island, walking around and around at least ten times. Patricia began grilling the steaks we had brought for the evening. 'If we wait too long,' she said, 'the meat will spoil.'

It was nine at night, completely dark.

'Maybe he can't come back until the morning,' I said again. I had said that a thousand times, I think.

Then, for the first time, there was an admission that something might possibly be wrong: 'I hope he's all right.' Patricia smiled weakly.

'Of course he is,' I told her, probably too quickly. 'He's fine. My father?' I tried to laugh, but it came out weird.

We chewed our steaks in silence. It was a meal, we both knew, that my father would have enjoyed more.

'There's wine,' Patricia said.

I only pointed to my head, indicating with a circle what could happen.

She laughed. 'You feel all right?' she said. 'Are you feeling—'

'Given the circumstances,' I told her, 'I feel just fine.'

Patricia walked around the fire, knelt beside me and put her arm around my shoulder. 'He never warns me,' she said.

I looked at her questioningly.

She said, 'He just takes off sometimes, sometimes quite literally, in his plane, you know. I'll wake up in the morning and he's just, he's just packing his things. I don't know if he's leaving me for ever or if he's coming back the next day.'

'He wouldn't leave you,' I said. 'He would never—'

'You don't know that.'

I didn't know. It was true. But I said, 'I know him well enough to know he would never leave you.'

'He left your mother. And he tells me he's going flying somewhere and I wait to see if he wants me to come and sometimes, you know, sometimes he doesn't.' Patricia smiled. 'And so I wait. I wait for him like an idiot, like we've been doing here all day. I mean, not doing anything but preparing things for when he gets home, making everything perfect, just for him. But not, you know, not doing anything for myself. I mean, nothing. Because his life is the life I'm living, you know what I mean? It's his life and I have to wait to see when and how I'll be a part of it.'

'I've always wanted to ask you', I said, 'what it was like before, before he left my mother and came to live with you.'

'It was like this,' Patricia said. 'It was a lot of pacing.'

'That couldn't have been fun.'

'I always imagined your mother was doing the same thing in New York.'

'She had things to occupy her.'

'Yes, but—'

'She wanted him to leave as much as he wanted to leave.' This wasn't true, but I said it, trying to make Patricia feel better.

'I can't imagine not loving him,' Patricia put her head against my shoulder. 'Where the hell is he?'

'It was different, it was different before.'

'Before?'

'Before Fiona.'

'Oh,' Patricia said.

'He was different.'

She sat back on her heels now, asking, 'How was he different?'

'He was more, it was a little more about other people, you know. He wasn't so—'

'Insular?'

'That's a good word.' I laughed a little bit. 'I was always so afraid of him, I was always feeling he was right about to beat me up.'

'Did he ever—'

'Oh, no,' I told Patricia, and this was the truth. 'He never hit me or Eric or, or Fiona. Never. I just always thought he was about to.' There were no stars in the sky at all. It was completely black, covered in clouds. 'I just thought it was everything he could do not to kill me.'

'He loves you,' she said. 'Did he ever tell you that?'

I remembered that he had always signed my birthday cards that way. But I could never remember him saying it directly. 'He must have,' I said. 'I just don't—'

'It's hard for him, you know,' Patricia said. She leaned forward, pushing a stick at the fire. 'Probably the less he says something, the more he means it, you know what I mean?'

'I do. I know what you mean,' I said. And I knew exactly what she meant, and I went ahead and let myself believe it, too.

Can you love someone so much that their memories are yours? Sitting by the fire, I looked at my hands and I thought of Eric's hands, so clean, and I remembered Fiona's hands, how small they were and delicate. And this was not my memory. It was my father's. Can love lay claim like that? Can it blur life at the edges?

It was a single moment, actually, pacing around the beach like the little prince, that I understood what had become of him. It was probably an irrational feeling and one that later, looking back, justified the events that followed, the way people say they have premonitions of things but only after the fact. Our greatest theory was that he had been forced to land somewhere in the ocean between here and the coast, and that, floating out there, he had radioed for help, and soon there would be someone coming to rescue us. But then it became more and more clear to me what really had happened because I saw the blue of the sky for a brief, flickering second through my father's eyes. I saw the sky from beneath the water, looking up, bubbles rising.

'The coastguards check places like this routinely,' I told Patricia. 'They fly over, making sure everything's OK.'

'I've never seen them do that.'

'That's what they do,' I reassured her. 'I've read about it.'

The feeling of being stranded, really alone on a desert island, was bizarrely liberating.

My father had committed suicide, I knew this now.

He was gone and I could say anything. I could *think* anything.

'You're not like him,' Patricia said a few nights later. She began by kissing my neck, her face all tears and her hands all trembling. She pulled my sweater and T-shirt over my head.

Then she sat up and pulled hers off, too.

I couldn't speak.

She pressed herself against me. 'You're not crazy,' she said. 'You aren't crazy at all.' Patricia's skin was against my skin, this woman my father had been with, had loved. She was between our ages, though, and she was letting it sink in, I believe, the realization that the man she had given up her life for, perhaps foolishly, was never coming back. She made love to me that night, every now and then saying, 'You're nothing like him, nothing like him at all.'

What was I supposed to do? How would I push her away? Her life was over, she believed, and she wanted to end it by doing something, by participating in something that the living do. I didn't think it was wrong. I still don't.

And the hands I touched her with were his hands.

And I looked at her with his eyes.

And my body was his body.

Patricia and I spoke the next morning as though it had never happened, of course. And the entire next day, as well as the day after, and the following day when we were rescued by the coastguard, the day we returned to the cottage and saw the sleeping bags resting in the carport, and the day a couple of weeks later when I went back to New York, it was never spoken of. Like so many things that have happened to me, this event disappeared like a frozen moment, a photograph in memory, time receding away like a wave that never comes back.

Maybe it's time, and not the woods, which lashes out, steals you.

She was patient, on top of me, rocking back and forth, guiding my hands – my father's hands – to her hips. We moved like this for more than an hour, it seemed, just tensing and relaxing, her hips like those of a woman riding out, I guess, the last night of her life, the last time she would be in contact with the flesh of someone she had loved unconditionally for so long – *his* flesh. Imagine how she waited for him all those years, the not knowing, the knowing only a little bit. She knew about his children, about me and Eric. She knew about his tragedies, about Fiona, and could only wait for his plane to land in Atlanta when she lived there, working in the airport lounge, and for him to come see her, in the years before and just after Fiona disappeared.

All that waiting.

And I whispered to her with his voice.

Only to be left waiting at the very end. Left waiting for ever. I would never blame a person for any action they had taken on the night that kind of realization occurred. Besides, I felt, I think, the same thing my father felt for her, or would have felt, had he known. Patricia was beautiful and womanly in ways my mother could never be. There was some bending, a melting quality inside her, a softness.

And I saw her with his eyes.

It was a long day's boat ride back to the mainland, and then we were taken to my father's – to Patricia's – cottage by van. I was to return home to New York immediately after the trip. But we decided, then, to have the memorial service for my father here, among his friends, all those *flyboys* and fishermen he liked to drink and watch sports with.

And, of course, so Patricia could be there, too.

If my father ever loved my mother – and I think he did, I *know* he did once – all that love disappeared with Fiona. It is the same love, not divided, but repeated whole again, that a man feels for his wife and his daughter. And when he had to give up his love for Fiona, he had to give up my mother, too. Naturally, Hannah had half-blamed him for Fiona's disappearance. I didn't know at the time that he had been a suspect in the case. I didn't know anything, to tell the truth, but one simple thing.

I had been off the medication now for seven days, and I was sane.

In the cottage the next morning Patricia asked if I wanted her to call my mother. 'No,' I said. 'I'll do it.' I would wait half the day, actually, and call Eric first and tell him that I wanted to tell her, that it should be me she heard it from.

'Why you?' Eric wanted to know.

'I was with him.' I was in the kitchen, half-expecting my father to walk in behind me at any moment and grab a beer from the refrigerator. 'I saw him last. He said his last words to me.' This was special. This was something Eric didn't have with our father.

'What were they?'

'He said if you wanted a good laugh, to think of him out there, flying with no pants.'

Eric didn't respond for a moment, and then he said, 'What?'

'He was kidding around.' I twisted the telephone cord in my fingers. Dad never kidded around with Eric. 'And that's what he said.' Only with me.

'That's ridiculous.'

'He didn't plan it,' I said. 'He must have made some last-minute decision.'

'What are you saying?' Eric had something weird and sarcastic in his voice. 'Are you saying there was some kind of Bermuda triangle bullshit, that there was some mysterious—'

'Eric,' I said, 'I'm not saying anything like that. I'm saying it was some kind of—'

'Pilot,' he said, 'why would he do this?'

'He didn't—'

'Are you taking your medication?'

'Yes,' I lied again.

'He was afraid of people finding out.'

'He had a will,' I said.

'I can't talk about this now.' My brother hung up.

Our mother was in her chair by the window when the nurse Eric had hired – her name was Thalia – brought in the telephone, heavy, rotary-dial, black. I said, 'Mom, Dad's—'

'I know,' she said. 'Fiona told me.'

'Mom,' I said again, 'it's Pilot.'

'I know,' she said, laughing, 'I know who you are, you're my own boy, aren't you? Wouldn't I know my—'

'He, he disappeared in his plane,' I said. 'He was flying back to get some things and he, he never made it to the mainland. They haven't found him.'

Was I crying?

'Your father loves to fly,' she said.

'Are you understanding this, Mom?'

'Fiona's out in the yard,' she said. 'I can hear her. Can you hear her, Pilot? She's playing with the girls next door. They're about the same age.' Through the kitchen window the light was changing, clouds rushing in front of the sun. I touched my face.

Tears.

'. . . how is she?' I asked, giving in. 'How is Fiona?'

'She comes and she goes,' Hannah said, tearful now. I could hear her voice breaking as if under the weight of something. 'Sometimes I see her, sometimes she, she whispers to me or comes into the room and puts her head on my lap, and looks up at me . . .'

'Mom,' I said. And then softly, '*Hannah.*'

'Sometimes I know she isn't there . . .'

'Mom,' I said.

'. . . isn't really there.'

'Dad's missing.'

'I understand. Your father's missing, I understand.'

'They've been searching for five days,' I said, 'and they think, they think that his plane went down and that he may have done it on purpose.' I was standing in my father's cottage, in Patricia's beige and white kitchen, tracing my finger across the strawberry-shaped magnets on the refrigerator door. And Hannah was sobbing. My mother, our mother, Eric's and Fiona's and mine, she was crying. 'I'm so sorry.'

'Does Eric know?'

'He knows.'

'And Patricia?'

'She's here,' I said. 'I'm with her now, in Florida, at their cottage.'

'Oh, yes,' my mother said. 'Oh yes.'

I waited before saying, again, softly, 'Mom?'

'I loved him, you know.'

'I know.'

'He left me.'

I watched the light passing in front of the window.

'He didn't love me . . . not the way I loved him. He never—'

'He loved you,' I told her. 'Hannah, he really did.'

Patricia was behind me. She put her hand on my shoulder. I turned, though, moving away.

'He was . . . he blamed me . . . for . . .'

'No,' I said. 'He didn't blame you. He never—'

'He wanted something . . . wanted someone . . . different,' she said, and I knew that was true. 'I could never be with someone else . . . Only him, only your father.' And I knew that was also true. She sobbed heavily, saying, 'I loved him so much,' as if this had never occurred to her before, as if she'd never said it out loud. And I could hear the nurse, could hear Thalia in the background asking if everything was all right. 'Pilot,' Hannah said finally, 'are you coming home?'

'As soon as I can.'

'What would have made him happy?'

'What do you mean?'

'What would he have wanted?'

I turned to Patricia. 'He had a will, apparently. He thought of everything. He planned everything.'

Patricia was nodding.

'You're like me,' our mother said, 'aren't you, my Pilot, stronger than you seem?'

'I'm better now, Mom.'

She said, 'I know you are.'

'I'm sane,' I said, the light in the kitchen turning gray, then white, then gray again.

'Come home.'

Our mother called him *flyboy* because he had been a fighter pilot. My father had flown experimental jets in the Air Force just before the Vietnam War. Luck and circumstance had prevented him from seeing any action, thankfully, and he'd spent his last tour of duty – this was shortly before Eric was conceived – at Langley Air Force Base in California. He had loved flying, however, the way some people love religion, and immediately upon his discharge went back to flight school, as so many ex-pilots did in those days, learning to operate those big jumbo jets for the airlines. It was either that, he'd always bragged, or become an astronaut, and 'I may be stupid,' he said, 'but I'm not crazy. Or maybe it's the other way around.' So, most of his career, my father was an airline pilot, traveling great distances in the world. He'd been to every continent, nearly every country, all the major cities. He had flown through every kind of bad weather, every possible condition, every type of storm. Therefore – and what I have been leading to is this – I doubt very much the wind, which was blowing strong in the early evening off the coast of Florida that day, was a major contributing factor. I do not believe the mild storm that seemed to come up out of nowhere that afternoon – out of the blue, the expression goes – blowing our hair around a bit, making the canvas of the tent in the clearing flutter, making the fire burn low, made any difference at all.

My mother, her eyesight deteriorating, was alone the first time she saw the apparition of her daughter running across the backyard. Alone up there in the sky, perhaps my father saw one, too. Maybe he saw Fiona's face shaded inside a cloud and he directed his plane toward her in a moment of absent-minded craziness. It sounds ridiculous, I know. But it is even more ridiculous to say that he ran out of gas or that his instruments failed or that he was blown away by a strong wind. It is too easy, for one, because there was no message from him, no mayday signal over his radio asking for help or even saying goodbye. There was nothing. His last words to me were, '. . . think of me out there, flying with no pants.'

These are the words of a person who is planning to see you again.

So, at what point did he decide?

When did he choose to leave us?

Was he sobbing? Did he have his head in his hands when the little seaplane finally ran out of gas somewhere over the water and dropped into the ocean? Was his face set, impassive? Was he screaming with rage? Was he calm? Was he finally, after all this time, satisfied? Did he allow panic to fill him at the last instant or did he remain accepting? Did he believe that Eric killed Fiona?

Did my father know, as I knew, that what must have happened, that the only thing that could have happened, was what I had told him?

Was it the truth that killed him?

I knew that day and in the weeks that followed, during the funeral – attended by me and Eric, my Dad's brother Rich, who came out from Phoenix, by Patricia and her two sisters, Marsha and Debra, and by the gruff, manly mechanics who worked in the airfield where he kept his plane – I knew that my father had been a man not much in control of things. He was a person who traveled around the world all his life, and the world is a sphere that spins and it goes nowhere.

It was the truth that killed him.

My father, our father, Eric's, mine, and Fiona's, disappeared, just like his daughter.

Did he go looking for her?

When Eric took the news from me, he panicked, his whole body developing an argument, and he hung up the phone quickly – too quickly, he thought later. He had to think. Things were different now. He had to *think*. Had Dad ever known what had really happened? he asked himself. Had he ever really figured it out? Eric was in his office, as always, thinking about his plans, his postures, positions, looking at his clean, brain surgeon's hands flat on the clear mahogany desktop in front of him, and the lifetime of lies he had created was complicating exponentially. Hannah, who for so many years had protected him, clear-eyed and cold, who had helped him with this, developed this with him, was coming undone – she was a blind old lady seeing the ghost of her long-disappeared daughter. And worse, his brother was going sane. I had become by accident of circumstance uncrazy, the spool of thread that was my mental health spinning together once again in such a way that, Eric knew, I could see through the bullshit, could see through to the truth and not turn it immediately into fear. Eric exhaled, trying to calm himself. Katherine, he knew, was going to believe me.

Katherine, he realized, had not been programmed as I was to believe every lie he told.

Things fall apart. The center cannot hold.

After hanging up on me, Eric had walked out of his office and into his examining room, where he had washed his hands again. But he wasn't washing away guilt, he thought. It was the bacteria, the flora and fauna, the organisms that lived out of sight range. He scrubbed his skin red, using only the hot water, water that to anyone else would feel scalding. 'Pilot,' he'd said, 'why would he do this?' He had tried to imply, just by asking, that there was guilt associated with our father's suicide, that it had something to do with Fiona, that our father had done something to her.

I hadn't bought it, though. I never would. And he knew it. Our father had been vain, arrogant, self-absorbed. But he was never abusive. He never hit us. He never laid an unkind hand on Fiona. And that night, the night of the party, he was the host. Eric knew this, knew all of this.

Jesus Christ, he had to think.

'Are you taking your medication?' he had asked.

'Yes.' It was a lie.

'Good.'

Eric looked out of his window. It was winter now, deep December, overcast and gray, a film of wetness covering everything. His view was of a parking lot and a small suburban office park. There were dentists, there were lawyers, a design firm. There was glass and steel, concrete and asphalt. As long as I stayed on the medication, Eric thought, things would be all right. If I got off it, if I realized that I was sane, if I knew that I wasn't crazy, I might figure things out for myself. That was the key, my own sanity, my own rationality.

He went back to his desk. Should he call Katherine? He imagined I was on the phone with Hannah now. He was right about that. He imagined Katherine was closing in on the evidence. He was right about that, too. He would have to plan this out carefully, he realized. He would have to find a way to get to it before she did.

Eric asked himself, where had Pilot – where had I – kept that evidence all these years?

Where?

He found himself angry, looking at his hands again. He laughed at himself. He had washed them clean enough, hadn't he? As he would say later, he was only protecting his brother. He was only doing what he thought was right. Shit. He would have to call Katherine. He would have to get to the evidence before she did. Eric remembered placing those things – the shoes and the bloody knife – inside the plastic Wonderbread bag and sliding it under his desk, a stupid place to put it. So incredibly stupid. He remembered coming back into the room and seeing it was gone.

And by then, I was gone, too.

'What did you do with it?' Eric asked me all those years ago.

'Do with what?' I said.

'Did you want a hunting knife?' He had me by the shirt. 'Is that all?'

'Will you get me one?'

Later that afternoon I had claimed to have found the red shoe in the woods, and the police were out looking for the other one, combing the forest floor for any sign of Fiona. Eric and I sat in the living room with our parents, our hands in our laps, waiting for the telephone to ring with news of something – of anything. It must have been difficult for him, knowing and not being able to say.

Right now in his office Eric remembered our father. Had he loved our father? There were patients scheduled for the rest of the day. There were people, Eric knew, who had cancer growing like weeds inside their brains, tendrils of death curling around the folds of tissue, twisting and burrowing into their nervous systems. He imagined having cancer himself, the waves of radiation therapy, like an unfurling blanket, passing over him.

Why had our father done this? He had never known about what happened. It had only been the two of us, and me only through the veil of near-sanity. Or had he known everything?

Yes, Eric loved his father, I believe, very much.

* * *

'Mom,' Eric said.

She reached out her hand, unable to see him.

He moved forward, saying, 'I'm so sorry.'

She pulled his hand to her puffy face. 'I look terrible,' she said. 'I must look frightening.'

'No.' Eric smoothed her hair. So much of it was gray now and her face had become so old.

'Pilot's still there,' she said. 'He's got to stay a few more days, set things up.'

'I know. I have to go down there, actually. Do you want to—'

'I don't want to go.' She shook her head. 'I can't see anything, anyway. It wouldn't make any difference. And Patricia. There's Patricia.'

She and our mother had never met.

'He mustn't remember too much.'

Eric moved his hands away from her. 'I'll take care of it.'

'How is the garden?' Hannah asked, letting go of his hand.

'The garden?' he said, somewhat confused. Then, 'Mom, it's the middle of winter. What difference does it make?' The weeds of autumn had overgrown, anyway, and the vegetables Hannah had planted had died and lay frozen in the earth which filled the old swimming pool. It was just a tangle of decay. 'It's fine,' he said after a while. 'It needs a bit of work, but I'll take care of it. When it gets warmer, I'll—'

'What will you do?' She kept her eyes closed now, he noticed, not even bothering to try to see. The light in the room was harsh. Every lamp was on.

'I'll talk to Katherine,' he said, shaking his head. 'This is crazy.'

'Has she been—'

'—talking to Pilot?' my brother said. 'Yes, I think so. She's helping him.'

'She doesn't know, though,' Hannah said.

'Not really.' Eric sighed. 'She thinks she knows something, but really, really she . . .' He trailed off. He lacked the strength, at the moment, to finish his sentence. 'Because Pilot doesn't really know anything, either, I guess.'

'Pilot knows,' Hannah said. 'It's all mixed up, but it's in there.'
Our mother opened her eyes, which appeared clear to Eric, completely normal.

'Mom, don't worry,' he said, sighing. 'I said not to worry, didn't I say—'

'I'm worried.'

'I know—'

'—and I think I'm—'

'—Mom, I'm sorry—'

'—going crazy, too, like Pilot,' she said. 'I think something's wrong with me, something's—'

'—but everything's going to be—'

'—really wrong, you know,' she finally told him, 'I've been seeing, seeing her, your sister. She comes to me. Fiona . . . she comes to see me.' Hannah was out of breath now, hyperventilating.

'Fiona comes to see you?'

'Yes.'

He was sitting on the canopy bed, rubbing his eyes. 'Fiona's gone, Mom, gone a long, long time ago.'

'I know, but, I know I'm crazy, it's crazy, but I keep seeing her, keep hearing her little voice. Do you remember her voice?'

She had a little girl's voice, nothing out of the ordinary – sweet, high-pitched, sometimes shrill. He moved, getting up, and Hannah's eyes, opening, sought him in the room. It meant she could only see shadows.

'You can't see anything at all,' Eric said. 'How can you see a ghost? How can you see—'

'There's no such thing, I know, but what if, what if a memory becomes too strong. Isn't there a neurological—'

'There's nothing,' he said frustratedly. 'There's nothing. It's not neurological. You're imagining things, that's all, just imagining.'

'But I see her.' She reached her hands out. My mother could see Fiona standing at the end of the bed now, actually, twisting one of the tassels that hung from the canopy, her little feet standing one on top of the other, fidgety. 'I see her right now.' Her voice was pleading.

My brother shook his head. 'You see her right now.'

Hannah had a large tear moving down her face, breaking into a thousand little rivulets. 'I'm so sorry,' she was saying. 'I was such a terrible person, such a stupid—'

Eric walked to her and put his hand on her hair again.

She looked up, her face a mess. 'Your father's dead.'

Eric brought her head to his chest.

'Just like I always knew he would die, in that stupid airplane, just exactly the way he always—'. And there emitted from her a sound unlike any Eric had ever heard her make, a squeal, like an animal sound. 'I hate you,' she said. 'I hate you like I hated him.'

'Mom.'

'You're just the same.'

She had the radio on full blast, was lying face down on the mattress on the floor of the *enclosure*, having kicked off her shoes. She still had all of her clothes on, except her overcoat, which she had allowed to fall from her shoulders the minute she entered. The pizza, thankfully, was on its way – extra olives, light sauce.

Katherine thought of the Tunnel Man. What was he eating tonight? Was he drunk? What had happened in his life to make him end up living in a tunnel under a highway? The knock at the door, she knew this time, was not the pizza guy. It was my brother. It was time, she thought, to tell Eric to stop coming over. Katherine let him knock twice before getting up.

'I'm coming,' she told the door.

When she opened it, Eric walked into the room without saying anything. He had a bruised look, his face troubled.

'What happened?' she asked. 'Is it Pilot?'

'It's my father.'

She closed the door behind him. She went to the radio and turned it off.

Eric sank on to the edge of her mattress, overcoat still on, hands rubbing together like a fly. 'I never imagined—' he began, and then he stopped.

There was something different about him. 'Just tell me,' Katherine said. 'Just say it.'

'He flew away.' It was more of a laugh than anything else, although his tone was unidentifiable.

Katherine pushed her hair out of the way and knelt beside him.

'He was with Pilot and, and Patricia. And apparently, he simply flew off somewhere. They haven't found his airplane.'

'Flew off—'

'Over the ocean. Into the fucking wild blue yonder.'

'On purpose?' Katherine said, checking.

'He knew.' Eric looked at her, eyes wide. 'He knew what Pilot was doing, that he was looking into all this, all this *shit*.'

'Eric, come on.'

Katherine wanted to ask him, wanted to know if he'd ever suspected his father, but she couldn't. Not now. 'Do you think it upset him?'

'That is the understatement of the fucking century.' Eric's head was shaking. 'He killed himself, didn't he?'

'How is Pilot?'

'I'm not so sure,' Eric said. 'I have to fly down tomorrow. We're having the memorial service in Florida. That's what he wanted.'

'He left a note?'

'Nothing that anyone has found yet.'

Katherine sat down on the mattress next to him and placed an arm around his shoulders. 'I'm sorry,' she said, knowing she sounded sincere but also knowing she didn't feel it. 'I really am.'

He leaned into her, dropping his head on to her neck. 'I'm like him,' Eric said. 'He and I, we're just alike.'

'I know,' Katherine said. 'I know.'

'What am I going to do? How am I—'. His voice broke.

'I don't know.' Katherine forced understanding into her voice. Whenever this happened, she realized, the world hardened a bit more around her. Whenever something like this happened, she felt herself become that much more cynical, out of touch. Why couldn't she feel as much sympathy as she wanted to? Was something wrong with her? 'I should tell you', she said, 'about what I've discovered.'

'Discovered?'

'When Pilot was, when he was lost in the woods—'

'Yes.'

'—he met someone.'

'What are you talking about?'

'There's a man, a homeless man, just an alcoholic, really, who lives in the drainage tunnel under the highway.'

'You're kidding me.'

'He knows Pilot.'

Eric shook his head, an expression of bewilderment. 'So?'

'So he knows, at least I think he knows, where Pilot put the evidence, or whatever it is Pilot put out there that he, that he thinks is evidence.'

Eric was looking at Katherine now, his eyes red, his face drained. 'Do you think I had anything to do with—'

Katherine said nothing.

'—with Fiona?'

Katherine stared back at him for a long moment, until finally she said, 'No, no, Eric, I don't.'

Eric sighed. 'I was starting to think the entire world was against me.'

'I'm going out there to talk to him again,' she said flatly. 'He told me to—'

'Who?'

'The man in the tunnel. He told me to come back in three days.'

'You're crazy. You're not going out to—'

'I can't help it. I think whatever Pilot may have hidden out there will help him clear everything up.'

'Katherine,' Eric said, 'look what this has already done to my family. My father has—'

Katherine couldn't respond. She just said, 'We have to find it. Whatever it is, we have to find it.'

'Why? What psychological reason do you—'

'We just do,' she said.

'That's enough, Katherine.' My brother rose from the mattress. 'This is coming to an end.'

The next day Katherine pulled into the Better-Than-New Auto World and asked the first salesman who approached her – a young man wearing a cheap suit and carefully combed red hair – where she could find Jerry Cleveland. 'He's with another customer right now, ma'am,' the young salesman said formally, touching his bangs. 'But perhaps I can be of service?'

Katherine smiled coolly. 'I'm not buying anything today.' She got out of her car, slammed the door behind her and walked into the sales office.

Cleveland had his foot up on a chair and was smoking a cigarette, waving it around like a wand, in the middle of a pitch. '—lime-green Mercury Monarch,' he was saying, 'a truly attractive automobile, beautifully maintained. We do all the detailing ourselves, you know, making sure everything's absolutely perfect before it even hits the lot.' He nodded in Katherine's direction, indicating that she should wait. The middle-aged couple looked hard at the agreement on the gray metal desk in front of them, then they looked at each other with expressions of grave concern. Everyone waited this way.

Come on, Katherine thought. Just buy the fucking lime green Mercury Monarch and let's get on with our lives.

'We'll have to think about it,' the man said sadly.

The woman looked up, eyes drowning in her face. 'Can we get back to you?'

Katherine pushed the hair out of hers. She bit her fingertip, chewing away a piece of flesh.

'There's been a certain amount of interest in this particular model,' Cleveland said. 'I don't know if—'

'But we can't just—'

'Ah hell, go ahead and take your time.' Jerry Cleveland smiled a broad, generous smile. 'You spend some time thinking about it and if it's still here when you're done we'll work something out, something that'll make you happy.' Then he pointed to Katherine.

'Would you two mind if I took a moment to speak with my daughter?'

'Oh,' the woman said, her eyes brightening, 'not at all.'

'Go right ahead,' her husband agreed.

Cleveland came toward Katherine then, his expression grim, his features as gray as his cigarette's ash.

'Your daughter?' she whispered.

'It makes me seem kinder.' As before, he led her into the manager's office.

'I don't know if you've noticed,' Katherine said when the door closed behind them, 'but I'm white.'

'You're adopted.' He winked. 'So what can I do for you today, Katherine DeQuincey-Joy with a hyphen?'

Katherine sat down in the metal folding chair, hands on her lap. 'I just wanted to, to get your opinion.'

'What on?'

'James Airie.' She didn't pause when she said, 'He killed himself last week.'

'Oh.' Cleveland sat down, too. 'Holy shit.'

Katherine looked at his face, the deep crevices, the worn lines, the colorlessness. 'I need you to tell me why you think he did it. Was there anything, any evidence—'

'That the father did it? There was certainly no proof.' Cleveland sighed. 'And like I told you, it was Bryce Telliman's theory more than mine. He just kept saying we should look closer to home, as if he knew something about Airie that he wasn't telling.'

'Closer to home,' Katherine repeated. 'Like what?'

He shrugged. 'I don't know. Hell, it was the Seventies. It could have been anything . . . drugs, pornography, just about—'

'But you never found anything incriminating.'

Cleveland looked at his hands. He flicked his cigarette into the bean-bag ashtray on the old desk. 'No. We never did.'

'Telliman was never charged?'

'All we had was circumstantial. He was a suspect, that's all.'

'Seems like there would have been circumstantial evidence for about two dozen people that night.'

'He was with the girl all evening. Everyone saw him and his footprints were found in the woods.'

'You never went after the father?'

'There was nothing leading to him – nothing besides Telliman.'

'What do you think now?'

Cleveland crushed his cigarette in the ashtray and lit another one. He began, 'I think—' and then he stopped, asking, 'Was there a note?'

'No.'

'Did he know?' he asked. 'Did he know you were investigating this?'

'I'm not investigating, I'm—'

'Young lady, you are investigating.'

Katherine gave in. 'He was with Pilot and Pilot is a talker. He probably told him.'

She was starting to know me. Katherine was understanding me more and more every day.

'Did Pilot find that evidence yet? The shoe or the knife? Or did you?'

She shook her head, curls quivering. 'Not yet.'

He leaned back. 'How'd he do it?'

'What?'

'The father. Did he shoot himself? Was it pills? Did he jump?'

'He flew out to sea, apparently,' Katherine said. 'He had an airplane, a little one.'

'That's right,' Cleveland said. 'He was a pilot. That's why he named the boy—'

'Pilot, yes.'

'Flew away, huh?'

'They still haven't found the plane.'

'Or the body?'

'Or the body.'

'I'll bet it connects the father,' Cleveland said, 'the evidence, I mean.'

Katherine sighed. She tried to gather a bunch of her hair into her hands, but it slipped away. 'It would mean I've been very wrong about, about this whole thing.'

'This kid has psychological problems, Katherine.'

'Well . . .'

'Right?'

Katherine shrugged. 'He does.'

'Always look to the parents for that stuff.'

Katherine laughed. 'You're a Freudian, too? Seems like everyone is these days.'

'I just know that if you've got a screwed-up kid, you've got screwed-up folks.'

'You're mostly right.' Katherine nodded. 'Mostly.'

'Did the police get the file from Albany?'

'The detective hasn't called yet,' Katherine said. 'I thought I'd give him a few more days.'

'Look at it. Read it. There's bound to be something in there that'll pop out, make you think of something you hadn't thought of.'

'But why would he do it?'

'The father? He was a drunk.' Cleveland rubbed his hand over his face.

This had never occurred to Katherine. 'How do you know that?'

'I was one, too.' Cleveland smiled. 'We recognize each other, us drunks. People do strange things when they're blacked out. Airie may not even remember what he did. He may have been the one to put that evidence in his kid's room and then totally forgot about it.'

'He wouldn't set up his own son, would he?'

'After killing his own daughter?'

'Jesus Christ.' Katherine put a hand to her mouth.

'Yeah.'

There was a knock on the door. It was the young man Katherine had met in the parking lot. 'Jerry,' he said, poking his head inside, 'I think they're ready to sign.'

Cleveland winked at Katherine again. 'It was the daughter thing,' he said. 'I owe you one.'

* * *

Katherine test-drove the idea: *The father did it.*

In an alcoholic rage James Airie killed his daughter, she thought, and hid the evidence in his son's bedroom, thinking no one would find it. The next morning, waking from a nightmare of abuse, he had forgotten everything. Was that possible? She remembered a story she'd heard about someone in rehab who had dreamed of killing his parents. He was sure he had done it. There were too many details for it to be an actual dream. But his parents were fine. Later, it was discovered that in an alcoholic stupor he had gone to the wrong house and killed another couple, thinking the whole time they were his parents. He had never remembered until his memory cleared up.

Had James Airie suddenly remembered killing his own daughter?

Katherine wondered what it would do to me to understand this. She didn't know that I already had thought of it a million times. Would I even believe it? she thought. Did she? Wouldn't someone have known? That night, the night of the party, wouldn't someone from the family – my mother, for instance – wouldn't she have heard something? Katherine wondered what kind of cop Cleveland had been. He had admitted that he was a better used-car salesman. He admitted he had been a drunk. She imagined Fiona, seven years old. What else did he do to her? Did he rape her? Where was the body?

The father did it. It made things easier.

It certainly made Eric more attractive.

The simplest explanation, Katherine told herself, is usually the right one. Isn't it?

She wanted to ask someone else. She needed another opinion. This had been Bryce Telliman's theory. Cleveland had said that, too. Of course, Telliman was the accused. He'd say anything, accuse anyone. Anyone in his position would. Unless, of course, he really was innocent. The innocent are usually compelled to tell the truth, or at least their version of it.

She realized she'd been chewing her fingers, and a fresh oozing of blood appeared on two of them. Katherine turned off Sky

Highway and into the hospital parking lot, swerving into the area reserved for the clinic. She got out of the Rabbit and walked to the glass entrance. She passed reception, strode down the hall and finally reached her office door.

The father did it.

What had happened to Bryce Telliman? She walked across the room to her cluttered desk, took a slip of paper out of her purse and dialed the phone. 'Better-Than-New Auto World,' a voice said cheerfully.

'Jerry Cleveland, please.' When he came on the line, Katherine said, 'What happened to him?'

'Who?'

She realized she'd been inside her head for too long. 'Bryce Telliman.'

'He moved away, I guess. I mean, where do those people go?'

'Those people?'

'You know.'

'What?'

'Homosexuals.'

Katherine laughed.

'By the time we gave up on the whole thing', Cleveland said, 'Telliman had an address in the city.'

'Thank you,' Katherine said.

Elizabeth was at the door. 'Oh, there you are,' she said. 'You have someone waiting.'

'One more minute.' On the phone again, Katherine dialed the number for New York information. 'Bryce Telliman, please,' she told the operator, 'a residence.'

'B. Telliman?' the operator asked.

'That will do.'

Katherine wrote down the number. She wanted to call him right away, but she had already canceled one appointment today and another was waiting in reception. She didn't have time. She would have to try later. Besides, her intercom was buzzing. She picked up. 'Hello?'

'Katherine,' Greg's voice said. 'I'm glad you're here.'

'Hi, Greg.'

'I tried earlier, but Elizabeth said you were out and she didn't know where—'

'Can I ask you something, Greg?'

'Sure.'

'Did you know James Airie?'

'Did I know—'

'He's dead.'

There was a pause. 'No. I never met him.'

'Shit.'

'What happened?'

'He flew into the ocean in his little airplane.'

'Oh my God.'

'I'm getting very confused,' she admitted. 'I'm wondering if—'

'Kate,' Greg said, 'why are you getting so involved in this family? Is it Eric?'

'No, it's Pilot,' she said, 'he's my—'

'I know he's your client, Kate, but for Christ's sake.'

'I need to know.' She looked around her office. It was a mess, she thought, such a terrible, stupid mess.

'Have you spoken to him about it – to Pilot?'

'We're scheduled for tomorrow, a telephone session, but now I don't know.'

'Are you thinking his father was confessing somehow?'

'I'm hoping,' Katherine said. 'I'm hoping that's what it was.'

'Why?'

'Knowing is better than not knowing, isn't it?'

Greg didn't answer. He just said, 'Kate.'

'I've got a client and I've got to get going. Did you want to ask me something?'

'Forget it,' he said. 'It can wait.'

On the phone Katherine asked immediately, 'The man who lives in the tunnel beneath the highway, do you remember him?'

'Beneath the tunnel?' I had been in it a million times as a kid, running through to the highway island on the other side. There was something familiar about it. I remembered the feeling of being swallowed by the woods, the forest lashing out like an enormous tongue. The tunnel like a throat.

But there was a man, a man who lived inside it.

'I remember—'. I looked around Patricia's kitchen, as if I could find the answer written on the wall somewhere. 'I don't know,' I said. 'I'm not sure.' I remembered the concrete sides of the tunnel curling upwards and over me and around me. I remembered the light coming through the other side like the light of heaven beckoning people who have died and come back.

'There's a man who lives out there,' Katherine said, her voice almost ashamed, 'the kids call him the Tunnel Man. He's homeless, an alcoholic – harmless, obviously. But, Pilot, he knows you. He knows your name.' She allowed a pause. 'He knows about the evidence.'

'Jesus Christ,' I said, touching my forehead. 'I was so incredibly deranged. How could I—'

'He knows what you did with the evidence, Pilot.'

I tried to picture him, the Tunnel Man, but there was nothing. 'How does he know?'

'He says he'll show me where it is. I'm going out there this afternoon to find him.'

I was still in Florida, waiting for the search for my father to end, for the coastguard to stop looking so we could simply get on with the memorial service. 'I don't know,' I said. 'I'm not sure if I remember the Tunnel Man.' As I said the words, though, they felt familiar, like words I had spoken before. I tried more of them. 'The tunnel by the highway,' I said. 'In a tunnel under the highway there's a man.'

'Anyway,' Katherine said, a sigh in her voice, 'how are you feeling?'

'I'm fine,' I told her. 'I'm just, I'm just waiting.'

'They haven't found it, the airplane?'

'No.'

Patricia had gone to her room and had started to weep. She hadn't stopped, really. Sometimes she came out and put her arms around me, saying how sorry she was. I told her she had nothing to be sorry about, she had done nothing wrong. The sleeping bags, she said. She forgot them. No, I told her, it was him, he did it on purpose, he wanted this. It made her cry again, hearing me say it, and she'd go back into her room and weep some more.

'Things are tense,' I said to Katherine. 'Patricia is very upset.'

'What about the medication?'

'I'm off it.' I hadn't taken anything since we had come back. My mind was clear as the hurricane-swept Florida sky.

'And do you know when you're returning to New York?'

'The service is soon,' I told her. 'As soon as they stop searching, we'll set it up. I'll be back the minute it's over.'

'I have things to talk about with you,' Katherine said.

'Good.'

'I have ideas about what you remembered, about what—'

'Excellent,' I said. 'What is it?'

Katherine sighed. 'Pilot,' she began. 'I can't—'

'I want to know.'

'You told your father?'

'About what?'

'About how you think Eric—'

'I told him,' I said, 'yes. I told him everything.'

'That you had the evidence hidden somewhere?'

'He didn't believe me.'

'You told him exactly what it was?'

'About the shoe and the knife, yes.'

'Pilot,' Katherine said gently, 'I don't want you to get upset, but I want you to ask yourself if you think it is possible that your father, that it was him who might have—'

'Killed Fiona?'

She was silent for a full half-minute. 'It was a theory,' Katherine said. 'According to Jerry Cleveland, it was, it was postulated that it might have been your father, at the time, you know. The police—'

'Oh,' I said.

'—believed it was possible that he might have . . . You should think about it, anyway, about what you remember from that night, if there was anything unusual about, about your father's behavior, anything strange. If there was—'

'He was a different person.'

Katherine said, 'I'm going to visit Bryce Telliman. Is that all right?'

'You are?'

'If nothing turns out from the Tunnel Man—'

'Oh shit,' I said. It was like a door opened up inside me and behind it I could see a face, the cloudy eyes under all that hair. I had sat with him inside the tunnel, given him all the money in my pockets.

'What?' Katherine said.

'I remember talking to him. I remember trying to make him understand me.'

'Trying to—'

'Just trying to get the words out,' I said. 'His name is Billy.'

I had been almost catatonic, like an animal in the last moment before giving itself up to a predator, its body exposed, its mind cut off.

And then they found him. They found everything – the plane, his body.

Our mother wasn't able to come. She couldn't see our father, anyway, she said, so what difference did it make? She said it was Patricia he had loved.

And since I had no response for that, I let it go.

Throughout the service I stood between Eric and Patricia and imagined my father killing Fiona. I thought of his hands around her neck, squeezing the air out of her tiny body.

The service was conducted at a Presbyterian church Patricia had forced our father to attend every Easter and Christmas. One after another, his friends, mostly old pilots, airplane mechanics, fishing-tackle shop owners, stepped up to the podium and said it was the way he wanted to go, old Jim loved flying so much. They all talked about how he was still flying somewhere out there. They actually believed this. But I saw in my mind our father's body not flying, but floating, bloated beyond recognition, his eyes open to the sea floor. Here were all of Patricia's friends, too. These were the wives of pilots and hunters. These were women more at home in blue denim than black nylon. Their sympathy was genuine, the expressions in their eyes far less maudlin, far more acknowledging of the disappearance, the deliberateness of it.

Patricia wept steadily and I found myself crying a little bit, too, the tears at first like surprises on my face. Eric stood beside me, impassive. I remembered that he didn't cry at the service for Fiona, either. I saw things with such clarity now that I thought I could see the obfuscation itself, my life's bizarre catastrophe playing out:

A girl disappeared, one brother accused the other, the father – guilty by action or the lack of it – follows the girl into the void. It had a symmetry. Why else would he kill himself?

It was never suggested at the service that he committed suicide, of course, that he would have even considered taking his own life. And the official police finding was death by misadventure.

I would leave Patricia here in Florida in the little cottage she had shared with him. More than likely, I would never see her again. She'd send me cards on all the right holidays, and I would call her on the anniversary of his fading away, just to make sure she was all right. Old soldiers don't die, the saying goes. It's the same for pilots. They don't die, they only get lost. Our mother had clouds in her eyes as long as I can remember. Perhaps that is what he saw in her, all those years ago.

But there I go, falling into the same trap as those old veterans.

Afterwards, Eric stood outside with his hands in his pockets and compared the weather to New York. 'It isn't frozen yet,' he said. 'It is colder, though, up there.'

It was just a week before Christmas. I had completely lost track. I wore only a black sports coat and old black corduroys. They were our father's, in fact, everything somewhat too big.

'I've been worried about how you were taking this,' Eric said. 'But I can see now that you're all right.'

'I've been crying a lot,' I admitted.

'You always cried a lot.'

'I spoke to Katherine.'

'Katherine DeQuincey-Joy.' It was odd the way he said it, just repeating her name.

'Are you still seeing her?'

He looked at the sky, which was blue and ignorantly bright. 'I don't know. I don't think so.'

I said, 'She's looking into things.'

'Yeah.'

'She has a theory.' I wanted to be cautious, but at the same time I wanted an ally and his opinion. 'She thinks Dad, thinks he did something—' I was whispering now '—something to Fiona.'

'What are you talking about?'

'She thinks that's why he—'

'Did you say anything to him?'

'I told him the truth.' I had to look away.

'You wouldn't know the fucking truth', Eric said, 'if it fell on you.'

'Eric,' I said, my head shaking, my hands trembling, 'I'm sane now.'

'Pilot—'

'I need to know what you think about that.'

My brother turned to me, the look of righteous conviction in his eyes I remembered from childhood, and in a way it frightened me and in a way it consoled me. 'It's what everyone always thought all along, you idiot.'

I shook my head.

He laughed. 'Pilot, you are so crazy. You have no idea how crazy you are.'

'Katherine believes me.'

'Katherine is looking for the reason you're crazy. Katherine is nurture. I am nature. Do you understand?'

'There's no such thing as crazy,' I said. 'You're a fucking neurosurgeon, you should—'

'Then there's no such thing as you, little brother.'

'Then there's no such thing as a old rusty knife with dried blood still on it and a red tennis shoe, either.'

'You don't have those things.'

I had been standing at the door, shaking the hands of these old pilots and mechanics. I only smiled at Eric now. I had been crying for so long, and now I smiled. I had been crying, I thought, all my life. 'Yes, I do.'

'Where?'

'Where is the last place, Eric, that you would look?'

'Do you want to disgrace our father's memory? What is the point of this, Pilot?'

'But what if he—'

'He took his own life, for Christ's sake. You don't think that's enough proof?'

I wasn't sure about the truth any more. But I was sure about what I had done with the evidence. 'Eric,' I said, 'where is the last place you would look?'

'What the fuck are you talking about, Pilot?'

I said, 'You tell me.'

The same day, but colder, a Saturday afternoon, nearly Christmas, the woods rustled and strained against a wind that came off the highway from the north, the thin branches black as Chinese calligraphy against the too-blue winter sky like an upside-down frozen-over lake, an arc of ice-brittleness above. Katherine hugged herself, not dressed for this in a light jacket and jeans. Three days earlier the weather had been completely different. Katherine had always loved winter in the city. Out here in the suburbs, though, there was no comfort in it. She moved steadily along the path that followed the highway, toward the concrete tube where the Tunnel Man lived. Would he remember her? She thought he was less crazy than his act indicated. He would remember her. The real question was, did he have the evidence? One seven-year-old girl's red drugstore sneaker, one hunting knife, both of these things gone in memory twenty years, fingerprints intact.

Katherine prayed those fingerprints belonged to my father.

She saw the tunnel up ahead of her, its mouth dark, water trickling like drool out into a puddle, bigger now than it had been three days ago. It had been raining that day. Did he know she was coming? Could he hear her walking down the path? When she rounded the corner and stood in front of the pool of filthy, cold water, she saw through the tube all the way to the highway island's daylight on the other side. Where the Tunnel Man's house had been was now only scattered debris, pieces of wood, a couple of crumpled, soggy blankets. There was a large piece of blue plastic sheeting stuck in the flow of the water.

'Hello?' Katherine said. It was a stupid thing to say, she thought. Clearly no one was there.

Clearly the Tunnel Man had left.

She trod across the edges of the pool and, her feet dry this time, stepped into the tunnel. It echoed, of course, announcing her aloneness. She found the plastic sheets and pulled them back. Underneath was an old shopping cart, a wet pile of rags and packing blankets. There was a smell emanating from it that was almost sweet, like an orchard of rotting apples. There were odd bits and pieces of things left behind. A few books, a bible, some Stephen King novels, a *Metropolitan Home* magazine. He had taken off, Katherine realized. He had gone. Had he left the evidence? No, he was probably using the knife, gutting road-kill raccoons and roasting them over a fire. Katherine pulled the edge of the wet packing blanket back and beneath it the Tunnel Man's face was clearly visible, eyes closed as if sleeping. His skin was made whiter, cleaner, actually, by the water washing over it. The dead man's image was presented to Katherine with the same banality as any inanimate object in the tunnel. She pulled the wet blanket back more and saw that he was fully dressed, his body deep in the mire of junk and dead leaves and garbage that flowed through. There were empty bottles all around him. He had killed himself by drinking, Katherine thought. She wondered if she should say anything to the police. What would be the point? Then she imagined those girls from the Junior High discovering the body. She could hear them shrieking. No, she would report it. She'd call that Vettorello guy. He would help.

Her mind blank, Katherine walked back to the car which she had parked in the junior high lot. Inside it, she dialed the number for the police.

'Detective Vettorello,' she said.

The receptionist asked her to wait.

'Vettorello.'

'Detective Vettorello,' Katherine said, 'this is Katherine DeQuincey-Joy.'

'I was going to call you,' he said. 'The file just arrived from upstate. We're ready to go. I talked to Cleveland, too. I'm glad he could help you. I wasn't sure if—'

Katherine broke in, 'I need your help in an entirely different way right now, at this moment—'

'What can I do for you?'

'I discovered a, a dead body,' she stammered, 'and I didn't want to just call the police, I mean, I wanted to call you—'

'Where is it?' Vettorello's voice contained within it an edge of calm, a tone belying a nearly untraceable undercurrent of thrill.

She said, 'It's in a concrete tunnel under Sky Highway. It's just past Exit 9.'

Vettorello shouted something across the office. 'Stay on the phone,' he told her. 'Where are you right now?'

'In my car,' Katherine told him. 'I have a car phone, but—'

'Did you move the body? Did you touch it at all?'

'No,' she said, 'I don't think so.' Did she touch it? She couldn't remember.

'Good. Now I want you to tell me exactly how you found it.' He was laughing a bit. 'What the hell were you doing in the concrete tube beneath Sky Highway?'

'It's complicated,' Katherine said. She looked at her hand. She had just torn a large piece of skin off her ring finger and a globule of blood was forming. She closed her eyes to the delicious feeling and placed her finger in her mouth.

'I'm listening.'

'The other day I was out walking around in the woods, in the woods where they found my client, Pilot Airie, just because I – well, because I was trying to get inside his experience, you know, and, and I met these girls, just kids from the junior high.' She sat in her sapphire-blue VW Rabbit with the black car phone to her ear and watched a boy, ten or eleven years old, walking across the junior high football field into the woods. It could have been me fifteen years ago. It could have been Eric, too. 'And I asked them if they knew about Pilot, if they had seen him, and they had heard about a man found raving out there and they also told me about the Tunnel Man.'

'The Tunnel Man.'

'I was curious,' Katherine said, 'so I went into the tunnel. And there was this man, an alcoholic, hopelessly deranged.' She was exaggerating, she knew. 'No,' she said. 'He wasn't so deranged, I guess. Just a drunk.'

'OK.'

'He said he knew Pilot, though. I think he might have helped him. I think they shared, shared something, something probably meaningless, but nevertheless—'

'Get to the part about him being dead,' Vettorello said.

'He told me he knew where Pilot put the evidence.'

'The shoe?'

'And the knife.'

'Excellent. Go on.'

'He told me to come back in three days, and that was—'

'Today, and you came back to find him and—'

'And it looks like he drank too much and his head fell into the water,' Katherine said. 'And he drowned. That's what it—'

'We'll figure out that part,' Vettorello said. He was smiling over the phone. She could hear him. 'I'll come out there, too,' he said now. 'There's a team on its way to you.'

'I'm in the parking lot at the junior high,' Katherine said. 'Should I return to the tunnel?'

'No, stay where you are,' Vettorello said. 'Stay right where you are.'

Katherine was smiling, too. It was stupid that she was smiling about this, she thought, a dead man – even terrible. But she couldn't help it. A man was dead and she was smiling, a professional counseling psychologist, and she couldn't stop herself.

Instead of taking me back to the airport, Patricia gave me the keys to our father's car, the rugged four-wheel drive he had picked me up in just a few weeks ago, the day I arrived. She didn't want to see it, she said, sitting in the driveway. So I drove it all the way back to New York in one steady blast of memories, stopping only for gas and Pepsi. I remembered everything – my whole life. I remembered Fiona, my little sister, and pulling her cool limbs in full cinematic motion from the wet pool behind the house, beads of glimmering water flying off her hair. I remember her smiling as I pulled her out, the bright little-girl giggle. This was a fully formed human being I remembered, not just a still photograph, an image from a catalog. I remembered Eric stalking me, the threats of death, the anticipation of violence. On each side of the highway that leads up the east coast of the United States, the thirteen colonies, I remembered my life. I remembered that he never carried them through, my brother, that his threats were just threats, that his violence was largely verbal.

Perhaps our father had remembered his life this way, too, his hands on the controls of the seaplane. Thinking of this, I wanted to turn the car off the highway, pedal pressed hard for the trees, my teeth clenched and my eyes closed. I didn't, though. That's what he did. I listened to the radio, instead, finding country music stations, the kind my father liked, the guitars all twangy and sharp, forcing myself to listen with his ears. I watched the sleek black sports cars of bachelors materializing in front of me. I crept by the old people in luxury sedans and college students in economy models returning home for the holidays. I examined the treeline, now moving by at sixty-five miles an hour, the cruise control set for easy driving, and saw how meaningless it had become, just a blur. When I got back, I thought, I would locate the evidence, I would have the police test it for fingerprints, blood, DNA, and then I would know. After twenty years, I wondered, would blood and fingerprints and DNA still exist? Would anything be detectable? Maybe not. It didn't matter. If I learned nothing, then nothing had changed. If I learned that it was my father who, in a fit of alcoholic rage, killed my little sister, then I would know everything I needed to know.

So I arrived at Hannah's house feeling tired but not numb, feeling sad but not morose—

This would be over soon, I was thinking.

—feeling sane.

It was late afternoon, but her light was on upstairs. She knew I was coming, and I knew she would wait for me. As soon as I opened the door, in fact, I heard her voice. 'Pilot?'

'I'm coming,' I called out. 'I have to unload the car.' I brought my luggage into the house and also the boxes of photographs Patricia had given me, pictures our father had taken from the seaplane, the faraway terrain of Florida he loved so much, the little island and white waves off the coast. When I was finished, I walked into her room. 'I'm here,' I said finally. 'Here I am.'

She sat in front of the window, an old woman in a chair, the radio playing softly, the air stuffy as the inside of an old trunk. 'Pilot,' she said. She'd been crying, of course. She reached out for me and I took her hand. 'I'm so glad you're back.'

'How are you?' I had asked her this every day on the telephone, but that was a different how-are-you, a telephone how-are-you. This one was real.

'I'm blind as a bat,' she said, a slight laugh in her voice.

'But you can see—'

'I can see your sister,' she said. 'During the day and then sometimes even at night she comes and sits beside me.' She was laughing at herself, saying this. She knew she'd been hallucinating. She knew she was going crazy. 'I'm afraid if I tell anyone', she said, 'they'll give me powerful medication of some kind and Fiona will disappear and I'll have to go years without seeing her again, and I couldn't—'

'It's just your memories, Mom.'

'I know, but they've been reborn.'

'You can see Fiona anytime you want. Just think of her, and then you can—'

'No,' she said. 'Not like this.'

'Is she happy?' I asked.

'She's a girl. She's as happy as girls ever are.'

'I have to ask you something,' I said.

'Pilot, please—'

'I have to,' I said.

'—I don't want to—'

'It's very important.'

She knew what it was.

'—talk about it now.'

'Did you ever think—'

'No.'

'—that Dad had anything to do with it—'

'Your father?'

'—with Fiona's disappearance?'

Hannah had been holding my hand. She let go of it now. 'Is that what you think?' she said. 'Have you given up blaming your brother? And what about Katherine DeQuincey-Joy?'

'Did you ever suspect him?'

Hannah turned her face to the window, eyes open and unfocused. 'Your father knew you were opening it all up again, knew you had the, the *things* somewhere,' she said now, 'didn't he?'

'I told him.'

'He either didn't want to learn the answer,' Hannah said, 'as I don't. Or he already knew the answer and didn't want to be around when you learned what it is.'

'I know.' I walked to the bed and sat down. 'I know those are the options. I'm just not sure what they mean.'

'Are you happy with either of them?'

'This is my life.'

'What about your sanity?'

'I don't know,' I said. 'I keep doubting that. I doubt it every minute.'

'I have gone blind,' my mother said. 'And now my husband is lost, too.'

'I'm going to give the shoe to the police.'

'Pilot,' she said.

'Mom, I have to.'

'Pilot.'

'And the knife.'

'Pilot—'. But she didn't finish. Her hand came to her mouth, and it seemed as if she couldn't say anything.

Shivering, Katherine waited in her car, her fingertips raw and scabby in her mouth. When the police arrived, she opened her door and stepped out. She had managed to stop herself from smiling, at least – smiling about a dead man. The cops seemed unhurried, serious but relaxed, doing something they did every day. Katherine introduced herself, hand extended, like a guest at a cocktail party, then led the two young police officers down the path into the woods she had taken just a half-hour earlier.

Inside the tunnel, one of the cops pulled the Tunnel Man out of the water, propping his head against the curvature of the concrete wall. 'Old Billy finally bit the big one,' he said with a grim smile.

'Billy,' Katherine repeated.

'He's been around for years,' the cop said sadly. The young policeman had introduced himself a moment ago, but now she couldn't remember his name. He had a fine mustache, dark skin and large, feminine eyes.

'You knew him?'

'He used to live in the dumpsite behind the Grand Union a few years ago,' the cop said, nodding toward the highway, 'then he moved into the tunnel.'

'Miss DeQuincey-Joy?' It was someone behind her.

'Detective Vettorello?'

He stretched out his hand from the backlit darkness. 'How are you?'

'I'm, I don't know,' she said. 'This is pretty weird.'

Vettorello wore a blue windbreaker over a yellow dress shirt and gray polyester pants. He wore big black rainboots and sloshed through the water in the tunnel. 'You'll have to fill out a report about finding the body out here, and, and I'll help you with that, so don't worry.' He was smiling, too. 'It shouldn't take too long.'

'Thank you.'

'Why don't you come out to my car for a moment?'

As Katherine followed, her feet got wet again, soaking her socks with the filthy water. She couldn't avoid it. The other night she'd thrown her things into the hamper and the chemical smell simply wouldn't go away.

Vettorello opened the door of an old red, boxy Volvo. 'Get inside,' he said. 'Go ahead.'

Katherine got into the passenger seat and watched Vettorello walk around to the driver's side. He got in, too, and shut the door hard. He turned to her now, saying almost teasingly, 'So can you tell me why the hell you were out here again?'

Katherine pushed her hair away from her face. 'I know it's weird,' she said, 'but, but the evidence I told you about, what I'm looking for—'

'The shoe.'

'And the knife.'

'Yes.'

'This crazy old guy said he knew where it was.' Katherine sighed. Vettorello lifted a single eyebrow.

'Let me back up,' Katherine said. 'Pilot Airie – he was found out here in the woods a few months ago, in the middle of a psychotic episode, right? So the other day I was walking around, just trying to understand things, perhaps from his point of view, I don't know, and there were these girls coming through the woods and they told me about the Tunnel Man.'

Vettorello raised both his eyebrows now. 'Did anyone else know you were going to see the Tunnel Man?'

Katherine shook her head. 'Why would—' and then she stopped. She stopped in the full horrible realization of what she was about to say. 'Eric,' she said.

'Eric Airie?'

And when she said it she knew what had happened. She knew he had been out here.

'Eric Airie,' Vettorello said. 'Your patient's brother.'

'Eric Airie.'

'Didn't you say he's the one Pilot is accusing of, of killing their sister all those years ago?'

Katherine nodded. 'He's the one.'

Vettorello put his hands over his face. 'This is the craziest thing I've ever heard,' he said. 'A homeless man dies. A man dies who I knew eventually would die like this, his head in the water, blood alcohol levels through the ceiling, no doubt, and now I have to go and question a brain surgeon about his whereabouts for the past few days.' He was shaking his head. 'This is ridiculous.'

'It gets worse,' Katherine said. 'Their father, well, he's disappeared, maybe suicide.'

'Disappeared.'

'Flew into the ocean.'

'By himself?'

'All alone.'

'Fuck me.'

'Tell me about it,' Katherine said. 'I'm beginning to think it was him all along – the father, you know, who hurt the girl. Pilot got confused and blamed Eric, and all the rest.'

'You've talked to Cleveland?'

'This was a theory,' Katherine said. 'This was a police theory.'

'That's what the files seem to indicate. After what's his name—'

'Bryce Telliman.'

'After him, it was the father they watched. An airline pilot.' Vettorello began to muse. 'I wonder where the little girl's body is. I mean, he could have gotten her on to a plane in a little suitcase and dropped her anywhere, somewhere no one would ever look, anywhere in the world.'

317

'It's possible.'

'Is it likely?' he asked now. 'I mean, forget hiding the body anywhere, is it likely, psychologically speaking, that the father did it and then hid the fact for all these years?'

'This family is deeply—' what was the word? she asked herself '—troubled.' It was all she could find, it would have to do. 'And I think anything is likely with these people, at this point.'

'They're here, you know,' Vettorello said. 'The files arrived from Albany.'

'Can I see them?'

'You have to come back to the station.' Vettorello paused for a moment, his hand touching the Volvo's dashboard. 'The shoelace was tested, as well, for being the right age and everything.'

'And?'

He looked at her steadily. 'It's not.'

'What?'

'It's made of some kind of nylon thread they didn't even have in the Seventies.'

'You're kidding me.'

'What does that mean?'

'It means I'm an idiot,' Katherine said, almost laughing. 'As far as evidence goes, we've got nothing.'

'What about the Tunnel Man?' Vettorello asked. 'Did he really know where the evidence is?'

'What evidence?' Katherine said, still laughing. 'I've been led down a road to nowhere.'

It wasn't as thick as she expected, just a slim stack of papers in a manila folder, typed statements from witnesses mostly, some forms filled out, a few pages of handwritten notes. 'I'm sorry you can't take it home,' Vettorello said, 'but I can let you read it here. I'm not even supposed to let you do that, really, but—'

'Thanks.' Katherine flipped through the pages until she found one with Bryce Telliman's name on it. There in the police station, she scanned through the single-spaced, typed lines, picking up key words and phrases.

'. . . saw Fiona at the party . . . cute little girl, she sat on his lap . . . likes children . . . left around two in the morning . . . didn't know the family well, very sorry to hear . . .'

Katherine continued to leaf through until she found what James Airie had told the police. He had gone to bed late, the statement said, didn't remember what time, must have been around three or four a.m., had been drinking a great deal. He really couldn't remember much.

She chewed a finger, the rich taste of blood in her mouth.

Memory seems to be such a problem for the Airie family, she thought.

There were other statements from Telliman. And lots of other ones from the party guests. There were statements from the Tischmans from next door, the Johnsons and the Brooks and the Daniers. There were the Jones and the Browns and the Ellimans and the Wells and the Malnerres. There were four bachelors, including Paul Davidson, Karl Fuchs, Arnold Desmond and of course Bryce Telliman, as well as four single women, including Celia Oblena, Sherry Meyerson, Tricia Caulder and Lacy Klugman. Finally, Katherine found what she was looking for. She held the slip of paper up for Vettorello to see. 'Did you read this one?'

'What is it?' Vettorello had been across the room, talking to another cop, styrofoam coffee cup in his hand. He walked back toward Katherine, still in his rubber rainboots, eyes focused on the sheet of paper.

'It's a warrant.'

'For what? Telliman's house?'

'No,' Katherine said. 'Something far more interesting. They searched Telliman's house, I presume, and found nothing. This is a warrant for searching the Airie house and it was denied.'

Vettorello took the piece of paper from her. He smiled thinly. 'Very interesting.'

'Why wouldn't the judge sign it?'

He took a sip of his coffee. 'Sometimes you have to have a lot of circumstantial before a judge will permit the search.' Vettorello sat down. 'They don't like to be wrong. They get in lots of trouble politically.'

'Opportunity,' Katherine said, more to herself than to Vettorello. 'Motive.'

'What motive would anyone have to kill their own kid?'

'It's usually rage,' Katherine said, 'anger, resentment.'

'An accident?' Vettorello said.

'Not possible, not with a knife.'

'We don't have a knife,' Vettorello reminded Katherine.

'You're right,' she said. 'You're right about that.' She slipped her hand into her pocket.

'Anyway,' he said, 'searching the Airie house in those days would have been very unpopular. They'd just lost their daughter, and to accuse the father—'. Vettorello winced.

Katherine thought for a moment. 'Cleveland said it was Telliman who first pointed to James Airie.'

'How did they know each other?'

'Did Cleveland ever ask that?'

'I'm sure he asked Telliman.'

Katherine was lost. 'Nothing makes any sense.' She looked at Vettorello. She looked around the suburban police station, the drab design, the sad Christmas decorations. The activity level was low right now, mostly people complacent at their desks, the radio tuned to a soft pop station. 'I don't understand any of this. How could there have been no real evidence?'

'There was the sneaker.'

'It led to nothing.'

'Listen.' Vettorello leaned toward Katherine. 'Sometimes in police work there is no good answer. Sometimes you don't find your bad guy.' He leaned back. 'It sucks, but it happens. It happens quite a lot, as a matter of fact.'

'The shoelace was from the Eighties?' Katherine could not understand this. Where had it come from?

She considered me. Why would I lie? To flush my brother out? It meant that she had been fooled into believing a crazy story by a paranoid schizophrenic. It meant Katherine had not only failed to help me with my psychological problems – she had, in fact, made them even worse.

'I should go,' she said now, shaking her head. 'I should go home.'

'I'll keep this around.' Vettorello indicated the file. 'And if you want to come back and read it again, just give me a call.'

On the drive home, Katherine decided to turn me over to another psychologist. She considered, for the long drive to the *enclosure*, leaving this job and going back to the city. And when she walked in the door, her feet cold, her hands shaking – full-blown winter now, freezing – Katherine was ready to quit. She set her things down and saw the message light was on. One message. It must be Michele, she thought. Or Mark.

Uncharacteristically, Katherine pressed the button.

'You have one message,' her answering machine said. 'Message one. Three fifty-seven p.m. . . .'

'Um,' a man's voice began, 'I, uh, I received a call from you the other day and I wasn't in town, so I just got this message this afternoon. My name is – is Bryce Telliman. If you want to call me back and let me know what, well, let me know what it is you called me for, that would be fine. I guess you have my number. Anyway, 'bye.'

It was almost Christmas. So I spent an afternoon at the Bed, Bath, and Beyond on the other side of the highway shopping for presents. It was almost impossible to pick anything out, but I finally settled on some beige-and-white striped towels for Hannah and a bathroom radio for Eric. Ordinarily I would have bought something for Patricia and my father, too, but it just seemed strange to get her anything. I'd send her a card, I thought. I walked through the aisles for what seemed like days, my hands stroking the sheets and blankets, my fingers running over the shelves of soap and bath salts. They had everything in this store. I paused in front of the chemical fire log display, wondering if Hannah would like to sit in front of a fire, if she could even see the flames. But then I imagined our house burning down, the ashes of my childhood rising into the air above Foxwood Court. And this was not a crazy thought, I told myself. This was a reasonable fear.

Fiona loved the news. How many girls that age even watch the news? She'd sit in front of the television and pay close attention to the stories – in those days it was Cambodia, the Carter election, the energy crisis. She'd fold her tiny legs underneath her minuscule butt on the floor and look up at the screen, her eyes rapt. And sometimes she'd turn around in amazement, her lower lip dangling. 'Pilot,' my little sister would say, 'look at this.' Perhaps other children are like that. But I doubt it. I think she was unique.

I'd shrug. 'Let's watch cartoons.'

And she'd tell me I was an idiot.

Sometimes I wonder what that meant about her, what that would have made of her. She was just a little girl, and it might have meant nothing. Everything can mean nothing.

On a trip to the library once she decided she wanted to learn French, and by the end of that afternoon she could count to ten. 'Uh, Du, Twa . . .' She skipped around the patio that day repeating the French numbers, lightly touching my head as she went by me. I was sitting on the flagstones popping a red spool of caps with a rock.

Sometimes I try to gather these memories all together in my head in an attempt to remember her whole. But something always slips away and I'm left with an incomplete picture. I would do anything to know where the photographs of her are, where Hannah put them, just so I could see her again.

Exhausted from the long drive into the city — Why had she moved so far away? What was she thinking of? — Katherine knocked on the door of the fourth-floor West Village walk-up and waited with her arms folded, fingers hiding beneath her jacket. From inside the apartment came the sounds of someone turning the television off and running to the door. '*Just a minute.*' It was the same voice from the telephone, a man's voice, but feminine. It was Bryce Telliman's voice. '*Just a minute,*' he said again. Katherine heard the door unlatching, the familiar New York sound of lock after lock after lock disconnecting. 'Are you Katherine?' It was open now.

She put her hand out. 'Nice to meet you, Bryce. Thank you very much for letting me come.'

He was an older man, thin as the dying, with long wavy gray hair and gray three-day stubble. 'Well,' he said, 'it's all right.' His skin hung off his neck like loose fabric.

'It's probably not easy for you to talk about this stuff, anyway.' She stepped into his little apartment, noticing the dozens of oil paintings hung on every wall, small abstract canvases made of thick, colorful smears of paint. Katherine looked around smiling.

'My paintings,' Telliman said. Then he motioned to a chair. 'Please, sit. Would you like something? Water? Tea? I have beer.'

'I'm fine,' she said. 'Thank you.' She took the canvas director's chair nearest the door. It was covered with flecks of paint.

Telliman took the one opposite. He sat for a moment, just looking at her, then shifted nervously. 'Where do we begin?'

Katherine took a deep breath. 'Like I said on the phone, I'm a psychologist and Pilot Airie is my patient. He's asked me to help him rediscover what happened to his little sister twenty years ago.' Katherine hadn't taken her jacket off and she still hid her fingers in the folds of her sleeves. 'And I know, believe me, I know that must have been a very painful experience for you, and I don't mean to dig up old injuries but—'

'I understand,' the man said. 'You want to know what I remember about that night.'

'Yes.'

'You want to know if I did it.'

Katherine shook her head. 'Pilot doesn't think you did it. Neither do I, if it means anything.'

'He doesn't?'

'He never thought it was you.'

'But he was just a kid.'

Katherine shrugged.

'And you?' Telliman said.

'It's all very difficult to understand.' Katherine heard the sound of steam hissing from a radiator in the next apartment. It made her miss the city. 'I don't have a theory or an opinion that I can really talk about yet.' She leaned forward a bit, asking, 'But why were you even at the Airie house that night?'

'I was a physical therapist in those days – a friend of a friend of a friend. It was the Seventies. People just went to parties. It didn't matter.'

Katherine nodded. 'Was it a good one? I mean, apart from the, from what happened?'

'There was a great deal of drinking, I remember. I remember doing a lot of that myself.'

'You played with her.'

'They seemed like nice kids.'

'Yes,' Katherine said, 'they probably were.'

'I've always loved children. I wanted to have them, myself, wanted to be a father, you know.'

'But—'

He sounded disappointed. 'But I'm gay and I could never have that kind of relationship with a woman, so I've had to enjoy children here and there. I've been more careful, though, since—'

Katherine nodded. She didn't know what to say.

'The little girl, Fiona, she was outgoing. She sat on my lap and talked, you know the way kids do, telling me her little secrets.'

Katherine thought she detected a southern accent in his voice, but she wasn't sure. 'Secrets?'

'She had a sip of someone's drink. She saw someone kissing someone. And the mother was OK with all of this.' Telliman's eyes were downcast. 'I mean, she saw me and the little girl and made a joke about Fiona being a flirt. But the father—'

'James Airie.'

'James.' Telliman shook his head. 'He kept telling her to leave me alone, you know, and by the tone of his voice I could tell that he meant for *me* to leave *her* alone.'

'Did you?'

'She went upstairs at some point.'

'And what happened next?'

'Just drinking. And I started to feel like I'd been drinking too much, you know, way too much.' It was the exact language from the police report. This had the sound, to Katherine, of something rehearsed, of something Telliman had said a million times. His voice was becoming monotonous, like he was singing a funeral dirge. 'So I walked around to the other side of the pool,' he continued. 'Fiona wasn't in there any more, you know, I don't know where she was, and I walked down to the trees they had in their backyard.'

'You went into the trees.'

'I thought I was going to throw up.'

'Why not use the bathroom?'

He sighed. 'I was embarrassed. I thought it would be more private in the woods. Besides, when you're drunk—'

'OK, and that's why your footprints were out there.'

'Obviously.'

'And was that it?'

The old man paused for a moment, his eyes glassy and wide. 'There was someone else out there, too.'

'James Airie?'

'No.' He smiled a bit. 'It was a kid.'

'Did you ever tell the police about that?'

'I told my lawyer. I don't remember if we—'

'What was the kid doing?'

'He was just sort of hiding, I think. Lurking around.' Telliman rolled his eyes. 'Anyway, I walked back out of the woods, and I think – I mean, I know people saw me do that. And I guess the little girl had either disappeared by then or something, because two days later I had the police at my door.'

'Jerry Cleveland.'

'What a moron.'

'He said you thought the father did it.'

Telliman chuckled, the gray skin of his neck jiggling slightly. 'Yeah.'

'What made you say that?'

'He never came after me.'

'What do you mean?'

'He never tried to threaten me, kill me, beat me up. I would have, I mean, if it were my daughter.'

'Which means—'

'Which means a couple of things. One, that he knew I didn't do it. And, two, that he knew she was gone for ever. Think about the way people act when their kids are missing. It's different from when they're dead. I'm telling you. You see it all the time on television, the hope in their eyes . . .'

Katherine nodded. 'Jerry Cleveland agreed with you about the father.'

'Really?'

'And James Airie has killed himself.'

Bryce Telliman sighed. His slapped his hands on his knees. 'Are you sure you wouldn't like something to drink, Katherine? I have lots of different kinds of tea.'

'I'm sure,' Katherine said.

'How'd he do it?'

'He flew his little airplane into the ocean.'

'His little airplane,' Telliman repeated.

Katherine realized now that she hadn't taken her jacket off. It was getting warm in here. 'Did you say you had beer?' she asked.

It almost never rang. She was in her Rabbit on the way back from the city when her cellphone rang. It was Dr Lennox, saying, 'There is something, Kate.'

Expectantly, Katherine asked, 'What? What is it?'

'I thought it was nuts,' Greg said, 'I thought *I* was nuts, but I took a second look at the blood test we gave Pilot Airie when he came in here.'

'And?'

'And, naturally, we only check for certain things.'

'And?'

'And I had the lab take a look, at great expense, mind you, but it's there in the test. It's in there.'

'Are you serious?'

'This stuff is not easily available. It's new. It's not entirely tested, as far as I know.'

Katherine held the phone to her ear and gripped the steering wheel tightly with her other hand. She had known it was possible, had known, in fact, that it was even likely. But now that it was true, she didn't know how to feel. She took a deep breath. 'This is getting weirder and weirder every second,' she said into the phone.

She could hear Greg Lennox sucking his teeth. 'I'm going to check and see if any of this stuff was given to Eric Airie. I know a sales rep from the pharmaceutical company that makes it.' Dr Lennox was grim. 'We have to remember, Katherine, it's not the kind of drug that would kill someone, even if he did—'

'It's worse,' she said. 'It's the kind of drug that makes you psychotic.'

'What are you going to do?'

'I'll wait.' Katherine pulled up to a light. 'Pilot should be back from Florida soon and I want to talk to him. Remember the shoelace?'

Dr Lennox was quiet.

'The one Pilot said was from the shoe he found, from the evidence?'

'I guess so.'

'It's not real.'

'So?'

'So I don't know if he has any actual evidence or not. In other words, Eric may have been successful in making Pilot crazier than he meant to. He may have made Pilot so crazy it came back to haunt him.'

Dr Lennox asked, 'Are you going to see Eric?'

'I'm going to avoid him, if I can.'

'There's nothing to worry about, Kate.' Dr Lennox's tone was unconvincing. 'Don't be frightened. This is between the family and Eric wouldn't, I'm sure – he wouldn't do anything, of course. He's a doctor.'

'Maybe there really isn't any evidence at all,' Katherine said, more to herself than to Dr Lennox. 'Maybe Pilot's using it as a story to flush his brother out, to make him do something—'

'That would be pretty—'

'Sane,' Katherine said. 'Wouldn't it?'

'Yes,' he said. 'In a way, I guess it would.' He paused, then said, 'I've never seen a family unravel like this.'

'They started unraveling twenty years ago,' Katherine said. 'Now it looks like everything's raveling back.'

Amazingly, it was Christmas Eve.

Eyes wide open, I was lying in bed. The only light coming in was a sliver of yellow driveway light through the mini blinds, and these sheets were too fucking new, I guess, or simply hadn't been washed enough, because they felt like sandpaper against my skin, abrasive as a scrubbing sponge. I lay awake listening to the irritating forced air hum of the central-heating system. It had become bitterly cold outside, a deep chill setting in, even invading my body in bed, insinuating itself under the covers the way Halley the Comet did when I was a kid. I usually slept perfectly, the sleep of the successful, deep and dreamless. I usually placed my head on my soft down pillow and one-thousand-thread-count sheets and miraculously discovered myself awake the next morning, the classical radio on, violins chattering, standing in front of the bathroom mirror, the shower filling the room with steam, my face full of recognition, razor in hand. That night, however, I was lying in bed staring at the tiled ceiling and I couldn't let go. Whether it was because of the sheets or the forced air hum or the light, I don't know, but I was wondering, couldn't stop wondering, where it could be, where the evidence was hidden, the fucking evidence – an old plastic Wonderbread bag, a little girl's red sneaker, a hunting knife, black handled – when I saw it. In a fraction of a second millions of neurons fired across my cerebellum, creating that single charge of realization, the burst of electricity that is a conscious thought, and I knew where it must be, had to be.

I saw it.

It was like something had come unlocked, a synapse had connected in just the right way, or disconnected, the right combination of serotonin and dopamine had been released. I could practically feel the pulsing of blood in my temples. I could almost hear the nerves crackling with electricity, the play of information along chemical routes through the ganglia of my nervous system. I found my feet on the hardwood floor. I found my hands reaching for the reading lamp. For some reason, I slipped into the clothes I had been planning to wear the next day – dress shoes, a gray suit, pinstriped, a pink shirt, monogrammed. But it didn't matter. Tomorrow didn't matter at all, I told myself. Tomorrow was canceled. I touched my face on the way out to the car and felt stubble, rough and sharp. I looked at my Patek Philippe in the yellow glow of the driveway light and saw that it was nearly three in the morning. I didn't remember putting this watch on, a watch that suddenly seemed alien. As I got in the car I realized that I had forgotten my overcoat. But I didn't care. I'd get this over with quickly. Now that I knew. Now that I knew where it was, exactly, precisely where it was.

How did I know where it was? Because I saw – for a fraction of an instant, I *saw* – through my brother's eyes.

For a fraction of an instant, everything had become clear.

Inside the Jag, it was like a freezer, and I held my hands to my mouth and blew, trying to warm the skin. I put my key in the ignition, turned the engine and waited a moment while the car thawed in the below-freezing temperature. Automatically, a compact disc came on in the stereo, one of the Brandenburg concertos, sweet and measured. But this was a night that didn't need a soundtrack. This was the part of my life story I didn't need in the documentary. I turned it off. I had an image of Fiona in my head, the way she had looked the night of the party through the trees, the people who had been standing all around the pool, cocktails and cigarettes in their hands, the mustachioed, blond Bryce Telliman standing alone off to the side, Hawaiian shirt open to his chest, eyes unfocused but flickering everywhere. I could see her tiny little-girl body in her red bathing suit with the white flower sewn between her two non-existent breasts. I remembered the sneakers on her feet, red high-tops, one of them tied, the other flopping around unlaced.

I pulled out of the long driveway and, without thinking, found myself on Sky Highway, the familiar whir of the tar road beneath the wheels, the yellow lines blurring by like lasers in a science fiction movie. I understood like no one in my family how the human eye apprehends the physical world. I knew more than anyone how an image distorts when it is converted from light and dark to discrete particles of information and then converted into a picture of something recognizable. I knew what could happen when this ordinary process breaks down. I knew the blurring that could occur and the rest of it: the panic, the sensations of fear, the psychological vertigo. I had been seeing double all my life. Through my own eyes and through my brother's.

I knew what our mother was experiencing.

I passed only three cars during the entire drive to the Thomas Edison junior high school parking lot. And, once there, I saw the same old orange BMW 2002, the same burgundy mist Buick Skylark, and same white early-Eighties Mustang, the same few poachers who parked back along the edge of these woods knowing that no one else used this part of the lot, so far from the school, way beyond the football field. Warmer now, even perspiring, I turned the engine off and cut the headlights. I knew that my brother would never find the evidence, that he had, in fact, never even remembered where he'd put it. Memory doesn't work that way. Details become cloudy, they switch around, become confused with so many other details that it is impossible to sort them all out. His brain was a blur, I thought. It takes someone else to decipher the memories, to find the shoelace of truth inside the snake-pit of recollection. I got out of my car into the fierce cold and closed the door without locking it. I stepped off the pavement and walked across the grass into the woods of my boyhood, where my life's experiment had begun.

When I was just a boy I found my father's old animal traps in the attic. Originally, they had been used for catching mink and muskrat, from the days – when our father was a kid – ordinary people sold animal pelts to Sears and Roebuck. When I was around twelve or thirteen I took three of these traps into these woods, setting them with bits and pieces of meat, carrots, cheese. Mostly, I caught squirrels and rabbits. In the mornings, I'd find the animals, their legs twisted and mangled from trying to get away, insane from the rage and pain of the rusty metal teeth. Sometimes, however, I'd find them catatonic, their undersides exposed, eyes all filmy and open, their bodies slack, wanting to die, I guess, or, often enough, already dead. Sometimes another animal would have come along, probably our cat, Halley the Comet, and they'd be gutted, their insides torn out, entrails exposed. I took these animals into the garage, usually, and experimented. I used a set of my mother's kitchen utensils to dissect their organs, categorizing each system with my old copy of *Gray's Anatomy*, trying to compare the animal equivalents to the organs of the human body. I have to say I became surprisingly knowledgeable about the structure of small mammals. But if one of them was still alive, I'd tack its body down by the fur and limbs to my father's workbench. Then I'd carefully remove the back of its skull with a serrated bread knife. If I was successful, the animal's brain would be exposed but its body still quivering, and I would touch different parts of its squirrel or rabbit or woodchuck nervous system just to see which parts of its body twitched. Bit by bit, I'd cut pieces away, seeing how long it took them to stop breathing.

Right now I took a few quiet steps into the woods, looking for the path I had taken home every day from school for so many years. Once I found it, I walked along confidently, more certain of my direction with every step.

The animals didn't last long without their brains, of course. But every now and then I found a squirrel or a rabbit who surprised me, who could live for quite a while – minutes, it seemed – without a central nervous system.

My father had given me the hunting knife when I was around ten, in secrecy. It was the knife I used to sever the legs off the little animals I had caught in his traps. It had a curved, steel blade, an ebony handle with a silver inlay of a rhinoceros. It came with a black leather sheath that attached to my belt and a small sharpening stone. Dad made me promise, when he gave it to me, never to tell my mother I had it, it was just between us guys. I carried this knife into the woods every day, checking the traps. And as the summers went by, I became more and more proficient at cutting the legs off the animals I caught, finding the right way to sever a clean line through the bone, slicing, and not tearing, through the surrounding flesh.

No one cared about that fucking cat, anyway.

I found him in the basement one day, sleeping on a pile of old blankets. I picked him up, petting his tangerine head and stroking the fur of his neck so he wouldn't be afraid. Halley the Comet loved everyone insanely, a glutton for affection. I could feel the sinewy cat muscles beneath his soft, orange-and-white-striped fur. His eyes were slits. He even seemed to smile at me and I could feel the little engine-like rumble inside him, his soft purr. I carried Halley the Comet into the garage and placed him on the workbench. He wanted to get down, suddenly panicked. I had to fight him now and Halley tore long, deep scratches into my arms. He even got my face, his rear-foot claw digging into the skin of my cheek as he tried to push off. I touched my cheek and saw the blood on my hands, more brown than red. The next thing I had to do was to find a way to keep him down and the only way was to hold him, pinning the cat's body with one hand and my chest against the workbench and reaching to my belt for the knife with my other. This was easier than it sounds. He was just a cat, after all. I could hear a strangling, gurgling sound coming from Halley's throat. It was like a baby screaming underwater. But when I did it, when I took the knife, which I had sharpened to a microscopic razor-thinness, and brought it down on his left rear leg, just below the joint, and cut, pushing down and through it like a carrot on the kitchen counter, Halley the Comet stopped making any noise at all. Like so many of the animals I had trapped, his body went catatonic, his muscles loosening beneath my grip. He even lost control of his bowels and bladder, shitting and pissing all over the workbench.

There was also more blood than I thought there would be. It spurted on to my shirt and the floor. So I cauterized the wound with my father's soldering iron. Then I carefully cleaned the area and wrapped it around and around with gauze and white tape. Halley was making a soft whining sound deep in his throat, not loud, so I stroked his neck again. He just started mewling then, one weak little cry after another, his eyes all filmy and despairing. I had been so absorbed in cutting off Halley's leg I hadn't been paying attention when the door to the kitchen opened. I looked up and saw my sister standing there, her jaw slack, her head shaking.

'It's all right,' I told her. 'Everything's fine.'

But she turned and ran back into the house, leaving the door to the kitchen ajar.

In the woods, more than twenty years later, the ground was hard beneath my feet, the mud frozen, and the air was dry and brittle. It felt as if my lungs were filling with ice crystals. There was no wind, thankfully, and the sky was clear, with a bright half-moon and pinpoint stars flickering like candlelight. It was a beautiful night, cold as it was. I could have walked through these woods with my eyes closed.

So I closed my eyes for a moment and just stood there, breathing in.

Everything had become so clear.

Later my mother came home and took me and Halley to see Dr Herman, the veterinarian, a man with large, clean, hairless hands, doctor's hands. I told him I had found the cat in the woods, caught in one of my animal traps, that the lower half of his leg was gone, I had dropped it in a panic. But I was congratulated. Dr Herman said that if I hadn't cut Halley's leg so cleanly and cauterized the wound so expertly, Halley probably would have died of blood loss. He said I had a great future as a doctor. He also said he wasn't sure how a cat could enjoy life without one of his rear legs. Dr Herman looked at our mother. He recommended putting Halley to sleep.

I remember that she sighed heavily.

But that's what this had all been about, I said, saving Halley, and I had an idea.

I opened my eyes and walked straight to the clearing, to where the evidence was hidden.

I had an idea.

A little girl's red sneaker, a hunting knife.

It was there, just as I knew it had to be. In my very own hiding place. I remembered reaching into the old broken concrete pipe so many times when I was a teenager to find the grass or speed I kept stashed inside a container. There was just enough room in the small space for a piece of Tupperware, one I had taken from my mother's kitchen. I used to come here every morning to pick up a couple of speed tablets and then I'd return again in the afternoon, after football practice, to smoke a joint or two before going home so I'd have an appetite for dinner. Right now I felt around for the Wonderbread bag.

There it was.

Inside it, even in the darkness of these woods, I could see the red shoe. It was small – much, much smaller than I had remembered. No bigger than my palm. Also, still in its leather sheath, was the hunting knife my father had given me, the one I carried in these woods, looking for animals, for experiments, learning opportunities. For a moment, I didn't know what to do with these things. They had worried me all my life, the only objects that had ever escaped me, and now they were in my possession. I stood in the clearing and removed the knife from the bag, holding its ebony handle. It felt smooth, fitting my grasp like a finely made surgical tool. I slipped it out of the sheath and ran my finger along the blade. There was no blood encrusted here, no dried matter, nothing to link anyone to anything. It was as clean as if it had been sterilized, the blade still sharp, the point unbroken. I may have even laughed to myself at this moment. I may even have been smiling when the flash of the camera went off and I heard my brother say, 'I thought these things weren't real, Eric. I thought you said there was no evidence.'

'Pilot?' Everything was blurry. What I had been able to make out

334

in the woods was now rendered completely opaque after the harsh flash of his camera.

'Eric,' he said, 'how will you explain this?'

'Pilot?' I said again. I wanted to stall him until I could see. I wanted to see him.

'If there was no evidence,' he said nervously, 'why would you come looking for it? And how would you know exactly where to look? If I'm insane, why would you believe my story?' Pilot's voice was quavering, excited. 'Because I'm not crazy, am I? I'm sane, Eric, completely, totally fucking sane, and you know it.'

'The hell you are.' My eyes had adjusted enough at this point to know that Pilot was standing only a few feet in front of me. 'Like fucking hell you are.' I held out the knife, *my* knife, the hunting knife I should have had all these years, and I took a step toward my brother in the dark.

But he jumped out of the way, more nimble than I expected. 'Forget it, big brother,' he said. 'You lose.'

'Pilot,' I said, 'you don't understand.' I stepped toward him again.

'No.'

'Pilot, Jesus Christ, it's for your own good.'

'I don't think so, Eric.'

'Pilot,' I said, and he took off running. I knew I would have to go after him. I knew I would have to catch him. I knew, in fact, that he wanted this – the chase. So I gave him a good head start, just as I had given him a head start millions of times when we were kids, knowing that I would catch him, knowing I had all the advantages. Then I started running, too, the knife in one hand, the Wonder-bread bag with the sneaker in the other, my eyes finally re-adjusted to the starlight coming through the inky treetops. I knew exactly where he was going. I followed him, the tiny tree branches scratching and stinging at my face. The ground was frozen beneath me. But my shoes were office shoes, and I had trouble getting the traction I needed to overtake him. It didn't matter, of course. I knew where we would end up. I knew exactly where this whole thing would end up. I would hold the blade of my old hunting knife

335

against his throat like I had when we were kids. I would not cut him. I had no interest in that, had never had any interest or intention of hurting my brother. 'Pilot!' I yelled after him. I could hear him ahead of me in the dark, thrashing through the trees. 'Pilot!' I called loudly. But then I had a better idea.

'You'll never catch me,' he said back. 'You will never fucking catch me, you piece of shit.'

'Pilot,' I said, 'you have to let me explain.' I knew he would be out of breath soon. I knew he hadn't exercised a day in his life. 'You don't understand,' I said. 'Let me tell you what happened.' We were nearing the path that led to the highway, toward the tunnel, exactly where I knew he would run. 'Pilot,' I begged, *please*. Let me tell you what happened to her.' Which is when I saw him disappear into the opening. And when I followed him in, I felt myself losing all reason, a numbness overtaking me, a physical absence, language itself leaving me, as if it was escaping through the pores of my skin, the sentences leaving my body through my hair follicles. *Pilot*, I wanted to say, but it was as if I couldn't remember my own brother's name.

He was in the tunnel, my brother, and the water beneath us was frozen, and there were bits and pieces of things – wood, trash, aluminum cans, cardboard boxes, an old packing blanket, what remained of the Tunnel Man's effects – all caught in the ice. It was animal-dark in here, but we could see each other, each of us silhouetted against an opening of the tube, with the grayish starlight coming in from behind. I lost everything but my senses then, my eyesight sharpening. My hearing intensified. I could listen to his breathing, heavy from running. I could even smell his sweat. Was there fear mixed in? I could make out his eyes, and I could see that he could see mine. The instant froze like the water we stood on. One of us said the other's name.

'Who do you think you are right now?' he said. But they were only sounds, meaningless noises erupting from his throat.

* * *

336

'Who do you think you are?' my brother asked. And I didn't know what he meant.

'Right now. Who are you? Who the fuck—'

I will tear out your carotid artery, I wanted to say, *with my bare hands.*

Can you love someone so much that you can see through their eyes, that – just for a fraction of an instant – you become him?
  Can love blur life at the edges?

I didn't know the answer. I didn't know who I was.

'You have to listen to me,' he said. 'Brother, you have to listen. *Please*, *please* listen.'
  I stood at the opening of the tunnel and saw his body easing, his muscles relaxing, his head drooping, his chest heaving, catching the cold air. I knew he was my brother and I knew I was his. I knew only that.
  'Do you remember pretending,' he said now, 'pretending to be a wolf? Do you remember that?'
  'It wasn't pretending,' I said. I had found the words somewhere, as if I had pulled them out of a well inside me.
  'Do you remember *being* a wolf, then?'
  'Yes,' I said. 'I remember.' I closed my eyes. I remembered crawling through the fall leaves, baring my teeth, my knees in the mud, the traps, the animals' traps—
  'Do you remember when that started?'
  'After Fiona. It was—'
  'No, it was before.'
  I shook my head, eyes still closed. I could smell my own skin beneath these clothes. There *was* fear.
  'It was before Fiona,' he said. 'It was right from the beginning, right from the time anyone could ever remember.'
  'No,' I said, 'it was after Fiona. It was a very common childhood response—'

'Brother, you have to—'

'—a response to trauma, very common.'

'—to listen, please. *Please*.'

'I'm listening.'

'Pilot, Jesus Christ, Pilot, it was you. Don't you get it?' I opened my eyes, shaking my head – not to say no, but as if to get something off of me, as if I had been walking through the woods and felt a spider drop on my head. He was coming toward me, feeling his way across the ice. 'That night you, you freaked out, Pilot, you went fucking crazy. You were just a little kid, I know, and that's why you don't remember, but that's what—'

'That's impossible.'

'—happened, you killed—'

'No,' I said.

'—her. You came and got the—'

'No.'

'—hunting knife and little brother—'

'There's no way,' I said. 'Because I—'

'—you cut her throat.'

'—remember.' I could hear my own breathing, loud. I could smell my own blood beneath my skin. I could feel my arteries pumping—

'You only think you're sane, Pilot.'

—pumping my own blood. I could feel my bones wrapped inside my muscles. I leaned back against the curvature of the tunnel and my body slid on to the ice. Eric stepped toward me, his hand touching the curved wall of concrete to guide him.

'I found her,' Eric said. 'That night I came home late from the party and found her body in the backyard, just there by the trees, and, and, and I went and got Mom, I got Hannah, and we wanted to protect you, brother. We knew that if people found out what happened, if the police knew what you did, you'd be in institutions for the rest of your life, and Mom, and Hannah, she didn't want that for you. I was just a kid, too, but, but neither did I, Pilot, neither did I.' He was near me now, standing over me. 'You have to understand that I loved you, that it was because—'

338

'Where did you put her?'

'—I loved you.' He sighed. 'We put her in the garage, for a while, for a few years, anyway, and then—'

'She didn't – I mean, didn't she—'

'We embalmed her. I did, anyway – with formaldehyde from school.'

'How did you – what about all the blood?'

'That night I had to work quickly, and Mom wasn't any help, you know. It all went down the drain in the laundry sink. I put her body in there and did what I could to keep things clean, pouring bleach down after it, and wrapping her in as many plastic trash bags as we had. I didn't want there to be a smell.'

'And what about the knife', I said, 'and the sneakers?'

'I forgot them.' Eric slid down beside me. 'I had left them by the patio that night, on the flagstones, and went out to get them later and then I just stashed them under the bed. And, and I guess you saw them there, and you didn't remember what happened, that's all. You repressed it. You thought you were a dog.'

'The wolf boy.' It suddenly felt cold. I had been out in this weather all night and only now did I feel the temperature. I looked up at Eric. 'She helped you?'

'Hannah helped me.'

He was calling her Hannah. 'Why don't I remember?'

'Who would want to remember something like that? That was your defense mechanism.'

'And what about later, is she still, still in the house?'

'Pilot,' Eric told me, and now it was him shaking his head, 'Fiona's in the pool.'

I did remember. I remembered being the wolf boy. I remembered my fearful childhood as Pilot Airie – Airie the Fairy. I remembered sitting at the back of all my classes, avoiding eye contact with other kids, walking as close to the wall as possible. And college, and working in the bookstore, and writing sad screenplays, and all the rest. I also remembered looking out through Eric's eyes and that the world was beautiful that way. How was this possible? Was it love? I remembered lying on the grass by the football field, arms wide open to the sky, thinking I was him.

Is that love?

'When I did it,' I told him now, 'when I killed Fiona, I didn't think I was the wolf boy.'

'No?'

'I thought I was you.'

This is the true nature of deception, to twist things around, persuade without persuasion – to complicate. It is too simple to create a lie, to say you were in one place and not another, to deny a series of events. Because the truth is a tangle, and you will get at it far more easily by raveling than by unraveling. So I sat slumped against the frozen wall of the tunnel with my brother and allowed him to convince me, the truths and untruths threading themselves around our bodies, binding us in such a complexity of yesses and nos and maybe-it-happened-that-ways that the actual truth seemed to become irrelevant, or at least impossible. And then we rose and walked out and we separated like two brothers – me toward the house, Eric in the direction of his car – each without saying a word, each without saying anything or even gesturing his respective goodbye, knowing we would be together again, that we were never really apart. The sunlight came through the branches overhead in impossible shafts of dazzling yellow and the air was so cold and clear there wasn't a mote of dust between the earth and sky. My hands were growing light. My chest expanded to capture more oxygen than seemed reasonable. I stepped on to the lawn of my childhood home and noticed a light crust of frozen dew on the grass. It crackled slightly with each step. The flagstones were frosted over, the whorling patterns of fractured ice like the iridescent visions of my boyhood when I pressed my hands into my eyes.

'Pilot,' Katherine had said, 'there's a way out of this.'

I had remembered everything.

She had leaned toward me, using those green eyes – eyes like Fiona's – to pull me in. 'There's a way.'

'What if I'm wrong?'

'Are you?'

In another lifetime I sat with my brother in the clearing of the woods and he showed me how to hold a joint between my finger and my thumb, how to pull the smoke into my mouth and then inhale, trapping it in my lungs. He sat close to me and put his hand on my back, tapping me there as I coughed. I didn't want to stop coughing if it meant my brother was touching me.

'No,' I had said to Katherine, 'I'm not.'

I stepped on to the frozen flagstones and looked at my mother's garden, Fiona's grave, the iced-over remains of the fall harvest broken and twisted on the hardened, cracked earth. The sun was fully up now. When I imagined her in there she wasn't below six feet of earth, she was swimming, legs moving like a frog's, sunlight flashing off the surface of the water. I saw the garden and pool at the same time, a double-vision, and I knew with a single clarity what had happened to my sister.

'Pilot, there's a way out of this.'

I knew I had not killed her.

'What if I'm wrong?'

'Are you?'

I knew it was him.

When my mother and I came home from the vet that day, Halley wasn't a comet any more. But I had already envisioned a special cat-sized prosthesis for his missing leg, made of molded model airplane plastic and elastic straps, and now it was just a matter of waiting until the wound healed. Once it did, I took Halley and his new leg to the Junior High Science Fair that year and then to the New York State Junior Scientist competition.

At the exhibition, I had to ask Dr Herman for special kitty sedatives to keep Halley from running away. He was happy to oblige.

I won, naturally. The enormous cup is still in my old bedroom. My mother keeps it on the top shelf, above all my football and swimming trophies. It's just a large bowl with my name and the year inscribed on it, nothing special. But it was winning that prize that made me realize my ambition in life. I'd already sensed it when I felt the hunting knife slicing through Halley's leg or when I removed part of a shrew's brain and watched its little gray body twitching on my father's workbench. Dr Herman had even come to the exhibition and explained that he had recommended putting Halley to sleep and that I had talked him out of it.

In the end, of course, it didn't work very well. Truthfully, Halley tore the elastic off with his teeth and limped into a corner. He died a few years later of an enlarged heart – very common for cats.

When they announced that I had won, I walked up to the podium with Halley in my arms. The cat was so heavily sedated his eyes were barely open. There was applause unlike any I'd ever heard on the football field, unlike any applause I could imagine. There were even people who thanked me, actually hugging me, for saving Halley's life. I realized I had to move up a notch, try something braver.

And then Fiona.

And then our parents in separate bedrooms and eventually in separate states.

And then I just studied, my head inside one textbook after another, for years and years. When I got to college I had few friends, only one or two girlfriends. Mostly I studied, biology and pre-med, eventually to graduate *summa cum laude*. In medical school it was even more studying, cramming vast amounts of information into my brain. And there was the neurology program at Columbia, graduate work, starting my practice in East Meadow. What was it Katherine said?

Praised be the fall. I'd heard that expression once before in an English class. But I don't know when the fall came for me. It wasn't when Fiona disappeared. It was long before that. My fall came when I realized I could detach myself, could separate my sympathy into its component parts. Even now, I can walk into the operating room, saw off the back of a human being's skull and perform incredibly delicate operations on a person's brain without feeling anything for them at all.

This is strength. This is what makes me more than just a good doctor. This is what allows me to perform.

To be a doctor is continually to test your resolve to suspend natural human sympathy. It is one thing to take apart a grasshopper and still another to remove and examine the organs of a baby squirrel. It is quite something else to cut the leg off the beloved family cat. Each notch up the great chain of being toward human requires greater and greater detachment. Unlike most doctors, I came to this realization early in life, and I asked myself, could I do it? Could I cut into a human body? Like my father had always encouraged me, I wanted to test myself early in life, so when eventually I encountered the real thing, I'd be prepared.

Like Pilot, I loved her, too. Who wouldn't love a little girl with fair hair and green eyes in a red bathing suit and red sneakers? Who wouldn't love that smile? I remember when she was born. I remember standing over her crib and seeing her green, green eyes leap up at me in unmitigated delight. Of course I loved her. She was my sister.

That day – Christmas Day – I just kept driving, driving all the way to the beach house, stopping only once for gas. I felt better, much better, knowing I had all the evidence with me, that Pilot was finally convinced, that I had a clear day – a clear life – ahead of me. I only hoped that Pilot would forget about it again, let it slip behind him like the yellow lines on the road beneath my Jag.

Pilot had slumped down against the side of the concrete tunnel when I told him, his body limp. He'd put his face in his hands. He was remembering, I think. He was seeing it the way I described it. His fingers on the knife. The knife at her throat. He was remembering himself as the wolf boy. There were new pathways forming along the synapse routes in his brain. There were images coalescing, memories congealing. And even though I felt terrible telling him, it was the only way. He'd left me no choice. 'But she was my sister,' he kept saying. 'Fiona was my sister.'

'*Our* sister,' I said. 'I know.' I put the knife back in the plastic bag with the tennis shoe and placed the whole thing on the ground. I was crouched down next to him, trembling with cold.

Outside the sun was rising. A shaft of orange light pierced the tunnel. This was what the Tunnel Man saw every morning, I thought. It was gorgeous.

'Why didn't you tell me?' Pilot said. 'Why didn't you help me remember?'

I said this as if I were ashamed: 'We didn't want you to.'

He sobbed into his hands. He wore a black overcoat and layers and layers of sweaters beneath it. He had been out in this cold waiting for me all night. The camera hung loosely around his neck.

'Have you been taking your medication?' I asked.

He shook his head. 'Not since the island.'

'Will you do me a favor, little brother? Will you please go home and take your fucking pills? Please?'

He nodded.

I helped him up.

'OK,' he said. 'OK.'

I walked with my brother through the tunnel, my hand on his shoulder, carrying the Wonderbread bag with the sneaker and knife inside it and I left him at the path that led to our mother's house. We didn't say anything. We didn't even hesitate, just separated smoothly into our opposite directions.

An hour and a half later, I was pulling into the long driveway of my beachhouse. I was getting out of the car with the same Wonderbread bag in my hand and walking without stopping, without even closing the door, to the water. No one was around. The wind and the sounds of the waves were blasting into my ears. Was it always this loud? I had no jacket, just that thin pink shirt, monogrammed. My shoes slipped in the sand, failing to gather traction. When I got to the edge of the ocean, where the waves licked the shore, I stepped in a few feet, the water rushing up around my shins, soaking my pants, and I didn't give a shit about the cold or ruining my Italian leather shoes. I looked up and down to make sure no one was watching. I reached into the bag and took out the knife.

This was the blade that cut so cleanly through Halley's leg, I thought. This was the way it felt in my hand.

In the daylight it seemed different. It had been years since I'd seen it, of course, but I didn't remember the handle being this sleekly black and the blade seemed oddly shiny. I guessed it was just a well-made object. It wasn't even the slightest bit rusty after all those years. I got the heft of it, momentarily tossing it up, and then I threw it as far into the ocean as I could, so far out I couldn't even hear the splash. I still had an arm, I thought. I took the plastic bag with Fiona's shoe in it and I filled it with a handful of wet sand. I twisted the plastic around the shoe and whipped it, like the knife, far out into the water. I knew it could come loose eventually and might even float back to the shore. But that didn't matter now. A single shoe, water-soaked, on a beach somewhere. The knife, I knew, would never resurface – not in this lifetime, anyway.

Stupidly, I stood in the cold water up to my knees for a few long minutes, and then I turned around and walked back to the beachhouse, my feet aching. It was extremely cold inside, so I made a fire and, after the furnace heated up, took a long, hot shower. I was probably in there for over an hour, just standing beneath the spray, my eyes closed, trying to let a lifetime of worry drain from my body. I had a change of clothes in the bedroom. I had a few cans of soup in the kitchen cabinet. I'd stay here tonight, I thought. I'd get some rest.

Hannah opened her eyes that Christmas morning to a dazzle of gold coming in at a sideways angle through her bedroom window. It was clear and uniform, a single shaft filled with individual particles of brilliance and glittering dust. It was late for Hannah, too, almost eight o'clock. From the bed she could see the minute hand on its way toward twelve, the hour firmly on eight, the red second hand gliding smoothly forward into the day. She could look across the covers of her bed and see the old maple bedposts, glossy and brown in the morning shimmer. She could see every green twist in the ivy motif of her duvet cover. She held up her hands. Her fingers were long, thinner than she remembered, the flesh translucent. The bones and muscles were plainly visible, the carpals and metacarpals, the joints and ligaments, the arteries and veins on clear display. Her fingernails were blunt, with ridges across their surfaces.

Hannah threw her legs on to the floor and stepped into the hallway, her ankles making a small *crick-crick-cricking* sound as she walked. With her eyes she followed the old oriental runner carpet and noticed with surprise and amazement how dirty it had become, flecked with bits of leaves and clods of dried mud. She looked at the black and white prints of forest scenes on the walls – remembering how she'd picked them out with my father at a photography gallery all those years ago – where was that? Martha's Vineyard – and saw them clearly, it seemed to her, for the first time since that afternoon. She could hear movement downstairs. It was Thalia, the nurse Eric had hired to take care of her in her blindness, preparing something in the kitchen. Hannah went in to the bathroom and closed the door softly, hoping Thalia wouldn't hear.

Inside, the full-length mirror revealed an old woman in a dingy, yellowed nightgown. Hannah put a hand to her face, touching her lower lip delicately. She was so pale. She ran a finger along the blue vein on her temple, noticing the way it disappeared into her hairline. She closed her eyes and rubbed them, and when she opened them up again the old woman was still there, still gray, singular and small – how small she had become, how frail – in the reflection.

Had she been breathing? She took a breath.

There was no wind outside, she noticed, no rattling in the treetops, no sound at all, so she went to the little bathroom window and looked out at the yard.

There were the flagstone patio, the pool/garden, overgrown with her dead plantings from the spring. She had known Eric would never get around to that. There was the patch of grass, still green, but fading to brown a bit in its winter cycle, and then there was the woods, the line of trees clear and solid against the grass. There were two girls' bicycles, one pink, one purple, with white handlebars, pieces of Christmas ribbon attached. Hannah strained, leaning her face against the glass, to see into the yard next door, wondering if the two girls were out there on this cold day, but she could not see from this perspective. Her forehead touched the glass of the bathroom window and she could smell the dust that had gathered there, the musty odor. She had never been a good housewife, she thought, had never been able to keep the house clean the way other women did. But Jim had never complained. That had been her own criticism. She turned and, as her body twisted toward the bathroom interior with the thought of its cleanliness, she was certain she heard something in the backyard, a voice, a small voice coming from where she had just been looking, just seen so clearly, with a singular, lucid vision, that no one was there. She thought she heard her daughter. Was it Fiona? And when she looked, she saw not only one, but two little girls, one ash-blonde, one brunette, each in their red woolly Christmas coats. Hannah could even see how pink the cold wind had made their little-girl cheeks. She could see how one of them sucked on a piece of her blonde hair like a string. She could see how one was stronger than the other, one quieter, one more brash, one more beautiful, one more sensitive. She could see these two little girls so clearly. They took their bicycles and rolled them away then, into their own yard, out of view.

'Mrs Airie . . . Hannah, are you in there?' It was the nurse out in the hall.

'I'm just, um, I'm just going to take a shower, Thalia, and then I'll be downstairs for breakfast, OK?'

'Can you find everything all right in there? Can I help you with anything?'

'I know just where everything is,' Hannah said. 'I can remember my own bathroom.'

'Trying to be helpful, that's all.' Thalia allowed a pause. 'And merry Christmas.'

Hannah stood at the window and focused on the trees in the distance, the bare branches of the perennials, the dark green needles on the evergreens. And as she looked at them she saw the familiar blurring of colors, the softening around the edges of things, the running together. But she could put her fingers into her eyes and wipe away the tears forming there, and when she did, everything became clear again. She could see. She could see it was winter outside and there was no water in the pool and there was no little girl in the yard.

I had told Thalia I just wanted to be alone, and she'd said I was just like my mother, merry Christmas to me, too. I had been sitting on the blue couch in the living room, still wearing my overcoat, the layers and layers of sweaters. I still had a chill under my skin from being outside all night. I still had the camera around my neck. I had been staring at my new sneakers, a pair of blue and silver Nikes. I had been imagining my brother up to his knees in the winter surf.

Hannah stood at the end of the stairs with her hand touching the banister and sang, '*I can see clearly now the rain is gone.*'

I lifted my head. 'You can see?'

'*I can see all the obstacles disa—*'

I got up. 'You're not kidding me, are you, Mom?'

'I can see everything.' She walked into the room. 'I can see better than I could before, I think. Why do you have that camera?'

'Come on, Mom.'

She pointed to the newspaper on the coffee table. She read the headlines. 'Chemical Spill in Westchester County.' She was smiling. 'Middle East Conflict Intensifies.' She came toward me. 'Popular Newscaster Implicated in Extortion Trial. You're better, too,' she said. 'I can see it in your face.'

'What happened?'

'I woke up,' she said. '*It's gonna be a bright, bright—*'

'You woke up and you can see?'

'That's what happened.' She reached to my face. Her hand was trembling. 'You look handsome.'

'You opened your eyes—'

'—and I could see,' she said. 'The ivy pattern on the bedspread, the trees in the yard, the little girls next door.'

'That's wonderful,' I said.

'Let me make you some breakfast.' She started to walk toward the kitchen, but I grabbed her arm, which felt like a thin branch.

'Wait,' I said. 'I want you to see something.'

348

'What is it?'

'Come upstairs.'

'Now?'

'Please,' I said. 'It's important.' I was like an astronaut. I was stepping on to the moon, my hands and feet growing lighter. I walked to the stairs, my overcoat still on. Hannah followed me. I had a feeling she knew where I was leading her. I had a feeling the force of gravity was growing less oppressive. 'It's in Eric's room.'

'Pilot—'

'It's in here.'

'—I don't think I want—'

I opened the door and she stood in the hallway.

'—to see this right now.'

'You have to come all the way in.'

She stepped into the room. 'Pilot,' she said, 'no.'

I reached up to Eric's top shelf, all the way up to the large silver bowl, the New York State Junior Scientist bowl he had won for designing a prosthetic limb for Halley the Comet.

'Pilot, please, I told you I—'

I pulled it down and removed the old plastic Wonderbread bag inside it. I put the silver trophy on the bed and held the plastic bag out toward my mother. 'This is it,' I told her. 'This is the evidence.'

She put a hand over her mouth.

I could feel the clothes lifting away from my body. I could feel the helium filling the inside of my veins, the buoyancy. Under the layers of dust, the Wonderbread bag seemed as new as it had the day I placed it there, all those years ago, standing on the same captain's chair that was now pushed under my brother's old desk. Maybe the colors had faded. Maybe the red, white and yellow Wonderbread graphics had changed since then, become more streamlined. But it looked as though I could have placed these things inside that silver trophy one minute ago. Inside the bag was a single red shoe, clearly visible, with no lace and, of course, the black-handled hunting knife with the silver inlay of the rhinoceros on the handle.

Hannah sat down on Eric's old bed. She looked around. A

million years ago, long before I could remember, she had decorated this room with a nautical motif and there were anchors and sailboats all over the wallpaper and drapes. I think she couldn't help – even at this strange moment – but to marvel proudly at the imagery of this room, the dozens of silver and gold trophies, the sea-blue decorator curtains, the brass, anchor-shaped handles on the dresser. She exhaled heavily. 'What are you going to do?'

I sat down beside her, pushing the old New York State Junior Scientist trophy out of my way. 'I'm going to do what I should have done when I was nine.' I felt like my body wasn't touching anything.

'Oh.'

'Did you know?' I said.

'*Pilot*.'

'Mom, did you know what he did?'

'Katherine,' I said, and I was holding the phone in the living room, rotary-dial, black, 'I'd like to meet Jerry Cleveland. I mean, I'd like to see him again.'

I took my father's sparkling blue four-wheel drive, blue like the sky that late December day, and drove it out to Sky Highway, traveling along the strip malls and shopping plazas, the apartment complexes and office parks that led to the Better-Than-New Auto Dealership where Katherine had told me the old police detective worked. In the passenger seat beside me was the evidence, the plastic Wonderbread bag, amazingly, still intact. I pulled into the parking lot next to a row of old Buicks, Mercurys and Lincolns and waved off the red-headed salesman who came toward me in a gray suit, his tie brightly patterned, his hand out for a shake. 'I'm looking for Jerry Cleveland,' I said.

His shoulders slumped. The guy hooked his thumb toward the lot, where car after car glinted and glittered in the bright winter sun. 'He's out there', the salesman said, 'with a customer.' He squinted at me. 'Sure there's not something I can show you?'

'Thanks,' I said, 'but no.' I climbed out of my four-wheeler, closed the door gently and walked off through the lot. It was jam-packed with dark late-model luxury sedans, Lincoln Continentals, one or two Cadillacs, their sleek, chromed bodies tucked together like a school of fish. Out toward the perimeter, there were the more practical vehicles, the mini-vans and four-wheel drives like mine, even a couple of old woodgrain-paneled station wagons. I could see him, an old man, gesturing toward one car after another, leading a young couple through the lot, car by car, describing past owners, delineating the features and extras, the miles driven, the detailing and tune-ups. He was commanding, I have to say. His voice boomed across the roofs all the way to me. When I finally reached them, Cleveland had opened a Ford Taurus and the couple – not much to describe, really, the woman was blonde, pregnant, the man was short, dark – were sitting inside it. The short, dark man was gripping the wheel, pretending to drive.

'Go on.' Cleveland was chuckling. 'Get a feel of it.' He was laughing at them, I thought. 'You look good in that color, ma'am. I have to say you were right about the red one. You look better in the green.'

The woman smiled at Cleveland, flattered. Her husband gripped the wheel, imagining a curving highway ahead of him.

'Mr Cleveland.'

He turned to me. His eyes flickered across my face and then down to the Wonderbread bag. 'Just a minute,' he said.

I knew that he knew me. I knew that he remembered.

'You do all the financing here?' the man asked him.

'Yes, we do,' Cleveland said. He stood with his hand on the roof of the car. 'Yes, sir, we do.'

'What do you think the monthly would be?' The man pretended to turn sharply to the left. Now to the right.

'The monthly. Can't say exactly,' Cleveland said, scratching his chin. 'But I imagine just shy of three hundred. Could be wrong.'

The woman put her hand over her husband's, which was still gripping the steering wheel. 'That's not bad,' she said encouragingly. 'Honey, that's not—'

'It's not bad at all,' Cleveland stated. 'As a matter of fact, I *challenge* any other dealership to do better.'

'Mr Cleveland,' I said again. 'Excuse me, but—'

'Mr and Mrs Kennedy,' Cleveland said, 'would you mind terribly if I took a moment to speak with my son?'

The couple turned to look at me, eyes wide, noticing me here for the first time. 'Oh, not at all.' The woman smiled warmly. From here I could see that she was pretty, with rounded features.

'We'll be here.' The man nodded, hands on the wheels, eyes focused on some imaginary point in the distance.

'Come on.' Cleveland put his arm around my shoulder and led me about fifteen cars away. He was wearing a wine-red blazer with large yellow stitching in the lapel. He smelled like cigarettes. I used to smoke – had quit the day I arrived in California. Was that an entire year ago now?

'Your son?' I said.

He winked. 'I don't want them to think you're another customer.'

'You remember me.'

'You're a lot older now,' Cleveland said, 'but so am I.' He laughed a little bit. 'And I've been expecting you.'

'You have?'

He reached out his hand. 'Can I see?'

I handed over the bag. 'Careful,' I said. 'There's a knife in there and it's still sharp.'

He looked inside it. He nodded, looking up. 'You ever touch these things?'

'No,' I said. 'No one has. Not since—'

'—they were put in the bag.' He furrowed his brow. 'Excellent. But I'm not a detective any more. You understand that, don't you?'

'But you know what to do with it.'

Cleveland rolled his neck, rubbing his hand on the back of it. He grimaced as if in pain. 'Yes,' he nodded. 'Yes, I do.' He paused now, looking at me directly, his eyes boring into mine. 'You knew what happened.'

'Yes.'

'You could have told me then.'

'Yes.'

352

'This is no recovered memory.'

'It's just a regular memory,' I said.

Cleveland nodded. 'That's good.'

Behind him the pregnant woman was approaching. She was beaming a look of pure joy in our direction. 'Mr Cleveland?' she said.

'It's Jerry.'

'Jerry,' she said, 'we'll take it.'

'That's good,' he said again, only this time to her, and grinning hugely. 'That's outstanding.'

Dawn Costello tore little strips off her napkin, creating a pile of white shreds on the red-checked tablecloth. Her lower lip trembled a bit. 'No one ever spoke to me about it,' she was saying, 'not from the police, at least, no one that was ever, you know, *official*.'

Katherine stirred a spoonful of sugar into her coffee. The restaurant was closed, but loud, banging noises and rich, garlicky smells came from the kitchen, the sound of saucepans hitting the stovetop, the smell of bread baking; a radio was tuned to a football game, crowds cheering, commentators announcing. 'Well,' Katherine said, placing her spoon in the saucer, 'can you remember much about that night now? I mean, I know it was a long—'

'Like it was yesterday.' Dawn exhaled roughly. 'Like it just happened.'

Katherine picked up her cup. 'Good. Tell me what you remember.' She took a sip.

Dawn Costello had eyes like a deer, enormous and dark brown. She had olive skin and wavy, ash-colored hair. She had a way of smiling with her mouth, kind of sideways, when she talked, her lips everywhere. She had the manner of an animal that has been hit one too many times, Katherine thought. She struck Katherine immediately as a good person, no doubt a kind mother – she had four children – and a good friend. Dawn reminded Katherine of the abused women she had met so many times in her career. 'He was taking speed.'

Katherine leaned forward. 'Do you remember what kind?'

'White cross. It was everywhere in those days. I mean, everybody in high school had it.'

'Did you take it, too?'

'Nah, I was too intimidated and it made me too jittery. I just smoked a little pot, drank a little beer, you know.'

'You were a cheerleader?'

'Yeah.' Dawn shrugged, placing another bit of torn napkin on the pile. 'I was one of the good girls.' She smiled her sideways smile.

'So Eric was on speed, and—'

'Well, no, let me back up.' Dawn took a drink of her own coffee. 'First we were at his house, in his bedroom,' she said. 'We used to go there and make out, you know, on his bed. But then the party downstairs started getting really loud and every now and then somebody would wander upstairs looking for the bathroom. You know how it is at parties.'

Katherine nodded.

'And *then* Eric started with the white cross.'

'Did he have any particular reason for taking it that night?'

'He just wanted to have some fun, I guess, and that's what he had.'

'Did he take a lot of it?'

'Oh yeah, that's how he did so well in everything. He was studying all the time and he was the best running back in the history of Albert Einstein, you know. Eric took speed practically every day.'

Katherine sipped her coffee. It was strong and hot. This would keep her up all night, she realized. 'Did you have sex with him that day?'

Dawn fluffed her little pile of napkin tearings. 'I remember I, I gave him, you know . . .'

'You gave him—'

'I can't say it.'

'—a blow job?'

She tore another bit of her napkin off. She made a small snorting noise. 'Yeah.'

'There's nothing wrong with that.' Katherine smiled reassuringly. 'And then you went to the party down the street.'

Dawn said, 'We went to Brian Kessler's house.'

'Were there a lot of people there?'

'Everybody was there.'

'All the popular kids,' Katherine said.

'Yeah, I guess so.' She looked up. 'All the popular kids.'

'What happened next?'

'We just . . . you know how kids are. We smoked pot. We drank beer. We listened to music. We made out.'

It was another life, but Katherine remembered parties at a girlfriend's mother's apartment on the east side, her sister Michele making out with two different boys in the same night. She remembered someone handing out yellow Valiums to all the girls. She remembered holding a cigarette in her fingers, that awkward feeling, knowing how foolish she looked. 'Can you tell me anything about Eric's mood? Was he different in any way? Was he agitated? Was he—'

'He was, he was the same, I suppose. He was the same until—'

'Until what?'

'It wasn't unusual.'

'What wasn't?'

Dawn looked around the restaurant. She smiled that sideways, trembly smile. 'Sometimes Eric would get kind of excited.'

'Like how?'

'Like he would get all pumped up about his future, start talking about being a doctor, how he was going to cure cancer, run for president . . .'

'Interesting.'

'He would say you have to, you have to prove yourself, prove you have the guts, that he had to prove himself and then he would just do something crazy.'

'Something crazy.' This is what Katherine had been looking for. 'Like what? Did he do anything crazy that night?'

'No, I guess not.'

'What do you mean by doing something crazy?' Katherine put

her hand on the table and her bitten fingertips were clearly visible. 'Can you give me an example?'

Dawn pushed the hair out of her eyes. 'What happened to your fingers?'

'I bite my fingernails.'

'I've never seen anything—'

'It's a problem, I know.' Katherine put her hand on her lap again. 'But what did you mean when you said Eric would—'

'One time he held his hand over a burner on a stove until his palm was all blisters, like in that movie . . . you know the one.'

'Oh, Jesus.'

'Yeah.'

'Anything else?'

'He would take the car out at night, when it was completely dark, and he would turn the lights off and put his foot on the gas pedal.'

'He couldn't see anything?'

'Not a thing.'

'Did you leave with Eric that night?'

'No.'

'What happened?'

'I couldn't keep up with him,' Dawn said. 'He was all wild, you know, because of the speed, I guess, and whatever else, and then he left.'

'On his own?'

'Yeah.'

'Did he say where he was going?'

'No, but I didn't think he was going home.'

'What time was it?'

'I think it was still early, around eleven-thirty.'

'Is there anything else about Eric that you can tell me, anything that might be—'

Dawn put her hand out, stopping Katherine. 'OK,' she said, 'but you have to promise never to tell anyone.'

Katherine nodded.

'Promise.'

'I *promise*,' Katherine said.

'I've never said this before, not to anyone.' Dawn looked around, and then lowered her voice, whispering, 'Eric got me pregnant. It was a few months before his sister, before Fiona disappeared.'

Katherine allowed a moment to pass and then she said, 'You had an abortion?'

'Yeah.'

'There's nothing wrong with that, Dawn.' Katherine reached across the table for Dawn's hand.

Dawn flinched, pulling away. 'I know, but—'

'But what?'

She finished tearing her napkin apart and now she looked at her empty hands. 'He didn't want me to go to the doctor.'

'But how did he—'

'He wanted to do it himself.'

Katherine asked, 'How old were you?'

'Sixteen.'

'Did you let him?'

She closed her eyes. 'Yes.'

Today it was mushroom soup, a tuna sandwich on coarse black bread, a tangerine. Eric laid out the wax paper his sandwich had come wrapped in across his desk and poured himself a glass of mineral water. 'Dr Airie,' Diane said through the intercom, 'there's someone here to see you.'

Eric put his spoon down. 'I don't have an appointment *now*, do I?'

'No,' his secretary said, 'I think this is personal. Her name is Katherine DeQuincey . . . DeQuincey-Joy.'

I was running. It was something I'd never done before, but I had these Nikes, blue and silver, and I was running – running around and around the track at the junior high. I didn't care that there were kids out there, either. I didn't care who the hell saw me. My legs hurt and my chest felt like it was on fire, but I kept on running sometimes for more than an hour. I'd stop eventually and put my palms on my knees and feel the cold air tearing through my body, the oxygen creating a barrage of new blood cells, my lungs exploding. I'd look up and see some junior high girls sitting on the bleachers, the dirty blondes and brunettes of East Meadow, shivering in their gym clothes, and I knew all of their thoughts. I could read their jealousies and fears and desires through the air. I could sense emotions coming off their bodies in waves. With each aggressive heartbeat I could sense my brother, too, faraway, his movements tracked in my consciousness like radar. If I closed my eyes I could see the world my mother was seeing – the dull, flickering glow of the television, the sharp sun coming through the trees in back of the house, a cup and saucer on the floor at her feet. And my thoughts were Katherine's, her sense of logic and loss, understanding and distrust, a bloody finger to her lips. So I'd start to run again, trying to get away from this omniscience, this sensitivity like raw skin. I'd circle the track one more time, trying to empty my mind, trying to make my thoughts my own. But I couldn't seem to run fast enough.

It was too sleek in here, Katherine thought, too futuristic, overly masculine, everything black or chrome. She said, 'I'll talk, and you just tell me if I'm wrong.' She was sitting across from Eric in the patient chair – small, modern, uncomfortable, with a stiff black leather seat and spindly silver arms and legs. She raised her eyebrows expectantly.

Eric pushed his sandwich away and leaned back in his large black leather swivel, smiling slightly, as if amused, as if he'd been expecting this, like the villain in a James Bond movie. 'All right, Katherine,' he said. 'Go ahead.'

She took a breath. 'You wanted desperately to be a doctor,' she began. 'All your life, growing up, you knew that's what you wanted to be. So you practiced. You practiced on little bugs and then small animals, and then you even cut off the leg of your family cat—'

'Halley the Comet.' Eric smiled. 'Named by Pilot, in fact.'

'Halley the Comet,' she said, 'so you could retro-fit a new leg on him and win the science trophy.'

'With the exception of animal cruelty,' Eric said, 'which most children are guilty of – especially boys – none of this means anything.'

Katherine ignored him. 'You'd been taking amphetamines to keep up with school and your heavy athletic schedule and all that partying, and that day the build-up was a little too much for you, wasn't it? You went a little bit crazy.'

Eric half-rolled his eyes, smiling.

'It's called amphetamine psychosis, Eric, but you know all about that. And remember, Dawn Costello saw you take the white cross.' She cleared her throat. 'Anyway, that night you decided to practice a little bit of surgery. I would guess that you cut her open with the old hunting knife, examined an organ or two, God knows what else. Did you open her skull, Eric? And then you hid her somewhere in the house. And when the search began the next day you pretended nothing had happened, quite expertly, as a matter of fact. And no one suspected you at all – why would they? – until your brother found the Wonderbread bag under your desk. But he was just a nine-year-old kid, and then he claimed to have found the shoe in the woods, so you thought he was protecting you, right? So then everything was fine, wasn't it? For years, in fact,' Katherine said, 'everything was just fine. Something about having done that, having—'

'—passed the test,' Eric said.

'What?'

'Something about having passed the test. It lets you do things other people can't do,' he said. 'When you push yourself.'

Katherine nodded. 'And then later it seemed that Pilot went crazy, pretending to be a dog in the woods, crawling around and growling, not having any friends, hardly ever washing his hair, no girlfriends, bad grades. He ceased to be a concern, it didn't matter, because no one would believe a crazy kid like him, anyway. And the truth was that he probably didn't even remember what happened, or was too crazy to put it together.'

Eric scratched his head. 'This is interesting,' he said. 'Go on.'

'But then, for some strange reason, Pilot did remember. Or maybe he had never forgotten. In any event, you poisoned him,

Eric, every day in his breakfast until he literally went over the edge. Did you want that? I'm not sure. Maybe Pilot became a little more crazy than you intended. Anyway, he wound up in the clinic, genuinely insane, claiming that twenty years ago you killed your little sister. But who would believe him, a paranoid schizophrenic? It's just like an old movie. Who would take this paranoid, delusional misfit seriously?'

'You, evidently.'

'So you seduced me.'

'I didn't have to try very hard.'

Katherine rubbed her face. She sighed. 'But you had to get your hands on the evidence. You knew enough about forensics that you didn't want to take any chances. And now, with DNA testing . . . So you went out of your way – way the hell out of your way. Eric, you even killed that poor man who lived in the tunnel.'

Eric rolled his eyes. 'This is ridiculous.'

'And then your father killed himself. After all those years bearing the loss of his daughter and the disintegration of his family, probably blaming himself for—'

'We don't know that it was deliberate, what my father—'

'No,' Katherine said, 'I guess we'll never know.'

Eric shook his head. 'And I wasn't anywhere near them when it happened.'

'But something made you remember the old broken concrete pipe. What was it, Eric?'

'What are you talking about?'

'You went into the woods, didn't you, looking for the evidence? And there it was. A plastic bag with a little girl's red sneaker and an old hunting knife. What made you think it was there?'

Eric made the smallest noise, more of a snort than anything else. It was obviously intended to be a snort of incredulity, but it came out strangled.

Katherine reached into her purse and dropped the snapshot on to Eric's desk. It was of him, in the woods, his eyes red in the camera flash, his hand inside a Wonderbread bag.

He closed his eyes momentarily. 'Pilot gave you that?'

Katherine reached into her purse again, pulling out an envelope. 'And here's what I gave Pilot.' She removed a stack of photographs, dropping them one by one on the desk. In the first one, Eric is standing up to his knees in the green-gray surf. In the following pictures he is throwing the shoe and the knife far into the water. He's wearing dark blue trousers, a pink shirt. 'These are video captures,' she said, 'stills from a video tape.'

'You followed me.'

'I was already there.' Katherine smiled. 'We knew that's where you would go. We had a good idea about it, anyway.'

'Just because I got rid of the evidence doesn't mean it was for—'

'Oh, yes,' Katherine said, 'you explained all that to Pilot. That you were protecting him. That all those years ago you were hiding the evidence because he had done it, and he didn't even know it, and you didn't want him to get in trouble. But that's bullshit, Eric.'

'But now we'll never know if it's bullshit,' Eric said. 'Because even if you find the shoe and the knife, there won't be any way to test them, they'll be completely—'

'Eric,' Katherine said, laughing, 'you may be a brain surgeon, but you're not that smart.'

'What do you mean?'

'What makes you think that stuff you threw in the ocean was the real evidence?'

When he came for me, I knew him. When he came for me, I was in my bed, the flannel covers pulled tightly up to my chin even though it was warm. I had my eyes closed, but I wasn't asleep. I had been listening to the grown-ups downstairs, the sounds of the ice cubes clinking in their glasses, the arguments between the men, the secrets whispered among the women. What were they saying? I had heard the sounds of the party slipping away, bit by bit, until there was nothing but the wind in the treetops and the faraway rushing sound of the highway, the wheels on concrete. I heard him say my name. I heard him say it was time to get up, and when I opened my eyes I saw him, saw his face, large and perfectly chiseled. I knew it wasn't time to get up and I said that it was pure bullshit. So he said that he had a surprise for me, that's why it was time. I took his hand and he said I should put my swimsuit on again. I told him I didn't want to go swimming. But he said to just put it on anyway. It was hanging on the end of my bed, on the bedpost, and I had been thinking of it as a red flag and my bed was a boat floating out in the ocean somewhere, lost. I took off my pink and yellow pajamas and made him turn around and not look at me and I got into the swimsuit. It was still damp and cold from swimming, but not too bad. I put my red sneakers on that I had kicked off on to the floor under the bed. I asked what we were doing now, were we going swimming? And he said we were going downstairs to the garage. And I said, why? And he said it was a surprise, he couldn't tell me. It was important that I be completely quiet, though, he said, and not wake anyone up. It was very important. If I wasn't completely quiet, he told me, there would be no surprise. So I stayed quiet, troubled even by the loudness of my breathing, afraid even to put my foot down on the carpet. It was so dark in the house, we couldn't see anything. And we stumbled over some things that were in the hall that led to the stairs. We went down through the living room and into the dining room, and, passing the family room, we saw our brother sleeping on the couch, his hand over his face, his chest heaving up and down violently just to get a breath. He slept like an animal, like Halley the Comet. Then we went through the kitchen – the whole time he was holding my hand tightly, more tightly than he'd ever held it, I thought, like he was afraid – and through to the garage. There was light in here, but just a little bit, coming from a flashlight that rested on the workbench. My brother said to close my eyes, and I did, and I could feel him moving behind me. And then really fast he put something over my mouth. It was tape, sticky and tight. He pulled it all the way around my head, around and around, and my hair got caught in it. I tried to scream – *I was screaming* – but there wasn't any sound coming out and I started to choke and cough, so I stopped screaming and concentrated on just getting some air in through my nose. I wasn't crying yet, but I was on the verge of crying. I could feel the water coming up to my eyes, rising up inside me. I tried to go to the door but he pulled me back by the arm, hard, jerking me back into him. He made me stand very still, his leg trapping my face against the workbench while he wrapped the tape around my wrists, around and around, so I couldn't move my arms at all. And then he picked me up, lifted me on to the workbench. I tried to kick him, thrashing my legs around, but he was too strong, and he got my legs down and he taped them together, too, twirling the tape around and around my ankles. I could only look at him now. In the light of the flashlight I could only try to seek out his eyes and get him to feel bad enough with my eyes to let me go. But he wouldn't look at me. I was going to run upstairs the minute he set my legs free and tell our mother, but then he wouldn't look at me. He wouldn't look at my eyes. He kept walking back and forth, walking back and forth in front of the workbench, saying, *You can do this*, repeating over and over, *You can do this you can do this, this is something, something you can do, do this, do this. Do this, do this, this this this*. And then he finally stopped pacing and he came to me and I tried to make a sound. He turned me over, and now my chin was on the surface of the workbench. I could feel him behind me pulling off my shoes and I heard one of them dropping on to the floor. He was still saying, *You can do this, you can do this*. I saw his hands flash in front of my face and I felt the string, the shoelace, around my neck. I felt it pulling tighter and tighter, cutting into my skin. I felt it cutting off the air, felt the veins in my neck straining and exploding against the string that he was pulling into me, into my skin. I tried to get oxygen. I opened my mouth inside the tape and I tried to lift my nostrils, but there was nothing. And my heart was pounding inside my body. And the blood was rushing into my ears, like my ears were pressed against the highway, listening up close to the sound of wheels on concrete. And my lungs went empty. And my whole body relaxed. I was in the pool, and it was the middle of the summer, just me and Mom in the house. I was pretending that I had drowned, my body relaxing, floating up up up. I was pretending, just letting my body float there, rising up to the surface, holding my breath. *Fiona*, my mother called. *Stop that*. She was calling from the kitchen door. She had the radio on in the kitchen. They were playing the news, the talk talk talk of the news announcer going on and on, it seemed, and never saying anything. I was just pretending to be dead, just pretending I wasn't dead, really, just letting my body go all slack, to fool my mother, my arms rising to the surface, my body rolling over. *Fiona*, she said. I could hear her, that faraway echoing sound that voices make through the water. I could hear her saying, *Fiona, Fiona*. And I wanted to stay in, but I couldn't hold my breath any more. And when I looked up I felt the back of my head being opened, the sawblade against my bone. *Fiona*, she said. I looked up. She was standing in the kitchen door, saying, *Don't scare me like that, sweetheart*. His fingers were reaching into my body, reaching in. She came out and stood at the edge of the pool. I went to the edge and put my hands on the flagstones, pulling myself out of the water. His hands were reaching in, so far in. *Do you want anything to eat yet?* she asked. I'm not hungry, I told her. The sun was warm, and I was standing now. She wrapped the towel around my shoulders, my favorite one, the one with the big white and yellow daisies all loopy and cartoony across it. *Put your sneakers on*, she said. *If you're going to walk around the yard I want you to put your sneakers on*. I was standing now in my sneakers, one lace tied, the other gone, water dripping off my swimming suit, and his fingers were reaching in, pulling my skin away from my body, pulling the muscles away from the bone, pulling the organs out from the inside of me. The sun was bright yellow. As I played in the yard I could see my mother walking back and forth in the kitchen, I could see her head moving by the window, her whole body by the door. She went in and out of the washing-machine room, her arms full of warm, clean clothes. Sometimes I ran upstairs and found her sitting in the chair by the radio, the soft voices talk talk talking. I would stand behind her and put my chin on her shoulder and tell her things about my day, tell her about how I was so afraid of the woods, the way they were going to lash out and take me, but that I was staying faraway, that I was safe in the yard, that I would never leave her. She just said, *Fiona, oh, Fiona, that's right, never leave, never leave me again*. I felt the shoe slipping away from my foot, dropping on to the floor. I was out in the yard playing, careful not to fall on the grass, or I was swimming, or standing on the flagstones, my body dripping water, the towel around me, covered in daisies. *Put your shoes on, dear,* my mother was saying. *I don't want you playing in the yard without shoes.* I saw her moving back and forth in the kitchen, her head through the window, her body through the door, back and forth with the clean laundry in her arms. I whispered into her ear. I heard her calling me from the water. *Fiona,* she said. *Don't scare me like that. Don't scare me.* But when I looked up, I felt the shoelace slipping away from my neck and the back of my head being opened, felt my skin peeling away, the sawblade cutting through the bone, his fingers reaching in, reaching in. I hung on to the lip of the pool, afraid to let go. Daddy, I said. *Daddy's sleeping,* he told me. He wore his aviator glasses and I couldn't see his eyes. He had a newspaper spread over his chest. There was a glass of ice tea resting on the flagstone beside him. Daddy, I said again. *Yes?* he asked. *What is it?* I didn't know. At the party, I said, thinking of something, of something to ask him, anything, just to talk, at the party will there be a lot of people? *We invited everyone,* he said. Can I stay up late? *You can stay up a little bit late,* he said. How much is a little bit? I could see clouds reflected in his sunglasses. He reached for his tea and removed the circle of lemon that was curled over the edge of the glass. I held on to the edge of the pool. *We'll see,* he said. Through the window I could see her, my mother, her head moving by, and then her body by the door. She'd look out every now and then to check if we were OK, did we need anything? And the woods encircled us, and even though I was afraid they would come too close and swallow us, I watched them, because I knew that soon my brothers would be walking through, stepping out of the trees and across the grass and the flagstones to the pool the way the astronauts walked on to the moon. How much, Daddy, I said, waiting for my brothers to come out of the woods, how much is a little bit late? He smiled, his mouth so wide and so handsome, like a movie star, his sunglasses full of clouds and blue sky, saying, *We'll see, sweetheart. We'll see.*

* * *

It was a wet day, and warm, as though spring had come in January, and the ground was soft and easy to dig through. Hannah had called Nathan Tabor, a tax lawyer she had known for years, who had, in fact, been a good friend of my father's. Detective Vettorello, arms folded, was presiding over the yard watching his team of police officers and forensics specialists shovel the earth out of the old swimming pool. It piled up on the lawn in large even slabs next to the rotten stalks of rhubarb that had been pulled out. Nathon Tabor paced back and forth across the flagstones, smoking a cigar. I was in my bedroom, watching all of this from the window. Eric had confessed, I guess, first to Katherine, and then to the police, that for a few years he had kept Fiona's body in my father's old wet suit that hung in the window of the garage, and then when Hannah had decided to fill in the pool, he had put her remains inside it, too, covering her with layers and layers of brown, mossy earth. And then came the vegetables my mother planted. Did the roots reach down to her? I wondered. Was there some comfort for my sister in the way that Hannah tended the garden? The police carved through the mud like archeologists, carefully removing it a foot at a time until someone yelled that he had found something, and then everyone went over to see if it was part of a child-sized human skeleton.

It was a beautiful day, at least. The sky was bright blue, the air warmer than it had been in months – humid, light jacket weather. When I turned from the window I saw Katherine Jane DeQuincey-Joy standing in the hallway.

'I let myself in,' she said. She was touching her lapel.

I nodded. I hadn't seen her in quite a while.

'I thought you might like some, some company right now.'

'Thanks.'

She walked into my bedroom. She looked around at all the race-cars on the wallpaper. She saw the piles of magazines and science fiction novels I had stacked up around the bed. I felt my face get hot. For some reason, I was embarrassed for her to see me here. 'Pilot,' she said warmly, 'you were right. You were right about everything.'

But I couldn't say anything. I sat down and looked at the rust-colored rag carpet. I was wearing those old Converse All-Stars, one of them with the lace missing. I felt my hands filling with helium. I saw Fiona, her body dripping wet, her skin all shiny, the daisy-patterned towel over her shoulders, the sun far, far behind her. 'I don't feel right,' I said finally. 'I don't feel normal.' I could have worn my Nikes, but I had decided not to today. 'Katherine Jane DeQuincey-Joy, I'm not myself right now.'

'You're not crazy, Pilot,' Katherine said and she almost put her hand on my shoulder. 'No one would feel normal today. I don't feel normal.' She sat beside me. 'Anyway,' she said, 'I wanted to apologize for, you know, for doubting you.'

'I doubted me. Why shouldn't you?' I shrugged. 'Besides, the shoelace wasn't even real. And I was wrong about a lot of things.'

'Like my name.' She smiled.

'Your name?'

'My middle name is Marjorie, after my grandmother.'

'It's not Jane?'

'Where did you get that?' She was almost laughing.

'Where did I get anything?'

'Were you just wrong about the shoelace?'

'You know how some people tie a string around their finger to remember things?' I said. 'That's all it was. And then I started to believe it myself.'

'You said you were omniscient.'

'I was crazy, that's all.'

'Do you still—'

I nodded, saying softly, 'I'm trying not to and I think it's fading.'

There was more shouting from the backyard. Someone was yelling, 'I found something. Over here. I found—'

'Do you want me to take you somewhere?' Katherine said. 'Would you like to get out of here? Would you like to be somewhere—'

'I'd like to see her.' I rose from the bed. I looked at Katherine. 'Wouldn't you like to see Fiona?'

Today she wore faded jeans, a simple black blazer, a white T-shirt beneath. Around her neck was the silver chain, the Celtic symbol. She looked at me questioningly for a moment and then she said, 'OK.' We walked downstairs together and the chain made a slight rattling noise. When I looked at it, Katherine put a hand to her neck. 'I'm sorry,' she said. 'I'll take it off.'

We were in the living room now. 'I was just noticing it,' I said. 'It's nice, that's all.' We walked through the dining room and through the sliding doors on to the mud-splattered flagstones. Detective Vettorello stood in a windbreaker with his arms folded over his chest. 'You found her?' I said.

He nodded.

Nathon Tabor paced back and forth in front of the pool, puffing his cigar.

'Can I see?'

Vettorello pointed to a group of police officers, covered in mud, carefully pulling out my sister's skeleton, piece by piece, bone by bone. I saw that someone had placed a part of her skull on a white piece of paper at the pool's edge. This is what all the yelling must have been about. A police photographer was taking pictures. Katherine was beside me and when I turned to look at her she was pushing tears off her cheek. A policeman put another bone beside the bit of skull, and then another and another. It would take all day, I could see that. It would go on like this for hours, the police finding the various parts of my sister's body, cleaning them and placing them on the white pieces of paper on the flagstones. There didn't seem to be much flesh left.

Vettorello looked at me. 'How is your mother?'

'I don't know.' I looked back at the house. 'She's been in her room all day.'

He and Katherine exchanged a look.

'When can I see my brother?'

'There's nothing preventing that,' Vettorello said. 'Unless his lawyer—' and then he stopped himself. 'Well, there's nothing preventing that.'

I nodded, standing there for a moment. Then I left Katherine with Vettorello and went back upstairs. Instead of going to my room, I went into Eric's, sitting on his old bed and looking at that case of trophies, the blue ribbons and silver cups. It was still in one of them, actually, Halley's prosthesis. I could see it protruding from the top of an old swimming trophy – a piece of molded gray plastic in the shape of a cat's rear lower leg, with a long piece of stretchy elastic attached. Halley had lived for quite a while, actually, learning to walk on three cat legs, but never leaving the house. He had died inside my mother's closet, curled in a ball.

Hannah touched her face. There was a throbbing behind her forehead. There was a pain forming, a pressure building in waves like a migraine. The cells divided and multiplied, the exponential increase of aberrant tissue curling like ivy around her optical nerve. She sat in her room and listened to the men pulling her daughter from the pool. She had done it herself so many times, holding Fiona's slim wrists and lifting her wet body on to the flagstones. At that moment, I knew how many years and months and days and hours and minutes and seconds my mother had left to live. At that moment – and I would forget later, mercifully – I foresaw the instant of her departure, a tube in her arm, hair white and thin. Right now, though, Hannah closed her eyes. She did not want to see Fiona this way.

There was a bright *two* glowing red and blinking on her answering machine and Katherine erased the messages without listening. She kicked off her sneakers and lay down, arms out, on the mattress. The brown stain on the ceiling hadn't changed. But at least it was warm in here. At least it wasn't frigid any more. She remembered that she hadn't paid her rent this month. Or her electricity. She hadn't done her laundry in so long she had been washing her underwear in the sink. There was no food in the refrigerator. Besides this mattress on the floor, there was no furniture, just those old boxes stacked along the wall. She would have to get it together, she told herself. She would have to get a better place, to begin with, and some new clothes and some furniture. Maybe she should just move back into the city, she thought. What was the point of staying? Still lying down, Katherine squirmed out of her black jacket. She was about to pull her jeans off when there was a knock on the door. She hadn't ordered a pizza and it certainly wasn't Eric.

'Yes,' she said loudly, 'just a minute.'

'Take your time, take your time.' It was an old voice, scratchy and warm.

Katherine opened the door smiling. Cleveland stood there with his hands in his pockets, wearing a coat too heavy for this weather, a mismatched tie, plaid pants. 'Come in,' she said. 'Please, come in.' She looked around. 'I'm sorry I don't have anywhere for you to sit. I've been here almost a year already and I haven't—'

'It's all right,' Cleveland said. 'I don't need to sit. I won't stay long, anyway.'

'Would you like some water?'

'No,' he said smiling. 'No, no. I just, I just wanted to come out here and, you know, and in person, and thank you in person, that's all.'

'Thank *me*? Really—'

He cleared his throat. 'That's a case that's bothered me for many years, probably the worst case I had in all the time I was with the police.'

'The person to thank, then, is Pilot Airie.'

He nodded. 'He lived with those memories all those years. That was the main thing.' Cleveland indicated the unopened cardboard boxes stacked in the corner. 'You going somewhere?'

Katherine laughed. 'I never unpacked them to begin with.'

'Not sure if you're going to stay?'

'Something like that.'

'It's a good enough place, East Meadow,' Cleveland said. 'You're from the city, though, aren't you?'

'Yeah.'

'Well, it's not like the city.'

Katherine sighed. 'No,' she said.

'What do you think made him do it now? I mean, that was twenty years Pilot went without saying anything.'

'They're brothers,' she said. 'And they're very close, in a way.

I'm not sure if I could turn my sister in for—'. She stopped herself. 'Well, maybe I could. I don't know.' She looked at the answering machine, which now said *zero*.

'Do you think he didn't remember, that he had repressed it all, like he said?'

'No,' Katherine said. 'Pilot remembered. It's almost like he remembered even more than he actually experienced.'

'I don't suppose you could forget something like that.'

'I don't think so, either.'

Cleveland looked around the room again, his eyes remaining on each object for an equal period of time. And then he said, 'Well, thank you again, Miss Katherine DeQuincey-Joy. And I believe you *are* the person to thank, no matter what you say.'

She smiled.

Cleveland turned to the door. He opened it. ''Bye now.'

'Goodbye.'

When the door was closed and Katherine was alone again, she ran her fingers through her hair, finding a nest of tangles. She looked at the telephone that sat on the kitchen counter. She wondered who had called and left those messages. She stared at that telephone, as a matter of fact, for quite some time.

And I was running. Later on I was running, wearing my blue and silver Nikes, around and around the track of the junior high. It was afternoon and soccer practice was under way. Kids with shin-guards and green and white kneesocks kicked a black and white ball across the field. I stopped, hands on my knees, panting like a dog – like the wolf boy – and tried to discern the point of this game. I lifted my head and watched these boys, each of them maintaining his respective position on the team.

'Are you all right?'

I was suddenly lying on the ground. Suddenly, I was looking up at the faces of two boys, the white sky behind them.

'Get the coach,' one of them said.

'I'm all right.'

'You just fell over. I was across the field.' He pointed excitedly. 'And you dropped like a rock.'

One of the kids ran off in the direction of the school.

I propped myself up on my elbows. 'I'm fine,' I said. 'I was just running too much.'

He had coarse brown hair, this kid, and crooked teeth. I tried to imagine his panic, the sensation of watching me, a stranger, drop to the ground – the thrill, almost. I tried to see inside him. He was sort of smiling now, encouragingly. But I could only imagine—

'Are you sure you're all right?'

—and this was amazing—

—what he was thinking, and I could only imagine the world outside this circle of grass, the soccer field, the rim of trees, because it was just me inside it, just me, *only* me – not my brother, not Hannah, not Katherine, not Fiona, not anyone, because I was alone now. I smiled at this kid. I got up. 'I'll be fine,' I said. I was alone now, gloriously beyond rescue.